Lilith Saintcrow was born in New Mexico, bounced around the world as an Air Force brat, and fell in love with writing when she was ten years old. She currently lives in Vancouver, Washington with three children and a houseful of cats. Find her on the internet at www.lilithsaintcrow.com

Find out more about Lilith Saintcrow and other Orbit authors by registering for the free monthly newsletter at www.orbitbooks.net

BY LILITH SAINTCROW

Dante Valentine Novels
Working for the Devil
Dead Man Rising
The Devil's Right Hand
Saint City Sinners
To Hell and Back

Jill Kismet Novels
Night Shift
Hunter's Prayer

LILITH SAINTCROW

WORKING FOR THE DEVIL

orbit

www.orbitbooks.net

ORBIT

First published in the United States in 2006 by Warner Books,
Hachette Book Group, USA
First published in Great Britain in 2006 by Orbit
Reprinted 2007, 2009

A CIP catalogue record for this book is available from the British Library.

ISBN 978-1-84149-466-1

Typeset by Palimpsest Book Production Limited,
Grangemouth, Stirlingshire
Printed and bound in Great Britain by CPI Mackays, Chatham, ME5 8TD

Papers used by Orbit are natural, renewable and recyclable
products sourced from well-managed forests and certified in
accordance with the rules of the Forest Stewardship Council.

Mixed Sources
Product group from well-managed
forests and other controlled sources
www.fsc.org   Cert no. SGS-COC-004081
© 1996 Forest Stewardship Council
FSC

Orbit
An imprint of
Little, Brown Book Group
100 Victoria Embankment
London EC4Y 0DY

An Hachette Livre UK Company
www.hachettelivre.co.uk

www.orbitbooks.net

To L. I.
I keep my bargains.

Acknowledgments

Writing is a solitary endeavor—and yet, no book is created in a vacuum. My thanks must go first and foremost to James, Maddy, and Nicky. Without them, the drive to create would be not nearly so strong in me—and the bonds of love that keep me together would not exist. For James, then-"Bananas." To Mom and Dad: bet you never guessed all those books would end up like this, huh?

Thanks are also due to Linda Kichline, one of the first to believe in me; Betsy Gallup and Ann MacDonald for the inception of AnotherChapter.com and for their editing, kindness, and great humor. The world of Danny Valentine would literally not be without them. Thanks to the best literary agent in the world, Miriam Kriss; I must also thank Devi Pillai at Warner, one of the best editors I've ever worked with. Without Miriam and Devi's enthusiasm and care, this book would be much worse and probably unpublished to boot. Special note to them both: thank you for putting up with this neurotic writer.

A roll call of the people who kept me sane while I wrote this book: Joe Zeutenhorst, who can always be counted on for a good time and a sharp tongue, who also gave me the key to unlock Jace; Chris Goodwin, who danced with me at the Alibi Room; my sisters Alison and Tricia (always and forever, you know); Jess Hartley, who has been a true-blue friend ever since we met; Jeff and Janine Davis for putting up with one mad forgetful writer (special thanks to Jeff for long talks about the nature of ghosts); Josh Carter for his clarity (pop!pop!) and Andrzej Karwacki for teaching me so much about my own characters; Akira, Lenore, and Sideeffekt at Dead-Journal, and Jonas Secher, who I will probably never meet face to face.

To Nicholas Deangelo, my heart still remembers your name. Thank you for teaching me about honor.

Big thanks to those creative people I've never met but who have informed the world of Dante Valentine: Joy Division and New Order, the Eagles, Moby, Mandalay, Garbage, Quentin Tarantino (who will never recognize himself in my books), Alex Proyas (who I want to direct some movies if we ever find the time), Jacqueline Carey (best damn fantasy author in the last decade), Jacques Cazotte, John Milton (of Lucifer's party without knowing it), and many others who must remained unnamed.

Lastly: thank you to everyone who reads my work and calls it good. You are who I write for. And to those who read my work and call it bad: thank you very much. You inspire me to keep going just to prove you wrong.

Nel mezzo del cammin di nostra vita
mi ritrovai per una selva oscura,
che la diritta via era smarrita.

—Dante

Hell hath no limits, nor is circumscribed
In one self place, for where we are is hell,
And where hell is must we ever be.

—Mephistopheles, by way of Marlowe

CHAPTER
1

$\mathcal{M}$y working relationship with Lucifer began on a rainy Monday. I'd just settled down to a long afternoon of watching the holovid soaps and doing a little divination, spreading the cards and runes out on the hank of blue silk I'd laid out, when there was a bashing on my door that shook the walls.

I turned over a card, my lacquered fingernails scraping. The amber ring on my left middle finger sparked. The Devil card pulsed, landing atop a pile of flat runestones. I hadn't touched it. The card I turned over was blank.

"Interesting," I said, gooseflesh rippling up my back. Then I hauled myself up off the red threadbare carpet and padded barefoot out into the hallway. My rings flashed, a drift of green sparks snapping and popping down my fingers. I shook them off, frowning.

The lines of Power wedded to my front door twirled uneasily. Something nasty was on my front step. I hitched up my jeans, then reached over and curled my fingers around the sword hanging on the wall. I lifted it down, chucked the blade free with my thumb against the guard.

The peephole in the middle of the door was black, no light spilling through. I didn't bother looking. Instead, I touched the door, spreading the fingers of my right hand against smooth iron. My rings rang and vacillated, reading the flow of whatever was behind the door.

Oh, gods above and below, I thought. *Whatever it is, it's big.*

Bracing myself for murder or a new job, I unlocked the door and stepped back, my sword half-drawn. The blue glow from Power-drenched steel lit up my front hall, glimmering against the white paint and the full-length mirror hung next to my coatrack. I waited.

The door creaked slowly open. *Let's have some mood music for effect,* I thought sardonically, and prepared to sell myself dear if it was murder.

I can draw my sword in a little under a second and a half. Thankfully, there was no need to. I blinked.

Standing on my front step was a tall, spare, golden-skinned man dressed in black jeans and a long, black, Chinese-collared coat. The bright silver gun he held level to my chest was only slightly less disconcerting than the fact that his aura was cloaked in twisting black-diamond flames. He had dark hair cut short and laser-green eyes, a forgettable face and dreamy wide shoulders.

Great. A demon on my doorstep, I thought, and didn't move. I barely even *breathed*.

"Danny Valentine?" he asked. Well, demanded, actually.

"Who wants to know?" I shot back, automatically. The silvery gun didn't look like a plasgun, it looked like an old-fashioned 9mm.

"I wish to speak with Danny Valentine," the demon enunciated clearly, "or I will kill you."

"Come on in," I said. "And put that thing away. Didn't your mother ever teach you it was bad manners to wave a gun at a woman?"

"Who knows what a Necromance has guarding his door?" the demon replied. "Where is Danny Valentine?"

I heaved a mental sigh. "Come on in off my front porch," I said. "*I'm* Danny Valentine, and you're being really rude. If you're going to try to kill me, get it over with. If you want to hire me, this is *so* the wrong way to go about it."

I don't think I've ever seen a demon look nonplussed before. He holstered his gun and stepped into my front hall, peeling through the layers of my warding, which parted obediently to let him through. When he stood in front of me, kicking the door shut with one booted foot, I had him calculated down to the last erg of Power.

This is not going to be fun, I thought. *What is a Lord of Hell doing on my doorstep?*

Well, no time like the present to ask. "What's a Lord of Hell doing on my doorstep?" I asked.

"I have come to offer you a contract," he said. "Or more precisely, to invite you to audience with the Prince, where he will present you with a contract. Fulfill this contract successfully, and you will be allowed to live with riches beyond your wildest dreams." It didn't sound like a rote speech.

I nodded. "And if I said I wasn't interested?" I asked. "You know, I'm a busy girl. Raising the dead for a living is a high-demand skill nowadays."

The demon regarded me for maybe twenty seconds before he grinned, and a cold sweat broke out all over my body. My nape prickled and my fingers twitched. The three wide scars on my back twitched uneasily.

"Okay," I said. "Let me get my things, and I'll be happy to attend His Gracious Princeship, yadda-yadda, bing-bong. Capice?"

He looked only slightly less amused, his thin grim face lit with a murderous smile. "Of course. You have twenty minutes."

If I'd known what I was getting into, I would have asked for a few days. Like maybe the rest of my life.

CHAPTER
2

The demon spent those twenty minutes in my living room, examining my bookshelves. At least, he appeared to be looking at the books when I came downstairs, shrugging my coat on. Abracadabra once called me "the Indiana Jones of the necromantic world," high praise from the Spider of Saint City—if she meant it kindly. I liked to dress for just about any occasion.

So my working outfit consists of: a Trade Bargains microfiber shirt, dries quickly and sheds dirt with a simple brush-off; a pair of butter-soft broken-in jeans; scuffed engineer boots with worn heels; my messenger bag strapped diagonally across my torso; and an old explorer coat made for photojournalists in war zones, with plenty of pockets and Kevlar panels sewn in. I finished braiding my hair and tied it off with an elastic band as I stepped into the living room, now full of the smell of man and cologne as well as the entirely nonphysical smell of demon—a cross between burning cinnamon and heavy amber musk. "My literary collection seems to please you," I said, maybe a little sardonically. My palms were sweating. My teeth wanted to chatter. "I don't suppose you could give me any idea of what your Prince wants with me."

He turned away from my bookshelves and shrugged. Demons shrug a lot. I suppose they think a lot of what humans do deserves nothing more than a shrug. "Great," I muttered, and scooped up my athame and the little jar of blessed water from my fieldstone altar. My back prickled with fresh waves of gooseflesh. *There's a demon in my living room. He's behind me. I have a demon behind me. Dammit, Danny, focus!*

"It's a little rude to bring blessed items before the Prince," the demon told me.

I snorted. "It's a little rude to point a gun in my face if you want me to work for you." I passed my hand over my altar—no, nothing else. I crossed to the big oak armoire and started flipping through the drawers. *I wish my hands would stop shaking.*

"The Prince specifically requested you, and sent me to collect you. He said nothing about the finer points of *human* etiquette." The demon regarded me with laser-green eyes. "There is some urgency attached to this situation."

"Mmmh." I waved a sweating, shaking hand over my shoulder. "Yeah. And if I walk out that door half-prepared I'm not going to do your Prince any good, am I?"

"You reek of fear," he said quietly.

"Well, I just had a gun shoved in my face by a Lord of Hell. I don't think you're the average imp-class demon that I very rarely deal with, boyo. And you're telling me that the Devil wants my company." I dug in the third drawer down and extracted my turquoise necklace, slipped it over my head, and dropped it down my shirt. *At least I sound good,* I thought, the lunatic urge to laugh rising up under my breastbone. *I don't sound like I'm shitting my pants with fright. Goody for me.*

"The Prince wishes you for an audience," he said.

I guess the Prince of Hell doesn't like to be called the Devil. On any other day I might have found that funny. "So what do I call you?" I asked, casually enough.

"You may address me as Jaf," he answered after a long crackling pause.

Shit, I thought. If he'd given me his Name I could have maybe used it. "Jaf," however, might have been a joke or a nickname. Demons were tricky. "Nice to meet you, Jaf," I said. "So how did you get stuck with messenger duty?"

"This is a sensitive situation." He sounded just like a politician. I slipped the stiletto up my sleeve into its sheath, and turned to find him watching me. "Discretion would be wise."

"I'm good at discretion," I told him, settling my bag so that it hung right.

"You should practice more," he replied, straight-faced.

I shrugged. "I suppose we're not stopping for drinks on the way."

"You are already late."

It was like talking to a robot. I wished I'd studied more about demons at the Academy. It wasn't like them to carry guns. I racked my brains, trying to think of any armed demon I'd heard of.

None sprang to mind. Of course, I was no Magi, I had no truck with demons. Only the dead.

I carried my sword into the front hall and waited for him. "You go out first," I said. "I've got to close up the house."

He nodded and brushed past me. The smell of demon washed over me—it would start to dye the air in a confined space, the psychic equivalent of static. I followed him out my front door, snapping my house shields closed out of long habit, the Power shifting and closing like an airlock in an old B movie. Rain flashed and jittered down, smashed into the porch roof and the paved walk. The garden bowed and nodded under the water.

I followed the demon down my front walk. The rain didn't touch him—then again, how would I have noticed, his hair was so dark it looked wet anyway. And his long, dark, high-collared coat, too. My boots made a wet shushing sound against the pavement. I thought about dashing back for the dubious safety of my house.

The demon glanced over his shoulder, a flash of green eyes in the rain. "Follow me," he said.

"Like I have another option?" I spread my hands a little, indicating the rain. "If you don't mind, it's awful wet out here. I'd hate to catch pneumonia and sneeze all over His Majesty."

He set off down my street. I glanced around. No visible car. Was I expected to walk to Hell?

The demon walked up to the end of the block and turned left, letting me trot behind him. Apparently I *was* expected to hoof it.

Great.

CHAPTER
3

*C*arrying a sword on the subway does tend to give you a certain amount of space, even on crowded hovertrains. I'm an accredited and tattooed Necromance, capable of carrying anything short of an assault rifle on the streets and allowed edged metal in transports. Spending the thirty thousand credits for testing and accreditation at the Academy had been the best step I'd ever taken for personal safety.

Although passing the final Test had turned a few of my hairs white. There weren't many accredited Necromances around.

The demon also granted me a fair amount of space. Although none of the normals could really tell what he was, they still gave him a wide berth. Normals can't see psychic power and energy shifts, but they *feel* it if it's strong enough, like a cold draft.

As soon as we started down the steps into the underground, Jaf dropped back until he was walking right next to me, indicating which stile to walk through and dropping two old-fashioned tokens in. I suppressed the shiver that caused—demons didn't usually pay for anything. What the bloody blue blazes was going on?

We got on the southbound train, the press of the crowd soft and choking against my mental borders. My knuckles were white, my fingers rigid around the scabbard. The demon stood slightly behind me, my back prickling with the thought—*he could slip a knife between my ribs and leave me here, gods protect me.* The whine of antigrav settled into my back teeth as the retrofitted train slid forward on its reactive-greased rails, the antigrav giving every bump a queer floating sensation.

Whispers and mutters filled the car. One little blonde girl in a school uniform stared at my face. She was probably examining the tattoo on my left cheek, a twisted caduceus with a flashing emerald set at the top. An emerald was the mark of a Necromance—as if anyone could have missed the sword. I smiled at her and she smiled back, her blue eyes twinkling. Her whey-faced mother, loaded down with shopping bags, saw this and gasped, hugging her child into her side a little harder than was absolutely necessary.

The smile dropped from my face.

The demon bumped me as the train bulleted around a bend. I jumped nervously, would have sidled away if the crowd had allowed. As it was, I accidentally elbowed an older woman with a crackling plastic bag, who let out an undignified squeak.

This is why I never take public transportation, I thought, and smiled an apology. The woman turned pale under her gray coif, coughed, and looked away.

I sighed, the smile again falling from my face. *I don't know why I even try. They don't see anything but my tat anyway.*

Normals feared psions regardless—there was an atavistic fear that we were all reading normal minds and laughing at them, preparing some nefarious plot to make them our mental slaves. The tats and accreditation were supposed to defray that by making psions visible and instituting tight controls over who could charge for psychic services—but all it did was make us more vulnerable to hatred. Normals didn't understand that for us, dipping into their brains was like taking a bath in a sewer. It took a serious emergency before a psi would read a normal's mind. The Parapsychic Act had stopped psions from being bought and sold like cattle, but it did nothing to stop the hate. And the fear, which fed the hate. And so on.

Six stops later I was heartily tired of people jamming into the subway car, seeing me, and beating a hasty retreat. Another three stops after that the car was mostly empty, since we had passed rapidly out of downtown. The little girl held her mother's hand and still stared at me, and there was a group of young toughs on the other end of the car, sallow and muttering in the fluorescent lights. I stood, my right arm wrapped around a pole to keep my hand free to draw if I had to. I hated sitting down in germ-laden subway seats.

"The next stop," Jaf-the-demon said. I nodded. He still stood very close to me, the smell of demon overpowering the canned air and effluvia of the subways. I glanced down at the end of the car and saw that the young men were elbowing each other and whispering.

Oh, great. It looked like another street tough was going to find out whether or not my blade was just for show. I'd never understood Necromances who carry only ceremonial steel to use during apparitions. If you're allowed to carry steel, you should know how to use it. Then again, most Necromances didn't do mercenary work, they just lived in shitty little apartments until they paid off their accreditation fees and *then* started trying to buy a house. Me? I decided to take the quicker way. As usual.

One of them got to his feet and stamped down the central aisle. The little girl's mother, a statuesque brunette in nurse's scrubs and Nikesi sneakers, her three plastic bags rustling, pulled the little girl into her side again as he passed.

The pimpled young man jolted to a stop right in front of me. He didn't smell like Chill or hash, which was a good thing; a street tough hyped on Chill would make the situation rapidly unbearable. On the other hand, if he was stone-cold sober and still this stupid—"Hey, pretty baby," he said, his eyes skittering from my feet to my breasts to my cheek and then back to my breasts, "Wassup?"

"Nothing," I replied, pitching my voice low and neutral.

"You got a blade," he said. "You licensed to carry that, sugar?"

I tilted my head slightly, presenting my cheek. The emerald would be glinting and winking under the harsh lights. "You bet I am," I said. "And I even know how to use it. So go trundle back to your friends, Popsicle."

His wet fishmouth worked a little, stunned. Then he reached for his waistband.

I had a split second to decide if he was armed or just trying to start some trouble. I never got to make the decision, though, because the demon stepped past me, bumping me aside, and smacked the youngster. It was an open-handed backhand strike, not meaning to do any real damage, but it still tossed the kid to the other end of the subway car, back into the clutch of teen toughs.

I sighed. "Fuck." I let go of the pole as soon as I regained my balance. "You didn't have to do that."

Then one of the punk's friends pulled out a Transom 987 projectile gun, and I crouched for nonexistent cover. The demon moved, stepping past me, and I watched events come to their foregone conclusion.

The kids boiled up from their seats, one of them yanking their injured, pimply-faced friend to his feet. They were all wearing black denim jackets and green bandannas—yet another minigang.

The demon blinked across intervening space and slapped the illegal (if you weren't accredited or a police officer) gun out of the boy's hand, sent it skittering against the floor. The nurse covered her daughter's ear with her hand, staring, her mouth agape. I moved forward, coming to my feet, my sword singing free of the sheath, and slid myself in between them and the gang, where the demon had broken one boy's arm and was now in the process of holding the gunner up by his throat, shaking him as negligently as a cat might shake a mouse.

"You want to get off at the next stop," I told the mother, who stared at me. "Trust me."

She nodded. Her eyes were wide and wet with terror. The little girl stared at me.

I turned back to find the demon standing in the center of a ring of limp bodies. "Hello!" I shouted, holding the sword in my right hand with the blade level across my body, the reinforced scabbard reversed along my left forearm to act as a shield. It was a highly unorthodox way to hold a katana, but Jado-sensei always cared less about orthodox than keeping alive, and I found I agreed with him. If the demon came for me, I could buy some time with the steel and a little more time with Power. He'd eat me alive, of course, but I had a chance—

He turned, brushing his hands together as if wiping away dust. One of the boys groaned. "Yes?" Same level, robotic voice.

"You didn't kill anyone, did you?" I asked.

Bright green eyes scorched the air. He shrugged. "That would create trouble," he said.

"Is that a yes or a no?" I firmed my grip on the hilt. "Did you kill any of them?" I didn't want to do the paperwork even if it was a legitimate kill in response to an assault.

"No, they'll live," he said, glancing down. Then he stepped mincingly free of the ring of bodies.

"*Anubis et'her ka,*" I breathed. *Anubis, protect me.*

The demon's lips compressed into a thin line. The train slowed, deceleration rocking me back on my heels. If he was going to attack, this would be a great time. "The Prince requested you delivered unharmed," he said, and sidled to the door, not turning his back to my blade.

"Remind me to thank him," I shot back, swallowing against the sudden dust in my mouth. I wondered what other "requests" the Prince had made.

CHAPTER
4

*W*e ended up on the platform, me sliding my sword reluctantly back into the sheath, the demon watching as the nurse hurried her little girl up the steps. The stop was deserted, sound echoing off ceramic tiles as the train slid along its reactive-greased tracks. I took a deep breath, tried to calm my racing heart.

When the last footstep had faded, the demon turned on his heel and leapt down onto the tracks.

"Oh, no," I said. "No way. Negatory." I actually backed up two steps. "Look, I'm *human*. I can't go running around on subway tracks." For a moment the station seemed to shrink, the earth behind the walls pressing in, and I snapped a longing glance at the stairs.

He looked up at me, his long thin golden hands shoved deep in his coat pockets. "There is nothing to fear," he said finally.

"Says *you*," I snapped. "You're not the one who could die here. Come on. No way."

"This is the quickest way," he said, but his mouth thinned even more once he stopped speaking. I could tell he was losing patience with my stupid human self. "I promise you, there is no danger. However, if you keep balking I will have no choice but to drag you."

I just saw him blast six neopunks without even breaking a sweat. And he's a demon. Who knows what he'll do?

"Give me your Name," I said, "and I will."

As soon as it escaped my mouth, I backed up another two steps, wishing I hadn't said it. It was too late. The demon made a sound that might have been a laugh.

"Don't make me drag you, Necromance," he said, finally. "The Prince would be most displeased."

"That isn't my problem," I pointed out. "No way. I can't trust you."

"You have left the safety of your abode and followed me here." His eyes narrowed. "Unwise of you, to cavil now."

"So I'm too curious for my own good," I said. "Give me your Name, and I'll follow you."

He shrugged, spreading his hands. I waited. If the Prince truly wanted me delivered unharmed, the demon would give me his Name. It barely mattered—I was no Magi, able to force a minor demon into working my will or able to negotiate a bargain with a greater demon for years of service in exchange for blood, sex, or publicity. I rarely ever dealt with demons. He was right, that I'd come this far and it wasn't exactly wise to start backing down now, but better to back down now while I still had a running chance at reaching the surface than have the demon drag me into a subway tunnel. At least with his Name I might be able to stop him from killing me.

"Tierce Japhrimel," he said, finally.

I blinked, amazed he'd given in, and did some rapid mental calculations. "Do you swear on the Prince of Hell and the waters of Lethe that your true, full Name truly is Tierce Japhrimel?"

He shrugged. "I swear," he said after a long tense sweating second of silence.

I hopped down into the dark well of the tracks, jolting my knees. *I'm too old for this shit*, I thought. *I was too old for this shit ten years ago.* "Good deal," I mumbled. "Fine, lead the way, then. I'm warning you, though, any tricks and I'll haunt you, demon or not."

"That would indeed be a feat," he said. I think he meant to say it quietly, but the entire station echoed.

With that said, my sword ready, and no more excuses handy, I followed the demon into darkness.

CHAPTER
5

If I had to say with any certainty where the demon opened the door that led into a red glare, I would be at somewhat of a loss. I lose a lot of my sense of direction underground. The demon's tearing at the fabric of reality to split the walls of the worlds . . . well, it's complex, and takes an inhuman amount of Power, and I've never seen anyone but a demon do it. Magi sometimes tried unsuccessfully to force doors between this reality and the world of demons lying cheek-by-jowl with it instead of pleading for a demon to come through and make an appearance, but I was a Necromance. The only alternate reality I knew or cared about was the world of Death.

Some of the Magi said that the higher forms of Power were a result of the leaching of substance between this world and the world of the demons. I had never seen that—humans and the earth's own well of natural Power were all I'd ever noticed. Even though Magi training techniques were used as the basis for teaching psions how to control Power, every Magi had his or her own kind of trade secrets passed on from teacher to student and written in code, if not memorized. It was like Skinlin with their plant DNA maps or a Necromance's psychopomp, personal information.

There was an access hatch, I remember that much, that the demon opened as if it had been deliberately left unlocked. Then again, who would be running around down here? A long concrete-floored corridor lit faintly by buzzing fluorescents, and a door at the end of it—but this door was ironbound wood with a spiked, fluid glyph carved deeply into the surface of the wood. The glyph smoked and twisted; I felt reality tearing and shifting around us until the demon was the only solid thing.

I was seriously nauseated by now, swallowing bile and nearly choking. *This isn't built for humans,* I thought, vicious little mouths nipping at my skin. It was akin to freefall, this walking between the worlds; that was why you were only supposed to do it astrally. The physical structure of my body was being stressed, the very building blocks of my cellular structure taking loads they weren't designed to handle. Not to mention the fact that the twisting of visual and auditory input screwed up my perceptions, and the *alienness* of the Power here made my aura compress close to my skin and shiver. When the demon opened up the door and red light spilled out, I almost lost the chicken soup I'd bolted for lunch. The demon grabbed my arm and hauled me through, and I understood why he'd been standing so close to me. As soon as the smell of demon washed over me, I felt a little better. The demon's aura stretched to cover me, and when the door closed behind us with a thud I found myself with a demon holding my elbow, volcanic heat lapping at my skin, and a gigantic hall with what appeared to be an obsidian floor and long narrow windows. Red light from spitting, ever-burning torches ran wetly over the floor and the ceiling, which I only glanced at and then back at the floor, shutting my eyes.

I heard, dimly, the demon saying something. The sense of sudden freefall stopped with a thump, as if normal gravity had reasserted itself. Nausea retreated—mostly. I choked, and tried to stop myself from spewing.

The demon pressed the fingers of his free hand against my sweating forehead and said something else, in a sliding harsh language that hurt my ears. Warm blood dripped down from my nose. I kept my fingers around my sword.

It took a few minutes for the spinning to stop and my stomach to decide it wouldn't turn itself inside-out. "I'm okay," I said finally, feeling sweat trickle down my spine. "Just a little . . . whoa. That's . . . oh, *shit*—"

"It's a common reaction," he replied. "Just breathe."

I forced myself to stand upright, swallowed sour heat and copper blood. "I'm okay," I repeated. "The sooner I get this over with, the sooner I can go home, right?"

He nodded. His lips were turned down at the corners now, and I saw that his long black coat was now in the same geometric scheme as the rest of the world. That was part of the problem—the angles of the floor and walls were just a little wrong, just a crucial millimeter off. My brain kept trying to make it fit and failing, and that made my stomach resemble a Tilt-A-Whirl, only without the fun part.

"Fine," I said. "Let's go."

He kept his hand closed around my elbow as we negotiated the vast expanse of the ballroom. *Is this the antechamber to Hell?* I thought, and had a difficult time not giggling. *I think I'm doing well with this. Really well.*

Then we reached the end of the hall, and the demon

pushed open another large ironbound door, and all thoughts of dealing really well went right out the window. I even dropped my sword. The demon made a quick movement, and had my blade . . . I never dropped my sword. *Never.*

"A *human,*" the Thing sitting behind the massive desk said. It had three spiraling horns sprouting from its head and wide, lidless, cat-slit yellow eyes that fastened on me. Its body was a shapeless mass of yellow blubber, festooned with long bristling black hairs in a few random places. Three nipples clustered on its chest, and the skin looked wrong, and greasy. The worst part was the hinged mouth and razor-sharp teeth—but even worse than that were the long spidery fingers that looked like maggots crawling among the papers on its desk. My brain went merrily rambling on—*a demonic bureaucrat, even Hell has its paperwork . . .*

"Not for you, Trikornus," the green-eyed demon said. "She's for the Prince."

"What a lovely present. Finally back in the good graces, assassin?" It was still staring at me. A dripping, purple-red tongue slid out, caressed its chin with a sound like screaming sandpaper. "Ooooh, give us a taste. Just a little taste?"

"She is *for the Prince*, Baron," Jaf enunciated clearly. I was too busy suddenly studying my boot-toes. *How did I get here?* I wondered. *If I'd known, I would never have been a Necromance. But jeez, they never told me dealing with dead people would get me here, I thought only Magi dealt with demons—*

"Very well, you greedy spoilsport," the horror behind the desk said. I had a vivid mental image of those sharp teeth clamping in my upper thigh while blood squirted out, and barely suppressed a shudder. I felt cold under the sick fiery heat coating my skin. The thing gave a snorting, hitching laugh. "The Prince is in his study, waiting for you. Second door on the left."

I felt more than saw Jaf's nod. *Who ever would have thought that he'd seem like the lesser of two evils?* I thought, then felt a chill finger touch the back of my sweating neck. That this Japhrimel looked a little more human didn't mean that he was any less of an alien being.

He guided me past the desk, and I was grateful that he was between me and the four-eyed demon. What would I have done if *that* thing had been sent to come fetch me? And what the hell would a demon need a Necromance for?

The world grew very dim for a few moments, but the demon half-dragged me through another ironbound door. "Keep breathing, human," he said, and stopped moving for a few seconds. "The Baron likes to dress in a different skin for each visitor," he continued. "It's normal. Just breathe."

If this is normal, don't let me see weird. "You mean you do this to other people, too?" I gasped out.

He made a brief snorting sound. "Not me. Sometimes people come without their flesh, Magi and the like. Very few are sent for. Only the desperate come here."

"I can believe that." I took a deep whooping breath. Felt bile burn the back of my throat. "Thanks," I said, finally, and he started off again. This hall was narrow but high, and there were paintings hanging on the wall that I didn't want to look at after catching a glimpse of the first one. Instead I stared at my feet moving under me, and had a brief flash of unreality—my feet didn't look like mine.

Jaf's fingers closed around my nape and I took in a deep breath. I'd stumbled and half-fallen. "Not long now," he said, releasing my neck, pulling me along by my arm. "Just hold on."

I was in bad shape, shivering and trying not to retch, when he opened another door and pulled me through a subliminal *snap*. My feet took on their normal dimensions, and I slumped gratefully into the demon's grasp. The only thing holding me up was his fingers.

Then I felt something in my hand. He closed his free hand around mine, the sword held by both of us now. "Here," he said. "Hold on to your blade, Necromance."

"Indeed, it wouldn't do to drop it." This voice was smooth as silk, persuasive, filtering into my ears. "She survived the Hall. Very impressive."

Japhrimel said nothing. I was actually kind of starting to like him.

Not really.

I opened my eyes. The demon's chest was right in front of me. I tilted my head back, looked up into his face. His eyes scorched mine. "Thanks," I told him, my voice trembling slightly. "That first step's a lulu."

He didn't say anything, but his lips thinned out. Then he stepped aside.

I found myself confronted with a perfectly reasonable neo-Victorian study, carpeted in plush crimson. Leather-clad books lined up on bookcases against the dark-paneled wooden walls, three red velvet chairs in front of a roaring fireplace, red tasseled drapes drawn over what might have been a window. A large mahogany desk sat obediently to one side.

A slim dark shape stood next to the fireplace. The air was drunk and dizzy with the scent of demons. I tightened my fingers on my sword, fisted my other hand, felt my lacquered nails dig into my palm.

The man—at least, it had a manlike shape—had an amazing corona of golden hair standing out from his head. A plain black T-shirt and jeans, bare golden-brown feet. I took a deep rasping breath.

"What though the field be lost? All is not lost; the inconquerable will, And study of revenge, immortal hate—" I trailed off, licked my lips with my dry tongue. I'd had a classical humanist as a social worker, and had been infected with a love of books at an early age. The classics had sustained me all through the schoolyard hellhole of Rigger Hall.

I shuddered, remembering that. I didn't like to think about the Hall, where I'd learned reading, writing, and 'rithmatic—and the basics of controlling my powers. Where I'd also learned how little those powers would protect me.

He turned away from the fireplace. *"And courage never to submit or yield,"* he finished. His eyes were like black ice and green flame at the same time, and there was a mark on his forehead that I didn't look at, because I found I had dropped my gaze.

The demon Jaf sank down to one knee, rose again.

"You're late," the Prince of Hell said, mildly.

"I had to paint my nails," my mouth bolted like a runaway horse. "A demon showing up on my doorstep and pointing a gun at me tends to disarrange me."

"He pointed a gun at you?" The Prince made a gesture with one hand. "Please, sit, Miss Valentine. May I call you Dante?"

"It's my name," I responded, uncomfortably. *The Devil knows my name,* I thought, in a kind of delirium. *The Devil knows my name.*

Then I gave myself a sharp mental slap. *Quit it. You need your wits about you, Danny, so just quit it.* "I would be honored," I added. "It's a pleasure to meet Your Lordship. Your Highness. Whatever."

He laughed. The laugh could strip the skin off an elephant in seconds. "I'm referred to as the father of lies, Dante. I'm old enough to know a falsehood when I hear one."

"So am I," I responded. "I suppose you're going to say that you mean me no harm, right?"

He laughed again, throwing his head back. He was too beautiful, the kind of androgynous beauty that holovid models sometimes achieve. If I hadn't known he was male, I might have wondered. The mark on his forehead flashed green. *It's an emerald, like a Necromance,* I thought. *I wonder why?* Necromance emeralds were set in the skin when we finished basic schooling at about eight; I didn't think the Prince of Hell had ever gone to primary school.

I was rapidly getting incoherent. "Excuse me," I said politely enough. "It's getting hard to breathe in here."

"This won't take very long. Bring the lovely Necromance over to a chair, my eldest, she's about to fall down." His voice turned the color of smooth cocoa mixed with honey. My knees turned to water.

Jaf dragged me across the room. I was too relieved to argue. The place looked normal. *Human,* without the weird geometry. *If I ever get back to the real world I'm going to kiss the ground,* I promised myself. *I've read about people going to Hell astrally. Lucky me getting to visit in the flesh.*

He dropped me into a chair—the one on the left—then stepped around to the side, his arms folded, and appeared to turn into a statue.

The Prince regarded me. His eyes were lighter but more weirdly depthless than Jaf's, a sort of radioactive silken glow. Thirty seconds looking into those eyes and I might have agreed to anything just to make it stop.

As it was, I looked down at my knees. "You wanted to see me," I said. "Here I am."

"Indeed." The Prince turned back to the fireplace. "I have a mission for you, Dante. Succeed, and you can count me as a friend all the years of your life, and those years will be long. It is in my power to grant wealth and near-immortality, Dante, and I am disposed to be generous."

"And if I fail?" I couldn't help myself.

"You'll be dead," he said. "Being a Necromance, you're well-prepared for that, aren't you?"

My rings glinted dully in the red light. "I don't want to die," I said finally. "Why me?"

"You have a set of . . . talents that are uniquely suited to the task," he answered.

"So what is it exactly you want me to *do*?" I asked.

"I want you to kill someone," he said.

CHAPTER
6

*W*hoa." I looked up at him, forgetting the hypnotic power of those green eyes. "Look, I'm not a contract killer. I'm a Necromance. I bring people *back* to ask questions, and lay them to rest when necessary."

"Fifty years ago, a demon escaped my realm," the Prince said mildly, his voice cutting through my objections. "He is wandering your realm at will, and he is about to break the Egg."

Did he say crack the egg? Is that some kind of demon euphemism? "What egg?" I asked, shifting uncomfortably in the chair. My sword lay across my knees. This felt too real to be a hallucination.

"The Egg is a demon artifact," the Prince said. "Suffice it to say the effects will be very unpleasant if this particular demon breaks the Egg in your world."

My mouth dried. "You mean like end-of-the-world bad?" I asked.

The Prince shrugged. "I wish the Egg found and the thief executed. You are a Necromance, capable of seeing what others do not. Some have called you the greatest death-talker of your generation, which is high praise indeed. You are human, but you may be able to find the

Egg and kill the thief. Jaf will accompany you, to keep your skin whole until you accomplish your task." He turned back to the fireplace. "And if you bring the Egg back to me I will reward you with more than a human being could ever dream of."

"I'm not so sure I want your reward," I told him. "Look, I'm just a working girl. I raise the dead for issues of corporate law and to solve probate questions. I don't do lone-gun revenge stuff."

"You've been dabbling in the bounty-hunting field since you left the Academy and with corporate espionage and other illegal fancies—though no assassination, I'll grant you that—for five years to pay off your mortgage and live more comfortably than most of your ilk," he replied. "Don't play with me, Dante. It is exceedingly ill-advised to play with me."

"Likewise," I said. "You've got a fully armed Necromance who knows your Name sitting in your inner sanctum, Your Highness. You must be desperate." My mouth dried to cotton, my hands shook. That was another lie.

Despite being more research-oriented than most of my kind, I didn't know the Devil's Name—nobody did. In any case, he was too powerful to be commanded around like a mere imp. I doubted even knowing Tierce Japhrimel's Name would do more than keep him from outright killing me. Lucifer's Name was a riddle pursued by Magi, who thought that if they learned it they could control the legions of Hell. The Ceremonials said Lucifer's true Name was more like a god's Name—it would express him, but didn't have power *over* him. The exact nature of the relationship between Lucifer and the gods was also hotly debated; since the complete verification of the existence of demons the various churches that had survived the Awakening and the Ceremonials had conducted experiments, largely inconclusive. Belief in the power of the words to banish imps was necessary—but sometimes even that didn't work unless the demon in question was extremely weak. As Gabe's grandmother Adrienne Spocarelli had remarked once in a footnote to her *Gods and Magi*, it was a good thing demons didn't want to rule the earth, since you couldn't even banish one unless it was a bitty one.

"And you must be greedy." His voice hadn't changed at all. "What do you want, Dante Valentine? I can give you the world."

It whispered in my veins, tapped at my skull. *I can give you the world . . .*

I actually thought about it, but Lucifer couldn't give me anything I wanted. Not without the price being too high. If I was sure of nothing else in this situation, I was sure of *that*. "Get thee behind me," I whispered, finally. "I just want to be left alone. I don't want anything to do with this."

"I can even," he said, "tell you who your parents were."

You son of a bitch. I rocketed to my feet, my sword whipping free. Blue runes twisted inside the steel, but neither demon moved. I backed around the chair, away from Jaf, who still looked like a statue, staring at my sword. Red firelight ran wet over the blade, blue runes twisting in the steel. "You leave my parents out of this," I snapped. "Fine. I'll do your job, *Iblis Lucifer*. If you leave me alone. And I don't want your trained dog-demon over there. Give me what information you've got, and I'll find this Egg for you."

For all I knew my parents had been too poor to raise

me; either that or they'd been too strung out on any cocktail of substances. It didn't matter—since my Matheson index was so high and they'd had me in a hospital, they hadn't been able to sell me as an indentured. That was the only gift they'd given me—that, and the genetic accident that made me a Necromance. Both incredible gifts, when you thought about the alternative. It wasn't the first time somebody had twitted me about being an orphan.

Nobody ever did it more than once.

Lucifer shrugged. "You must take Japhrimel. Otherwise, it's suicide."

"And have him double-cross me once we find this Egg? You must not want word to get out that someone took off with it." I shook my head. "No dice. I work alone."

His eyes came up, bored into my skull. "You are under the illusion that you have a choice."

I lifted my sword, a shield against his gaze. Sweat trickled down my back, soaking into my jeans. It was damnably hot—*what else, in Hell? You were expecting a mint julep and a cool breeze?*

I didn't even see Jaf move. In one neat move he had the sword taken away, resheathed, and the gun pressed into my temple. One of his arms was across my throat. My feet kicked fruitlessly at empty air.

"You are intriguing," the Prince of Hell said, stalking across the room. "Most humans would be screaming by now. Or crying. There seems to be a distressing tendency to sob among your kind."

I spat an obscenity that would have made Jado-sensei, with his Asiano sense of decorum, wince. Jaf didn't move. His arm slipped a little, and I fought for breath.

He could crush my windpipe like a paper cup. I stopped kicking—it would waste what little oxygen I had left—and *concentrated*, the world narrowing to a single still point.

"Let go of her," the Prince said calmly. "She's building up Power."

Jaf dropped me. I hit the ground and whirled on the balls of my feet, the sword blurring free of the sheath in an arc of silver, singing. *No think,* little nut-brown Jado in his orange robes yelled in my memory. *No think, move! Move!*

I didn't even *see* Jaf move again. He stepped in close, moving faster than a human, of course, twisted my wrist just short of breaking it, and tore the sword from my fingers. I punched him and actually connected, snapping his head back. Then I backed up, shuffling, away from the two demons, my two *main-gauches* whipping out, one reversed along my left forearm, the other held almost horizontally in front of me, ready for anything.

Anything except this.

Jaf dropped my sword. It chimed, smoking, on the floor next to the scabbard. "Blessed steel. She *believes*," he said, glancing at the Prince, who had stopped and was considering me.

Of course I believe, I thought, in a sort of delirium. *I talk to the god of Death on a regular basis. I believe because I must.*

"Do you think you can fight your way free of Hell?" the Prince asked.

"Do you think you could be polite?" I tossed back. " 'Cause I have to say, your treatment of a guest kind of sucks." I gulped down air, a harsh whooping inhalation.

It was slow suffocation, breathing in whatever gas these demons used for air.

Lucifer took a single step toward me. "My apologies, Dante. Come, sit down. Japhrimel, give her sword back. We should be polite, shouldn't we, since we are *asking* her for her help."

"What's in the Egg?" I asked, not moving. "Why is it so important?"

Lucifer smiled. That smile made me back up until my shoulders hit a bookcase. "What's in the Egg?" he said. "None of your concern, human."

"Oh, boy." I gulped down air. "This is *so* wrong."

"Help me, Dante, and you will be one of the chosen few to claim my friendship." His voice was soft and persuasive, fingering at my skull, looking for entrance. I bit savagely at the inside of my cheek, the slice of pain clearing my head slightly. "I swear to you on the waters of Lethe, if you retrieve the Egg and kill the thief, I will consider you a friend for eternity."

I tasted blood. "What's the demon's name?" I asked. "The one that stole it."

"His name is Vardimal," Lucifer said. "You know him as Santino."

I considered throwing my left knife. It wouldn't kill him, but the blessed steel might slow him down long enough for me to juke for the door or the window. "Santino?" I whispered. "You slimy son of a—"

"Watch how you speak to the Prince," Jaf interrupted. Lucifer raised one golden hand.

"Let her speak as she wishes, Japhrimel," he said. For the first time, he sounded . . . what? Actually weary. "Value the human who speaks truth, for they are few and far between."

"You could say the same for demons," I said numbly. "Santino . . ." It was a longing whisper.

—*blood sliding out between my fingers, a chilling crystal laugh, Doreen's scream, life bubbling out through the gash in her throat, screaming, screaming*—

I resheathed my knives.

Lucifer examined me for a few more moments, then turned and paced back to the fireplace. "I am aware that you have your own score to settle with Vardimal," he continued. "You help me, I help you. You see?"

"Santino was a demon?" I whispered. "How—" I had to clear my throat. "How the *hell* am I supposed to kill him?"

"Japhrimel will help you. He also has a . . . personal stake in this."

Jaf gingerly picked up my sword, slid it into the sheath. I watched this, sweat trickling down my forehead. A drop fell into my eyes, stinging. I blinked it away. "Why doesn't *he* just kill Santino?" I asked. My voice trembled.

"A very long time ago, during the dawning of the world, I granted this demon a gift in return for a service," Lucifer said. "He asked for an immunity. Neither man nor demon can kill him."

I thought this over. "So you think I can, since I'm neither."

"It is," Lucifer pointed out, "worth a try. Japhrimel will protect you long enough for you to carry out your mission."

Awww, jeez, isn't that sweet of him. I was about to say that, had a rare second thought, and shut my mouth. After a moment I nodded. "Fine." I didn't sound happy. "I'll do it. It's not like I have much of a choice." *And I'll*

*get free from this Jaf guy as soon as I've got the scent.
How hard can that be?*

"The rewards will be great," Lucifer reminded me.

"Screw your rewards, I'll be happy just to get out
alive," I muttered. *Santino was a demon? No wonder I
couldn't find him.* "Can I go back to Earth now? Or is
this Vardimal hanging out in the Infernals?" The thought
of hunting for a murderous demon through the lands of
the not-quite-real-but-real-enough made suicide seem
like a pretty good option.

"He is among your kind," Lucifer told me. "Your
world is a playground for us, and he plays cruel games."

"Gee, imagine that." I swallowed, a dry dusty click.
"A demon who likes hurting people."

"Let me tell you something, Dante Valentine," Lucifer
replied, staring into the flames. His back was rigid. "I
saw your kind crawling up from mud yesterday, and
pitied you. *I* gave you fire. *I* gave you civilization, and
technology. *I* gave you the means to build a platform
above the mud. *I* gave you the secrets of love. My
demons have lived among you for thousands of years,
teaching you, molding your nervous systems so you
were no longer mere animals. And you spit on me, and
call me evil."

My mouth couldn't get any drier. We called them
demons, or djinn, or devils, or a hundred other names,
every culture had stories about them. Before the Great
Awakening they had been *only* stories and nightmares,
despite the Magi who had worked for centuries to clas-
sify and make regular contact with them. Nobody knew
if demons were gods, or subject to gods, or Something
Else Entirely.

My vote went for Something Else. But then again, I'd

always been the suspicious type. "Lucifer was the very first humanist," I said. "I'm well aware of that, Your Highness."

"Think of that before you open your mouth again," he continued as if I hadn't spoken. "Now get out, and do what you're told. I give you Japhrimel as a familiar, Dante Valentine. Go away."

"My lord—" Jaf began, and I rubbed my sweating hands on my damp jeans. I would need a salt tablet and a few liters of water—the heat was physical, pressing against my skin; sweat drenched my clothes.

"Get *out*," Lucifer said. "Don't make me repeat myself."

I wasn't about to argue. I looked at Jaf.

The demon stared at Lucifer for a moment, his jaw working, green eyes burning.

Green eyes. They both have green eyes. Are they related? Jeez, who knows? I swallowed again. The tension buzzed against the air, rasped against my skin.

Lucifer made an elegant motion with one golden hand. It was a rune, but not one I recognized.

Fire bit into my left shoulder. I screamed, sure that he'd decided to kill me after all, me and my big mouth—but Jaf stalked across the room, holding my scabbarded sword, and grabbed my elbow again. "This way," he said, over my breathless howl—it felt like a branding iron was pressed into my flesh, the *burning*—and he hauled me back toward the door we'd come in through. I struggled—*no not that again it HURTS it HURTS it HURTS*—but when he opened the door and pulled me through there was no hall, just an icy chill and the blessed stink of human air.

CHAPTER
7

$\mathcal{M}$y shoulder ached, a low dull throbbing. It was dark. Rain fell, but I was dry. My clothes were dry, too. I was covered with the smoky fragrance of demon magic.

I blinked.

I was lying on something hard and cold, but something warm was against the side of my face. Someone holding me. Musk and burning cinnamon. The smell drenched me, eased the burning in my shoulder and the pounding of my heart, the heavy smoky pain in my lungs. I felt like I'd been ripped apart and sewn back together the wrong way. " . . . *hurts*," I gasped, unaware I was talking.

"Breathe," Jaf said. "Just keep breathing. It will pass, I promise."

I groaned. Kept breathing.

Then the retching started. He rolled me onto my side, still holding me up, and I emptied my stomach between muttering obscenities. The demon actually stroked my hair. If I tried to forget that he had just held a gun to my head, it was actually kind of comforting.

I finished losing everything I'd ever thought of eating. Retched for a little while. Then everything settled down, and I lay on the concrete listening to sirens and hovers passing by while the demon stroked my hair and held me. It took a little while before I felt ready to face the world—even the real human world—again.

I said I'd kiss the ground, I thought. *Not sure I'd want to do that now that it's covered in puke. My puke. Disgusting.*

"I suppose this is pretty disgusting," I finally said, wishing I could rinse my mouth out.

I felt the demon's shrug. "I don't care."

"Of course not." I tasted bile. "It's a *human* thing. You wouldn't care."

"I like humans," he said. "Most demons do. Otherwise we would not have bothered to make you our companions instead of apes." He stroked my hair. A few strands had come loose and stuck to my cheeks and forehead.

"Great. And here I thought we were something like nasty little lapdogs to you guys." I took a deep breath. I felt like I could stand up now. "So I guess I've got my marching orders, huh?"

"I suppose so." He rose slowly to his feet, pulling me with him, and caught me when I overbalanced. He put my sword in my hands, wrapped my fingers around it, then held the scabbard there until I stopped swaying.

It was my turn to shrug. "I should go home and pick up some more stuff if we're going to be chasing a demon down," I told him. "And I need . . . well."

"Certainly," he said. "It is the Prince's will that I obey."

The way he said it—all in one breath—made it sound like an insult. "I didn't do it," I said. "Don't get mad at me. What did he *do* to me, anyway?"

"When we get to your house, you should look," the demon said, infuriatingly calm. "I hope you realize how lucky you are, Necromance."

"I just survived a trip to Hell," I said. "Believe me, I'm counting my blessings right now. Where are we?"

"Thirty-third and Pole Street," he answered. "An alley."

I looked around. He was right. It was a dingy little alley, sheltered from the rain by an overhang. Three dumpsters crouched at the end, blocking access to the street. Brick walls, a graffiti tag, papers drifting in the uncertain breeze. "Lovely," I said. "You sure have a great flair for picking these places."

"You'd prefer the middle of Main Street?" he asked, his eyes glowing in the darkness. I stepped sideways as soon as my legs seemed willing to carry me. His hands fell back down to his sides. "The Prince . . ." He trailed off.

"Yeah, he's a real charmer, all right," I said. "What did he *do* to my shoulder? It hurts like a bitch."

"You'll see," was the calm reply. He brushed past me, heading for the mouth of the alley. "Let me move the dumpster, and we'll call a cab."

"Now you'll call a cab, where before you had to drag me through the subway?" I chucked my blade free of its sheath, checked the metal. Still bright. Still sharp.

"It was necessary. Leaving Hell is not the same as entering it, especially for a human. I had to find an entrance you would *survive*, but falling back into mortality is not so hard." He stopped, his back to me. "Not so very hard at all." The light was dim—*I've been in Hell all afternoon*, I thought, and felt an insane giggle bubble up inside me and die away. *Why do I always want to laugh at*

times like this? I wondered. All my life, the insane urge
to giggle had popped up at the worst times.

"Great," I muttered, shoving the blade back home.
"All right, let's go."

He shoved one of the dumpsters aside as easily as I
might have moved a footstool. I concentrated on putting
one foot in front of the other without keeling over.

Neon ran over the wet street. Thirty-third and Pole
was right in the middle of the Tank District. I wondered
if it was a demon joke—but then, there was likely to be
a lot of sex and psychoactives floating in the air here. It
was probably easier to open a door between here and
Hell around that kind of energy charge.

We splashed through puddles, the demon occasionally
falling back to take my elbow and steer me around a corner. He seemed content to just walk silently, and I hurt
too much to engage in small talk. I'd ditch him soon
enough.

He hailed a cab at the corner of Thirtieth and Vine,
and I fell into the seat gratefully. I gave my address to the
driver—a bespectacled, mournful Polish man who hissed
a charm against the evil eye when he saw my tattooed
cheek. He jangled the antique rosary hanging from his
faredeck and addressed all his replies to the demon; he
couldn't See that the demon was more of a threat than
little old human me.

Story of my life. Guy didn't mind the demon, but
would have thrown me out of the cab if he could.

CHAPTER
8

$\mathcal{G}$o ahead and make yourself at home," I said as I locked the door. "There's beer in the fridge. And wine, if you like that. I've got to take a shower."

He nodded. "I should speak of Vardimal," he said. "To familiarize you with—"

"Later," I told him. My shoulder twinged. "Hey."

He turned back to me.

"What did he do to me?" I lifted the sword a little, pointing at my left shoulder with the hilt. "Huh?"

"The Prince of Hell has granted you a familiar, Necromance," Japhrimel said formally, clasping his hands behind his back. He looked a little like a priest in his long black high-collared coat. I wondered where he hid the guns. I'd never heard of a demon with guns before. *I should have studied harder, I suppose. But how the hell was I supposed to know that a demon would show up at my front door? I'm a bloody Necromance, not a Magi!*

"A fam—" My brain started to work again. "Oh, no. I'm not a Magi. I don't want—"

"Too late," he informed me. "Go take your shower, I'll keep watch."

"Keep watch? Nobody knows I'm working for—" I

put my back against the door. *How did I get into this?* I wondered—not for the last time, I might add.

"Your entry into Hell may have been remarked," the demon said. "I'll make coffee."

I shook my head and brushed past him, heading for the stairs. "Gods above and below," I muttered, "what did I do to deserve this?"

"You have a reputation for being honorable," the demon supplied helpfully. "And your talents as a Necromance are well-known."

I waved a hand over my shoulder at him. "Fine, fine. Just try not to set anything on fire, okay? Be careful with my house."

"As my Mistress wishes," he said. It would have been hard for him to sound more ironic.

I climbed the stairs, my legs aching. Even my teeth hurt. *An hour into this job and I'm already wishing I was on vacation.* I had to laugh, trailing my fingers along the painted wall. My sword seemed far heavier than it should be. Halfway up the stairs, under the altar niche, was a stash of three water bottles, and I snagged one. I fumbled in my bag for a salt tablet, took it. Dried sweatsalt crackled on my skin. I probably smelled like I'd been stuck in an oven. It was a miracle I hadn't been hit with heatstroke.

I drained the water bottle, dropped my sword on my bed, put my bag inside the bathroom door, and started stripping down. I paused halfway to turn the shower on, and examined my left shoulder in the mirror.

Pressed into the skin was a sigil I'd never seen before, not one of the Nine Canons I knew. I was no demonologist, so I didn't know what it meant, exactly. But when I touched it—the glyph shifting uneasily, ropy scar like a burn twisting under my fingertips—I hissed in a sharp breath, closing my eyes against a wave of heat.

I saw my kitchen as if through a sheet of wavering glass, the familiar objects twisted and shimmering with unearthly light. He was looking at my stove—

I found myself on my knees, gasping. *I've read about this,* I thought, oddly comforted. *I've read about seeing through a familiar's eyes. Breathe, Danny. Breathe. Breathe in, breathe out. Been doing it all your life. Just breathe.* The tiled floor bit into my knees, my forehead rested against the edge of my bathtub. Steam filled the air. *Gods,* I thought. *So that's what they're talking about when they say . . . oh, man. Heavy shit, dude. Can't take the scene; gotta bail.*

I'd just been given a demon familiar. Magi everywhere would be salivating—it was the high pursuit of every Magi, to achieve a working relationship with one of the denizens of Hell. I'd never done much in that arena—I had more than enough work to keep me busy inside my own specialty. But occult practitioners are a curious bunch—some of us like to fiddle around with everything when time permits. And a lot of the standard Magi training techniques were shared with other occult disciplines—Shamans, Journeymen, Witches, Ceremonials, Skinlin . . . and Necromances. After all, Magi had been the ones pursuing occult disciplines since before the Awakening and the Parapsychic Act. So I'd been given something most Magi worked for years to achieve—and I didn't want it. It only complicated an already fucked-up situation.

The steam shifted, blowing this way and that. I looked up to see the water running in the shower. I was wasting hot water.

That got me moving. I stripped off the rest of my clothes with trembling fingers and stepped into the shower, loosing my hair with a sigh. I've been dyeing my hair black for years, to fit in with Necromance codes, but sometimes I wondered if I should streak it with some purple or something. Or cut the damn mess off. When I was young and in the Hall, every girl's hair was trimmed boy-short except for the sexwitches. I suppose growing it out when I reached the Academy was another way of proving I was no longer required to follow any rules other than the professional ones. Purple streaks would look nice on me.

I'd been mousy blonde at the Hall. Dyeing your hair to fit in with the antiquated dress codes rubbed me the wrong way, but part of being an accredited Necromance was presenting a united front to the world. We were all supposed to look similar, to be instantly recognizable, dark-haired and pale with emeralds on our cheeks and accreditation tats if possible, carrying our swords like Shamans carried their staves.

Once I retire I'll let it grow out blonde, maybe, I thought, and then the shock of unreality hit me again. I slumped against the tiled wall, my teeth chattering.

I traced a glyph for Strength on the tiles with a trembling finger. It flushed red for a moment—I was dangerously close to shock. And if I went into shock, what would the demon do?

I finished washing up and got out, dried off, and padded into my bedroom, carrying my bag. I was dressed in a few minutes, moving automatically, sticking my feet back into my favorite pair of boots. The mark on my shoulder wasn't hurting now—it just ached a little, a flare of Power staining through my shielding and marking me like a demon to Sight. Black diamond spangles whirled through the trademark glitters of a Necromance's aura, and I could see the mark on my shoulder, a spot of pulsing darkness.

Great. This will make work so much easier, I thought, and sighed. I needed food. My stomach was rumbling, probably because I'd puked everything out in a back-street alley. I yawned, scratched under my wet hair, and scooped up my sword, dumping my salt-crusted clothes in the hamper.

Then I paced over to my file cabinet, passing my hand over the locked drawer. The locks—both electronic and magickal—clicked open, and I dug until I found what I needed. I didn't give myself any time to think about it.

The red file. I held it in a trembling hand for a moment and then slammed the drawer shut. Scooped up my bag from the bed and stood for a moment, my knees shaking slightly, my head down, gasping like a racehorse run too hard.

When I could breathe properly again, I stamped down the stairs, pausing halfway to touch the Anubis statue set in the little shrine tucked in the niche. I'd need to light a candle to him if I survived this.

I found the demon in my kitchen, contemplating my coffeemaker with a look of abstract horror. It was the closest to a human expression he seemed capable of, with his straight saturnine face. "What?" I asked.

"You drink *freeze-dried*?" he asked, as if he just found out I'd been sacrificing babies to Yahweh.

"I'm not exactly rich, Mr. Creepy," I informed him. "Why don't you just materialize some Kona fresh-ground if you're such a snob?"

"Would you like me to, Mistress?" There was the

faintest suggestion of a sneer in his voice. He was still wearing the long black coat. I took a closer look at him. Long nose, winged cheekbones, strong chin . . . he wasn't spectacular like Lucifer, or horrific like the thing in the hall. I shivered reflexively. He looked *normal*, and that was even more terrifying, once you really thought about it.

"Just call me Danny," I mumbled, and stamped over to the freezer, pulling it open. I yanked the canister out. "Here's the *real* coffee. I only get this out for friends, so be grateful."

"You would call me a friend?" He sounded amazed now. It was a lot less like talking to a robot. I was grateful for that.

"Not really," I said. "But I *do* appreciate you holding me up out of my own puke. I understand you're just doing what Lucifer tells you and something tells me you don't like me much, so we'll have to come to some kind of agreement." I tossed the canister at him, and he plucked it out of the air with one swift movement. "You're pretty good," I admitted. "I'd hate to have to spar with you."

He inclined his head slightly, his ink-black hair falling back from his forehead. "My thanks for the compliment. I'll make coffee."

"Good. I'm going to go think about this," I said, turning my back on him. He looked like a piece of baroque furniture in my sleek, high-tech kitchen. I almost wanted to wait to see if he could figure out the coffeemaker, but I wasn't that curious. Besides, demons have been fooling with technology for hundreds of years. They're good at it. Unfortunately for humans, demons don't like *sharing* their technology, which is rumored to be spotless and perfect. It occurred to me now that the demons probably were doing now what the Nichtvren had done before the Parapsychic Act—using proxies to control certain biotech or straight-tech corporations. Cloned blood had been a Nichtvren-funded advance; lots of immortal bloodsuckers had grown very rich by being the stockholders and silent partners in several businesses. I guess when you're faced with eternity, you kind of have to start playing with money to assure yourself a safe nest.

I carried the file into the living room and collapsed on the couch. My entire body shook, waves of tremors from my crown to my soles. I balanced the file on my stomach, flung my arm over my eyes, and breathed out, my lips slackening. Training took over, brainwaves shifting. I dropped quickly into trance, finding the place inside myself that no genemap or scan would ever show, and was gone almost immediately.

CHAPTER
9

*B*lue crystal walls rose up around me. The Hall was immense, stretching up to dark, starry infinity, plunging down below into the abyss. I walked over the bridge, my footfalls resounding against the stone. My feet were bare—I felt grit on the stone surface, the chill of wet rock, the press of my long hair against my neck. Here, I always wore the white robe of the god's chosen, belted with silver, the mark on my cheek burning. The emerald flamed, a cocoon of brightness, kept me from being knocked off the bridge and into endless wells of the dark. The living did not come here—except for those like me.

Necromances.

On the other side of the bridge the dog waited, sleek and black; His high pointed ears focused forward, sitting back on His haunches. I touched my heart and then my forehead with my right hand, a salute. "Anubis," I said in the not-dream, and my lips shaped the other sound that was the god's personal name, that-which-could-not-be-spoken, resonating through me.

I am the bell, but the god puts His hand upon me and makes me sing.

I breathed out, the warmth of His comfort descending

on me. Here in this refuge I was safe even from Lucifer—demons did not tread in Death. At least, I'd never seen one here.

Sometimes, especially after a long stint of working one apparition after another, I wanted to stay. Almost needed to stay. No other Necromance could enter my Hall, even those that could speak to Anubis as their psychopomp. Here I was blessedly alone, except for the dead and the god.

The cipher of the god's presence in the form of a dog pressed closer. I stroked His head. Silently, I felt Him take the crushing weight of the problem and consider it. Blue crystal walls and floors sang a tone that washed through me, pushing away fear and pain as they always did. The souls of the dead rushed past, crystal draperies fluttering and sliding past the edge into the well of souls, impelled down the great expanse of the ballroom of infinity, I curled my fingers in the dog's fur and felt a jolt of warmth slide up my arm.

My left shoulder twinged. The dog looked up, sleek black head inquiring; then nodded, gravely. I found myself laughing. It was all absurd. The demon's mark did not rob me of my ability to walk in Death. I was under the protection of my patron, the Lord of the Dead, what did I have to fear?

Nothing.

I sat straight up, bright metal peeking out between hilt and scabbard. The demon looked down at me, his green eyes subdued now. The file started to slide off my stomach.

I grabbed for the red file, propping the sword to the side, using the floor to brace the end of the scabbard so I could slide the metal back in. It took me a few moments to get situated, but Jaf waited patiently, then handed me a cup of steaming coffee. "Were you dreaming, or Journeying?" he asked.

"Neither." The contact with the psychopomp is private; other Necromances don't talk or write about it easily—and never to strangers or other psis. I would most definitely *not* tell this demon about it. I accepted the coffee cup, sniffed delicately at it. Good and strong. He'd even added a little bit of creamer, which is how I like my coffee. "Thanks."

He shrugged, folded his hands around the mug he'd chosen. It was the blue one, an interesting choice. Most people chose the white one, a few chose the red geometric TanDurf mug. Only one other person I'd allowed in my house had chosen the blue Baustoh mug.

Maybe the gods were trying to tell me something.

I yawned, scrubbed at my eyes, reached over and hooked up the phone. I'm one of the few people left without a vidshell. I don't want anyone seeing my face unless it's in person. Call me a Ludder, but I distrusted vidshells. And in the privacy of my home, if I wanted to answer the phone naked it was nobody's business but mine.

I keyed in the number. The electronic voice came on, I punched in a few buttons, the program checked my balance and informed me the pizza would be at the door in twenty minutes. I hung up, yawning again. "Pizza's on its way," I said. "You can eat human food, right?"

"I can," he agreed. "You're hungry?"

I nodded, took a sip of coffee. It burned my tongue, I made a face, settled the file in my lap. The tapestry hung on my west wall fluttered uneasily, Horus's eyes shifting back and forth. "I lost lunch *and* breakfast back in that alley, and I need food or I start talking to dead people." I shivered. "*Without* meaning to," I added. "Anyway, I hope you like pepperoni. Make yourself at home while I take a look at this."

He backed away without looking, dropped down in a chair next to a stack of Necromance textbooks holding up a potted euphorbia. Then he just sat, his eyes narrowed, holding the coffee under his nose but not drinking it, watching me.

I opened the file.

Seconds ticked by. I really didn't have the courage to look down yet.

I sipped at my coffee again, slurping, taking in air to cool it. Then I looked down at the file. There was the grainy police laseprint that made my stomach flipflop—Santino getting out of a car, his long icy-pale hair pulled back and exposing his pointed ears, the vertical black teardrops over his eyes holes of darkness. I shut my eyes.

"Get down, Doreen. Get down!"

Crash of thunder. Moving, desperately, scrabbling . . . fingers scraping against the concrete, rolling to my feet, dodging the whine of bullets and plasbolts. Skidding to a stop just as he rose out of the dark, the razor glinting in one hand, his claws glittering on the other.

"Game over," he giggled, and the awful tearing in my side turned to a burning numbness as he slashed, I threw myself backward, not fast enough, not fast enough—

I shook memory away.

Last seen in Santiago City, Hegemony, it said, and gave a date five years back. *That's the day Doreen died,* I thought, taking another slurp of coffee to cover up my sudden flinch. *He could be anywhere in the world by now.* He had been using the name Modeus Santino, rich

and elusive owner of Andro BioMed . . . we'd thought he
was cosmetically modified; the rich got altered to look
like whatever they wanted nowadays. After the murder
investigation, we found out Andro BioMed was a front
for another corporation. But the paper trail stopped cold,
since the parent corporation had filed Andro under the
Mob corporate laws, effectively rendering itself anonymous.

I hated the Mob like I hated Chill. It wouldn't have
hurt any of them to tell us where Santino had gone, it
wasn't like we were trying to bring down the Mob as a
whole.

We'd squeezed every Mob connection in town and
made ourselves a few enemies and finally had to admit
defeat. The ancient law of *omerta* still reigned even in
this technological age. Santino had vanished.

More pictures.

Pictures of victims.

The first one was the worst because the first one was
Doreen lying under the photographer's glare, her legs
twisted obscenely aside, her slashed throat an awful gaping smile. Her chest cracked open, her abdominal cavity
exposed, her right thigh skinned all the way down to the
bone and a chunk of the femur excised by a portable
lasecutter. Her eyes were closed, her face peaceful, but it
was still . . .

I looked up at the ceiling. Tears pricked behind my
eyes.

*Someday someone's going to find out what a soft
touch you are, Danny*, Reena's voice echoed through
years. I hadn't thought of her in a while, no more than I
would think of any other deep awful ache. Someone had
once accused me of being unfeeling. It wasn't true—I

felt it all the way down to the bone. I just didn't see any need to advertise it.

The doorbell rang, chiming through the silent house. I was halfway to my feet before Jaf reached the hallway. I sank back down on the couch, listening. The pizza delivery boy's voice was a piping tenor—*must be the kid with the wheelbike*, I thought. The murmur of the demon's voice replying, and a shocked exclamation from the tenor. *Maybe Jaf tipped him*, I thought, and forced a shaky smile. I already could smell cheese and cooked crust. Yum.

The door closed, and a hot stillness took over the house. The demon was checking my house shields. It was faintly rude—he didn't trust me to have my own house guarded?—but then I set my jaw and turned Doreen's picture over.

Santino hadn't had time to do his usual work-up on Doreen, but there were other pictures, familiar from the case. He had taken different things from each—blood, different organs—but always the femur, or a piece of it. As serial killers went, he was weird only in that he took more numerous trophies than others.

That had been back when the police could afford my services. I still did a turn every now and again, mostly on cases Gabe was working.

I owed Gabe. More important, she was my friend.

He was a demon, I thought. *It all makes sense now. Why didn't he taste like a demon? I wasn't THAT inexperienced . . . and why hasn't Lucifer tracked him down before now?*

I looked up. Jaf stood at the entrance to the living room. My tapestry was shifting madly now, woven strands moving in and out, Horus shimmering, Anubis calm and still, Isis's arms beckoning. "Why hasn't Lucifer tracked him down before now?" I asked. "Fifty years is a long time."

"Not for us," he said. "It might as well have been yesterday."

"Because only *humans* were being carved up." I felt my eyes narrow. "Right?"

He shrugged. The coat moved on him like a second skin. "We don't watch every serial killer and criminal in your world," he said. "We have other ways to spend our time. Our business is with those who want to evolve."

"Get some plates for the pizza, please." I rubbed at my forehead, delicately, with my fingertips. Looked back down at the file.

A teenage girl's eviscerated body peered up at me. Her mouth was open, a rictus of terror. They'd called him the Saint City Slasher in the holovids, lingering over each gory detail, theorizing why he took the femurs, plaguing the cops for information.

I reached for the phone again. Dialed.

It rang seven times, then picked up. "Mrph. Gaar. Huck." Sounded like a monkey with horrible bronchitis.

"Hello, Eddie," I said. "Is Gabe there?"

"Murk. Guff. Ack."

I took that to mean "yes." There was the sound of sliding cloth, then Gabriele's breathless voice. "This had . . . better be good."

"You got some time tonight for me, Spook?" I asked.

More sliding sounds. A thump. Eddie's cheated growl. "Danny? What's up?"

"I've got a lead," I said. "On the Slasher case."

Silence crackled through the phone line. Then Gabe sighed. "Midnight, my place?" She didn't sound angry.

"You know I don't have time for a wild-goose chase, Danny."

"This isn't a wild-goose chase." My jaw ached, I was almost grinding my teeth.

"You have new evidence?" Gabe's voice changed from "friend" to "cop" in under a heartbeat.

"Of a sort," I said. "Nothing that will stand up in court."

"Doesn't follow the rules of paranormal evidence?" She sounded sharp now, sharp and frustrated.

"Come on, Gabe. Don't ride my ass."

The demon paced into the room, carrying the pizza box and two plates. I nodded at him. He stopped dead, watching me.

"Fine." Click of a lighter, long inhale. *She must really be pissed.* "Come over at midnight. You alone?"

"No," I said. I owed her the truth. "I've got company."

"Living, or dead?"

"Neither."

She took this in. "All right, keep your little secret. Jesus. Fine. Come over around midnight, bring your new thing. We'll take a look at it. Now leave me alone."

"See you soon, Spocarelli."

"Fuck you, Dante." Now she was laughing. I heard Eddie growl another question, and the phone slammed back into the cradle.

I hung up and looked across at the tapestry. Horus shifted, Isis's arm raised, palm-out. The great goddess held the ankh to Her chest, protectively. I saw Anubis's head make a swift downward movement.

As if catching prey.

Well, the gods were with me, at least.

"We've got an appointment in two hours with a friend

of mine," I told the demon. "Let's go over the file to-gether beforehand, so we're prepared." *Never mind that I'm going to ditch your immortal ass as soon as possible.* I had to fight back the urge to giggle again. "Bring the pizza over, share some space." I patted the couch.

He paused for just the briefest moment before pacing across the room, settling next to me on the couch. I laid the file aside and flipped the pizza box open. Half pep-peroni, half vegetarian—I took a slice of either, plopped it on my plate. "Help yourself, Jaf." I prodded him, and he took a single slice of pepperoni. Looked at me. "Haven't you ever had pizza before?"

He shook his head, dark hair sleek and slicked-back. His face was blank, like a robotic mask. A muscle twitched in his smooth cheek. Had I somehow violated some complicated demon etiquette?

I folded the vegetarian slice in half, set the open pizza box on the floor, and took a huge bite. Melted cheese, crust, garlic sauce, and chunks of what used to be veg-etable matter. "Mmmh," I said, helpfully. The demon took a bite. He chewed, meditatively, swallowed, then took another bite.

I swallowed, tore into another chunk. Licked my fin-gers clean. Hot grease and cheese. The food made me a little more solid, gave me some ballast. I had three slices in me before I started to slow down and really taste it. I alternated between chunks of pizza and long gulps of less-scorching coffee. The demon copied me, and be-tween us, we polished off the whole gigantic pizza. He ate three-quarters of it.

"You must have been hungry," I said, finally, licking my fingers clean for the last time. "Damn. That was good."

He shrugged. "Unhealthy," he said, but his green eyes shone. "But yes, very good."

"How long has it been for you?" I asked. "I mean, you don't seem like you get out much, you know."

Another shrug. "Mortal years don't mean that much," he said, effectively stopping the conversation. I squashed a flare of irritation. Served me right, for getting personal with a demon.

"Okay, fine," I said. "How about you tell me why Santino doesn't smell like a demon?"

"He does," Jaf replied. "Just not the kind that's allowed out of Hell. Santino's a scavenger, and a plague, one of the Lower Flight of Hell. But he served the Prince well, and was rewarded for it." Jaf popped the last bit of crust in his mouth, his eyes half-lidding. "That reward allowed him to eventually escape the Prince's strictures and come to this world, with the Egg."

"So what's in the Egg?" *I might as well ask him now,* I thought, *I might not get a chance to later.*

"The Prince told you it's none of your concern," Jaf said, staring blankly at the pizza box. "Is there more?"

"What, three-quarters of a gigantor pie isn't enough for you?" I stared at him. "Why would breaking the Egg be bad?"

"I've rarely had human food," the demon said, and hunched his shoulders, sinking into the couch. "Vardimal must not be allowed to break the Egg. The repercussions would be exceedingly unpleasant."

I blew out a dissatisfied snort. "Like what?" I asked. "Hellfire, brimstone, plagues, what?"

"Perhaps. Or annihilation for your kind," he replied. "We like humans. We want them to live—at least, most of us do. Some of us aren't so sure."

"Great." I toed the empty pizza box. "So what side are you on?"

He shrugged again. "I don't take sides. The Prince points and says that he wants a death, I kill. No philosophy for me."

"So you're on the Prince's side." I wiggled my toes inside my boots, then rocked up to my feet. "You're hungry, huh? That wasn't enough?"

"No." His mouth twisted down on one side.

I scooped up the pizza box and my empty coffee cup. "Okay. Let me see what else I've got. What else do you know about Santino?"

He spread his hands, indicating helplessness. "I can give you his Name, written in our language. Other than that, not much."

"Then what good are you?" Frustration gave my voice an unaccustomed sharp edge. It's usually better to speak softly while a Necromance. Some of us tend to affect a whispery tone after a while. I took a deep breath. "Look, you show up at my door, threaten me, beat up six street punks, drag me through Hell, and finish off the job by eating most of the pizza. The least you can do is give me a little *help* tracking down this demon-who-isn't."

"I can give you his Name, and can track him within a certain distance. Besides, I am to keep you alive," Japhrimel said. "You might find me useful, after all."

"Lucifer said you had a personal stake in this." I balanced the pizza box in one hand. "Well?"

He said nothing. His eyelids dropped a millimeter or so more over burning green eyes. *Lucifer's eyes were lighter*, I thought, and shivered. *Lighter but more awful.*

"You aren't going to tell me anything," I said, finally.

"You're just going to try to manipulate me from place to place without telling me anything."

Nothing, again. His face might have been carved out of some golden stone and burnished to a matte perfection. It was like having a statue of a priest sitting on my couch.

That's the last time I try to be nice to a demon, I thought, said it out loud. "That's the last time I try to be nice to a demon." I turned on my heel and stalked away, carrying the empty pizza box. *Fucking demons,* I thought, *rip me away from a nice afternoon spent doing divination and watching the soaps. Now I've got a demon to catch and another goddamn demon sitting on my couch and Doreen . . .*

I folded the pizza box in half, barely noticing. Then I jammed it in the disposer and closed the lid, pressed the black button. "Fucking demons," I muttered. "Push you from square to square, never tell you a goddamn thing. You can take this job and shove it up your infernal—"

Dante. A touch like a breath of cool crystal against my cheek.

I whirled.

The world spun and wavered like a candle flame. I looked down at my hand on the counter, my fingers long and pale, red molecule-drip polish on my nails glimmering under the full-spectrum lights. Necromances can't handle high-end fluorescents on a daily basis.

I could have sworn I heard Doreen's voice, felt her usual touch on my cheek, her fingernails brushing down toward my jaw.

My house is shielded to a fare-thee-well; it would take the psychic equivalent of a thermonuclear explosion to get inside.

A demon could do it, I thought. I blinked.

My sword was in the other room. The living room. I'd left my blade with a demon.

I sprinted down the hall and skidded on the hardwood, turning the sharp corner and bolting into the living room. My sword was where I'd left it, leaning against the couch. The demon sat still with his hands upturned on his knees, his eyes half-closed, a sheet of white paper in one golden hand.

I scooped my sword up and turned on the balls of my feet, metal ringing free from the sheath. Green sparks flashed—my rings were active again, spitting in the charged air. I dropped below conscious thought and *scanned*.

Nothing. Nothing there.

I heard it, I know I heard Doreen's voice. I know I did. I let out a short choppy breath. I'd heard her voice.

My sword rang, very softly, in the silence. The metal was blessed and rune-spelled, I'd spent months pouring Power into it, shaping it into a psychic weapon as much as a physical one, sleeping with it, carrying it everywhere until it was like an extension of my arm. Now it spoke, a chiming song of bloodlust and fear filling the steel, pushing outward in ripples to touch the defenses on my house, making them shiver slightly.

My left shoulder twinged sharply. I glared at the demon, who still hadn't moved.

"Are you expecting a battle?" he asked, finally.

A single drop of sweat rolled down my spine, soaked into the waistband of my jeans. I tried to look everywhere at once.

I heard it. I know I did.

I sheathed my sword, backed up toward my altar,

scooped up my bag, and slid it over my head. I needed my knives, would have to go upstairs.

"I'm going upstairs," I told him. "Someone's playing games with me, and I don't like it. I *hate* being played with."

"I am not playing," he told me. He sounded robotic again.

"You wouldn't tell me if you *were*," I pointed out, and backed out of the room. *Looks like I'll be ditching him right about now,* I thought. *Christ, I'm going to have to leave a demon in my house. This really sucks.*

I made it up the stairs and had my knives on in less than twenty seconds. Then, carrying my sword, I padded to my bedroom window. The chestnut tree that shaded my window had a convenient branch I could drop from.

I had the window open and my foot out when Jaf's hand closed around the back of my neck. "Going somewhere?" he asked in my ear. His fingers were hard, and too hot to be human.

Oh, no, I thought.

CHAPTER
10

I wanted to walk to Gabe's, and the demon had no preference either way. So we walked. The rain had stopped, and the pavement gleamed wet. At least it wasn't dark-moon—that would have been bad all the way around. I get cranky around darkmoon, even with the Espo patch to interrupt my menstrual cycle and keep me from bleeding while I'm on a bounty or just can't be bothered.

I stole glances at the demon as we walked down Trivisidiro Street. Gabe's house was in a bad part of town, but she still had the high stone walls that her great-great-something-or-another had put up. The *real* defenses were Gabe's shields and Eddie's rage. Not even a Chill junkie would intrude on a house held by a Skinlin and a Necromance. Skinlin were mostly concerned with growing things, the modern equivalent of kitchen witches; most of them worked for biotech firms getting plants to give up cures for ever-mutating diseases and splicing together plant DNA with magick or complicated procedures. Skinlin are as rare as *sedayeen* but not as rare as Necromances; most psions are Shamans. Another hot debate between the Ceremonials and Magi and genetic scientists: Why were Necromances and *sedayeen* so rare?

The only real drawback to Skinlin is that they are berserkers in a fight; a dirtwitch in a rage is like a Chill-freak—they don't stop even when wounded. And Eddie was fast and mean even for a dirtwitch.

The demon said nothing, just paced alongside me with even unhurried strides. It was uncomfortably like walking next to a big wild animal.

Not that I'd ever seen a big wild animal, but still.

I lasted until the corner of Trivisidiro and Fifteenth. "Look," I said, "don't hold it against me. You can't blame me for being cautious. You're just here to yank my chain and take this Egg thing back to Lucifer, leaving me in the dust and probably facing down Santino alone to boot. Why shouldn't I be careful?"

He said nothing. Laser-bright eyes glittered under straight eyebrows. His golden cheeks were hairless and perfect—demons didn't need to shave. Or did they? Nobody knew. It wasn't the sort of question you asked them.

"Hello?" I snapped my fingers. "Anyone in there?"

He still said nothing.

I sighed, and looked down at my feet, obediently stepping one after another on the cracked pavement. We had to wait for the light here, Trivisidiro was a major artery for streetside hover and pedicab traffic. "All right," I finally admitted, while we waited for the light. "I'm sorry. There. You happy?"

"You chatter too much," he said.

"Fuck you too," was my graceless and reflexive reply. The light changed, and I didn't look, just stepped off the curb, already planning how to ditch him after Gabe's house.

My left shoulder gave one hot flare of agony. His hand closed around my arm and jerked me back as a warm rush of air blasted up the street. The telltale whine of hovercells crested, and a sleek silver passenger hover jetted past, going well over the speed limit, a sonic wash of antipolice shielding making me cringe.

I should have sensed that, I thought.

I ended up breathless and stunned, staring after the car. Sooner or later a cop cruiser would lock onto it and the driver would end up with a ticket, but right now my skin tingled and roughened with gooseflesh. The demon's fingers unloosed from my arm, one by one.

My breath whooshed out of me. I wasn't focusing on my surroundings. I was too busy grousing to myself over being stuck with a demon. It was unprofessional of me—but more important, it could get me killed. I couldn't afford to lose my focus.

I closed my eyes, promising myself I would *pay attention from now on, okay, Danny? It's no skin off the demon's nose if you fucking well get yourself run over by a frat boy in his daddy's hover.*

I should say thanks, I thought, and then, *If it wasn't for him I wouldn't be standing here, I'd be at home nice and warm and dry. And going on with my life.*

"Thanks," I said finally, opening my eyes and taking a slightly calmer look at the world. "I know you're just doing what you're told . . . but thanks." *I won't pull a stupid stunt like that again.*

He blinked. That was all the response I got from him.

I checked the street and was about to step out, cautiously, when he caught my arm again.

"Do you hate demons?" he asked, looking out over the empty street. The "don't walk" sign began to flash.

I jerked free of his hand, and he let me. "If what you tell me is true, it was one of yours that killed my best friend," I told him. "She was *sedayeen*. She never hurt anyone in her *life*. But Santino killed her all the same."

He stared across the street as if he found the traffic signals incredibly interesting.

"But no," I continued finally, "I don't hate demons. I just hate being jacked around, that's all. You could have simply asked me nicely instead of sticking a gun in my face, you know."

"I will remember that." Now instead of "robot" he sounded faintly surprised. "Santino killed your friend, then?"

"He didn't just kill her," I snapped. "He terrorized her for months and nearly killed me too."

There was a long silence filled with city sounds—the wail of sirens, distant traffic, the subwhine of urban Power shifting from space to space.

"Then I will make him pay for that," he said. "Come, it's safer now."

I checked again and followed him across the street. When we reached the other side he dropped back to walk beside me, head down, hands behind his back while he paced. My thumb caressed the guard on my sword, wanting to pop the blade free.

If they were right, and I *could* kill Santino, this was the blade that would do it.

Wait until Gabe sees this, I thought, and found myself smiling, a hard delighted smile that would not reach my eyes.

CHAPTER
11

I laid my hand against the gate, let the shields vibrate through me. Gabe's work recognized me, and the gate lock clicked open. I pushed before it could swing closed, slipped through. The demon stepped through almost on my heels, and Gabe's shielding flushed red, swirled uneasily. I bit down on the inside of my cheek and waited.

Gabe's shields settled, turned a deep blue-violet. She'd read what was with me, and wasn't amused.

"Come on," I said, and the demon followed me up the long paved drive. "Keep your mouth shut, okay? This is important."

"As you like," he said. It would be hard for him to sound any more flat or sarcastic.

Just when I was starting to think I might like him, too.

I walked up to the house, my footfalls echoing on pavement. The grounds were ragged, but still evidently a garden. Eddie kept the hedges down and the plots weeded.

I went up the steps to the red-painted door. Gabe's house had layers and layers of shielding—her family had been Necromances and cops for a long time, since before the Parapsychic Act was signed into law, giving psis protected status and also granting citizenship for several other nonhuman races. Gabe's trust fund was humongous and well-managed; she didn't even have to work as a Necromance, let alone as a cop. She had this thing about community service, passed down from her mother's side of the family. I admired that sense of responsibility in her; it made up for her being a rich brat.

I knocked, courteous, feeling a flare of Power right inside the door.

Eddie tore the door open and glowered at me, growling. I smiled, keeping my teeth behind closed lips. The demon, fortunately, said nothing, but a slow tensing of his diamond-flaming aura warned me. The same aura lay over mine, tensing as if to shield me, too.

The shaggy blond Skinlin stood there for a long ten seconds or so, measuring us both. His shoulders hulked, straining at his T-shirt, and the smell of wet earth and tree branches made the air heavy around him. I kept my hands very still. If he jumped for me he wouldn't stop until one or both of us was bleeding.

Gabe resolved out of the shadows, her sword out, soft light sliding on the blade's surface. "You didn't tell me you were bringing a demon," she said, her low soft voice a counterpoint to Eddie's growling.

Gabriele Spocarelli was small and slender, five foot two inches of muscle and grace. Her Necromance tat glittered on her cheek, the emerald spitting and twinkling a greeting that my own cheek burned, answering. She wore a scoop-necked silk sweater and a pair of torn jeans, and looked casually elegant in a way I had always secretly envied. I always wondered what she saw in a dirty misanthropic hedge-wizard, but Eddie seemed to treat her well and was almost fanatically protective of her. Gabe needed it. She got into a lot of trouble for a homicide detective—almost as much trouble as I did.

Almost.

"I'm kind of surprised by that myself," I said. "Truce?" I reached up slowly and pulled cloth away from my shoulder, exposing about half of the red, scarred brand that was the mark of a demon familiar. "I've got a story to tell you, Gabe."

Gabriele considered me for a long moment, her eloquent dark eyes passing over the demon and back to the mark on my shoulder. Then her sword flickered back into its sheath. "Eddie, can you get us some tea?" she asked. "Come in, Danny. You've never pulled a mickey on me before; I suppose you're not pulling one now."

"You can't be serious," Eddie started, his blond eyebrows pulling together. *Why does he never seem to shave?* I thought, letting go of my shirt. I felt better with the mark covered up.

"Oh, come on, Eddie," she said. "Live a little. Tea, please. And you—whoever you are—" Her eyes flicked over Jaf. "If you bring trouble into my house, I'll send you back to Hell posthaste. Got it?"

I saw the demon nod out of the corner of my eye. He said nothing.

Good for him.

Inside Gabe's house, the scented dark pulled close. She'd been burning kyphii. I closed my eyes for a moment and filled my lungs. She wasn't the most powerful Necromance around, but she had a quality of precision and serenity most Necromances lacked. Necromances don't often like hanging out with each other. We tend to be a neurotic bunch of prima donnas, in fact. To find someone I actually liked who understood what it was like to see the dead . . . that was exceptional.

She led us into the kitchen, where Eddie had the kettle on. He had my regular cup out, too, the long sinuous black mug reserved for me. "Tea?" I asked the demon, and he spread his hands, helplessly. "He'll have tea. I've told him not to open his mouth, it'll get us all in trouble."

"Good thinking." Gabe set her sword down on the counter. I prefer a katana-shaped blade, but Gabe went for a two-handed longsword that seemed far too big for her slim hands. And believe me when I say I never want to face her across that edged metal. "So you said, about that case . . ."

I dug the file out of my bag and handed it to her. "The Prince of Hell wants me to track down this guy. His name's Vardimal—our old buddy Santino."

"The Prince of—" Her eyes stuttered past me, fastened on Jaf.

"Apparently this is the Devil's errand boy," I said, trying to strangle the mad giggle that rose up inside me. It didn't work; I snorted out half a laugh and shivered. "I've had a *really* rough day, Gabe."

She flipped the file open, even though she knew what it contained. Her face turned paper-white.

"Gabriele?" Eddie's voice held only a touch of a growl.

Gabriele fumbled in her pocket, dug out a crumpled pack of Gitanes, and fished one out with trembling fingers. She produced a silver Zijaan and clicked the flame into life. The smell of burning synth hash mixed with the pungent spice of kyphii. "Make some tea, Eddie," she said, and her voice was steady and husky. "Goddamn."

I perched on a stool on the other side of the breakfast

counter. "Yeah." My own voice was husky, maybe from the smoke in the air.

Gabe slapped the file closed, not even looking at the demon's addition—the single sheet of paper with silvery lines marking Vardimal-Santino's name in the demon language. "You really think . . ."

"I do," I answered. "Honestly."

She considered this, took another drag off her smoke. The emerald set in her cheek flashed, popped a spark out into the air; my rings answered with a slow steady swirling. Eddie poured hot water into the cups. I sniffed. Mint tea. "What do you need?" Gabe finally asked.

"I need a paranormal-Hunt waiver on my bounty hunter's license." That was fairly standard and carried no liability for her; all I'd have to do was have her sign off on the paperwork. Now came the big stuff. "I need two H-DOC and omni-license-to-carry, and I need a plug-in for the Net." I licked my dry lips. If I was going to go after a demon, I needed all the policeware I could beg, borrow, or steal. The H-DOC and the plug-in would give me access to Hegemony cop computers and the treaty-access areas of Putchkin cop nets, and the omni license would be nice to have if I needed a plascannon or a few submachine guns to make sure the demon stayed down.

"Christ," Eddie snorted. "And a partridge in a pear tree. Want her fucking left kidney too, Danny?"

I ignored him, but the demon shifted his weight, standing right behind me. My left shoulder throbbed, a persistent fiery ache.

Gabe's dark eyes half-lidded, and she inhaled more smoke. "I can get you the para waiver and one H-DOC and maybe an omni, but a plug-in . . . I don't know. This doesn't constitute new evidence."

"What if I made a donation?" I asked. My rings spat and crackled. "This is *important*."

"Don't you think I know that?" she snapped. "What the fuck, Danny?"

I accepted my tea from Eddie, who slammed a pink flowered ceramic mug down for the demon. My mouth quirked, turned down at the corners. "I'm sorry," I said. "I just . . . Doreen, you know."

"I know." Gabe flipped over another page. "I can't get a judge to sign a plug-in for you on the basis of this . . . but I can ask around and see what the boys can do on the unofficial side. Might even be able to get you some backup. What do you say?"

"I work alone." I jerked my head back at Jaf. "The only reason I let him tag along is because I've been forced into it. You should have seen it, Gabe. It was awful."

She shuddered, a faint line beginning between her perfect charcoal eyebrows. "I have no desire to ever see that, Danny. Graeco Hades is enough for me."

I had never asked who her personal psychopomp was. Now I wondered. It wasn't a polite question—each key to unlock Death's door is different, coded into the deepest levels of breath and blood and consciousness that made up a Necromance. It was like looking in someone's underwear drawer to the *nth* degree.

I blew across the top of my tea to cool it. Gabe flipped grimly through the rest of the file. Her fingers shook a little; she tapped hot ash into a small blue ceramic bowl. Eddie hovered in the kitchen, running his blunt fingers back through his shaggy blond-brown hair, his eyes fixed on Gabriele's drawn-back lips and tense shoulders.

"Gods above and below," she said, finally. "Can that thing actually track Santino?"

I half-turned on the stool. Jaf's eyes met mine. Had he been watching the back of my head? Why?

"Can you track him?" I asked.

He shrugged, spreading his hands again to indicate helplessness. I glared at him. "Ah." He cleared his throat. It was the first almost-human sound I'd heard from him. "Once I am close enough, I can track him. The problem will be finding the part of your world to look in."

"I *need* a plug-in to get information on who's in whatever town I go to," I said softly, swiveling back to look at Gabe. "The nightside will help me trace him, especially if he's up to his old tricks. Dacon can do me up a tracker, but if Santino's a fucking demon and notices me using Magi magick, he might be able to counter." I paused. *"Hard."*

Gabe chewed at her lower lip, considering this. She looked over at Eddie, finally, and the Skinlin stilled. Motionless, barely even breathing, he stood in the middle of the clean blue-tiled kitchen, his blunt fingers hanging loosely at his sides.

She finally looked up at me. "You'll get your plug-in. Give me twenty-four hours."

I nodded, took another sip of my tea. "Good enough. I'm going to visit Dacon and the Spider, and I need to kit myself out. Has Dake moved?"

"You kidding? You know him, can't stand to walk down the street alone. He's still in that hole out on Pole Street," she answered. "You've got to get some sleep, Danny. I know how you are when you hunt."

I shrugged. "I don't think I'll get much sleep for a

while. Not until I rip his spleen out—Vardimal, Santino, whoever he is. *Whatever* he is."

"If he was a demon, why didn't we know?" Gabe tapped her short, bitten nails against her swordhilt.

I tipped my head back, indicating Jaf. "*He* says Santino's a scavenger, and they aren't allowed out of Hell. This one escaped with something Lucifer wants back."

"Great." Her mouth turned down briefly. "One thing, Danny. Don't bring that *thing* here ever again."

My rings spat green sparks. It was small consolation that Gabe understood how much more dangerous the demon was than me. I would have thought she'd be a little more understanding, knowing what it was like to be pointed and sneered at on the street.

But then again, a demon *was* something different. "He's not a thing," I remarked acidly, and Japhrimel gave me a sidelong look. "He's a demon. But don't worry, I won't."

CHAPTER
12

I needed to shake out the fidgets and think, and I thought best while moving. I doubted the demon could ride a slicboard, so we walked. The demon trailed me, his boots echoing against pavement. My fingers locked so tightly around my scabbard they ached.

Bits of foil wrappers and discarded paper cups, cigarette butts, the detritus of city life. I kicked at a Sodaflo can, the aluminum rattling against pavement. Little speckles from quartz in the pavement, broken glass, a rotting cardboard Cereon box, a pigeon hopping in the gutter, taking flight with a whir of wings.

Two blocks fell away under my feet. Three.

"That went well," Jaf said finally.

I glanced up at him from my boot toes. "You think so?" I settled my bag against my hip. "Gabe and I go way back."

"Gabe?" His tone was faintly inquiring. "And you're . . . Danny. Dante."

"I had a classical humanist for a social worker." I stroked my swordhilt. "I tested positive for psionic ability, got tossed into the Hegemony psi program. I was lucky."

"Lucky?"

"My parents could have sold me as an indentured, probably in a colony, instead of having me in a hospital and automatically giving me to the foster program," I said. *Though a colony would have been preferable to Rigger Hall.* For a moment the memory—locked in the cage, sharp bites of nothingness and madness against my skin; or the whip burning as it laid a stroke of fire along my back—rose to choke me. The Hall had been hell—a true hell, a human hell, without the excuse of demons to make it terrifying. "Or sold me to a wage-farm, worked until my brain and Talent gave out. Or sold me as a breeder, squeezing out one psi-positive baby after another for the colony program. You never know."

"Oh."

I looked up again, caught a flash of his eyes. Had he been looking at me? His profile was bony, almost ugly, a fall of light from a streetlamp throwing dark shadows under his eyes and cheekbones. His aura was strangely subdued, the diamond darkness folding around him.

Like wings.

I was lucky. I didn't know who my parents were, but their last gift to me had been having me in a hospital and signing the papers to turn me over to the Hegemony. Even though the Parapsychic Act was law and psis were technically free citizens, bad things still happened. Psis were still sold into virtual slavery, especially if their Talent was weak or their genes recessive. And most especially if they were born in backroom clinics or in the darkness of redlight districts and slums.

His black coat made a slight sound as he moved. He had a habit of clasping his hands behind his back while walking, which gave him a slow, measured gait. "So what do you do?" I asked. "In Hell, I mean. What's your job?"

If I thought his profile was ugly before it became stonelike and savage now, his mouth pulling down and his eyes actually turning darker, murderously glittering. My heart jumped into my throat, I tasted copper.

"I am the assassin," he said finally. "I am the Prince's Right Hand."

"You do the Devil's dirty work?"

"Can you find some other title to give him?" he asked. "You are exceedingly rude, even for a human. Demons do not conform to your human idea of evil."

"You're an exceeding asshole, even for a demon," I snapped. "And the human idea of evil is all I've got. So what is such an august personage doing hanging out with me?"

"If I keep you alive long enough to recover the Egg, I will be free," he said through gritted teeth.

"You mean you're not free now?"

"Of course not." He tilted his head up, as if listening. After a few moments, I heard a distant siren. My left shoulder twinged. "Where are we going?"

"I'm going to see Dacon. He's a Magi, he'll just *love* you." My jaw ached and my eyes were hot and grainy. "After that I'm going to get some sleep, then I'll visit the Spider. And by then Gabe should have everything together, and I'll start hunting."

"I suppose you will try to escape me as soon as possible," he said.

"Not tonight," I promised him. "I'm too tired tonight."

"But afterward?" he persisted. "I don't want to lose my chance at freedom for your petty human pride."

"You say 'human' like it's a dirty word." I tucked my

free hand in my pocket. My rings were dark now, no longer glittering and sparking. Out here, in the flux and ambient static of city Power, the atmosphere wasn't charged enough to make them react. Instead, they settled into a watchful gleam.

"That's the same way you say 'demon,'" he shot back, immediately. Was he *scowling*? I had never seen a demon scowl, and I stared, fascinated.

I'm not going to win this one, I realized, and dropped my eyes hurriedly back down to the pavement. "You stuck a gun in my face." It was lame even by my standards.

"That's true," he admitted. "I did. I thought you were a door-guard. Who knows what the best Necromance of a generation has guarding the door? I was only told to collect you and keep you alive. Nothing else, not even that you were a woman."

I stopped short on the sidewalk and examined him. He stopped, too, and turned slightly, facing me.

I pulled my free hand from my pocket, stuck it out. "Let's start over," I said. "Hi. I'm Danny Valentine."

He paused for so long that I almost snatched my hand back, but he finally reached out and his fingers closed around mine. "I am Japhrimel," he said gravely.

I shook his hand twice, had to pull a little to take my hand back. "Nice to meet you." I didn't mean it—I would rather have never seen his face—but sometimes the little courtesies helped.

"Likewise," he said. "I am very pleased to meet you, Danny."

Maybe he was lying, too, but I appreciated the effort. "Thanks." I started off again, and he fell into step beside me. "So you're Lucifer's Right Hand, huh?"

He nodded, his profile back to its usual harsh almost-ugly lines. "Since I was hatched."

"Hatch—" Then I figured out I didn't want to know. "Never mind. Don't tell me, I don't want to know."

"You're very wise," he said. "Some humans pester us incessantly."

"I thought you liked that," I said. "Demons, I mean, as a whole."

He shrugged. "Some of us have leave from the Prince to answer the calls of the Magi. I have not had much traffic with humans."

"Neither have I," I told him, and that seemed to finish up conversation for a while. I was glad. I had a whole new set of things to worry about—how Dacon would react, and how the news of me hanging out with one of Hell's citizens would get around town *really* fast, especially if I saw Abra. I couldn't leave the demon behind—he might get into trouble, and besides, I didn't think he'd take to waiting in an alley while I went into Dake's club.

CHAPTER
13

I was right. "Absolutely not," he said, his eyes turning almost incandescent.

"Okay, fine, keep your hat on." I looked across the rain-slick street. A few sleek cigar-shaped personal hovers drifted in a parking pattern overhead, and there were several slicboards leaning against the side of the old warehouse, reactive paint glowing on their undersides. I scanned them out of habit and noticed one had a hot magtag; evidently some kid had jacked it. I clucked out through my teeth. Kids stealing slicboards, what next? Then again, since hovers had palmlocks and bodyscans built in standard now, a slic was all a kid could steal.

Pole Street rang with neon and nightlife around us. I shivered, hunching my shoulders, and sighed. "If you want to go in with me, you're going to have to do what I tell you, okay? Let me do the talking and *don't start a fight* unless I start one first. Okay? And try not to kill anyone—just hurt them bad enough to keep them down."

He nodded, his dark hair stuck to his head with dampness. A fine drizzle had started around Trivisidiro and Eighteenth Street, and followed all the way out into the Tank. A block down from us, a group of freelance hookers huddled under an overhang, the neon running wetly off their pleather sheaths and go-go boots. A cop cruiser slid by like a silent shark, bristling with antennas and humming with riotshields. It drifted to a stop by the hookers, and I wondered if they were scanning for licenses or looking for a little fun.

I licked my dry lips, nervous. "Actually," I said, "can you look scary? It would help."

He bared his teeth, and I had to fight down the urge to step back.

"Okay," I said. "You win. You just look scary and I'll do the talking."

We crossed the street, the demon keeping step slightly behind me, and stepped up on the pavement on the other side. There were two bouncers there—shaved gorillas with black-market augments, three times my size. My fingers itched.

Don't let there be any trouble, I prayed silently.

I came to a stop right in front of the bouncers. The one on the left paled visibly, seeing my tat. The one on my right looked the demon over, his fat cheeks quivering with either terror or silent laughter. I inhaled deeply, tasting night air, hash smoke, and the salt-sweat-sweet smell of Chill. Did Dake know one of his bouncers was on Clormen-13? That shit was nasty, it made addicts psychotic after a while. Taking down a Chillfreak was hard work.

I tilted my head so my tat was visible to both of them. "Dacon Whitaker," I said, pitching my voice loud enough to slice through the pounding bass thudding out the door.

The bouncer on the right nodded. I saw the telltale

glint of a commlink glittering from his right ear, and his throat swelled. He had a subvocal implant, too.

Great. Dake knew I was coming.

"He's indisposed," Shaved Gorilla #1 said. He had muttonchop and some very nice custom-made leather pants straining at his massive legs.

"Either he sees me now, or I tear his club apart and bring the cops down here. He can be charged for interfering with a legitimate hunt." My lips peeled back from my teeth. "I'm doing a bounty, and I'm in a bad mood. It's up to him."

The demon's hot silence swelled behind me. Five seconds. Ten. Fifteen.

"Come on in," the gorilla on the right said. "Go up to the office, the big man says."

I nodded and passed between them, the demon moving close. Together we plunged into a swirling migraine attack of red and orange light, skitters of brightness from the blastball hanging from the ceiling, hash smoke and the reek of alcohol mixing with the smell of sweat and the psychic assault of a warehouse full of people, sunk in the music, most of them dancing. A thin edge of red desperation curled over a smile, a razor-flick against a numb arm.

I was used to the sensory assault, barely paused, my mental shields thickening. There were ghostflits in the corners, riding the air, a few of them silently screaming.

People think that when they die, the Light opens up and takes them. A majority of the time, that's what happens. But sometimes—often enough—the soul is chained here. Sometimes confused, or held by violent death, and sometimes just unable to leave without a loved one, the souls of the dead crowd toward the living any place there's Power enough to feed them and make them more than just a cold sigh against the nape, more than just a memory.

Back before the Parapsychic Act, there was about fifty years of psionics being bought and sold by corporations like chattel—even Necromances. And before that, Necromances were generally locked in asylums or driven to suicide by what we saw—what nobody else could see. Some, like Gabe's ancestors, made it through by keeping mum about their talents, blending in. Others just assumed they were crazy.

I forced my way through the crowd, each person a padded sledgehammer blow, laid completely open by hash and trance music. I recognized the track—it was RetroPhunk's "Celadon Groove".

If I could stand being around a crowd again, I could dance to this, I thought, and felt a sharp twisting pain. I hadn't danced for three years. Not since Jace.

Don't think about that. My head came up; I scanned the crowd. Like most psis, I disliked crowds, especially riot-crowds or large groups all stoned on hash. Sure, I could jack in and ride the Power created by that much wide-open emotional energy—but I had no need of it. Other psis knew enough to keep their thoughts to themselves, but most normals were sloppy broadcasters, hammering at even the best of shields with the chaotic wash of sense-impressions and thoughts. It was like walking through a field of unmuffled hovers; even if you had earplugs the noise still settled against the pulse and bones, and hurt.

No. Maybe it wasn't the dancing or the crowd that hurt, maybe it was only my heart. I hadn't thought of Jace in at least six months.

Writhing bodies pulsed on the lit-up dance floor. I saw couples twisted around each other, a few shadowed booths in back full of bodies that could have been swooning in love or death. A sharp strain of desperate sex rode the air. My nostrils flared and my rings sparked. I could have jacked into the atmosphere and *used* that Power for a Greater Work, if I'd needed to. I slid between two tarted-up, rail-thin yuppie girls so doped-out on hash it was a wonder they were still vertical; nodded to the bartender.

Behind the bar was a moth-eaten red velvet curtain that the bartender—a skinny nervous man in a red jumpsuit, a cigarette hanging from his lips—pushed aside. A safety door was slightly open, a slice of yellow light leaking out and into the smoky air.

The music shifted. My skin prickled with heat and uneasy energy.

Goddammit, that bastard at the door warned Dake and now he's getting ready. I wanted him off-balance.

I jumped forward, darted through the door, and ran lightly up the stairs. I wasn't in the best shape—my stomach was still bruised and tender from puking and my entire body felt just a fraction of a second too slow—but when I spun into Dake's plasglass-walled office, my sword already drawn, he *did* look surprised. He was up to his pudgy elbows with venomous green snapping Power, and was just turning away from the open iron casket on his desk.

Dacon was a Magi, albeit a weak one. He'd been a few years behind me at Rigger Hall, and I still thought of him as the same pudgy-faced kid with his uniform all sloppy and his mouth loose and wet from too much synth hash. He'd barely managed to produce a low-level imp to qualify for Magi-accreditation, and his tat was a plain round Celtic symbol with no taste. All in all, he wasn't the best for this type of work, but he was the only Magi I could conceivably bully into doing me a tracker for a demon without having to pay an arm and a leg for it.

Even though Dake was a lousy Magi when it came to calling up demons, he was pretty good at the offensive magicks. He couldn't fight much physically, but with enough of a Power charge he was fast and nasty. That, I suspected, was why he rarely if ever left his nightclub. I hadn't heard of him being on the street in years. He was as close to a shut-in as it was possible for a psion to get.

And that was also why he was the perfect choice to do a tracker for me. It was a passive offensive piece of magick, which meant it was right up his alley—and he didn't have to leave his nightclub to do it.

"You son of a *bitch*," I said, pleasantly. "You were planning on giving me a little surprise, weren't you, Dacon? Just like the little bitch you are." My blade spat blue-green, light running along its razor edge. The runes I'd spelled into the steel sparked into life, twisting fluidly along the length of the blade. And the demon's aura laid over mine sparked and swirled.

Dacon squeaked, his round pale face suddenly slick with sweat. I felt more than heard the arrival of the demon behind me, and Dacon nearly passed out, swaying, his expensive Drakarmani shirt wet and clinging under his armpits. "You—*you*—" he spluttered, and the green glow arced between his fingers. Sloppy of him.

"Me," I answered. "Of course. Who else would come and talk to you, Dake? Nobody likes you, you have no friends—why are you so fucking surprised?"

Dake's eyes flicked past me. He wore a pair of shiny

pleather pants straining to hold his ample legs in. "You have a . . . that's a . . . you've got—"

"A demon familiar." My voice was edged with a hard delight that I didn't really feel. "Jealous, Magi? I'll have him talk to you up close, if you like."

The demon moved past me, almost as if reading my mind. The diamond flares of his aura spread, filling the room, closing around the unlucky Magi. I held my sword slanting across my body, the blessed steel a defense from the demon who bore down on Dacon with slow, even steps.

"What the *fuck* you want?" Dake yelled, scrambling back and almost leaping on top of his desk. "*Christ*, Danny, what you *want*? Just tell me!"

The demon paused, again as if reading my mind.

"Information," I said, scanning the room. Something was off here, one instrument was out of tune, screwing up the whole damn band.

My nostrils flared.

Salt-sweat-sweet. The odor of Chill.

I fumbled the paper out of my bag. Silver flashed from my rings. I approached Dake carefully, brushing past the demon, who stood taut and ready. I unfolded the paper, glanced down at the twisted rune that was Vardimal's name. The African masks Dake hung on the walls ran with wet red light through the plasglass windows. People downstairs were dancing, strung out on hash and sex, unaware of the drama going on right overhead.

"I want you to give me a tracker keyed to this name, Dake. And if you're a very good boy, I won't call the Patrols in to get rid of your Chill stash." *You lousy, stupid motherfucker,* I thought. *Chill's going to eat you alive. And how many lives are you going to destroy, dealing*

*here? No wonder one of your bouncers is on that shit.
Gods damn you, Dake.*

His round, brown eyes rolled. I held up the paper,
ready to jump back if the green glow around his hands
struck for me. He stuttered.

"I ain't—I'm not—*Danny*—" A thin thread of spittle
traced down his stubbled chin. His mouth worked.

"Don't fucking lie to me!" I snarled, my sword whipping up, stopping just in time. Razor steel caressed his
wet double-chin. "Now, are you going to do me a tracker,
Dake, or do I get all catholic and burn this goddamn
place down?" *Where did the demon go?* I wondered. *Too
much static, where did he go?*

The demon's arm shot past me, fingers sinking into
Dake's throat under its slab of fat, pushing my sword
aside. I resheathed my blade. "Put. It. Down," the demon
said, in a low throbbing impossible-to-ignore voice.

Something metallic clattered on the floor. I didn't
glance down. The green glow lining the Magi's hands
drained away.

Dake's face crumpled. He began to sob.

Oh, Sekhmet sa'es. *If he starts to cry I'll be here all
night calming him down.*

"Let go of him," I snapped. "He won't be good for
anything if you make him cry."

The demon made a low, growling sound. "As you
like," he finished. Dake whined, gibbering with fear.

I was perilously close to losing my temper. Instead, I
curled my fingers into Dake's shoulder as the demon retreated. "Oh, c'mon, Dake, we're just playing around,
right? You don't mean to hurt me. You *like* me. You want
to be my *friend*, don't you, Dake?" Exactly as I would
talk to a four-year-old.

Dake whined and nodded, his lank brown hair flopping forward over his sweaty forehead. Just like school. I'd interfered once when some of the bigger Magi kids had been pushing Dake around, and had to suffer his pathetic attachment for the rest of my career at Rigger Hall. The trouble with Dake was that he had no grit in him; if he hadn't already been broken Mirovitch and Rigger Hall would have wrecked him. For a Magi to lack a magickal Will was bad news; the Power wouldn't obey and his or her spells would go awry. I was of the private opinion that it was a good thing Dake hadn't been able to call up more than an imp inside a chalk circle with a whole collection of more experienced Magi standing guard in case things went wrong; an unwary, cowardly Magi would be easy prey for anything larger than an imp.

And I wondered what would have happened if something like Jaf had shown up in response to Dake's summonings. A Greater Flight demon could kill even from within a chalked circle; that's why they were so hard to call up. Lucky me, getting to hang out with one.

The demon made a low grinding sound, a growl. "Good," I said. "Good. You'll be my good boy, Dake, and give me a tracker. Then I'll be out of your hair and you can go back to selling Chill and waiting for it to burn out your fucking brain and your Talent as well."

"I'm not *on* Chill," he lied, his eyes shifting back and forth.

I cursed internally. *Does he have enough Talent left to do a decent tracker?* I stepped back, and Dake slid down from the desk, his boots hitting the floor. I half-turned, looked at the demon. Japhrimel's eyes were incandescent green. "Make sure he doesn't move," I said, and didn't wait for the answer.

Below conscious level, the spinning vortex of darkness that was the demon focused on a red-brown pulsing smear. Dake.

My own aura under the demon's shielding held the trademark glitters of a Necromance. I watched those glitters swirl, reacting to the presence of the demon and the nervous spatters of red-brown Dake was giving off. On this level, Dacon Whitaker was visibly in trouble, gaping holes in his aura, Power jittering and trembling out of his control. Dake's Power would escape him, eat him alive as the Chill consumed his nervous system. But not yet—not yet. He had his Power—but not for very much longer.

I snapped back into myself. The demon was absolutely still and silent, his shoulder touching mine, his eyes eating into a trembling Dake.

I held the paper up. "I need a tracker, Dake. Get your kit, and be quick. I've got other shit to do tonight."

When it was finished, the tracker looked like a globe of spun crystal and silver wire, a crystal arrow inside it, pulsing faintly reddish as it spun. "What's the range on this thing?" I asked, almost forgetting that Dake was a Chillfreak now. When he was motivated he did good work, and it was always nice to see another magickal discipline perform.

"Worldwide, baby, it's a Greater Work. Let it settle for about twenty-four hours, then give it the keyword and it'll go live. Use sparingly." Dake coughed into his palm, scuttling back toward his desk. The odor of burning blood in the air had bothered me for the first ten minutes, but my nose was acclimated now.

I've never seen anyone grind up a frog before, I thought, and shivered. I dropped the tracker in a small leather pouch and settled it carefully around my neck. "Okay, Dake. Thanks."

I did not tell him I owed him one.

He blinked at me. "You're not going to kill me?" he whined.

The thudding bass beat of the music downstairs made me nervous. "No," I said. "Of course not, you idiot. Why would I kill you?"

As if he was a goddamn normal instead of a Magi who should know better.

"I know how you feel about Chill," he stuttered, "and if you think I—"

No shit you know how I feel about Chill, everyone knows how I feel about that shit. "I don't *think*, Dake." I turned on my heel and started for the door. "I know. And you'll get yours soon enough. The Chill's going to eat you, Dacon. There's no detox for it. You're a stupid motherfucker."

"It's not my *fault!*" he yelled after me as I swung out the door. "It's *not!*"

"Yeah," I said, and stamped down the stairs into the womblike starred dark of the club below. "Sure it's not, Dacon. Nothing ever is."

Hot salt spilled down my cheeks as I pushed through the crowd of people and finally, blessedly, achieved the coolness of the street outside. One of the bouncers— probably the Chillfreak—sniggered something behind me, and for a single heartbeat I considered turning around and separating him from his liver.

I wrestled the urge down, still striding along the cracked pavement, my shields resounding. I waited until I turned the corner to stop, head down, my ribs heaving. I had jammed my sword into the loop on my belt, not trusting myself with edged metal right now.

"Are you injured?" the demon asked.

I almost flinched. The hard impenetrable darkness of his aura swirled once, counterclockwise, brushed against my aura's sparkling. Checking for damage. I shivered, my shields thickening reflexively, pushing the touch away. It was bad enough to smell like a demon, I didn't want him pawing at me. Even on an energetic level.

"I'm fine," I forced out through a hard lump in my throat. "I just wanted to . . . I'm fine."

He didn't say anything else. Instead, he only stood there. Another human being might have asked me useless questions, tried to say something comforting. Apparently a demon wouldn't.

I finally wiped my cheeks and scanned the street, deserted except for me and a demon. "Okay," I said. "We've got our tracker. Let's go."

"Is he a friend of yours?" The demon tipped his chin back, indicating the vague direction of the club with one elegant motion. His eyes were darker now, strange runic patterns slipping through the depths of green light.

"Not any more," I said, casting around for a callbox.

There was one down at the end of the street, and I set out for the lighted plasteel box. The demon followed me, moving as silently as a manta ray slipping through dark water.

I passed my hand over the credit square, flushing my palm with Power. The door clicked open, and I stepped into the callbox. It was one of the older ones without a vidshell. *Thank the gods for small favors.* "Hold the door," I said, and the demon put out his golden hand, held the folding door aside.

I picked up the handset and dialed the copshop.

"Vice, Horman speaking," Detective Lew Horman snarled on the other end.

"Horman? It's Danny." My voice sounded normal. A little husky, but normal.

"Aw fer Christ's sake—"

I didn't know he was a Christer. "Don't blaspheme, Detective. Look, I've got a word for you."

"What the fuck now, deadhead? I ain't Homicide!" The high edge of fear colored his voice.

"You know the Chill that's been soaking the South Side? I found out a major distributor."

That got his attention. He literally gasped.

I waited a beat. "Of course, if you're not interested—"

"Goddammit, you deadhead freak. Give it up."

"Dacon Whitaker, out of his club. One of his bouncers is a Chillfreak and so is he now."

"A fuckin magician's a Chillfreak? I thought they didn't—"

"They don't last long, but they're nasty while they do. I'd take some para backup with you. Don't mention my name, okay?"

"Quiet as the grave," Horman snorted.

I let it pass. "You owe me one, Horman," I said, and hung up without waiting to hear his reply.

The demon still said nothing.

I took my hand off the phone and looked out the wavering safety-glass at the dark street, pools of streetlamp glow shivering on wet pavement. "Fuck," I said finally, and clenched my hand. "*Fuck!*"

My fist starred the safety glass in a spreading spider-web, I pulled back and let another one fly. This punch left a bloody print on the cracked glass.

Then I stopped, gasping for breath, fighting for control. My pulse pounded in my ears.

When I had swallowed the last of my rage, I opened my eyes to find the demon studying me. His eyes were even darker. "What did you do?" he asked, mildly enough.

"I just turned Dake in to the cops," I told him through gritted teeth.

"Why?" It was a passionless inquiry.

"Because he'll kill people with that Chill shit."

"A drug?"

"Yeah, a nasty drug." *A drug that makes mothers abandon their infant babies at the hospital, a drug that eats people whole, a drug that makes punk kids shoot social workers on the street in broad daylight, a drug that swallows whole families and smashes psions. A drug the Hegemony won't get serious about outlawing because the Mob gets too much taxable income off it, a drug the cops can barely stem the tide against because half of them are on the take anyway and the other half are so choked with paperwork they can't stop it.*

Between Chill and the Mob, it was hard to tell which I hated more.

"Why not let those stupid enough to take it, die?"

I considered him, my bleeding hand curled tightly in my unwounded hand. Dake had been at Rigger Hall; I suppose I couldn't blame him for wanting some oblivion. My own nightmares were bad enough; just the thought of that place made my shields quiver.

Valentine, D. Student Valentine is called to the head-master's office immediately.

And the Headmaster's chilly, precise, dry little voice. *We've got something special for those who break the rules today, Miss Valentine.* The smell of chalk and spoiled magick, the feel of a collar's metal against my naked throat and collarbones . . .

Thinking about it made the scars on my back ache again, an ache I knew was purely psychic. Three stripes, running down my back; and the other scar, the burn scar, just at the bottom crease of my left buttock. Dake probably had his own scars . . . but that was no excuse to drown them in Chill. After all, I managed to live without drowning mine, didn't I? It was no excuse.

Was it? Or had I just turned him in because I was having a pissy day?

"Because I'm human," I informed him tightly, "and I operate by human rules. Okay?" I wasn't about to tell him about Lewis bleeding to death on the sidewalk, dead by a Chillfreak's hand, his antique watch and Rebotnik sneakers stolen to hawk for more Chill. It was private. And anyway, why did he care why I hated Chill? It was enough that I hated it.

He shrugged. "Your hand."

I stared at him. "What?"

"Give me your hand."

After a moment's consideration, I extended my hand. He folded his fingers over it, still holding the door of the callbox open with his other elbow. My entire hand fit inside his palm, and his fingers were hard and warm.

A spine-tingling rush of Power coated my entire body. His eyes glowed laser-green. The pain crested, drained away.

When he let go of my hand, it was whole and un-wounded under a mask of blood. I snatched it back, examined it, and looked up at him.

"I will endeavor to remember human rules," he said.

"You don't have to," I found myself saying. "You're a demon, you're not one of us."

He shrugged. Stood aside so I could exit the callbox.

I let the folding door accordion shut behind me. The light inside the callbox flicked off.

"Okay," I said.

"What next?"

I took a deep breath. Looked at my hand. "Next I go home and try to get some sleep. Tomorrow I'm visiting Abracadabra—a friend. I'll see if she can give me a direction to go in and some contacts. Better not to use the tracker until I'm sure I need it."

"Very well." He still didn't move, just stood there watching me.

A gigantic lethargy descended on me. Why did it all have to be so *hard*? The pressure behind my eyes and throat and nose told me I was a few minutes away from sobbing. I set my jaw and scanned the street again.

Empty. Of course. Just when I needed a cab.

"Okay," I said again. "Come on."

He fell into step behind me, silent as Death Himself.

CHAPTER
14

I lay on my back, holding my sword to my chest, looking up at the dark ceiling. My eyes burned.

I slept with my rings on, and the shifting blue-green glow sliding against the ceiling told me I was agitated.

As if I don't already know, I thought, and my fingers clasped the sword more tightly.

Downstairs the demon sat in front of my fireplace. My shields buzzed and blurred; he was adding his own layers of protection. Even my home wasn't mine anymore. Of course, on the plus side, that meant a better shielding for my house.

If I'd been born a Magi, I would have at least some idea of how to deal with a demon in my house. I probably would have even been excited. Magi worked with circles and trained for years to achieve regular contact with Hell after passing their Academy test and calling up an imp. They paid the rent by working as consultants and doing shielding for corporations, like Shamans. They also ran most of the training colleges and did magickal research. Finicky eyes for detail, most Magi; but when dealing with demons you wanted to be a perfectionist when it came to your circles and protections. The Greater

Demons were like *loa*, only more powerful—they didn't exactly have a human idea of morals. And while the *loa* might mislead, it was an axiom of Magi practice that demons outright lied sometimes for the fun of it—again, because their idea of truth wasn't the same as ours.

I sighed, burrowed my back deeper into my bed. I was retreading the same mental ground, going over and over what I knew of demons, hoping I would somehow think of something new that would make me feel better about this.

If I was a Christer, I'd be peeling the paint off the walls screaming, I thought sardonically. Some normals were still Christers, despite the Awakening and the backlash against the Evangelicals of Gilead; the Catholic section, of course, would have tried reading from old books and blessing water to get rid of a demon. Sometimes it might have worked—even normals were capable of belief, though they couldn't use it like a tool as a Shaman or a Necromance could. And the Christers had even believed that demons could get *inside* people, not understanding the mechanics of shielding and psychic space very well.

None of this got me anywhere.

How the hell did this happen? How did I end up working for the fucking Devil?

I didn't have a clue. There had been no warning, from my cards or runes or any other divination. Just a knocking on my door in the middle of a rainy afternoon.

So did they sneak up on me, or are my instincts getting rusty?

Or both?

I stared at the greenshift shadows on the ceiling, my mind ticking, sleep a million klicks away.

Breathe, Danny. Start the circle like you were taught. In through the nose, out through the mouth. Breathe deep, deeper, deeper—

The ritual was comforting, born of too many sleepless nights. Outside my window a gray rainwashed dawn was coming up. I yawned, settled myself more comfortably between white sheets.

I wondered if the cops had visited Dake yet. Or if Dake had dumped his stash in panic, guessing I'd turn him in even though we went way back together. Back to the Hall.

Don't think about that.

Mirovitch's papery voice whispering, three lines of fire on my back—the whip, the smell of my own flesh searing—

Do not think about that. I shifted on the bed, the sheet moving, my fingers white-knuckled on the swordhilt. "Don't think about that," I whispered, and closed my eyes. "What you cannot escape, you must fight; what you cannot fight, you must endure. Now think of something useful if you're going to stay awake."

You weren't warned because they haven't been preparing this, the deep voice of my intuition suddenly whispered. *This doesn't have the feel of a well-planned expedition.*

It was a relief to have something else to think about. So even the Devil was scrambling to keep up with current events, so to speak. Maybe he'd gone to use this Egg or look at it, and found out it was gone. Hell was a big place; you couldn't keep track of every artifact and demon.

Which means Santino probably has Lucifer by the balls. And how does this Japhrimel fit in? He's Lucifer's agent. Why wouldn't Lucifer come out on this job him-self?

It would do me no good to fret over it. I was well and truly caught.

I closed my grainy, burning eyes, consigning the question to my unconscious mind. With any luck, the bubbling stew of my subconscious would strike me with the answer—right between the eyes—soon enough.

Even Japhrimel has no idea what's going on, I thought. *Even Lucifer. They're playing blind. Which is why they need me.*

They need me. I'm calling the shots here.

The thought was enough to press a smile to my face as I kept breathing, deeper and deeper, waiting for dawn. When I finally fell asleep, the sky was turning gray with morning.

The house was full of the smell of demon, amber musk and burning cinnamon creeping through the air like gas. I came downstairs after a long shower and fresh clothes to find his scent rippling and dyeing the psychic atmosphere with golden darkness.

He handed me a cup of coffee. He looked just the same as he had last night, except a little of the robotic blankness was gone from his face. Now he looked thoughtful, his green eyes a shade darker and not quite meeting mine.

I blew across the steaming mug and yawned, contemplating the kitchen. Late-afternoon sunlight slanted in through the window. The rain must have fled, because golden sunlight edged the wandering Jew hanging over the sink. "Morning," I finally said, slipping past him to stalk to the toaster. "How are you?"

"Well enough," he replied. "Did you sleep well?" He actually sounded interested.

"No. I hardly ever do. Thanks for the coffee." I dropped two slices of wheat bread into the toaster and pressed the button for "just short of charcoal."

"Where is your sword?"

I shrugged. "I don't think I need it in a demon-protected house, do I?" I yawned again. "When we go out to hunt I'll be taking my sword. I won't put it away again until I've brought Santino down. I haven't started yet—this is just saddling my horse." My rings sparked again. This time the shower of sparks was pure gold.

I smell like a demon now, I thought with a sort of grim amusement. *That should make things fun.*

"I see." He still sounded thoughtful. He hadn't moved from the kitchen door.

"Before we go," I continued, "I need you to tell me exactly what having a demon familiar means. I was going to ask Dake, but we didn't have time last night. So I'm forced to ask you."

"I'll do my best not to disappoint you," he said sardonically.

I swung around to look at him, the coffee sloshing in my cup. I fished a butterknife out of the drying rack next to the sink. "You're starting to develop a sense of humor," I said. "Good for you."

"We will get exactly nowhere if we cannot reach an agreement," he pointed out. "I am responsible for your safety, and my physicality is now tied to you by the grace of the Prince. If I allow you to be harmed, it will be most unpleasant for me." His lean saturnine face didn't change, but his voice was colored with a faint sneer.

"Mmh." My toast popped up as I was getting the

peanut butter down. "Guess it's bad luck all *over* you, huh?" I set the coffee cup down after a quick, mouth-burning gulp. It was, at least, decent coffee.

"On the contrary," he said. "It is very *good* luck. It appears you need a familiar and I need my freedom. You appear tolerable, at least, despite your foul mouth. And you are occasionally thoughtless, but not stupid."

I looked over my shoulder. He had his hands behind his back again, standing military-straight, his long black coat buttoned up to his chin. "Thanks," I replied, as dryly as I could. "Have you had breakfast?"

He shrugged. "Human food is pleasant, but I don't *need* it."

I was just about to say something snide when the phone rang. I hooked up the kitchen phone and snarled into it. "*What?*"

That was my hello-good-morning voice.

"And a good bloody morning to you too, Danny," Trina chirped. She was the agent for the Parapsych Services Unlimited Message Agency; most psions in Saint City used them. Since I did bounties as well as apparitions, Trina managed my schedule and acted as a buffer between me and the cranks and yahoos who sometimes decided to prank-call psions. I didn't have the time or energy to keep track of when I was supposed to be where, so Trina would coordinate with my datpilot and datband as well as monitor my datband while I was on a bounty. Magick was a full-time job; even Necromances needed secretaries nowadays and it was cheaper to just freelance-contract with an agency. "Quick word?"

"What, another job?" I looked down at my toast, picked up my coffee. "How much?"

"Fifty thousand. Standard."

That would take care of another few mortgage payments. "What kind?" I swirled the coffee in the cup, the steam rising and twisting into angular shapes.

"A probate thing. Shouldn't take more than a coupla hours. Old coot named Douglas Shantern, died and the will's contested. Total estate's fifteen mil, the estate itself is paying your fee."

I yawned. "Okay, I'll take it. Where's the body? How fresh?"

"Lawyer's office on Dantol Street has his cremains. Died two weeks ago."

I made a face. "I hate that."

"I know," Trina replied, sympathetic. "But you're the only one on the continent who can deal with the burned ones, since you're so talented. I'll schedule you for midnight, then?"

"Sounds good. Give me the address?"

She did. I knew the building; it was downtown in the legal-financial district. The holovid image of a Necromance is all graveyards and chanting and blood, but most of our work is done in lawyers' offices and hospital rooms. It's very rare to find a Necromance in a graveyard or cemetery.

We don't like them.

"Okay," I said. "Tell them I'm bringing an assistant."

"I didn't know you had an apprentice." She actually sounded shocked. I have never met Trina face-to-face, but I always imagine her as a stolid, motherly woman who lived on coffee and Danishes.

"I don't," I said. "Thanks, Trina. I'll hear from you again, I'm sure."

"You're welcome," she said, barely missing a beat. "Bye."

"Bye." I hung up. "Well, that's nice. Another little job."

The demon made a restless movement. "Time is of the essence, Necromance."

I waved a hand over my shoulder at him. "I've got bills to pay. Santino won't get anywhere quickly. He escaped fifty years ago; you guys didn't jump right on the bandwagon to bring him down. So why should I? Besides, we're going to visit Abra too, and after I do this job Gabe will have all the things I need and we can start hunting. Unless you're going to pay my power bill this month."

"You are infuriating," he informed me coldly. The smell of demon was beginning to make me dizzy.

"Tone it down a little, Japhrimel." I curled my fingers around the edge of the counter and glared at him, reminding him that I knew his Name. "I don't have a whole hell of a lot to lose here. You make me angry and you lose your big chance to shine."

He stared at me with bright laser-green eyes. *I think he's angry,* I thought, *his eyes just lit up like a Yulefestival tree. Or is that just me?*

The plate holding my peanut butter toast chattered against the countertop. I held his gaze, wondering if the Power thundering through the air would burn me. My rings popped and snarled, my shields shifting, reacting to the charged air.

He finally glanced down at the floor, effectively breaking the tension. "As you command, Mistress."

I wondered if he could sound any more sarcastic.

I shrugged. "I'm not your mistress, Japhrimel. The sooner I can get rid of you and back to my life, the better.

All I want you to do is stay out of my way, you dig? *After* you explain what a demon familiar does."

He nodded, his eyes on the floor. "When would you like your explanation?"

I wiped a sweating hand on my shirt, my combat shields humming as they folded back down. "Let me finish my coffee first."

He nodded, his hair shifting, wet dark spikes. "As you like."

"And pour yourself a cuppa coffee or something," I added, grudgingly. Might as well be polite, even if he wasn't.

CHAPTER
15

*A*shton Hutton," the lawyer said, his grip firm and professional. He didn't flinch at the tat on my cheek or at the sight of Japhrimel—of course, lawyers in the age of parapsych don't scare easily. "Nice of you to come out on such short notice, Ms. Valentine."

"Thank you, Mr. Hutton." I smiled back at him. *You fucking shark,* I thought. He was slightly psionic—not enough to qualify for a trade, but enough to give him an edge in the courtroom—and his blond hair was combed back from a wide forehead. Blue eyes sparkled. He had a disarming, expensive grin. The wet ratfur smell of some secret fetish hung on him. I filled my lungs, taking my hand back, smelling something repulsive and dry.

Not my business, I thought, and looked past him into the tasteful meeting room. The windows were dark, but the lights were full-spectrum, and the table was an antique polished mahogany big enough to carve up a whale on.

The family was there: bone-thin, sucked-dry older woman who was probably the wife dressed in a peach linen suit, very tasteful, a single strand of pearls clasped to her dry neck; there were two boys, one of them round and wet-eyed, greasy-haired, no more than thirteen, a ghost of acne clinging to his skin. The other was a college-age kid, his hair cut into the bowl-shape made popular by Jasper Dex in the holovids, leaning back in his chair while he tapped at the table's mirror polish shine with blunt fingertips.

On the other side of the table was a woman—maybe thirty-five, her dark hair in a kind of spray-glued helmet, ruby earrings clipped to her ears. *Mistress,* I thought. Then my eyes flicked past her to the two plainclothes cops, and a whole lot more about this situation started to make sense.

I looked at the lawyer. "What's with the cops?" I asked, the smile dropping from my face like a bad habit.

"We don't know yet," Hutton replied. "Miss Sharpley requested a police presence here, and it was not denied by the terms of the will, so . . ." He trailed off, spreading his smooth well-buffed hands.

I nodded. In other words, the cops were here because someone was suspected of something, or relations between the wife and mistress were less than cordial. Also none of my business. "Well," I said, and stepped into the room, digging in my bag. "Let's get to work then."

"Who's your associate?" Hutton asked. "I didn't catch his name."

"I didn't throw it," I replied tartly. "I'm here to raise a dead man, not talk about my accessories." I was already wishing I hadn't accepted this job either.

In the center of the table stood the regulation box, heavy and made out of steel, holding the remains of the man I would be bringing back out of death's sleep. I shivered slightly. I hated cremains, worked much better with a body . . . but you couldn't afford to be picky when you had a mortgage. I wondered why an estate worth fifteen million didn't have an urn for the hubby, and mentally shrugged. Also none of my business. It wasn't my job to get involved, it was my job to raise the dead.

The first time I'd raised an apparition out of ash and bone had been at the Academy; I hadn't been prepared for the silence that fell over the training room when I'd done it. Most Necromances need a whole body, the fresher the better; it was rare to have the kind of talent and Power needed to raise a full apparition out of bits. It meant steady work, since I was the only Necromance around who could do it—but it also meant that I pulled more than my share of very gruesome remains. One of the worst had been the Choyne Towers fiasco, when a Putchkin transport had failed and crashed into the three towers. I'd been busy for days sifting through little bits and raising them for identification, and there were still ten people missing. If I couldn't raise them, they must have been vaporized.

And that was a singularly unpleasant thought. That hadn't made my reputation, though. My reputation as a Necromance had been cemented when I'd almost by accident raised the apparition of Saint Crowley the Magi. It was supposed to be a publicity ploy by the Channel 2004 Holovid team, but I'd actually done it, much to everyone's surprise. Including my own.

But most of what I was stuck with were the gruesome ones, the burned ones, and dead psions. It was Hegemony law that the remains of a dead psi had to be cremated—especially Magi and Ceremonials, because of the risk of Feeders.

I shivered.

I had the candles out and placed on the table when the

wife suddenly made a slight choking sound. "Do we have to?" she asked, in a thready, husky voice. "Is this *absolutely* necessary?"

"Chill out, Ma," the college boy snapped. His voice was surprisingly high for such a husky kid. He leaned back in his chair, balancing on two legs. "Smoke and mirrors, that's all, so's they can charge for it, you know."

"Ms. Valentine is a licensed, accredited Necromance," Hutton said thinly, "and the best in the country if not the world, Mrs. Shantern. You *did* ask to have the . . . questions . . . resolved."

The stick-woman's mouth compressed itself. On the other side of the table, the mistress's dark eyes rested steadily on the steel box. She was as cool and impenetrable as a locked hard drive, her smoothly planed cheeks coloring slightly as she raised her eyes to mine.

That's one tough cookie, I thought, and looked over at the plainclothes. They didn't look familiar.

I shrugged. Once the candles were secure in their holders I snapped my fingers, my rings sparked, and blue flame sputtered up from the wicks, glowing like gasjets.

I always got a kick out of doing that.

The wife gasped, and the college boy's chair legs thudded down on the expensively carpeted floor.

"If you'd be so kind as to kill the lights, Mr. Hutton," I said, drawing my sword free of its sheath, "we'll have this done in a jiffy."

The lawyer, maybe used to Necromances working in semidark, moved over to the door, brushing nervously past the demon, who stayed close, almost at my shoulder. I hopped up on the table and sat cross-legged, the sword in one hand, and rested my free hand on the steel box. This put my head above everyone's—except the demon and the taller of the plainclothes cops in his rumpled suit. *What are they here for?* I thought, dismissed the question.

"Dante?" the demon asked. It was the first time he had truly used my name.

"It's okay," I said. "Just wait. I'll let you know if I need you."

I am your familiar, the demon had told me, *and I may act to defend you. Any harm that comes to you, I will feel as if committed to my own flesh. I am at your command as long as you bear that mark. If it is possible for me to do, your word will make it so. I am not free to act, as you are.*

I understood a lot more now. No wonder Magi wanted familiars. It was like owning a slave, he had explained, a magickal slave and bodyguard. The trouble was, I didn't want a slave. I wanted to be left alone.

I closed my eyes. Deep circular breaths, my sword balanced across my knees. After the uncertainties of the last few days, it was a relief to have something I *knew* how to do and understood doing. Here, at least, was a problem I could solve. Dropped below conscious thought, the blue glow rising, my hand resting on the steel box.

The words rose from the deepest part of me. *"Agara tetara eidoeae nolos, sempris quieris tekos mael—"*

If you were to write down a Necromance's chant, you'd have a bunch of nonsense syllables with no real Power. Necromance chants aren't part of the Canons or even a magical language—they're just keys, personal keys like the psychopomp each Necromance has. Still, someone always tries to write them down and make them follow grammatical rules. The trouble is, the chants *change* over time.

Blue crystal light rose above me, enfolded me. My rings spat sparks, a shower of them, my left shoulder twinging. Riding the Power, crystal walls singing around me, I reached into the place where the cremains rested, hunting. Small pieces of shattered bone and ash a bitter taste against my tongue.

To taste death, to take death into you . . . it is a bitter thing, more bitter than any living taste. It burned through me, overlapping the ache in my shoulder from the demon's mark.

I've seen the tapes. While I chant, my head tips back, and the Power swirls counterclockwise, an oval of pale light growing over the body—or whatever is left of the body. My hair streams back, whether caught in a ponytail, braided, or left loose. The emerald on my cheek glitters and pulses, echoing the pulsing of the oval of light hanging in front of me, the rip in the world where I bring the dead through to talk.

My hand fused to the steel box. My other hand clamped around the hilt of my sword. The steel burned fiercely against my knees, runes running like water up the blade. My tattoo would be shifting madly, serpents writhing up the staff of the caduceus, their scales whispering dryly.

Blue crystal light. The god considered me, felt through me for the remains, and the thin thread that I was stretched quivering between the world of the living and the dead. I became the razorblade bridge that a soul is pulled across to answer a question, the bell a god's hand touches to make the sound out of silence . . .

There was a subliminal *snap* and the wife gasped. "Douglas!" It was a pale, shocked whisper.

I kept my eyes closed. It was *hard,* to keep the apparition together. "Ask . . . your . . . questions . . ." I said, in the tense silence.

The chill began in my fingers and toes. I heard the wife's voice, then the lawyer taking over, rapid questions. Shuffle of paper. The mistress's husky voice. Some kind of yell—the college kid. I waited, holding the Power steady, the chill creeping up my finger, to my wrists. My feet rapidly went numb.

More questions from the lawyer, the ghost answering. Douglas Shantern had a gravelly voice, and he sounded flat, atonal, as the dead always do. There is no nuance in a ghost's voice . . . only the flatline of a brain gone into stormdeath, a heart gone into shock.

There was another voice—male, slightly nasal. One of the cops. The numb chill crept up my arms to my elbows. The sword burned, burned against my knees. My left shoulder twisted with fire.

The ghost replied for quite some time, explaining. My eyelids fluttered, the Power drawing up my arms like a cold razor.

There was a scuffle, something moving. The lawyer's voice, raised sharply. I ignored it, keeping the ghost steady.

Then the lawyer, saying my name. "Ms. Valentine. I think we're finished." His voice was heavy, no longer quite as urbane.

I nodded slightly, took a deep breath, and blew out between my teeth, a shrill whistle that ripped through the thrumming Power. The cold retreated.

Blue crystal walls resounding, the god clasping the

pale egg-shaped glow that was the soul to His bare naked chest, dog's head quiet and still. White teeth gleaming, eloquent dark eyes . . . the god regarded me gravely.

Was this the time that He would take me, too? Something in me—maybe my own soul—leapt at the thought. The comfort of those arms, to rest my head on that broad chest, to let go—

"Dante?" A voice of dark caramel. At least he didn't touch me. "Dante?"

My eyes fluttered open. The sword flashed up between me and the pale egg-shaped blur in the air. Steel resounded, chiming, and the light drained back down into the steel box, fluttering briefly against the flat surfaces, limning the sharp corners in a momentary pale glow.

I sagged, bracing my free hand against the polished mahogany of the table, the smell of my own Power sharp and nose-stinging in the air. I could *feel* the demon's alertness.

When I finally looked around the dark room, one of the cops had the younger son—the acne-scarred wet-eyed boy with the greasy hair—in plasteel cuffs. The boy blinked, his fishmouth working. *Goddammit*, I thought sourly, *if I'd known this was a criminal case I'd have charged the estate double. Got to have Trina make a note about this lawyer.*

The wife sat prim and sticklike still, but her eyes were wide and wild with shock, two spots of red high up in her dry cheeks. The mistress sat, imperturbable. The older boy stared at his younger brother as if seeing a snake for the first time.

I managed to slide over to the edge of the table and

put my legs down, sheathing my sword. Surprisingly, the demon put his hands up, held my shoulders, and steadied me as I slid down. My fingers were numb. *How long?* I thought, numbly.

"How long?" I asked, forcing my thick tongue to work.

"An hour or so," Jaf replied. "You . . . Your lips are blue."

I nodded, swayed on my feet. "It'll pass soon, I'll be fine. What *happened*?" I deliberately pitched my voice low, a whisper. Jaf caught the hint, leaned in, his fingers digging into my shoulders.

"The mistress was accused of killing the man," he said softly. "The ghost said it was his son that beat him to death with a piece of iron."

"Ms. Valentine?" the lawyer interrupted, urbanely enough. The cops were dragging the limp kid away. He hung in their hands, staring at me. The shorter cop—curly dark hair, dark eyes, he looked Novo Italiano—forked the sign of the evil eye at me, maybe thinking I couldn't see.

Lethargy washed over me again. I swayed. *An hour? I kept the ghost talking—a full manifestation—for an hour? From a pile of ashes? No wonder I'm tired.* I took deep, circular breaths. The air was so cold from the ghost's appearance my breath hung in a white cloud, and little threads of steam came from Jaf's skin. "I hate the ash ones," I muttered, then faced the bland-faced lawyer. "It just happened to slip your mind that this was a criminal affair?"

"Consider your . . . ah, fee, tripled." His eyes were wide, his slick blond hair ever-so-slightly disarranged. Maybe I'd scared him.

Good. He'd think twice before trying to cheat a psi out of a decent fee again.

"Thanks," I said, and blinked deliberately.

He was sweating, and his face was pasty white. "I've never—I mean, I hardly—" The lawyer was all but stammering. I sighed. It was a transitory pleasure to scare the shit out of a little scumbag like this.

"I know. I'll be going now. I suppose I can just let myself out?"

"Oh, well—we could—"

"No worries." I was suddenly possessed of the intense urge to get the hell out of this bland, perfect, antique office and away from this stammering frightened man. Maybe he wasn't quite as used to Necromances as he'd thought.

I never thought I would be grateful for a demon. But Japhrimel apparently had grown impatient waiting for me to finish making the lawyer stumble and sputter, because he put his arm around me and pulled me away from the table. I stumbled slightly; the demon's arm was a warm weight.

As soon as he led me past the empty secretary's desk and into the office lobby, I ducked out from under his arm. "Thanks," I said, quietly. My knees were still a little shaky, but my strength would return quickly. "That was a little draining. I had no idea they wanted a full hour from a bunch of ashes."

"You appear to be most exceptional." Japhrimel's arm fell back to his side. His eyes were half-lidded, glowing so fiercely that the skin around them seemed to take on a greenish cast. Again, there were runic shapes glittering in their infinite depths.

"I don't know," I said. "I'm just a girl looking to pay off her mortgage."

"I am sorry I doubted your ability," he continued, falling in step beside me as I headed for the stairs. The elevator dinged, nearly sending me through my skin; Japhrimel's hand closed around my upper arm. Steel fingers sank into my flesh. "Easy, Dante. There is nobody there."

"Not . . . the elevator." I forced the words out. If I had to be closed in a small space—

At least he had his own shields, and could keep his thoughts to himself. Raw as I was, if he'd been human I might have torn my arm out of his grasp to escape the onslaught of someone else's emotion. As it was, I let him steer me through the door and into the echoing, gray-painted stairwell. "So you've decided I'm not so bad?" I asked, trying for a light tone. The ghost's voice echoed in my head, just outside my mental range, shivering, a deep husky sound. I would hear him for another few hours, until my psyche recovered from the shock of holding someone else so closely. Training helped lessen the shock, but could not deaden it completely.

"I have decided that you need a familiar," he said flatly. "You seem foolhardy."

"I'm careful," I protested. "I've survived this long."

"It seems like luck instead of care," he remarked. I stumbled, my feet feeling like huge blocks of cold concrete—he steadied me, and we began down the stairs, my footsteps echoing, his silent.

"I don't like you very much."

"I supposed as much."

By the time we reached the bottom floor, my boots were beginning to feel less like concrete and more like they belonged to me. The awful cold retreated slowly, the mark on my left shoulder a steady flame that dispelled the ice. My energy was returning, the Power-well of Saint City flooding me with what I'd expended on the apparition. The ground-floor lobby was plush and quiet, water dripping down a tasteful Marnick wall fountain. I kept my fingers curled around my sword, my bag bumping my hip. As soon as I could walk by myself I shook his arm away. It was a good thing the weakness never lasted long. "Thanks."

"No thanks necessary." He opened the security-lock door, sodium-arc light shining against glass. The parking lot was mostly empty, the pavement drying in large splotches. Night air touched my face, a cool breeze sliding through pulled-loose strands of my hair. I tucked one behind my ear and checked the sky. Clearing up from the usual evening shower. That was good.

"Hey." I stopped, looking up at him. "I need to do something. Okay?"

"Why ask me?" His face was absolutely blank.

"Because you'll have to wait for me," I replied. "Unless you can ride a slicboard."

CHAPTER
16

*H*ey, deadhead," Konnie said, stripping green-dyed hair back from his narrow pasty face. "Whatchoo want?"

The Heaven's Arms resounded with New Reggae music around me, the sweet smell of synth hash from the back room filtering out between racks of leathers in garish colors, shinguards, elbow pads, helmets. "Hi, Konnie," I said, ducking out of my bag. The demon accepted the strap—I felt a thin thread of unease when I handed my sword over. "I need a board and an hour."

Konnie leaned back, his dead flat eyes regarding me over the counter. "You got credit?"

"Oh, for *fuck's* sake." I sounded disgusted even to myself. "Give me a board, Konnie. The black one."

He shrugged. "Don't suppose you're gonna wear any pads."

"You've got my waiver on file." I ran my fingertip over the dusty counter, tracing a glyph against the glass. Underneath, blown-glass hash pipes glowed. There were even some wood and metal hash pipes, and a collection of incense burners. Graffiti tags tangled over the walls, sk8 signs and gang marks. "Come on, Konnie. I've got a job to do."

"I know." He waved a ringed hand. His nails were painted black and clipped short—he played for a Neoneopunk band, and had to see his hand on the bass strings in pulsing nightclub light. "You got that look again. Who you hunting down this time, baby?"

"*Give* me the goddamn board," I snarled, lips pulling back from my teeth. My emerald sparked, my rings shifting crazily. The demon tensed behind me. "I'll be back in an hour."

Konnie bent briefly, scooped up a slicboard from its spot under the counter. He slid the chamois sheath free, revealing a sleek black Valkyrie. "I just tuned it up. Had a Magi in here not too long ago told me to 'spect a deadhead; I hate that precog shit. You're the only deadhead crazy 'nough to come to the Arms. Why dontcha keep this thing at home?"

I snatched the board. My hands were trembling. The ambient Power of the city helped, soaking into me, replacing what I'd spent in bringing Douglas Shantern back from the dry land of death. But I still wasn't convinced I was still living . . . "Fine. Thanks."

"Hey, what to do with the stray here?" Konnie called after me as I headed for the front door.

"Try not to piss him off," I tossed over my shoulder, then hit the door. I was running by the time cool night wind touched my hair, my fingers pressing the powercell. I dropped the board just as the cell kicked in, and the sound of a well-tuned slic hummed under my bones.

My boots thudded onto the Valkyrie's topside, the board giving resiliently underneath me. My weight pitched forward, and the board hummed, following the street.

No, I don't want streetside, I thought. *I want to fly. Tonight I need to fly.*

I pitched back, the slic's local antigrav whining. Riding a slicboard is like sliding both feet down a stair rail, weight balanced, knees loose and relaxed, arms spread. It's the closest to flight, to the weightlessness of astral travel plus the gravity of the real world, that a human body can ever attain.

Hovercells thrummed. Up in the traffic lanes, hovers were zipping back and forth. The thing about hover traffic is that it's like old-time surfing waves—catch the right pattern, and you can ride forever, just like jacking into a city's dark twisted soul and pouring Power into a spell.

But if you miscalculate, hesitate, or just get unlucky, you end up splashed all over the pavement. Hovers and freights have AI pilot decks that take care of keeping them from colliding, making driving mostly a question of following the line on your display with the joystick or signing the control over to the pilot deck, but slics are just too small to register. The intricate pattern of mapped-out lanes for hover traffic was updated and broadcast from Central City Hall in realtime to avoid traffic jams, but the slics couldn't tune in to that channel. There wasn't room on a slic for an AI deck, sk8ers and slic couriers disdained them anyway.

I stamped down on my left heel, my weight spinning the slicboard as it rocketed up, and I streaked between two heavy hover transports and into the passenger lane, missing a blue hover by at least half an inch, plenty of room. Adrenaline hammered my bloodstream, pounded in my brain, the Valkyrie screamed as I whipped between hovers, not even thinking, it was pure reaction time, *spin* lean down kick of wind to the throat like fast wine, I dove up out of the passenger traffic pattern and into the freight lanes.

Riding freight is different, the freight hovers are much bigger and their backwash mixes with more hovercells and reactive to make the air go all funny. It requires a whole different set of cold-blooded calculations— freight won't kill you like a passenger foul-up will. Slicboard fatalities in the passenger lanes are called "quiksmaks." Freight fatals are "whoredish." They're tricky, and a mistake might not kill you instantly. It might kill you three feet ahead, or six behind. You never know when a freight's backwash will smack you off your board or tear your slic out from under your feet.

—*watch that big rig there, catch,* fingernails screeching on plasteel, hovercells whining under the load, *board's got a wobble, watch it, lean back stamp down* hard *going up,* ducking under a whipping freight hover, my hair kissing plasteel, rings showering golden sparks, coat flying, weaving in and out of the hovers like a mosquito among albatrosses, *this is what it feels like to be alive, alive, alive . . .*

Heart pounding, copper laid against my tongue, Valkyrie screaming, lips peeled back from teeth and breath coming in long gasps, legs balancing the slic, the friction of my boot soles the only thing between me and a long fall to the hard pavement below.

I fell in behind a police cruiser that was whipping between freights, going siren-silent. They'd already scanned me—an unhelmeted head on a slic isn't a crime, but they like to know who's riding suicidal—and I played with their backwash, riding the swells of turbulence until they dropped out of the traffic patterns. I rode a little while after that, almost lazily, darting down into traffic and swooping back, tagging hovers.

When I finally dropped back to streetside, hips swaying, body singing, I brought the Valkyrie to a stop right outside the Arms and hopped down. My hair fell in my face, my shoulders were loose and easy for the first time since a booming knock on my door had sounded in the rain.

Japhrimel leaned against the window of the Arms, neon light spilling through the glass and glowing against his wetblack hair. He held my bag and my sword, and his knuckles stood out white against the scabbard.

I tapped the board up, flipping off the powercell, and let out a gusty sigh. "Hey," I said. "Anything cool happen while I was gone?"

He simply stared at me, his jaw set and stone-hard.

I carried the board back inside and gave it to Konnie, used my datband to transfer the rent fee to him, and came out into the night feeling much more like myself, humming an old PhenFighters song. After every Necromance job, I ride a slicboard. I fell into the habit years ago, finding that the adrenaline wash from riding the antigrav worked almost as quickly as sex; the fight-or-flight chemical cascade wiping the cold leaden weight of dead flesh away and bringing me back to full screaming life. Other Necromances used caff patches or Tantra, took a round in a sparring cage, visited a certified House like Polyamour's or any cheap bordello—I rode slics.

Japhrimel handed my bag over, and my sword. His silence was immense, and it wasn't until I looked closer that I noticed a vertical line between his coal-black eyebrows. "What?" I asked him, slightly aggrieved. Rainwashed air blew through the canyon streets, brushing my tangled hair and making his long coat lift a little, brushing his legs.

This is a demon, I thought, *and you're not screaming or running, Danny, you're treating him just like anyone else. Are you insane?*

"I would rather," he said quietly, "not do that again."

"Do *what* again?"

"That was foolish and dangerous, Dante." He wasn't looking at me; he studied the pavement with much apparent interest.

I shrugged. I couldn't explain to a demon that a slicboard was the only way to prove I *was* still alive, after lying cheek-by-jowl with death and tasting bitter ash on my tongue. Neither could I explain to him that it was either the slic or the sparring cage, and I didn't like cages of any kind. Besides, it didn't matter to the demon that I *needed* to prove I was alive after bringing a soul over the bridge and feeling the cold stiffness of rotting death in my own limbs. "Come on. We've got to visit Abra."

"I would like your word that you will not leave me behind again," he said quietly. "If you please, Mistress."

"Don't call me that." I turned away from him, slinging my bag against my hip, and was about to stalk away when he caught my arm.

"Please, Dante. I do not want to lose my only chance at freedom for a human's foolishness. *Please.*"

I was about to tear my arm out of his hand when I realized he was *asking me politely*, and saying please as well. I stared at him, biting my lower lip, thinking this over. A muscle flicked in his smooth golden jaw.

"Okay," I said finally. "You have my word."

He blinked. This was the second time in my life I'd ever seen a demon nonplussed.

We stood like that, the demon holding my arm and staring at my face, for about twenty of the longest seconds of my life so far. Then I moved, tugging my arm away from him, glancing up to check the weather. Still mostly clear, some high scudding clouds and the relentless orange wash of citylight. "We've got to get moving," I said, not unkindly. "Abra gets mean later on in the night."

He nodded. Did I imagine the vertical crease between his eyebrows getting deeper? He looked puzzled.

"What?" I asked.

He said nothing, just shrugged and spread his hands to indicate helplessness. When I set off down the sidewalk he walked beside me, his hands clasped behind his back, his head down, and a look of such profound thoughtfulness on his face I half-expected him to start floating a few feet off the pavement.

"Japhrimel?" I said finally.

"Hm?" He didn't look up, avoiding a broken bottle on the pavement with uncanny grace. I readjusted my bag so the strap didn't cut into my shoulder. I'd left both my sword and my bag with him, and he hadn't tampered with either.

"You're not bad, you know. For a demon. You're not bad at all."

He seemed to smile very faintly at that. And oddly enough, that smile was nice to see.

CHAPTER
17

$\mathcal{A}$bra's shop was out on Klondel Avenue, a really ugly part of town even for the Tank District. *Abracadabra Pawnshop We Make Miracles Happen!* was scratched on the window with faded gilt lettering. An exceptionally observant onlooker would notice that there were no graffiti tags on Abra's storefront, and that the pavement outside her glass door with its iron bars was suspiciously clean.

Inside, the smell of dust and human desperation vied with the spicy smell of beef stew with chili peppers. The indifferent hardwood flooring creaked underfoot, and Abra sat behind the counter in her usual spot, on a three-legged stool. She had long dark curly hair and liquid dark eyes, a nondescript face. She wore a blue and silver caftan and large golden hoops in her ears. I had once asked if she was a gypsy. Abra had laughed, and replied, *Aren't we all?*

I had to give her that one.

Racks of merchandise stood neatly on the wood floor, slicboards and guitars hung up behind the glassed-in counter that sparkled dustily with jewelry. Her stock did seem to rotate fairly frequently, but I'd never seen any-one come into Abra's to buy anything physical.

No, Abra was the Spider, and her web covered the city. What she sold was *information*.

Jace had introduced me to Abra, a long time ago. Since then we'd been friends—of a sort. I did her a good turn or two when I could, she didn't sell too much infor-mation about my private life, and we edged along in a sort of mutual détente. I'll also admit that she puzzled me. She was obviously nonhuman, but she wasn't regis-tered with any of the Paranormal voting classes—Nichtvren, Kine, swanhilds, you name it—that had come out when the Parapsychic Act was signed into law, giv-ing them Hegemony citizenship. Then again, I knew a clutch of nonhumans that weren't registered but man-aged to make their voices heard the old-fashioned way, by bribe or by hook.

The bell over the door jingled as I stepped in, wooden floor creaking. The demon crowded right behind me.

"Hey, Abra," I began, and heard a whining click.

The demon's hand bit my shoulder. A complicated flurry of motion ended up with me staring at the demon's back as he held two silvery guns on Abra, who pointed a plasrifle at him.

Well, this is exotic, I thought.

"Put the gun down, *s'darok*," the demon rumbled. "Or your webweaving days are over."

"What the *hell* did you bring in here, Danny?" Abra snapped. "Goddamn psychic women and their goddamn pets!"

"Japh—" I stopped myself from saying more of his name. "What are you *doing*?"

"She has a weapon pointed at you, Dante," he said,

and the entire shop rattled. "I will burn your nest, *s'darok*. Put the gun down."

"Fuck . . ." Abra slowly, slowly, laid the plasrifle down and raised her hands. "Psychic women and their goddamn pets. More trouble than anything else in this town—"

"I need information, Abra," I said, pitching my voice low and calm. "Jaf, she's not going to hurt you—"

"Oh, I know that." His voice had dropped to its lowest registers. "It's *you* she'll harm, if she can."

"Isn't that sweet." Abra's face crinkled, her dark eyes lighting with scarlet pinpricks. The shop's glass windows bowed slightly under the pressure of her voice. Dust stirred, settled into complicated angular patterns, stirred again. The warding on Abra's shop was complex and unique; I'd never seen anything like it. "Dante, make him go away or no dice."

"Oh, for the love of—" I was about to lose my temper. "Japhrimel, she's put the gun down. Put yours away."

There was an eye-popping moment of tension that ended with Japhrimel slowly lowering his guns. His hands flicked, and they disappeared. "As you like," he said harshly, the smell of amber musk and burning cinnamon suddenly filling the shop. I had quickly grown used to the way he smelled. "But if she moves to harm you, she'll regret it."

"I *think* I'm capable of having a conversation with Abra that doesn't lead to anyone killing anyone else," I said dryly. "We've been doing it for years now." My skin burned with the tension and Power in the air. The smell of beef and chilis reminded me I hadn't eaten yet.

"Why does she have a gun out, then?" he asked.

"You're not exactly kind and cuddly," I pointed out, digging my heels into the floor as the weight of Power threatened to make me sway. "Everyone just *calm down*, okay? Can we do that?"

"Make him wait outside," Abra suggested helpfully.

"Absolutely *not*—" Japhrimel began.

"Will you *both* stop it?" I hissed. I'd be lucky to get *anything* out of Abra now. "The longer you two do this, the longer we stay here, and the more uncomfortable it'll be for *all* concerned. So *both* of you *just shut up!*"

Silence returned to the shop. The smell of beef stew, desperation, and dust warred with the musky powerful fragrance of demon. Japhrimel's eyes didn't leave Abra's face, but he slowly moved aside so I could see Abra without having to peek around him.

I dug the paper scored with Santino's name out of my bag. "I need information on this demon," I said quietly. "And I need to know about Dacon Whitaker. And I'm sure we'll find other things to talk about."

"What you paying?" Abra asked, her dark eyes losing a little bit of their crimson sparks.

"That's not how things stand right now. You owe me, Abra. And if you satisfy me, I'll owe *you* a favor." She more than owed me—I had brought her choice gossip last year after that Chery Family fiasco. The information of just who was stealing from the Family had been worth a pretty penny, and I was sure she'd sold it to the highest bidder—without, of course, mentioning that I'd been the one to bring her the laseprints. After that, I'd watched the fireworks as the Owens Family lost a good chunk of their holdings from an internal power struggle. It always warmed my heart to do the Mob a bad turn.

Her dark eyes traveled over Japhrimel. "You aren't a

Magi, Danny. What are you doing hanging out with Hell's upper crust?"

So she recognizes him as a demon, and what kind of demon, too. That's interesting. "Just call me socially mobile," I said. "Look, *they* came and contacted *me*, not the other way around. I didn't ask for this, but I'm in it up to my eyebrows and sinking fast, and in order to collect on all my balloon payments I need to be breathing, okay? And I need information to keep breathing, Abra." My voice was pitched deliberately low, deliberately soothing. "We've been colleagues for a long time now, and I made you some cash during that Chery Family thing last year, and I'd *really like* to get some usable information. Okay?"

She measured me for a long moment. The demon didn't even twitch, but I felt him tense and ready beside me. My left shoulder was steadily throbbing, the mark pressed into my flesh responding to his attention.

"Okay," she said. "But you'd better not ever bring that *thing* here again."

He's not a thing. I didn't say it, didn't even wonder why I'd thought it. I had all I could handle right in front of me. "If I had a choice, I wouldn't have brought him in the first place," I snapped, my temper wearing thin. "Come *on*, Abra."

She made a quick movement, slipping the plasrifle off the counter. The demon didn't move—but my shoulder gave a livid flare. It had been close. Very close. "Okay," Abra said. "Give me whatever you've got."

I laid the paper down on the counter, face-down. I gave her everything I had—Santino/Vardimal, the Egg, being dragged into Hell, Dacon's addiction to Chill, and the job I'd just been on. That was an extra, for her—she could sell the information that Douglas Shantern had been murdered by his son. I laid the pattern out for her, and Japhrimel drew closer during the recital until his hand was on my shoulder and his long black coat brushed my jeans. Oddly enough, I didn't mind as much as I might have.

Abra took it all in, one dusky finger tapping her thin lips. Then she was silent for a long moment, and put her hand down, fingers stretched, over the paper I'd laid on the counter. "Okay," she said. "So you have a tracker, and Spocarelli'll give you a waiver and a DOC and an omni . . . and you need a direction, and not only that, you need contacts and gossip."

I nodded. "You got it."

"And your tame demon there is supposed to keep you alive until you kill this Santino. Then all bets are off."

Japhrimel tensed again.

"That's my personal estimation of the situation," I said cautiously.

Abra chuffed out a breath between her pearly teeth. It was her version of a sarcastic laugh. "Girl, you are fucked for sure."

"Don't I know it? Give me what you got, Abra-cadabra, I've got work to do tonight."

She nodded, dark hair sliding forward over her shoulders. The gold hoops in her ears shivered. Then she flipped the paper over, regarded the twisting silvery glyph. "Ah . . ." she breathed, sounding surprised. "This . . . oh, Dante. Oh, no."

The color drained from her dark face. She spread her hand over the paper, not quite touching it, fingers trembling. "South," she said in a queer breathless voice. "South, where it's warm. He's drawn to where it's warm . . . hiding. He's hiding . . . can't tell why. A woman . . . no, a girl . . ."

Japhrimel tensed next to me. I didn't think it was possible for him to get any tighter strung. He moved a little closer, I could feel the heat breathing off him, wrapping around me. If he got any closer he would be molded to my side.

"What about the Egg?" I breathed. Abra's eyes were wide and white, irises a thin ring around her dilated pupils, splotches of hectic color high up on her now-pale cheeks.

"Broken . . . dead . . . ash, ash on the wind . . ." Abra's hand jerked, smacking down on the counter. I jumped, and Japhrimel's fingers bit my shoulder. She didn't get these flashes often, but when she did, they were invariably right—though usually not precise enough to be of any real help.

I had an even more important question. "How do I kill the sonuvabitch, Abra? How do I kill Santino?"

Her eyelids fluttered. "Not by demon fire . . . neither man nor demon can kill him . . . *water*—" She took in a long gasping breath, her lips stretched back over strong white teeth. "Waves. Waves on the shore, ice, I see you, I *see* you, Dante . . . face-down, floating . . . you're floating . . . floating—"

I leaned over the counter, grabbed Abra's shoulders, and shook her. When that didn't work, I slapped her— not hard, just hard enough to shock her. Her eyes flew open, and Japhrimel yanked me back, hissing something low and sharp in what I guessed was his own language. Abra coughed, rackingly, grabbing on to the counter with white-knuckled fingers. She said something quiet and harsh that I didn't quite catch, then looked me full in the eyes. "This is going to kill you, Danny," she said, with no trace of her usual bullshit. "Do you understand me? This is going to *kill* you."

"As long as I take out the fucker that did Doreen I'll be okay," I grated out. "Information, Abra. Where the fuck is he?"

"Where else?" Abra snapped back, but her chin trembled slightly. She was paler than I'd ever seen her. "Nuevo Rio di Janeiro, Danny Valentine. That's where you'll find your prey."

I scooped up the paper and shoved it in my bag. Abra stared at me, trembling, her teeth sunk into her bottom lip. It was the first time I'd even seen her even remotely close to scared.

She looked *terrified*.

"What about Dacon and the Chill?" I asked. "How the hell did—"

"Whitaker's hand-in-fist with the Owens Family, has been for years now. He got hooked last year and started skimming from their shipments," she replied shortly, reaching up to touch her cheek where the mark of my hand flushed red. "You *hit* me!"

"You were getting boring," I said before I thought about it. "Contacts in Nuevo Rio?"

"I don't have any," she said. "But as soon as you get there, you might want to look up Jace Monroe. He moved down there a while ago. Doing work for the Corvin Family. He's gone back to the Mob."

I hadn't known that. Then again, I'd never asked Abra about Monroe, even though he'd introduced me to her. I knew he'd been Mob, and suspected he'd gone back to the Mob—but hearing it out loud was something else entirely. I made a face. "I'd rather talk to a spasmoid weasel with a plasrifle," I muttered. "Okay. So what about gossip?"

Abra shrugged. "Word on the street is you're into something big, and there's a warning out there, too. *Don't mess around with Danny Valentine.*"

"I thought that was common knowledge."

"You've got a demon for a lapdog, Danny. Nobody wants that kind of static." She grimaced, rubbing her cheek. "Not even me. Can you go away now?"

I nodded, frustration curdling under my collarbones. "Thanks, Abra. I owe you one."

Her response was a bitter laugh. "You're not going to live long enough for me to collect. Now get the fuck out of my shop, and *don't* bring that thing back here." Her hand twitched toward the plasrifle leaning obediently on her side of the counter. Japhrimel pulled me away, dragging me across the groaning wooden floor, my bootheels scraping. The temperature in the shop had risen at least ten degrees.

He's not a thing, Abra. "I'll leave him at home to crochet next time," my mouth responded smartly with no direction from my brain. "Thanks, Abra."

"If she dies, *s'darok*," Jaf tossed back over his shoulder, "I will come hunting for you."

"Stop it. What's *wrong* with you?" I tried to extract my arm from his hand, with no luck. He didn't let go of me until we were outside the pawnshop and a good half block away. "What the *hell*—"

"She predicted your death, Dante," he said, grudgingly letting me slip my arm away from him. I felt bruises starting where his fingers had been. I dug my heels into the pavement and jerked my arm all the way free of his grasp, irritation rasping sharp under my breastbone.

"What the hell does it matter to *you*?" I snapped. "You're more trouble than you're worth! I could have gotten *twice* the information out of her if you hadn't gone all Chillfreak! You're fucking *useless*!"

A muscle in his cheek twitched. "I certainly hope not," he answered calmly enough. "You walk into a *s'darok*'s den with no protection, you court death with no conception of the consequences, and you blame *me* for your own foolhardiness—"

"I blame *you*? You don't even make any *sense*! If you had just been a little less set on 'psychotic' we could have gotten twice as much information from her! But no, you had to play the demon, you had to act like you know everything! You're so arrogant, you never even—"

"We are *wasting time*," he overrode me. "I will not let you come to harm, Dante, despite all your protests. From this moment forth, I will not *allow* this foolishness."

"*Allow?* What's this 'allow'? What the bloody blue hell is wrong with you?" It wasn't until the streetlamp in front of us popped, its glass bulb shattering and dusting the pavement below with glittering sprinkles, that I realized I was far too upset.

I need to fucking well calm down, I thought. *Too bad it looks like that's not going to happen soon.*

He said nothing in reply, just staring at me with those laser-green eyes, his cheek twitching. The cold wind was beginning to warm up, little crackles of static electricity in the air.

Necromances and Ceremonials both tended to affect a whispery tone after a while. We live by enforcing our Will on the world through words wedded to Power—and a Necromance shouting in anger could cause a great deal of damage. One of the dicta of Magi training ran: *A Magi's word becomes truth.* And for trained Necromances, who walked between this world and the next, discipline was all the more imperative.

I took a deep breath, tasting ozone, my shields flushing dark-blue with irritation, annoyance, and good clean anger. "Okay," I said, struggling for an even tone. "Look, I think we can make some progress, if you just tell me what's wrong with you. Okay? You're making this much harder than it has to be."

His jaw worked silently. *If he keeps that up he might grind his teeth down to nubs,* I thought, and had to bite back a nervous giggle.

I rubbed at my arm. It *hurt*, and so did my left shoulder. The burning, drilling pain reminded me of how quickly my life had grown incredibly-fucked-up. Even for me. "I wish I'd never seen you," I said tonelessly. "That *hurt*, you asshole." I was far too angry to care about calling a demon who could eat me for breakfast an asshole.

He reached out for my arm again, and I flinched. His hand stopped in midair, then dropped back to his side. He looked—for the first time—actually chagrined. Or as if he was hovering between chagrin and fury. I'd seen that look before, but only on Jace.

I didn't want to think about Jace.

My hand shook as I massaged my new bruise. "Look," I said finally. "I'm going to call Gabe and set up a meet so we can get our supplies. Then I'm packing for Rio and catching a morning transport out there. I can't be taking time to educate *your* dumb ass on how to catch a gods-be-damned demon in my world. Stop fucking up my hunt, okay?" My emerald spat a single spark out into the night, a brief green flash making his pupils shrink. "I am going to find Santino and kill him. It's *my* revenge. When I tear his spleen out through his nose, you can have your fucking Egg and go back to your fucking Prince and *stay out of my life.* But until then, *quit fucking up my hunt*! You got it?"

He stared at me for another ten seconds, that muscle in his cheek twitching. "As you like," he finally grated out.

"Good," I said. "Now follow me. And keep your goddamn motherfucking mouth shut."

CHAPTER
18

I met Gabe in a noodle shop on Pole Street. I was starving, and managed to get most of a bowl of beef pho into my stomach before Gabe and Eddie drifted in the front door, Eddie silently snarling, Gabe looking cool and impenetrable in a long black police-issue synthwool coat.

Gabe slid into the booth across from me, and Eddie lowered himself down with a single glance at the demon, who sat utterly straight next to me, staring into the distance, a teacup steaming gently in front of him. The tattered red velvet and black-and-white photographs of ancestors and movie stars hung on the walls made the entire place feel warmer than it was, and the sticky plastic of the booths made squealing sounds as they made themselves comfortable.

The waitress brought coffee for Gabe, and Eddie ordered seafood soup. I slurped down another mouthful of noodles. Eddie smelled like dirt and violence, and Gabe had one hell of a black eye. Probably fresh, since she would have used a healcharm on it if she'd had time. I studied her for a long time before letting my eyebrows raise.

"I got called in to do para backup on a Chill raid last

night," she said finally, tossing her dark hair back over her shoulder. "Some motherfucking dumbass Magi dealing Chill out of his nightclub. Wouldn't you know."

I nodded. "Sorry about that."

She shrugged. Her sword was propped between her knees, and Eddie was probably carrying some hardware, too. "Not your fault, sweetie. You did the right thing." She slid a bulky package wrapped in brown paper across the table. "An official bounty hunter's license, two H-DOC and omni-license-to-carry, and a plug-in for the Net. A sanctioned plug-in."

My jaw dropped. Japhrimel's lip twitched. He looked down at the table, one gold-skinned finger tracing a single symbol I wasn't able to decipher over and over again on the Formica.

"What the hell?" I asked.

"Someone's put some pressure on the department. Apparently anything you need is okay. You're a real golden girl right about now." Gabe's lips quirked up at the corners. "Knowing the Devil personally has some benefits, I'd guess."

I let out a gusty sigh and slurped some more noodles. "You want to get on my shit list, too?" I asked her. "'Cause the number of people on that hallowed list is growing rapidly tonight."

"Poor baby," she laughed, while Eddie glared at me. "So where we going? What did Abra say?"

"Abra said Nuevo Rio," I said shortly. "And what's this *we*?"

Japhrimel stared out from the booth, his eyes moving over the entire restaurant in smooth arcs. I got the feeling that even the flies buzzing in loose spirals over the tables and the pattern of grease speckles and neon on the front window were receiving his full attention. Behind us, an old Asian man slurped loudly at his noodles, a curl of cigarette smoke rising slowly into the air. I'd been eating noodles here for six years, and no matter what time of the day or night, the old man was here, and he was always smoking. It was a dependable thing in a very undependable universe.

"Well," Gabe said finally, after studying the demon's impassive face for a few moments, "Doreen was my friend, too, and it was my case. Eddie and I have talked it over, and we're coming with you."

I put my chopsticks down and took a deep breath. "Gabe," I said, as kindly as I could, "I work alone."

She jerked her chin at the demon. "What, he's good enough to come along, but not me?"

"It's not like that," I said. "You know it's not like that." The familiar tension began in my shoulders, drawing tighter and tighter.

"I know you're going to get yourself killed chasing Santino down, and you need backup. Have you read your cards lately?" Her elegant eyebrows raised.

"My last divination session was kind of rudely interrupted," I said dryly.

"Come on, Danny." She batted her long, coal-black eyelashes at me. "I've got some vacation time, and I want to bring this fucker *down*."

"Gabe—"

"She says she's going," Eddie growled. "Means it too. Can't dissuade her."

Since when does Eddie use the word "dissuade"? I thought. *This is lunacy.* "Since when do you use the word 'dissuade,' Eddie? You get yourself a Word-A-Day holovid pro? Come on, Gabe. I don't want to have to watch out for Eddie on a hunt like this—"

"Eddie's got his own hunter's license," she pointed out, "and he's perfectly capable. You're grasping at straws, Danny. We're coming."

I threw up my hands. "Oh, *Sekhmet sa'es,*" I snarled. "If you must, I suppose. Gods above and below damn this for a suicidal idea, and Anubis protect us *all.* What did I do to deserve this?"

"You were Doreen's best friend," Gabe reminded me. "You got her out of that—"

I shivered, all levity and irritation disappearing. "Don't," I said tonelessly, looking down at the table. "Don't talk about that. I failed when it mattered, Gabe, that's what I did. So don't go patting me on the back. If I'd been stronger, smarter, or faster, Doreen might still be alive."

Silence descended on the table. Eddie's chopsticks paused in midair, noodles hanging from them. Steam drifted up. The smell of fried food, soy sauce, grease, and dust warred with the smell of demon, making my stomach flip.

The demon looked over at me. He reached out, deliberately, and touched the back of my wrist with two fingers.

Heat slid through my body. The mark on my left shoulder tingled. My other arm, where the bruise was swiftly developing, gave a crunching flare of pain and then eased. He said nothing.

I licked at dry lips and finally jerked my wrist away from him, almost upsetting my almost-empty soup bowl. I caught it, gathered my chopsticks, and dropped them into the plasglass bowl with a clatter.

"I'm catching a transport out in the morning," I said, picking up my bowl.

"We've already got the tickets, for you, too," Gabe replied. "And we're bringing munitions. Being a cop is good for *something*."

"It better be," Eddie muttered darkly, munching on his noodles. I took a long drink of hot beef broth, holding my chopsticks out of the way with my thumb. The demon still watched me.

I ignored him.

When I finished and set my bowl down, Gabe was staring into her coffee cup. "Better go home and get some sleep," she said. "We're scheduled for a 10:00 A.M. jumpoff."

"Charming," I muttered, then poked at the demon's shoulder with the hilt of my sword. "Okay. Come by my house about eight-thirty tomorrow. All right?" I took the bulky package with me, following the demon as he rose gracefully to his feet and moved aside, offering his hand to help me stand. I didn't take it, squirming out of the booth on my own.

"Don't get any ideas about stranding me, kid." Gabe peered around Eddie, who had his face buried in his bowl, supremely unconcerned. "It's hard enough to find a friend nowadays. I don't want you to go all *banzai* on me."

Oddly enough, that made a lump rise in my throat. "You win, Gabe," I said. "You win."

I turned around and headed for the door.

"Nice to be working with you," Eddie burbled through his soup.

We made it out onto the hushed street. The noodle

shop's neon-lit windows threw a warm red glow out onto the drying pavement. The demon still said nothing.

My arm didn't hurt anymore.

I could feel the demon's eyes on me. Wouldn't you know, he wasn't bothering looking at where he was going; he was busy looking at me, stepping over a drift of wet newspaper without even looking.

"What?" I finally asked, my eyes on the pavement under my feet. I kicked a Sodaflo can out of the way. "I can feel you wanting to say something, so spit it out."

We walked for maybe half a block until he spoke. "You're distressed," he said quietly. "I hurt your arm. My apologies."

"We could have gotten a lot more out of Abra if you hadn't threatened her," I pointed out.

"I did not want you injured."

"Because it'll foul up your own carefully laid plans," I flared. "Fine."

He was quiet for another half minute, during which we crossed Pole Street. I looked both ways this time. The old feeling of being on a hunt, adrenaline and sour boredom and fierce determination, was beginning to come back.

"You are the most infuriating human I have ever met," he said.

"I thought you didn't often leave Hell." I was so out of sorts that my neck was starting to tingle.

"Why must even an apology be a battle, with you?"

"I thought demons didn't apologize."

"You are testing my patience, Dante."

"Go back to Hell, then."

"If I were human, would you be so cruel to me?"

"If you were human you wouldn't have shown up at

my house and dragged me to Hell with a gun pointed at my head and gotten me involved in this mess." I stamped against the pavement, my boots echoing. *Get over it, Danny. You're losing your focus. What is wrong with you?*

Nothing's wrong with me. It wasn't quite true. I thought I had made my peace with Doreen's death, but the ghosts of the past were standing up, shaking out their dusty clothes, and emerging into my life again. I didn't want to face any more memories of pain and terror and death—I had too many already.

And if the memories of Doreen were coming back, why not the other memories I thought I'd locked up and buried for good? *Let's make it a party for Danny Valentine, let's get out all the old terrors and shake her to and fro, how about that?*

"How would you have preferred it, then?" he asked.

"I would have *preferred* to be left alone," I snapped at him. "I thought you were going to apologize."

"I already did. If you weren't so determined to hate me, perhaps you would have noticed."

"You arrogant—" I was again paying no attention to where we were going, so the slight scuffle in the alley made me stop midstride and whirl. Metal sang as my sword cleared the sheath. A good fight was just what the doctor ordered. My lips peeled back from my teeth. *Come on out,* I thought, dropping into guard position, my blade suddenly aflame with blue light. Even the thought of the paperwork it would take to clear up the mess wasn't enough to deter me from stepping forward, unconsciously putting the demon behind me as if to protect him, the blue glow of my sword suddenly reflecting on eyes and teeth and glints of metal.

The demon turned, too, an oddly graceful movement, peering into the alley. He held up a hand, and sudden light scored the darkness, making my eyes water.

Shit, he's destroyed my night vision, dammit—I flicked my sword up into the blind guard, readying myself for a strike. Here on Pole Street, it wasn't likely to be a minigang like on the subway. Here it was likely to be a full-fledged pack of street wolves, and even though I had a sword and a Necromance's tat, it could get really ugly, really quickly.

Then again, ugly was just fine with me. The flood of copper adrenaline was almost as good as riding a slicboard, my breath hissing out through my teeth.

Unfortunately, the demon's little light-ball showed six dark shapes fleeing down the alley, one with a metal glint in his hands. Switchblade or gun, didn't matter. I stood there as the demon calmly flicked his wrist, bringing the white-hot glowing sphere back to rest obediently in his palm. Another flick of his wrist and the light was gone, making me blink my dazzled eyes. Power hummed through the air, the smell of ozone and rain mixing with the sharper smell of garbage, and fear. And over it all, the smoky smell of demon.

"As I said," he said quietly, "you appear to need a caretaker. Were you unaware of being followed? And did you think to protect me?"

His face resolved as my pupils expanded, green eyes glowing and half-lidded, his mouth curled up faintly at the corners. Laughing at the poor stupid human.

"I don't need to be taken care of, especially when it's only a grunge-smelling pack of Pole Street wolves. I need to get this *over* with so I can go back to my life, pay my mortgage, and retire." I resheathed my sword, the blue glow draining from the blade as unspent adrenaline wound my nerves up like a slic set on high. "I'm going home to get some sleep."

He nodded.

I set off down Pole Street, vaguely wishing there *had* been a fight. The demon's disdain was infuriating, even though I shouldn't have cared. It took me about a block to realize I'd been rude. "Hey," I said, looking up at the demon, who paced beside me silent as a shark.

"Yes?" Wary. But he looked puzzled, too, as if I had just done something extraordinary.

"Thanks for the apology," I gave him, grudgingly. "And I tend to take point to protect whoever I'm with. It's not a comment on your ability. I'm sure you're able to take care of yourself."

Did he stumble slightly, or was it just my imagination? He didn't say a word.

CHAPTER
19

Get down, Doreen. Get down!"

Crash of thunder. Moving, desperately, scrabbling . . . fingers scraping against the concrete, rolling to my feet, dodging the whine of bullets. Skidding to a stop just as he rose out of the dark, the little black bag in one hand, his claws glittering on the other.

"Game over," he giggled, and the awful tearing in my side turned to a burning numbness as he slashed. I threw myself backward, not fast enough, not fast enough, blood exploding outward, copper stink.

"Danny!" Doreen's despairing scream.

"Get out!" I screamed, but she was coming back, hands glowing blue-white, still trying to heal.

Trying to reach me, to heal me, the link between us resonating with my pain and her burning hands—

Made it to my feet, screaming at her to get the fuck out, and Santino's claws whooshing again as he tore into me, one claw sticking on a rib, my sword ringing as I slashed at him, too slow, he was something inhuman, something inhuman—

"Dante. Wake up." A smooth, dark, old voice. "Wake up."

I sat bolt upright, screaming, my fingers hooked into claws, scrambled back until my shoulders hit the wall, sobbing breaths hitching in through my mouth because my nose was full. My back burned, the three whip scars full of heat, the burn scar on my left ass cheek twinging, and the scars across my belly and up my right side pulsing with awful fiery remembered numb pain.

Japhrimel's hand dropped back down to his side. "You were dreaming." His hair was slightly mussed, as if he'd been sleeping, too. His eyes glowed, casting dim shadows under his nose and cheekbones and lower lip. "I heard you scream . . ."

My left shoulder ached most of all, a deep desperate pain. I gasped. Blinked at him. The sheet had come free; I clutched it to my chest, trying to control my jagging breath. My rings spat green-gold swirls of light. I rubbed at my left shoulder with a fistful of sheet, my silk nightgown wadded up at my hip. The phantom pain drained away, each wound giving a final vicious sear, promising a return. The whip scars went first, and the clawmarks on my left side lingered until I took another sobbing breath in through my mouth and reminded myself that I was not bleeding.

Not anymore.

I reached for the box of tissues on my nightstand, blew my nose. It was my only admission of the tears, having to wad up the tissue and toss it in the general direction of the bathroom. My heart rate dropped to something like normal, and I found my voice. "You heard me?" I sounded husky, not like my usual self. Frightened.

"Of course I heard you. You bear my mark." He pointed to my left shoulder. He was still wearing that long black coat. *He must not have much of a dry-cleaning bill*, I thought, and a traitorous giggle almost escaped me.

"You're still wearing that coat."

"I usually do. What were you dreaming about?"

"S-s-Santino. When he k-killed D-Doreen . . ." I rubbed at my shoulder. "Why does it hurt?"

I sounded childlike.

"How did he kill her?" he asked.

I shrugged. "He kills psionics. We thought he was a serial killer, he eviscerates—"

Japhrimel stiffened. "He bleeds psychics? Not just ordinary humans?"

I nodded, pushed strands of my hair back over my shoulders. "He took trophies. Internal organs . . . he took the femur, or parts of it. It was his trademark . . . We couldn't figure out what his victims had in common, until I did a reconstruct of a crime scene and we found out all of his victims were psis. Then we went back through . . . *gods* . . ." I took a deep breath. "He sent each one flowers. Flowers!"

Japhrimel nodded. His eyes were so bright they cast little green sparkles against his cheekbones. He settled on the edge of my bed. "I see."

"I figured out he was the Saint City Slasher by going through some security tapes on one of the victims' buildings. By that time Gabe was on the case. I think . . . I think it was my being on the case that made Santino fixate on Doreen. He s-s-sent those f-f-flowers . . . Gabe agreed with me that Doreen was a target, and we outthought him . . . gods, it must have just made him more angry . . ." I relaxed, muscle by muscle. Took deep breaths. *In through the nose, out through the mouth . . .*

Moving Doreen from safehouse to safehouse, one step ahead of the killer; living out of our suitcases, me lying awake every night with my hand curled around my swordhilt, listening, my entire world narrowing to keeping Reena alive one more day . . .

Japhrimel touched my shoulder with two fingers, warmth spreading through my cold bones. Gooseflesh prickled at my skin. "That's a nice trick," I managed around the lump in my throat.

He shrugged. "We are creatures of fire."

The way his eyes were burning, I believed it.

I shut my eyes. That was a mistake, because Santino's face hung in the darkness behind my lids. I stared at the face, the black teardrops over the eyes, the high-pointed ears, long nose, sharp teeth—

I thought he had rich-boy cosmetic augments to make himself look like a Nichtvren, I thought he was psionic and overrode me while I was losing consciousness, even though the cops couldn't find any sign of a memory wipe, I thought he was just a sick twisted human psionic . . .

"Dante. Come back." His fingers were still on my shoulder, bare skin scorching against mine.

My eyes flew open. He leaned across my tangled bed, his fingers almost melded to my shoulder. My other shoulder—the one that bore his mark—twinged sharply. "Why does it hurt?" I asked, tipping my chin down to point at my shoulder.

He shrugged. "I am your familiar. I suspect it's one of the Prince's jokes."

What the hell is that supposed to mean? "What are you talking about?"

"How much do you know of the bond between Magi and familiar?"

My heart rate calmed down. Sweat dried on my skin. I tasted copper adrenaline and blood—I'd bitten my lip. "I told you, not much. Just that some Magi get familiars, it's the great quest for every Magi . . . mostly imp-class demons, just little guys. Barely enough to light a candle."

"It's my duty to obey you. It's *your* duty to feed me." He didn't sound like it was any big deal.

"You know where the kitchen is." I took in a deep breath. "Thanks for . . . for waking me up. I haven't had a bad nightmare like that in . . . in a couple of years." The lie came out smoothly. The nightmare returned almost every night, punctually, unless I was exhausted. I had plenty of nightmares, from Rigger Hall, from some of the jobs I'd been on, from any number of horrible things I'd witnessed or had done to me. But the replaying of Santino's last assault had top billing for the last few years.

It was my heaviest regret, not being strong enough or fast enough when it counted.

He was quiet, and still. "I don't need *human* food," he said.

I touched my bleeding lip. My sword lay on my other side, safe in its sheath. "So what are you talking about? Power?"

"Blood. Sex. Fire." His fingers fell away from my shoulder. "Imps can feed on alcohol and drug intoxication, but I wouldn't recommend that. You need your wits about you."

"*Anubis et'her ka,*" I breathed. "You're not serious. Why tell me this now?"

"There hasn't been a better time." He settled back, the

bed creaking underneath him. "I think you would be most comfortable with blood instead of sex."

"You've got *that* right," I muttered, my head still ringing with the dream. That chilling little giggle, while he took what he wanted, his satisfied wet little sounds while he—

A new and terrible thought occurred to me. We had assumed Santino took trophies. What if he was . . . *eating* the parts he took? I shivered, opening my eyes as wide as I could.

"How badly did he hurt you?" he asked. "Santino. *Vardimal*."

I shut my eyes again. "He eviscerated me," I whispered. "If Doreen hadn't . . . she had her hands on me when he slit her throat. He didn't have enough time to do his entire ritual on her . . . he just bled her dry and cut out part of her femur . . . she had her hands on me . . . she used her last breath to heal me."

"Blood. Why blood? And a human bone . . ." he asked, very softly, as if to himself.

"You tell me," I said. "What does he need to murder psionics for? Does it have anything to do with the Egg?"

"It is useless to him," Japhrimel said quietly.

"What happens if he breaks it? Apocalypse, right?"

"Of a sort." Japhrimel folded his hands. The mark on my left shoulder gave another deep twinge. "The Egg holds a piece of . . . of the Prince's power. Decoded on Earth instead of in Hell, it could . . . upset the order of things. It is a violation of the way things should be."

"Okay." I took a deep breath. This was almost interesting enough to make me forget my heart was still hammering from a nightmare. Was this Egg a Talisman? The way he was talking about it, it seemed likely. "I guess I understand the magickal theory behind that, if it's heavy-duty demon stuff. But what's in it? Why does he want it? If word gets out that it's been stolen, what will—"

Japhrimel's teeth showed in one of those murderous, slow grins he seemed so fond of. "It will mean that the Prince is not strong enough to rule Hell. Demons will test his strength as they have not done for millennia. A Rebellion might succeed . . . and Vardimal might become the new Prince of Hell."

I chewed on this for a moment. He wasn't precisely answering the question, but his answer opened up so many other questions I decided to let the first one go for now. "So that's why Lucifer can't have anyone know that someone's stolen the Egg," I said. "Funny—I thought you guys were in Hell because you rebelled in the first place."

My attempt at levity failed miserably. He didn't even look like he got the joke. Then again, not many psis studied classical literature and the pre-Awakening Christos Bible Text, which had been discredited and gone out of use in the great backlash against the Evangelicals of Gilead.

"I have heard that story," he answered slowly. His eyelids lowered over his glowing eyes as he glanced down. "Human gods do not trouble us overmuch. It is only that humans were frightened of us, and mistook *us* for gods. There was a rebellion—the Fallen defied Lucifer's will, and died on earth because of the love they bore for the brides . . . but that is not something we speak of."

I absorbed this. If I was a Magi I'd be peppering him with questions, trying to get him to say more, but I was too tired.

Silence thundered through the dark bedroom. The mark on my shoulder ached, pounding. I was finally beginning to believe that I was awake. The scars went back to sleep until the next nightmare; maybe I could sleep, too. Maybe.

"If he manages to destroy this Egg," I thought out loud, "does that mean you'll be free?"

"Of course not." He dropped his eyes, studied the bed. Little green shadows danced on my blanket, showing me his gaze moving in an aimless pattern from my knee to my hand to the edge of the bed, back to my knee. "Should Vardimal's rebellion fail, I will be left as your familiar, perhaps. Then after your death—which might be swift, since the Prince is not one for slow punishment—I will be punished, for as long as the Prince's reign is secure. If by some stroke of chance Vardimal succeeds, I will be executed—after your death as well. If the Prince wins, I wait another eternity for a chance at my freedom—if another chance is granted me at all."

"You just can't win, can you." I didn't want to sound snide. I swallowed dryly. It seemed like I couldn't win either, since both scenarios involved my sudden demise, too.

"No," he said. "I can't."

"So you really have a lot invested in this."

"It would appear so."

Another long, uncomfortable silence. The world was hushed outside, in the deepest part of night before the flush of false dawn. I didn't feel sleepy, though I knew I should be trying to catch some shut-eye before the morning transport. Once I left the house tomorrow, I'd be on the hunt. I didn't sleep much while hunting.

"You must be pretty hungry," I said finally. "This mark hurts like a bitch."

"My apologies."

It took more courage than I thought I had to extend my hand, flipping my palm up and making a fist. My wrist was exposed, pale in the dimness of my bedroom. The nightlight in the hall shone in through the door, a cool blue glow. "Here," I said. "Blood, right? You need me to cut myself, or . . ."

He shrugged. "Many thanks for the offer, Dante, but . . . no."

"You're hungry. I don't want a weak demon. I want a kickass demon who can help me deal with Santino."

"I fight better when I'm a little hungry."

"Fine." I dropped my hand, feeling foolish. "I'm okay now. You can go back downstairs. Get yourself something in the kitchen. If you want."

"As you like." But he didn't move.

"Go ahead," I finally said. "I'm fine. Really. Thank you."

"You will have no trouble sleeping?" he asked, still looking at the bed. The burning intensity in his eyes seemed to have lessened a bit. He ran his hand back absently through his hair—the first sign of nervousness I'd ever noticed in him. Was he nervous? Was it just me, or was he seeming a little more . . . *human* . . . with every passing hour?

I managed to dredge up an uneasy laugh. "I always have trouble sleeping. It's not a big deal. Go on and catch some shut-eye yourself. Tomorrow's going to be a busy day."

He unfolded himself from the bed and stood up, hands behind his back. *Why does he stand like that?* I wondered.

And why doesn't he take that coat off? "Thanks." I scooted back down, pulled the covers up, rested my hand on my sword, still lying faithfully next to me. "For checking on me, I mean."

He nodded, then turned on his heel and stalked for the door. There was a moment of shadow, his bulk filling the doorway, his coat like a shadow of dark wings. I heard his even tread going down the hall, then down the stairs. He went into the living room, and silence pervaded my house again, broken only by the faint hum of traffic and the subliminal song of the fridge downstairs.

I snuggled back into bed and closed my eyes. I expected to be lying awake for a long time, shaking and sweating in the aftermath of the dream, but strangely enough I fell into sleep with no trouble at all.

CHAPTER
20

*E*ddie dug his fingers into the armrests. He was as pale as I'd ever seen him, his cheeks chalk-white under his blond sideburns.

Gabe, leafing through a magazine, didn't appear to notice, but Japhrimel was studying Eddie intently, his green eyes glittering. The demon lounged in his seat next to me, occasionally shifting his weight when the transport rattled. I tapped my fingers on my swordhilt and looked out the window. Seeing the earth drift away underneath the hover transport was no comparison to a slicboard, but it was nice to sit and watch city and water drift away, replaced by pleated folds of land, the coastal mountains rising and falling.

"I can't believe I made a ten o'clock transport." I rested my head against the seat-back. Gabe had actually scored first-class tickets. We had a whole compartment to ourselves—Gabe's tattoo and mine took care of that. "I haven't even had coffee yet, goddammit."

"*Someone's* a little cranky." Gabe hooked her leg over her seat-arm and rubbed her ankle against Eddie's knee. "Bitch, bitch, bitch. I had to drag this big shaggy guy out

of bed and onto a transport before noon. I should be the
one whining."

"You're always trying to one-up me," I mumbled. The
demon glanced at me, then leaned forward to look out
the window. I caught a wave of his scent and sighed, my
eyes half-closing. Once you started to get used to it,
being around a demon was kind of absurdly comforting.
At least the most dangerous thing in the vicinity was
right where I could see it.

"Fucking transports," Eddie said, closing his eyes.
"Gabe?"

"I'm here, sweetie." Gabe rubbed her ankle against
his knee. "Just keep breathing."

I looked away. So there *was* something Eddie was
afraid of.

"What's he doing in Rio?" I asked the air, thinking out
loud. "Not a particularly good place to hide . . ."

"No, not with all the *santeros* down there," Gabe answered dryly, flipping another page. A holster peered out
from under her left shoulder, a smooth dark metal butt.
Plasgun, I thought, and looked over at the demon again.
He had disappeared as we navigated the security check-
points and rejoined us just before boarding, his hands
clasped behind his back and his face expressionless.
"Hey, you know their Necromances kill chickens to get
Power like the vaudun? Then everyone eats the chicken."

I'd studied vaudun at the Academy, so I wasn't entirely unfamiliar with it. "That's weird," I agreed, my
eyes snagging on the demon's face. He was looking at
me now, studying intently. "What?"

"Why does he reek of fear?" Japhrimel asked, jerking
his chin at Eddie.

"He doesn't like high places," Gabe said, "and he

doesn't like enclosed spaces. Most Skinlin don't." Her dark eyes came up, moved over the demon from head to foot. "What are you afraid of, demon?"

He shrugged, his coat moving against the seat. "Failure," he said crisply. "Dissolution. Emptiness." His mouth twisted briefly, as if he tasted something bitter.

Silence fell for about thirty seconds before the first inflight service came along—a blonde stewardess in a tight magenta flightsuit, paper-pale and trembling. Her eyes were the size of old credit discs, and she shook while she poured coffee, probably thinking that we were all going to read her mind and expose her most intimate secrets, or take over her mind and make her do something embarrassing—or that Gabe and I would suddenly start to make ghosts appear to torment her. Instead, I selected a cream-cheese Danish, Gabe got a roast-turkey sandwich, Eddie asked for the chicken soup in its heatseal pack. Oddly enough, Eddie seemed to scare her the most in his camel coat and long shaggy hair, his Skinlin staff braced against Gabe's sword. She looked like she expected him to go berserk at any moment. Japhrimel accepted a cup of coffee from her with a nod, and it was strange to see her give him an almost-relieved smile. Being normal, she couldn't see the dangerous black diamond flaming of his aura.

Sometimes I wished I'd been born that oblivious.

We waited until she was gone. I dumped a packet of creamer into my coffee. "So do you have contacts in Rio, other than a plug-in? Abra couldn't give me any." I settled back, wrinkling my nose at the reheated black brew.

"A few," she said, tearing into her sandwich. "Guess who else is down Rio way? Jace Monroe."

I made a face. "Yeah, Abra told me. Go figure."

"He's good backup."

"Too bad we're not going to use him."

"Aw, come on," Eddie piped up. "You two are so cute together."

I shrugged. "I don't go near the Mob. I thought you knew that."

"He's not Mob no more." Eddie slurped at his steaming soup, wiggling his blond eyebrows at me. He seemed to have forgotten he was on a transport.

"I fell for that line the first time. Once Mob, always Mob." I nibbled at my Danish, finding it bearable. "You remember that when you're dealing with him, Eddie, 'cause I sure as hell won't ever be messing around with him. Once was enough for me."

"I'll bet," Gabe muttered snidely, and I threw her a look that could have cut glass.

My rings swirled with lazy energy. We settled down to a long flight, Gabe flipping through her magazine again while she sipped at her coffee, Eddie finishing his soup in a series of loud smacking slurps, crunching on the crackers. I fished a book out of my bag—a paperback version of the Nine Canons, the glyphs and runes that made up the most reliable branch of magick. You can't ever study too much. I was secondarily talented as a runewitch, and I firmly believed that memorizing the Canons trained the mind and opened up the Power meridians, and why waste power creating a spell when you could use a Canon glyph as a shortcut?

The demon settled himself in his seat, alternating between watching me and studying his cup as if the secrets of the universe were held inside the nasty liquid passing for coffee. At least it was hot, and it had enough caffeine.

It was going to be a long, long flight.

CHAPTER
21

*W*e touched down in Nuevo Rio not a moment too soon. "Eddie, if you don't quit it, I'm going to fucking kill you," I snarled, standing and scooping my sword up.

"You're the one tapping your fingernails all the time," Gabe retorted. "Don't get all up on him."

"Stay out of this, Spocarelli," I warned her.

The demon rose like a dark wave. "Perhaps it's best to have this conversation outside," he said mildly. "You seem tense."

That gave us both something to focus on. "When I want your opinion, I'll ask you for it," I snapped.

"Oh, for the love of Hades, leave the damn demon alone!" Gabe almost yelled. "Off. Get me *off* this damn thing—"

"You're like a pair of spitting cats," Eddie mumbled. "Worse than a motherfucking cockfight."

"Now I know why I don't travel," I muttered, making sure my bag fell right. The airlocks whooshed, and we would have to wait our turn to get out.

Fuck that, I thought, and jammed the door to our compartment open. There are some *good* things about being a Necromance. One is that people get out of your way in a hell of a hurry when you come striding down a transport corridor with a sword in your hand and your emerald spitting sparks. Being accredited meant being able to carry edged metal in transports, and I had never been so glad.

Japhrimel followed me. By the time I stalked through another pair of airlocks and onto the dock, I was beginning to feel a little better. Eddie was next off, with Gabe right behind him, dragging her hand back through her long dark hair. "Fuck," she said, turning to look at the bulk of the transport through the dock windows. Hovercells were switching off, a subliminal hum loosening from my back teeth. "We're in Nuevo Rio. Gods have mercy on us."

"Amen to that," I answered. "Hey, what hotel are we staying at?"

"No hotel," she said, still trying to push her hair back, "I got us one better. We're going to stay with a friend. Cheap, effective, and safe."

"Who?" I was beginning to suspect something wasn't quite right by the way Eddie was grinning, showing all his teeth.

"Who else?" A familiar voice echoed along the dock. People began to pile out of the transport, casting nervous glances at us—two Necromances and a Skinlin, armed to the teeth, and a man in a long black coat. I closed my eyes, searching for control. Found it, and turned on my heel.

Jason Monroe leaned against a support post, his blue eyes glowing under a thatch of wheat-gold hair. He wore black, even in Rio, a pair of jeans and a black T-shirt, a Mob assassin's rig over the T-shirt, two guns, a collection of knives, his sword sheathed at his side. I prefer to carry my blade; he wore his thrust through his belt like an old-time samurai.

He was taller than me, and broad-shouldered, and wore the same kind of boots Gabe and I did. The thorny-twisted tattoo on his cheek marked him as an accredited Shaman just as the leather spirit bag on a thong around his neck marked him as a *vaudun*. Small bones hung from raffia twine clicked together as he moved slightly, twirling his long staff. I caught a glimpse of red in his spiky aura—he must have just offered to his patron *loa*. "Hey, Danny. Give an old boyfriend a kiss?"

CHAPTER
22

I can't *believe* you did this," I hissed at Gabe. She looked supremely unconcerned.

"It's *safe*," she repeated for the fifth time. "And neither of us has endlessly deep pockets. Who's going to mess with an ex-Mob *vaudun* Shaman in Nuevo Rio? He's established, Danny. He's letting us stay for free and feeding us as well as running interference with the locals. What more do you fucking want?"

"A little warning next time you decide to drop shit like this on me," I said, glancing out the window. Jace had reserved us a cab, said he'd meet us back at his place, and hopped on a Chervoyg slicboard, rocketing away. Leaving us to pile into the cab with our luggage and get dumped at his house like a package delivery.

One thing hadn't changed; the man certainly irritated me as much as he ever had.

Eddie was grinning broadly. "He's still got it for you, you know." He settled back, stretching his legs out, bumping my knee. I kicked him back. For a claustrophobe Skinlin, he seemed extremely comfortable in the close quarters. Maybe it was just big transports he didn't like.

Nuevo Rio sprawled underneath us in a haze of smoke and noise. Here, the Power was more raw, not like Saint City's cold radioactive glow. This was a different pool of energy, and I would have to spend a little time acclimating. As it was, I felt a little green, and when the cab swooped to avoid a flight of freight transports, I grabbed at the nearest steady thing—which just happened to be Japhrimel's shoulder. I dug my fingers in.

He said nothing.

"I don't care *who* he's got *jackshit* for," I snapped. "I told you I never wanted to see him again. And you— *you*—" I was actually spluttering.

Gabe regarded me coolly, her dark eyes level. "What's the big deal, Danny? If you were so truly over him, it wouldn't *be* a big deal, y'diggit?"

"One of these days," I forced out between clenched teeth, "I will make you pay for this."

She shrugged. "Guess we'll be even when all's said and done, won't we?" She looked out the window at the sweltering smoghole that was Rio. "Gods. I hate the heat as much as I hate travel."

I could kill her, I thought. *No jury would ever convict me.* I realized my fingers were still digging into Japhrimel's shoulder and made them unloose with a physical effort. "Sorry," I said, blankly, to the demon.

He shrugged. "He was once a lover?" he asked, politely enough. "He seemed very happy to see you."

"We broke up," I said through gritted teeth. "Long time ago."

"She hasn't dated since," Eddie offered helpfully. "They were a hot team when they did work together—if they could finish a job without ripping each other's clothes off."

I gave him a look that could have drained a hovercell. "*Will* you *quit* it?"

He shrugged, settling back in the seat, bumping my knee again with his long legs. The smell of dirt and growing things filled the car, and the musky perfume of demon that I had only just become accustomed to. "Not my business," he said finally. "Hey, I wonder what time's dinner?"

"Soon," Gabe said. "He told me he'd feed us. Since we're on business."

"What else did you tell him?" I was forced to ask.

"Not much. Said you'd brief him on the hunt. That was his condition, that he get a piece of the—"

"Oh, *Sekhmet sa'es*," I hissed. "You *didn't*."

"What is your motherfucking *problem?*" Gabe snarled.

"Here we go again." Eddie at least pulled his legs up out of the way.

"Strictly speaking," the demon said, "the more cannon fodder, the better your chances, Dante."

I looked at him, my jaw dropping.

Silence crackled in the cab for a good twenty seconds, during which the driver—a bespectacled Hispanic normal with an air-freshener of Nuestra Dama Erzulie de Guadalupe hanging from his farecounter—did his level best to commit suicide by taxi. I stared out the window until my stomach rose in revolt and then shut my eyes, breathing deeply and trying to get a handle on my rage. It would strike at anyone around me if I lost control, my anger taking physical form—and I didn't want that.

Not yet.

"You invite yourself along on my hunt," I said slowly and distinctly, "and you give me trouble about the tech I ask you to supply, and you finish up by inviting *someone else* into my hunt too, someone who may or may not be trustworthy. This is not looking good for future collaborations, Gabe."

"You're the one dragging around a fucking demon," Gabe replied tartly. "And he's right—the more cannon fodder, the better the chances that your sloppy ass will get through this alive. You're losing your touch, Valentine. *Don't* make me come over there and smack some sense into your hard head. Besides," she continued, "sparring with Monroe will take some of your edge off. You haven't had a good sparring partner in years, and you won't eat him alive the way you'd do anyone else. Way I recall it, he always gave you a good run for your money—in and out of the sack. I never saw you so relaxed."

"Do we have to drag my sexual history into this?" I asked. " 'Cause if we do, you're going down with me."

Silence. The cab began a wavering descent. My ears popped.

"Do you need combat to ease your nerves?" the demon asked.

I shrugged, keeping my eyes firmly shut as my stomach lurched.

"Hades," Gabe breathed. "Does he live *there*?"

I opened my eyes to look; wished I hadn't.

Jace had either done well for himself or was renting from a Nuevo Rio druglord. The house was large, with an open plaza made of white stone, green garden growing up to the stone walls, a red-tiled roof and the glitter of shielding over it.

The shielding slid briefly through the taxi, flushing

slightly as the demon stilled. The mark on my shoulder gave another spiked burst of pain.

"The mark's hurting," I said. The demon's attention fixed on me.

"My apologies."

"What's up?" Gabe asked.

"Don't even talk to me," I said without any real heat. The anger had drained helplessly away. "Not until after dinner, Gabe. *Fuck.*"

She shrugged and stared out the window again.

"Thank the gods," Eddie mumbled.

I was just beginning to seriously contemplate drawing a knife when the cab touched down and we scrambled out onto the glittering hard-baked white marble plaza— above the city's smoghole stink, but still blazing under the hammerblow heat of Nuevo Rio.

CHAPTER
23

Jace Monroe hadn't just done well for himself.

He'd gotten absolutely, filthy, marvelously, stinking rich.

I took a long bath in a sumptuous blue-tiled bathroom while the demon laid his own protections in the walls and windows of the suite a hatchet-faced butler had led us to. Gabe and Eddie had their own set of rooms right next door, done in pale yellow instead of blue and cream. I wondered if Jace had picked the furnishings himself or had an assistant do it.

I wondered who he'd bought the house from, and how he'd managed to accumulate enough credit. Mob free-lancers usually don't get rich—they usually die young, even the psionics.

I closed my eyes, resting my head against the back of the tub. The water was hot, the soap was sandalwood-scented—I knew that was Jace, he had to remember that I'd always used sandalwood soap—and I felt as safe as it was possible to be, in a Shaman's mansion with a demon carefully laying warding everywhere.

I wondered what Jace would make of Japhrimel. He

hadn't seemed to even notice the demon. I wondered what Gabe had told him.

I lifted my toes out of the silky hot water. Examined the blood-red molecule-drip polish on my toenails. The heat was delicious, unstringing muscle aches and soothing frazzled nerves.

Gabe was right, really. This was better than a hotel. And if Jace would feed us, it would mean that we wouldn't have to spend a fortune tracking down Santino. We could spend our credit on *finding* the demon instead of hotels and food . . . and maybe hiring some merc talent to make things uneasy for him.

Feeding, I thought, and grimaced. *What am I going to do about the demon? Blood, sex, fire. I can't give the last two . . . and he's refused the first.*

A knock on the bathroom door interrupted me. "Dante, I've finished shielding the room."

"Come on in," I said, sinking down in the milky water. "We've got to have a little talk."

He opened the door. A burst of slightly cooler air made the steam inside the bathroom billow slightly. "Are you certain?"

"For God's sake. I'm sure you've seen a naked woman before. I'm under the water, anyway. Sheesh."

He stepped into the bathroom, his long coat moving slightly. He didn't seem to sweat, even in the fierce Nuevo Rio heat. He examined the mirror over the sink across from the bathtub as if he'd never seen one before, and I thought of asking him to sit down but the only place was the counter next to the sink or the toilet—and the image of a demon sitting on the toilet and looking at my profile was too much. While he studied the mirror I studied his broad back, turned to me and covered with that coat. "You wanted to talk?"

"You need blood," I said, wiggling my toes against the cobalt tiles. My sword leaned against the tub, a comforting dark slenderness. "The mark's hurting me, and I can't do my job with that kind of unnecessary distraction. Okay?"

He nodded, his dark hair beginning to stick to his forehead. He wasn't sweating—the steam in the air was weighing his hair down. "It may be uncomfortable for you."

"Well, you won't take mine, so . . . Um, how many pints do you need?" *I should have suggested a Nichtvren haunt,* I realized, kicking myself for not thinking of it sooner. Since the advent of cloned blood, Nichtvren social drinking had taken on a whole new context and popularity.

"I can visit a slaughterhouse," he said. "You still have slaughterhouses."

"Oh." I absorbed this. "You don't . . . oh. Okay." *Silly me. I thought he meant* my *blood.* I slipped my toes back into the water, yawned. Oddly enough, I was tired. "How about tonight? I need to do some recon anyway, get used to the whole place."

He nodded. His eyes were darker, their luminescence veiled. "Very well."

"Is it going to be really messy?" I asked. "We can't afford *him* being warned of our intentions."

"I think it would be best if I went alone, Dante."

I shrugged, water rippling against the side of the tub. "Fine." Another yawn caught me off-guard. "I'm going to finish up in here, and then you can have a turn."

"Not necessary. But thank you." He didn't sound

robotic—his tone was merely polite, shaded with some human emotion. Which emotion? I couldn't tell.

I shrugged again. "Okay. Scoot along, then."

He turned to leave, then stopped. "I would not have you see me feed, Dante."

Why should I care? I thought. "Thanks," I said out loud, not knowing what else to say.

He ducked back out the door, steam drifting behind him. *He didn't even sneak a peek,* I thought, and smiled, ducking under the sandalwood-scented water.

When I emerged into the bedroom, wrapped in a towel and carrying my sword, the demon stood by a window looking down into a courtyard full of orange trees. Up here above the main bulk of the city, the smog wasn't so bad, and the heat was bearable due to the high ceilings and chill stone walls. Jace had climate control. But I was going to have to get used to the heat if we were going to be hunting here.

"It's pretty, isn't it?" I said, dropping down on the bed. Water weighed my hair, sandalwood smell drifting around me and warring with the heavy smell of demon. "I wonder how Jace affords this."

"Ask him," the demon replied. "You're tired, Dante. Sleep."

I yawned again. "If I asked him, he'd probably think I was interested."

"Are you?"

"We broke up a long time ago, Japhrimel. Why are you asking?"

"He seems to evoke a response from you." Did he sound uncertain?

"I suppose loathing might be a response," I admitted. "He's infuriating."

"Did you leave him?"

"No," I yawned again, closing my eyes, surprised. I didn't sleep much on hunts. And who would have thought that it could be comforting to have a demon in the same room? "He left me. Three years ago. Came down here, I guess . . ."

"Foolish of him," Japhrimel said, before I fell asleep.

CHAPTER
24

*G*abe settled down cross-legged on the rug across from me. I balanced the tracker in one hand, examining its crystalline glitter. The arrow was spinning lazily, not yet triggered. I wouldn't use it unless I absolutely had to—but it was nice to have. If we didn't find any whisper of the demon here, we could trigger the tracker and see where it led us.

"Where's the demon?" Eddie asked.

"Went out," I replied absently, staring at the tracker. "Needs feeding."

"Hades bless us," Gabe snorted, "Feeding?"

"Well, he said he was going to go to the slaughter-houses. Efficient, right?" I shifted on the green and blue Persian rug, uneasy. "Where's Jace?"

Gabe pulled a black satin card-pouch from the bowels of her blue canvas bag. Her fingers moved with the ease of long practice as she extracted the tarot cards, shuffled them with loud gunning snaps, then turned one over. "He said he'd be back by dark. It's dark, so I suppose either he lied, or—"

"You have no faith in me either," Jace said from the door. He stalked into the room, the bones on his staff clicking together. His hair was damp, sticking to his skull and darker than its usual gold, and his eyes were dark too. *He's upset,* I thought, automatically cataloguing the set of his shoulders, the way his left knee moved a little stiffly, the way his aura shifted through violet and into blue. We'd been lovers once, and it was a mixed relief to find out I could still read him with a glance.

I looked back down at my palm, at the tracker's lazy spinning.

We were downstairs, in a huge high-ceilinged living room holding two long blue velvet couches and a collection of silk and satin floor pillows, ceiling fans turning lazily. The staff of the house were Nuevo Rios, lean brown women in starched uniforms, a black-jacketed butler, none of whom spoke any English.

Gabe glanced up at Jace. "Hey, Monroe. Nice digs." Her tone was neutral, and her expression might have been a warning.

"Anything for the famous Spocarelli. And the pretty Danny Valentine." He paced over to the wet bar holding up one end of the room. "Drinks?"

"Scotch on the rocks for Eddie, vodka Mim for me, and Danny looks like she's in the mood for a brandy," Gabe replied promptly. "What's the word, Shaman?"

He waved his staff briefly, a clicking rattle. "Give me a minute, Gabe. 'Kay?"

I studied the tracker, worrying my lower lip with my teeth. If I could still read Jace . . .

No. He had never been able to read me.

My left shoulder throbbed. Japhrimel had left as soon as dusk fell. I didn't want to know what he was doing. I kept my fingers away from the mark, not wanting to see through his eyes.

Gabe's eyes rested on me. The clink of glasses, liquid pouring from place to place. "Aren't you going to say anything?" she stage-whispered.

I darted her a murderous glance. She grinned, her emerald twinkling, and a completely uncharacteristic desire to laugh came over me. She was acting just like a high-school girl—or at least, like the high-school girls I'd seen in holovids, blinking innocently and giggling over boys.

I shrugged. I didn't have a reputation for small talk, so I simply concentrated on stuffing the tracker back in its leather bag. *If I have to use this, it had better work,* I thought, *or I'll go back to Saint City and find whatever cell they've stuck Dake in, and I'll make him wish he'd never been born.*

If he hadn't died from Chill withdrawal by the time I got back.

How long would it take to hunt down Santino anyway?

Not long. Not once he finds out I'm looking for him. My skin went cold, my nipples tightening and gooseflesh breaking out over my skin. All at once memory rose, swallowed me, was pushed down.

Jace turned around at the wet bar, and his blue eyes met mine. I hadn't even known I was staring at his back. "I hear you're hunting Santino, Danny," he said quietly. "Is that why you brought a demon into my house?"

I rocked up to my feet, carrying my sword. "Okay," I said quietly. "That's *it.*"

Gabe sighed. "I didn't want—"

"Let's get this over with," I snapped, and my thumb caressed the katana's guard. One simple movement would slip it free. "I didn't want to be here in the first

place, Monroe. I'd rather live in the filthiest sink of
Nuevo Rio than stay in *your* house." I took a deep breath.
"And that demon's saved my life more than once since
this whole filthy mess started. More than I can say for
anyone else here."

Silence. Jace carried two glasses instead of his staff.
He walked across the room, handed one glass to Eddie,
who was watching me, his hazel eyes narrowed. Gabe
turned over another card, accepted the other glass.

I started to feel a little foolish, standing up. Gabe
hummed under her breath, a snatch of classical music.
Berlioz, I placed it, and took a step back, turning on my
heel.

"So you're in a bit of a mess," Jace said quietly. "You
always did have a talent for getting into trouble."

I rounded on him, my unbraided hair swinging heavily against my back. "It's none of your concern. I wasn't
the one that wanted to contact you."

"I know," he answered, straightening a little. His fingers tapped his swordhilt. "Gabe told me as much. I
talked her into staying here. It's safer all the way around,
especially if you're hunting Santino." His voice dropped.
"I heard enough of your nightmares to know that name."

My thumb rested against the guard.

There was a slight sound, and the black-clad hatchet-
faced butler bustled in. I took a deep breath, eased my
hand away from the guard, clasped the hilt loosely. He
directed a stream of liquid Portogueso at Jace, who
shrugged and gave a clipped answer. The butler, his dark
eyes resting on me for just a moment and skittering
away, bowed and scuttled out.

Jace shrugged. "Dinner's in fifteen minutes, sweetheart. I was just curious. He's a tough one, your demon."

I swallowed dryly. My left shoulder gave one last spiked flare of pain; then a wave of warmth slid over my body, my neck easing its aching. "I guess so," I said. "Look, I didn't want this."

He nodded, his eyes holding mine. "I know. It's okay. Come on, let's get something to eat. It's been a long day. I've cleared my calendar for the next month or so, and there's a few contacts we can start on tomorrow—"

"You're inviting yourself in on my hunt, *too*?" My jaw clenched.

Jace's mouth curled up into a half smile. It was his "I-know-best" expression, and the sight of it tightened my hand on the hilt. "Why not? You're a hell of a lot of fun to work with, Danny."

I looked down at Gabe. Her hair fell forward over her face, unsuccessfully hiding her smirk. Eddie still stared at me with narrowed eyes. He was tense, too tense. Eddie expected me to go after Gabe.

That managed to hurt my feelings.

I took another step back, bare feet shushing against the Persian carpet. If I'd been wearing my boots, I might have stalked out of the house. "If everyone's finished having some fun at my expense," I said tightly, "I think I'll excuse myself."

"Dinner," Jace said softly.

"Not hungry," I countered.

"You don't eat, you start seeing ghostflits without wanting to," he reminded me. "Come on, Danny. Don't let that stupid pride ruin a lovely reunion."

I kept my temper with a physical effort of will, my hand clenching on the hilt. Gabe scooted back and made it to her feet, hooking her arm through Eddie's. "Come

on, Eddie. Let's let these two have a moment alone." She
looked enormously pleased with herself.

"No need," I said. "I'm leaving."

"Don't." Jace said. "Come on, Danny. Bend a little."

I shrugged. "I was never very good at that, was I?
That's why you left."

Gabe all but dragged Eddie out of the room, whispering something to him. The shaggy blond Skinlin cast a
doubtful look over his shoulder. Gabe kicked the door to
the hall closed behind them. And for the first time in
three years, I was alone with Jace. His face was interested and open, his eyes now bright blue. His tattoo
shifted a little, thorny lines twisting.

"Dante—" he began.

My sword leaped half free of the scabbard, my arm
tensing. "Don't."

His own hand drifted down, touched his swordhilt.
"That's what you want?"

"I won't hold back," I warned him. "Don't push me,
Jace. I'm on a hunt, and Gabe seems determined to bring
every halfass mercenary in the world in on it. And I've
been dragged through Hell for this, I even have to have a
demon tag along with me." I resheathed my blade, then
reached up and dragged my shirt down, exposing a slice
of the branded mark on my left shoulder.

"Fuck," Jace breathed. "Dante—"

I let go of my shirt. "So don't push me, Jace. Got it?"

The ceiling fans turned lazily, drafts of cooler air sliding across my skin. "I never did," he said. "You were always the one pushing."

"We're old news, Jace. Get over it." I turned away
again, but was unable to resist a final parting shot. "At
least the goddamn demon can't betray me."

He grabbed my arm, sinking his fingers in hard, his weight perfectly balanced. I recognized the stance—he was ready for me to attack him. I wondered grimly if I should. "I didn't betray you. I would *never* betray you."

I shrugged. My rings crackled in the tension, reacting uneasily with the Power in the air. "Get. Your. Hand. Off. Me."

"No."

"Get your—"

There was no warning. One moment I was yanking my arm away from Jace's grip, screaming, and the next Jace stumbled back, sword ringing free, Japhrimel's right hand up, arm outstretched, the shining gun held level. The demon was between us, his long black coat fuming with Power, the rumbling thunder of his arrival shattering the air inside the room. Jace's defenses re-sounded, humming into life, crackling with Power, gathering like a cobra gathers itself to strike.

"Stop!" I yelled, and the demon paused, though the gun didn't move.

"Are you injured?" he asked, and his eyes didn't waver from Jace. I thought for one lunatic instant that he was asking *Jace* if he was injured.

"Call him off, Danny," Jace said grimly. He carried a larger sword than mine, a *dotanuki* instead of a *katana*; the steel shimmered under the full-spectrum lights. Second-guard position, balanced and ready, Jace's jaw was set and his eyes burned blue. Burning—but still human.

I curled my left hand around Japhrimel's shoulder. The subliminal hum of that much Power in such a con-fined space roared through me, heady whine like the kick of a slicboard's speed against my stomach. "It's okay," I said. "Really. Stand down, Jaf, it's all right." It was an effort of will to keep from using more of his name. When had I started to think of him as *human*?

Japhrimel considered Jace for a few moments, then eased the hammer down with his thumb. The gun was bright silver, glittering under the lights. "You're all right?" he asked again.

"I think so," I replied, taking another deep breath. "Where were you?"

"Returning from my feeding," he answered, still not looking at me, his eyes glued to Jace. "I felt your distress."

"I'm not distressed. Just pissed off and tired and hungry and wishing this was all over." I kept my hand on his shoulder. If he dove for Jace, what would I do? Stab him in the back? "Okay? Thanks, Jaf. I mean it. Easy, okay?"

The gun disappeared. Japhrimel half-turned, examined me with one laser-green eye. His mouth turned down at both corners. "You have no further need of me?"

My chest tightened. "Thank you." I meant it. "I'm going to go do some recon."

Japhrimel's shoulders tightened slightly. If I hadn't been staring at his throat, I wouldn't have seen it. *What's with him? He looks ready to explode.* "I will accompany you, then, as is my duty."

I decided it would be wiser not to fight over this one, set my jaw. My head rang with the tension and Power humming in the air. If Jace moved on Japhrimel, or if Japhrimel decided Jace meant to hurt me—

"Danny." Jace's sword slid back into its sheath, whispering. "Get something to eat. And I'll spar with you tomorrow, I'll even let you kick my ass if it'll make you feel better about this."

"Good," I slid my hand down Jaf's arm, found his elbow. "I'll do that. I'll be back in a few hours."

"Hey, demon." Jace's chin tilted up. "Take care of her."

Japhrimel studied him for a bare second, then nodded once, sharply.

I don't need anyone to take care of me, Jace, shut your stupid mouth. I hauled on Japhrimel's elbow. "Shut *up*, Jace. Just shut up. Have a nice fucking dinner and I'll talk to you tomorrow, okay?"

He didn't respond. Japhrimel followed me obediently out into the hall, then pointed to the right. "The front door is that way."

"I need my boots," I said, harshly. My throat hurt, for some reason. As if there was a big spiky lump in it.

"The stairs." Japhrimel pointed, again. I was grateful, even though I had Jace's house mostly figured out. I've deciphered enough city street grids that one overblown Nuevo Rio mansion wasn't a hassle.

I nodded, and we set off. Just to be sure, I kept my hand on his elbow. He didn't object.

CHAPTER
25

Once we alighted from the hovercab Japhrimel had somehow had waiting for me at Jace's front door, I chose a few streets at random. Walked along feeling my shields thicken and thin, taking in the atmosphere. It's a strange process to get accustomed to another city; it takes normal people months. Psionics process a lot faster; it takes up a few days—or if we deliberately sink ourselves into a city's Power-well, a few hours.

We walked, the demon and I, his coat occasionally brushing me. I sweated freely, heat still trapped in the streets, my coat's Kevlar panels heavy against my back. My bag's strap cut into my shoulder. I carried my sword, tapping my fingernails on the hilt.

I might not have held back this time, I thought, as we turned into the redlight district.

Down in the smoking well of Nuevo Rio, I found a *taqueria* and ordered in passable pidgin with a soupçon of pointing. The demon stood uncomfortably close, his heat blurring and mixing in with the heat of the pavement giving back the fierce sun of the day. He said nothing as we stood aside between a bodega and a closed-up cigar shop. Crowds pushed past, Nuevo Rios in bright colors, most of them wearing *grisgris* bags. Vaudun and Santeria had taken over here after the collapse of the Roman Catholic Church in the great Vatican Bank scandal in the dim time between the Parapsychic Act and the Awakening; the revelation that the Church had been funding terrorist groups and the Evangelicals of Gilead had been too much for even the Protestant Christians traditionally opposed to the Catholics. And the Seventy-Day War had put the last nail in the coffin of the tradition of Novo Christos.

Nuevo Rios understood a little more about Power than other urban folk, and would no more go outside without defense from the evil eye or random curse than they would go out without clothing. So Nuevo Rio was heat and the smell of tamales and blood, copper-skinned normals with liquid dark eyes speaking in Portogueso, old crumbling palatial buildings standing cheek-by-jowl with new plasteel skyscrapers, pedicabs and wheelbikes making a crush of traffic on the streets. Sweat, heat, and more heat; I could see why the city seemed to move so damnably fast and slow at the same time. Slow because the heat made everything seem like it took forever to do; fast because the natives seemed unaffected by the thin sheen of sweat on everything.

I bolted the food, hoping I wouldn't get sick. I had the standard doses of tazapram in my bag, but I rarely needed them. Most Necromances had cast-iron guts. You'd think that a bunch of neurotic freaks like us would have delicate stomachs, but I'd never met a queasy Necromance.

When I finished, licking hot sauce from my fingers, the demon glanced down at me. "Did he hurt you?" he asked, incuriously. But his shoulders were tense; I saw it and wondered why. Of course, if anything happened to me Jaf was screwed . . . I wondered if he thought Jace was that dangerous.

I shrugged. "Not really." *Not physically, anyway,* I added, looking away from the demon's green gaze.

He handed me a cold bottle of *limonada* and watched as I opened it with a practiced wrist-flick. We stepped out into the flow of foot traffic, the demon still uncomfortably close, moving with weirdly coordinated grace so he didn't bump or jostle me. "Why was he holding you?" Japhrimel asked in my ear, leaning close so he didn't have to shout.

"I don't have any idea," I said. "I think he's upset at me."

"Do you?" Even though the street was crowded, we were still given a few feet of breathing room. My emerald glowed under the streetlamps, and my rings swirled with color, my shields adjusting to the different brand of Power pulsing out from the people and pavement. "Why did he leave you?"

I shrugged. "I have no idea. I came home from a job and he was gone. I waited for him to come back for a few weeks and . . ." I glanced up as slicboards hummed overhead. The hovertraffic here was chaotic outside of a few aerial lanes, taxis screeching through banzai runs, gangs of slicboarders whooping as they coasted through the smoggy air. "I got over it."

"Indeed." The demon bumped my shoulder slightly. I wished I'd thought to tie my hair back—a stray breeze blew a few strands across my nose. "He seems very attached to you, Dante."

"If he was attached, he wouldn't have left. Don't *you* start in on me, too."

"Understood." He sounded thoughtful. We started to walk, oddly companionable.

I stopped to watch a three-card-monte game, half-smiling when I saw the man's brown hands flick. Streams of liquid Portogueso slid past me. The demon leaned over my shoulder, his different heat closing around me and oddly enough making the sweaty smoggy atmosphere a little easier to handle.

Down the street from the monte, a *babalawao* drew a *vevé* in chalk on the pavement. The crowd drew back to watch, respectful, or hurriedly slipped away, giving her a wide berth. The woman's dusky hair fell forward over her dark shoulders, her wide-cheeked ebony face split with a white smile as she glanced up, feeling the demon's glow and my own Power.

I nodded, the silent salute of one psionic to another. She was too engaged in her own work of contacting her guardian spirit to do much more than give the demon a brief glance—and anyway, Shamans aren't nearly as scared of demons as they should be. To them, the demons are just another class of *loa*. I didn't think so— if demons were just another type of *loa*, Magi techniques for containing a spirit should work for the spirits like Erzulie and Baron Samedi. They don't—only the Shamanic practice of going through an initiation and gaining an affinity for a *loa* of your own does.

I watched the *vevé* take form under her slender fingers, a curl of incense going up. A rum bottle stood to one side, and a wicker basket that probably held a chicken.

"What will she do?" the demon asked, quietly, in my ear.

"She's probably fulfilling a bargain with a *loa*," I

replied, tilting my head back and turning so I could whisper to him while still watching the *babalawao*. My knuckles ached, I was gripping my sword so tightly. "Just watch. This should be interesting."

Little prickles of heat ran over my skin. It was uncomfortable, but being this close to a contained burst of Power would help me adjust to the city. I'd studied vaudun, of course, at the Academy. The Magi training techniques borrowed heavily from Shamanism, vaudun, and Santeria in some areas; vaudun and Santeria had been interbreeding ever since before the Parapsychic Act. Eclectic Shamans like Jace picked up a little here, a little there, and usually had two or three *loa* as incidental patrons; this *babalawao* would be sworn to two *loa* at the very most, and would probably intensely dislike being compared to Jace—who was, after all, only a gringo Shaman trained by the Hegemony, not heir to an unbroken succession of masters and acolytes like the *babalawao* would be. Even though the basic techniques were the same, this woman's Power felt different; here in Nuevo Rio she was on her home ground, and her Power was organic instead of alien.

I wish I'd thought to learn Portogueso, I thought, and blinked.

The *vevé* to call the *loa* done, the woman took up the rum bottle, her bracelets and bead necklaces clicking together. She took a mouthful of rum, swirled it, then sprayed it between her lips into the air, the droplets caught hanging, flashing over the *vevé*.

Power spiked, scraping across my shields and skin, prickling in my veins.

A cigar laid across the chalk lines started to fume as the woman flipped open the wicker lid and yanked a chicken from the basket. The bird made a frantic noise before she cut its throat with one practiced move, blood spraying across the *vevé*.

"She'll cook it tonight and eat it for lunch tomorrow, probably," I told him. A swirl of air started, counter-clockwise, the chicken's body still scrabbling mind-lessly. The blood slowed from a spray to a gush and then to a trickle, and the *babalawao*'s voice rose, keening through a chant very similar to a Necromance's. But this chant would complete the job of making the offering to the *loa*. The rum droplets vanished, eaten up by Power. I felt insubstantial fingers touch my cheek, saw a vague shape out of the corner of my eye—a tall man, with a top hat over his skull-white face, his crotch bulging, capered away through the crowd. A breath of chill touched my sweating back. I didn't mess around with *loa*.

Power tingled over my skin, a wash of fever-heat, the sickening feeling of freefall just under my stomach. The Power-burst would force my own energy channels to change to acclimate to the different brand of Power here if I just gave it enough time. I kept my breathing even. *Just a few minutes*, I told myself. *It'll go away. Just need to relax long enough for it to work , that's all. Stay cool, Danny. Just stay cool.*

It was while I was staring at the *vevé* and waiting for my body to acclimatize to the resident Power, my mind tuned to a blank expectant humming, that the precogni-tion hit.

The demon had my shoulders, drew me back away from the clear space in the pavement, the *babalawao*'s chanting rising against the backdrop of city noise. "Dante?"

My gods, does he sound concerned?

"What's wrong? Dante?"

"Nothing," I heard my voice, dim and dreamy. Precog's not my main Talent; if it was I'd be a Seer. But I had enough of it to be useful sometimes. "Nothing." Darkness folded over me, a quiet restfulness, the sound of wings. The vision trembled just outside my mental grasp. If I simply relaxed and let my minor precognitive talent work, it would come to me, and I would be warned . . . but of what?

What did I need a warning for? I already knew I was in deep shit.

"Nothing . . ." I whispered. Hot fingers touched my forehead; my fingers curling around my scabbard, head lolling, I sank into the candleflame of the future, guttering, held in a draft—

"Don't lie to me," he snarled, and I found myself dimly surprised. *Why should he give a shit if I lie to him?* I thought. I snapped back into myself, hot prickles running over my skin, my stomach flipping uneasily, my eyes fluttering. "Dante! *Dante!*"

"I'm fine," I said irritably. "Just give me a minute, okay? Will you?"

"As you like." Heat roiled over my skin. Was it him? A flood of hot, rough Power slid down my spine from the demon's hands. It knocked the premonition—and my hold on relaxation—away like a *jo* staff slamming into my solar plexus. There went any hope of seeing the future.

"—*fuck*—" was all I could say, digging my heels into pavement, curling around the scorching pain in my middle. The Power tipped back and slid into the hungry well of Nuevo Rio. "Gods *damn* it—"

"What's wrong?"

It was too dark. What had—

I opened my eyes slowly. The demon stood, feet planted, green eyes glowing like chips of radioactive gemstone. "I lost it," I said. "A premonition, and I lost it. Ask me before you do that next time, all right?"

The demon shrugged. I looked up. Brick, plasteel, cardboard, and aluminum sheeting, tenements sloped crazily up. Instead of the street, it was an alley. Why wasn't I surprised? Had he dragged me here, thinking I was about to have some sort of fit? "I acted for your safety," he said, quiet but unrepentant. "I feared you were being attacked."

"Who would be stupid enough to attack me with a demon right next to me?" I snapped, and wriggled out of his hands. He let me go, clasping his hands behind his back again, standing straight, his eyelids dropped, hiding his eyes. "Great. A premonition usually means something nasty's on its way, and now I'm not even forewarned. Perfect."

Japhrimel said nothing.

I sighed, filled my lungs with the heavy carbon stink of Nuevo Rio. Curdled smells of garbage and human misery rose around me. My shields were paper-thin, the premonition draining me; I forced myself to breathe through the stink. "*Anubis et'her ka,*" I breathed, shaking my head. "I'd better get back. I think I'm going to crash."

"Very well." Japhrimel took my elbow, guiding me toward the mouth of the alley. "You should take more care with yourself, Dante."

"Nobody ever got rich by being cautious," I muttered. "Besides, what do *you* care? As soon as we find this Egg, you'll be on your way back to Hell, and I'll probably be left to clean up the mess. I'll be lucky to get out of this alive, and you're telling me to be careful." I snorted, concentrating on placing one foot in front of the other.

"I would not leave you without being sure of your safety," he replied, quietly enough. "It would grieve me to learn of your death, human."

"Bully for you," I muttered ungracefully.

"Truly," he persisted. "It would."

"Fuck," I said, the beginnings of a backlash headache starting behind my eyes. "Just get me back to Jace's, okay? My head's starting to hurt."

"Backlash," he said. "Dante, there is something I would—"

If he kept talking I was going to scream. "Just get me back to Jace's, all right?"

His hand tightened on my elbow. I closed my eyes. "Understood."

CHAPTER
26

I stamped into the practice room just as the afternoon heat began to get thick and heavy, black-stacked clouds massing over the city. There would be rain soon, a monsoonlike downpour. Thunder and lightning would accompany the rain, and by the time full dark fell the steaming city might get some relief.

I wasn't wearing my bag or my coat, just jeans and a fresh microfiber shirt, boots and my rings. My hair was wet, braided back tightly, and I'd relacquered my fingernails with the molecule drip that made them tough as claws.

The practice room was a long hall floored with tatami, weapons racked on the wall and three heavy bags ranged in a row near the door. One wall was mirrored, a ballet barre bolted to the mirror (*Now that probably wasn't here before, Jace must have put that in,* I thought snidely) and Eddie faced Jace in the center of the room.

Jace had a *jo* staff, and Eddie had one, too. They both wore black silk *gi* pants, and Eddie wore a white cotton tank top that did nothing to disguise just how hairy he really was. I stopped, leaning against the doorjamb to watch.

Jace, stripped to the waist, held his staff with both hands. Muscle flickered under his skin, the scorpion tattoo on his left shoulderblade moving slightly, his golden hair plastered down with sweat.

Gabe was stretching out, well away from them. She went into a full front split, then leaned forward to touch her forehead to her front knee. *Showoff,* I thought, the ghost of pain behind my eyes reminding me of backlash.

Japhrimel, his arms folded, leaned against the wall on the other side of the heavy bags. The windows were covered with sheer curtains, but the sun pouring in still made it a little too warm. Nobody had flipped on the climate control in here.

I watched as Eddie moved in, Jace parrying strikes, low sounds of effort from both men. I watched the fight, almost feeling the wood balanced in my own hands, jagging in a breath when Eddie smacked upward, meaning to catch Jace in the face. It was a dirty move, but they were both good enough—and with two Necromances standing by, if someone caught a bad strike we were well prepared to handle it.

Japhrimel approached me slowly. "Better?" he asked. Behind him, the sunlight coming through the windows dimmed. The clouds had arrived. That didn't break the heat, though; it just made one more conscious of the awful humidity pressing against skin and breath.

I don't know why heat rose to stain my cheeks. "Yeah," I said, glancing up at his unremarkable, saturnine face. "Thanks."

"I've seen backlash before," he replied quietly. "The best thing for it is Power, and letting the pain pass."

"Thanks," I said again. "It helps, to have someone there during—"

Crack. Eddie's strike wrenched Jace's staff out of his hands. I clicked my tongue. *That's the first time I've seen Jace lose at staves with Eddie.*

Eddie growled. "Quit fuckin' around and give me a fight, hoodoo! Goddammit! You ain't no fuckin good to us distracted!"

"Shut up, dirtwitch." Jace snarled back. "Want to switch to blades?"

"You'll fuckin' kill yourself," Eddie scooped up Jace's staff, tossed it at him. Jace's hand flashed up; he caught the smooth wood, then turned it vertically. "Thanks anyway. Been a while since I saw you make an amateur move like that. Hey, Danny!" He glanced over Jace's shoulder at me. "Come on over here and work his fidgets out, will you? Goddamn boy can't even hold his staff."

I sighed. I had expected this. "Fine," I said, shrugging. "We'd come to this sooner or later." I looked up at the demon's face, quiet and shuttered. "I'm going to spar with Jace. I want you to stay out of it, all right?"

Japhrimel nodded his dark head.

"Cool," Gabe said, bouncing to her feet. "I've missed watching you two fight. Better than a holovid."

I ignored her. *What would piss Jace off most?* I thought, looking up at the demon again. A faint breeze swept through the room, carrying the promise of thunder with it. *Okay.*

I stepped close to the demon, went up on tiptoe, my hand curling around his shoulder, the smell of musk and dark Power enveloping me. "Hey." I pulled on his shoulder and he bent a little, obediently. I kissed his cheek— just a peck, but I heard Jace's indrawn breath and knew I was halfway to winning.

He fought better when he was angry, anyway.

"Thanks." I repeated to Japhrimel, whose eyes had half-closed. He looked surprised. "It helps to have some-one there while I'm in pain." My tone was a little more intimate than I'd planned. "I appreciate it."

He nodded once, sharply, and straightened, his gaze flicking away from me. I turned back to the practice room.

Gabe's jaw dropped. She sidled back, almost to the mirrored wall. Eddie followed her, watching Jace, white teeth showing in a wide grin.

Jace walked deliberately over to a rack near the win-dows and put his staff up, scooped up his scabbarded sword. "I'm game for it, if Danny is," he said quietly, and I had to fight the smile that wanted to pull my lips up. *Careful, Danny. You haven't fought him in a while, ease into this.*

I made it to the center of the room and yawned. I hadn't even stretched out beyond my usual morning rou-tine. Jace carried his sword, approached me cautiously, his booted feet shushing over the tatami. "Hi, sweet-heart," he said, his blue eyes locking with mine. It was his usual greeting, usually followed by a kiss. My body remembered the sound of that voice. I let myself smile, then. My rings gave out a low, sustained humming.

"You're in for a treat," Gabe said to the demon. "Jace and Danny are the best in the biz. They used to do naked-blade slicboard duels, back in the day. And—"

"Shh," Eddie said. "I wanta see this."

"Hi, baby," I said quietly, holding my sword, fingers curled loosely around scabbard and hilt. "Missed me?"

"Every damn day." Jace's face was set. His shoulders

were loose and easy. *Maybe I didn't piss him off as much as I thought.* "Every single motherfucking day."

"Hmm." I smiled sweetly. "Shouldn't have left."

"Didn't have a choice," he returned.

We circled each other, wary. I shifted my weight forward, playing through the sequence that would end with his head separated from his body. He countered almost immediately, and we went back to circling.

Point for him, he'd made me twitch first.

"Yeah," I said. "You were in such a hurry you didn't even leave a note. Must have been really deep and hot, Jace, for you to just get up and leave." I let my smile broaden. "What was her name?"

"I've been a fucking monk since our last time, sweetheart," he said, the easy smile dropping from his voice.

Second point for me. I'd pushed him too far.

"I hope it's made you a better fighter . . . than you were as a lover." I tacked that on just to goose him.

"You had no complaints."

"None I told you to your face."

He was smiling again. He moved in, testing, and I countered.

"When are they going to—" Eddie began. I tuned him out.

"Wait." Gabe replied.

I caught a flash of Japhrimel watching, hands behind his back, his eyes almost spitting sparks.

"Try me again, sweetheart," Jace said, his tone low and purring. "I've been dying for it."

"Good for you." I shuffled back, to the side; things were rapidly heating up. "Get used to disappointment."

"You don't want an explanation?"

"Three years too late, Jace. All I want to do now is

forget you ever existed." My own voice dropped to a whisper. His eyes narrowed.

"Good luck," he said. "I just bought myself free of the Corvin Family, sweets, and I have some time on my hands. Want to help me fill it?"

"I'd rather turn into a Chillfreak whore." My blade whispered free of the sheath just as his did.

"Now?" Eddie asked.

"Just wait," Gabe whispered back.

"Mmh." Jace said. "You say the sweetest—"

He moved in then, with no warning. Metal clashed and rang. We separated, both of us breathing fast and deep.

"You've gotten quicker," he said.

"And you still talk too goddamn much," I said, wishing I could spit. That would add something to the festivities.

"I should put my tongue to better use," he muttered, and gave me a flash of the famous Monroe grin, the one that had Mob groupies following him around all the time.

"Try it on someone who cares, fucker," I spat at him, and that broke the tension.

We moved in on each other, feet shuffling, sparks spraying from the metal and the Power in the air. He wasn't trying very hard, and I almost got him twice before he realized I was serious and began to scramble. Cut overhand, spin-kick, he tried to lock me into a corps-a-corps where his height and weight could overpower me but that was an old trick, *move move move*, scabbard flying in to jab him in the ribs, it was a cheap shot but every little bit told, I had speed and endurance, he had power and a different type of endurance—

Parry, parry, a short thrust he had to shuffle back to escape, metal sliding, wall coming up fast, was I going to cheat or was I going to—

I cheated.

I popped my left hand forward, the scabbard held horizontal, and a dart of Power flashed from my rings, spattered on his defenses.

We separated, both breathing hard now. It bought me some breathing room.

"Cheater," he said. Sweat rolled down his forehead, his hair truly soaked now. Thunder rumbled outside.

"Anything for you," I answered, showing my teeth. Sweat dripped down the shallow channel of my spine. My ribs flared with deep rasping breaths. "You going to come and get me, baby?"

"You should be so lucky," he said. "We're full-on now, sweetheart? You sure? Last time we did this I spanked your ass."

"I was holding back," I said. "Since you always bitched when you lost."

He grinned. "You sure, Valentine?"

"Come over here and find out, Monroe," I dared him, katana dipping into *guard*. He was coming in low, his shielding swirling with the peculiar spiky turbulence of a Shaman, impossible to predict. I was glowing, glitter spattering through my aura; reacting to his nearness and to my own defenses springing up, locking with his.

We closed in again, and this time he was serious. Metal screamed and Power tore through the air, ozone, smell of musk, the mark on my shoulder suddenly coming alive. Spray of sparks, he was using a pattern I didn't recognize but muscle memory took over again and it was like riding a slicboard, trembling on the outer edge of adrenaline control, fully alive, fully *aware*, kiss of breeze against my sweaty forehead, clap of thunder like angels striking and neither of us flinched, spin, half-falling, *get up get up,* kicked his bad knee, felt the flare of sick pain from his shielding but he was too hyped on adrenaline to slow down, we closed again but I had momentum, *push*, Power crackling, across the room, running, his face inches from mine, eyes locked, my lips peeled back with effort, familiar, every other time we'd fought blurring under my skin, memory and intuition and action—

Glass. Shattering. I drove him through the window, separating from him for long enough to gain footing on the stone walk outside, heavy scent of wet green air rising from the garden on the other side of the strip of stone flags. Boot soles gripping, sliding, cut overhand, he batted it away with more luck than strength. Harsh gasps of air tore at my throat. His shielding flared, trying to throw me off, I reacted without thinking, tearing Power from the air and smashing at him.

Rain spattering against my skin, stinging-hard. Rivulets of water down Jace's face. We were outside now, booted feet crunching in glass, the wild rain pounding on both of us, soaked to the bone and suddenly chill, breath steaming, sparks flying like water as we danced.

Flying. I didn't have to hold back. The rhythm of the fight changed, became insistent, *no think! No think! Move!* Jado-sensei screamed in my memory and I fell, landing on the wet stone scrambling, scrambling, throwing aside one of his strikes, on my feet again, whirling, his scabbard coming in, deflected, I was going to bruise there by tomorrow, didn't care, *alive, alive, see you stay that way, alive, alive—*

Thunder.

He fell, blood striping his face, landing sprawled on the marble. My blade kissed his throat. For a moment I was tempted—*push the blade in, no resistance, you can watch him bleed, watch the soul leave the body, watch the sparks fly, and then*—

"Do you give?" I asked, my voice a harsh croak. My ribs flared.

"Of course," he said, his eyes closed, head tipped back, throat exposed. Steel caressed the vulnerable place where his pulse beat. My hands weren't shaking, but they were close. "Anything you want, Valentine."

"Stay off my case, Monroe." I let the temptation slide away. Not today. I wouldn't kill him today.

Thank the gods, think of the paperwork . . . I sheathed my blade, suddenly aware that the rain drenched both of us, my shirt stuck to my body, my jeans chafing, boots sloshing in foaming water. I offered him my hand, still tuned to combat, watching his blade just in case.

"Sure." He took my hand; I hauled him up from the stone walk-turned-river. "You still look good when you fight, sweetheart."

I tore my fingers out of his, watched as he sheathed his sword. Both of us were bloody—scraped knuckles, a cut on his scalp, his knee, a shallow slice on my shield arm, my back on fire. "Good match," I said grudgingly. "You've been practicing."

"So have you. That double-eight thing kicked my ass."

"Where'd you learn that little shuffle-trick? That's nice." I pushed a strand of wet hair out of my face—no matter how tightly I braided it, sometimes little bits worked free.

"Around and about. You still do knife-work?" His hair streamed with water, dark and plastered against his forehead.

"When the occasion calls for it." I stepped through the shattered window. "Sorry about that."

"It's okay. It's just a window." I could hear the smile in his voice. "Goddamn, you're good."

"I train with Jado almost every day when I'm not on a job."

"That old dragon? Chango love you, girl, no wonder you're good." He stepped through, shaking the water off his hair and hands, stamping his feet. *That'll foul the mats,* I thought, and wondered if broken glass ground into tatami was a bad idea. *Of course it is. But maybe he can afford it.* "I couldn't even get time with him. Some say he only trains women."

"No, there's men too. But he says women are better. Quicker reaction time. More evil." I found myself smiling. Adrenaline laid its thin copper taste against my palate. Now I wanted a hot bath, and I wanted sex.

Too bad. Nobody here but unavailable men. And I don't want to trust the local escorts.

Jace's hand closed around my wrist. His skin was warm, almost too warm, his shields rubbing against mine. His thumb drifted over my skin, an intimate touch. "Danny."

I tore my hand away again. He tried to keep it. Again. "Danny—" Again.

"No, Jace. Forget it. That's all you're going to get from me."

He shrugged. "It's a shame. I remember how good it used to be after a sparring session." His eyebrow quirked a little. Even with blood running down his face—head wounds are messy—he was still beautiful. I'd always liked blonds. Maybe because I had to dye my hair to fit in with Necromance codes.

"Well, if you hadn't dumped me three years ago you might be a little luckier now," I said, and turned away.

Gabe and Eddie were watching us. Gabe's eyes were round. Eddie's were narrowed, and he looked about ten seconds away from a growl. He had his arm over Gabe's shoulders; she leaned into his body as if she belonged there.

Japhrimel stood bolt-upright, his hands behind him. His eyes were half-lidded and the smell of demon filled the entire practice room, warring with the tide of rain-washed air pouring in through the broken window. His coat smoked and fumed with darkness, a psychic stain spreading out from him.

I don't know if that's really a coat, I thought, and stopped short, staring at him. *What else could it be? Wings? An exoskeleton?*

Jace went utterly still beside me. "Is that it?" he asked. "You're dating a demon?"

"Don't be ridiculous," I snapped, and stalked away from him. "Your dick always gets the better of you, Jace, maybe you should try thinking with your *brain* next time. Thanks for the sparring, I needed it. Next time I'll spar with Japhrimel—he's a real challenge." I was so happy with myself I used more of Jaf's name, and sounded as if I was talking about someone else. The name fit smoothly against my tongue. *Japhrimel.* I wondered what it meant, and if I called him by his full name, what would happen?

"Fucking *hell*—" Jace began, his voice hitting a pitch I recognized.

He'd lost his temper.

"That's enough," Gabe snapped, even though Eddie pulled back on her shoulders. The emerald in her cheek flashed, sending a spear of green light through the heavy air. "Hades, haven't you two finished flirting? Get over it already so we can find the fucking demon and get rid of our Happy Little Pet here!"

"Japhrimel," I said, over the last half of her sentence, "come on. The rest of you, we're going recon in two hours when the rain stops and it gets darker. I'll expect you all to be ready."

"Oh, for fuck's—" Gabe began. Eddie shushed at her.

"Danny?" Jace's voice.

I stopped. Didn't turn around. Japhrimel hovered near my shoulder. I hadn't seen him blink across the intervening space, and that made me vaguely nervous.

"Thanks for the sparring," Jace said. "I love working with you."

"Sorry, Jace," I answered. "It's too late. I work alone."

Then I strode out of the practice room, my anger crackling on the air, hearing Jace's awful silence behind me. I'd won both battles.

Good for me.

CHAPTER
27

*J*aphrimel didn't say anything until we reached the blue suite. He closed the door behind us, precisely, locking it, the defenses he'd set in the walls humming as soon as I entered the room. "That was not wise," he said quietly. "A jealous man does not work well."

"Jace works better when he's under pressure," I said, unwinding my wet hair from its braid. "And he deserved it." My rings lay dark and silent against my fingers now. I felt better, the headache eased out by pulling on Power from the well of the city now that my body had acclimatized, my back stopping its low-level cramping. I'd stretch out after a hot bath, and be ready for recon.

My hands shook. I'd just faced Jace over a sword again. Three years. Three *years*—and he hadn't even tried to explain yet. Just acted as if—

I took a deep breath. I could feel the weight of Japhrimel's green gaze on my back. Jace didn't matter. I'd said he didn't matter, that I didn't care anymore. I'd sworn many times, out loud and silently, that I was over Jason Monroe. Period. End of story, end of spell, so mote it be, amen, *finis*.

"Nevertheless," Japhrimel persisted. "You should not have used me to prick his jealousy."

I shrugged. "It's his problem. Not mine. My problem is finding Santino and getting that Egg back to Lucifer. Besides, he's only human. It's not like he can hurt you if he decides to do something stupid."

"Perhaps," he replied. "But even demons understand jealousy, Dante."

I started to unbutton my shirt, tossing my sword on the bed. *Safe enough*, I thought. *At least for now.* "Next time I'll spar with you. At least you'll give me a workout."

If my voice had been any more brittle, it would have snapped. If I was over Jace, I was *over* him. Right?

Right?

"You were not sparring with him," the demon pointed out. He leaned on the door, his arms folded on his chest, his eyes half-lidded. There was a faint red stain on his caramel cheeks. Dear gods, was he blushing? "You were trying to kill him."

"I don't see any other way to play," I tossed over my shoulder as I headed for the bathroom. "I'm going to clean up."

"As you like." He didn't sound too pleased.

I stopped and looked back at him, my shaking fingers pausing on the fourth button. *I didn't do anything wrong,* I repeated to myself. *I simply sparred with Jace and made it clear he doesn't affect me anymore. Now everyone knows what's going on, it's official, it's all aboveboard and time-stamped. I didn't do anything wrong.* "What? Go ahead and say it."

Japhrimel didn't move. He might as well have been a statue, leaning against the door. Warm electric light caressed the planes of his face, sparked in his eyes. The faint reddish stain had drained from his cheeks. "You are . . . trifling with his affections, and using me to do so. The game is exceedingly dangerous."

I examined him. "What are you really trying to tell me, Tierce Japhrimel? That Jace has some sort of feeling for me? Why did he leave, then? Huh? You answer me that."

"If you like, I will find out."

I clutched my shirt together. "I don't want to know. If it was important, he would have sent me a message or something. I'm not interested in his excuses now."

"Then stop needling him. Treat him as an equal."

"Hey, demon, I didn't know if you noticed, but everybody gets the short end of the stick from me."

"Do not use me to make a human jealous, Dante. It is very unwise of you."

"*Sekhmet sa'es,*" I hissed. "I *didn't.* Don't get your girdle in a twist."

"You *did,* Dante. I would advise you not to trifle with him, and not to trifle with me either." He didn't move, but the air swirled uneasily. Thunder boomed outside, muted by the bulk of the house but still enough to raise the hairs on my nape. The demon's stain on my aura moved, drawing closer to my skin, a gentle brush against the edges of my awareness.

"Like *you* care," I said, and turned on my heel, stalking for the bathroom. "Leave it alone, hellspawn. This is a *human* thing."

He said nothing. I stamped into the bathroom and slammed the door, then started peeling off my wet clothes. "Gods *damn* it, " I hissed, yanking my jeans down, kicking them into the corner. *I could really hate them both, couldn't I? I sure could. Especially the gods-be-damned demon. Because?*

I found myself staring in the mirror, wet lank dead-black seaweed hair, indeterminate dark eyes, pale face, dark rings under my eyes, my mouth pulled tight in a bitter grimace, my fingernails *skritch*ing against the counter as my hands tensed. My tattoo shifted uneasily, serpents writhing against winged staff, the emerald turning dark and glittering angrily.

Because he's right. I want Jace to suffer. I want him to lose his temper. I want to win, goddammit. Even if it's a hollow victory. I want him to hurt.

"Fuck," I breathed, looking at my eyes. Dark circles, mouth drawn tight, Power trembling at the outer edge of my control. *Deep breath, Danny. Take a deep breath and get cool with the program, okay? Chill down. Chill down.*

I'm going to die.

"Shut up," I whispered. "If I die, I'm taking Santino with me. I owe Doreen. And I've lived long enough."

It sounded good, but the woman in the mirror didn't believe it. I had a mortgage. I had a life I was just beginning to piece together and go on with. I didn't want to die.

"How much longer would you live anyway going up against Santino, Danny?" I asked myself. "Huh?"

Not very much longer, some deep voice replied. *Just long enough to make him regret it.*

"Good," I said. "So stop fooling around."

I don't want to die.

"I don't have a choice. If the god takes me, He takes me."

I still don't want to die.

"Too bad," I whispered, turning away from the mirror. I couldn't take looking at myself any longer.

CHAPTER
28

El diablo Santino," Jace said, the knife pressed against the thin Hispanic's throat. "Okay?"

Gabe and Eddie had the mouth of the alley and the demon stood behind me. I watched the man's eyes flicker, white rolling around their edges. He was sweating, great drops of water sliding down his face. The reek of fear warred with the smell of demon. The alley was piled with garbage, hot and rank and wet from the afternoon's rain. It was only slightly cooler. My hair, trapped in a braid, was twisted into a knot at my nape. I looked down at my wrist, having just scanned the man in.

The plug-in, clear plasilica smoothed over my datband, lit up with a string of code. "He's got a warrant, Jace," I said quietly. "Do we haul him in?"

The omni and the first H-DOC, slim squares of plasilica with clear Hegemony military-tech flexcircuits, I'd already plastered over my datband. I'd smoothed the second H-DOC over Japhrimel's wrist. We were officially on a hunt now, plugged into the Hegemony police nets and immune to a few laws having to do with general murder and chaos—as long as the murder and chaos served the purpose of bringing our bounty in. The night sky was choked with clouds though the downpour had stopped, and steaming heat closed us in a bubble of damp discomfort. Now I knew what the inside of a rice cooker felt like.

The man babbled in Portogueso, sweating, his eyes rolling. He wore a loose white cotton shirt and frayed khakis, his huaraches digging into the pavement as he tried to back through the rough earth-brick wall behind him. One of his hands hit the dumpster Jace had trapped him beside, and a hollow boom punched the air.

Jace was shaking down his contacts, and none of them looked happy to see him. Considering he was walking around with two Necromances, I didn't blame them. Still, Jace was savage. He was in his element here. The first contact had tried to dive out a fourth-story window onto bare concrete to get away from him.

I was beginning to think that he had a reputation.

Jace said something very low. The man's eyes flicked past his shoulder, fastened on me, and he gibbered something.

Jace went very still. He asked a couple more questions, both answered in a high whine.

Jace laid the knifeblade against the man's cheek. He said something very low and quick, and I caught my name—*Dante Valentino*—and his own name, accented strangely. Then he let the man go, tossed him onto the floor of the alley, the knife disappearing.

As soon as he turned around, his eyes thoughtful, I knew there was trouble. "What was that?" I asked incuriously, looking down at the man moaning on the pavement. He seemed to be in an ecstasy of fear. "And are we hauling him in?"

"No, let him go, he's wetting his pants anyway. Come

on, Danny." Jace straightened his shoulders. "We've got
to pow-wow."

Gabe and Eddie drifted in from the mouth of the alley.
We left Jace's contact scrambling against the cracking
pavement and moaning to himself. "Good news," Gabe
whispered. "There's a set of heavies coming through the
neighborhood, Jace. Not sure if they're looking for you
or—"

"They aren't," he said grimly. "Word is the Corvin
Family's looking to capture Danny. Alive and unharmed.
Someone is putting the squeeze on the Mob down here."
Jace's eyes didn't move from mine. He wore dark blue,
shirt and jeans, blending into the night. He dropped his
hand to his swordhilt, tapped blunt fingers in a pattern I
recognized. "Wonder who that could be."

"Santino?" I asked. Why would the Mob get involved,
expecially a Mob Family I hadn't ever tangled with?
*Then again, the Mob didn't want us to go after Santino
last time, because they were in the same corporate bed
with him when it came to illegal augments.* The memory
made my lip curl. Gods above and below, how I hated the
Mob.

Behind me, Jace's contact monkeyed up a splitting,
rotten wooden fence and dropped down on the other
side.

"Don't think so. I've got enemies too, and you came
in on a public transport as Saint City police irregulars.
Fun. About as stealthy as a Skinlin berserker." He
grinned, lips stretching back from his teeth in a grimace
I remembered. Jace was *furious.*

Why? Why would *that* make him furious?

"So what do we do now?" Eddie asked. "They're get-
tin' kind of close, Monroe."

"Do?" Jace shrugged. "I just told Jose to spread the word that Danny Valentine's under my personal protection. As for those clumsy fuckers moving in, we either run, or we send a message that she ain't going to come cheap. My vote goes for the latter. It will make it easier to get information, scare some people. What do you say?"

Eddie shrugged. "I'm up for a fight."

"Me, too," Gabe chimed in. "Lucky you, Danny, you've got an admirer or two. Or a hundred."

"I can't think of why," I grumbled. "Look at this, I just blew into town and already people want to kill me."

"Not *kill*," Jace corrected. "Capture. Alive and unharmed."

"For how much?" the demon asked suddenly.

"Five million standard credits," Jace replied easily.

Silence. I looked at Gabe. Her jaw dropped. She had her hair in two braids like a demented schoolgirl. One hung forward over her slim shoulder, the other dangled in back. Her emerald glittered in the darkness. Even in a police rig and synthwool coat in the boiling heat, she looked cool, calm, and precise.

Eddie let out a low whistle.

"Take her back to the house," Jace said to the demon. "*Watch* her. Don't even send her to the bathroom alone."

"Now just wait one goddamn second," I objected, relieved that Japhrimel made no move to obey Jace. "This is *my* hunt, I'm not going to be hauled around like a piece of baggage."

"Give us some time to clear the street and do some recon, Danny," Jace said reasonably. But a tic in his cheek was jumping. That meant trouble. *Heavy* trouble.

There was something Jace wasn't telling. "It's best. You know it's best."

"This is *my* hunt," I repeated in a fierce whisper. "You are not taking over. Is that clear?"

"This serves no purpose," the demon said. "Dante?"

"Let's go kick some ass," I answered. "Don't fuck with me on my hunt, Jace."

"Danny, you should get under cover until we can sort out who's looking for you." Jace sounded calm and reasonable, but his hand curled around his swordhilt. He was two steps away from rage, and I'd only seen Jason Monroe in a rage twice before.

"I'm not backing down, Jace," I hissed. "Come on."

"Fine," he said. "But after that we're going back and hashing this out."

"Good enough," I gave in. I was hungry anyway, and I wanted a quiet place to think. "Let's go rumble."

"Standard form?" Gabe asked.

"Yeah. Watch out for Danny, everyone, they'll look to net her." Jace didn't look away from me, even when my lip lifted and I snarled openly at him.

"I can take care of myself," I said, thumbing my blade free of the scabbard with a small sound. "Japhrimel, we're going to mix. Kill the opposition, as long as they're not innocent bystanders. Okay?"

"As you like," Japhrimel said quietly. "I will watch over you, Dante. They are coming quickly; we had best go now."

"Oh, *Sekhmet sa'es*," I hissed. "Get moving, standard form. Jace, you take point; Gabe, keep Eddie from going berserk—"

"Danny?" Gabe turned, her right hand sliding below her left armpit. "They're here."

with sudden pain as the demon let out a shattering roar. Jace drove past me, engaging the *vaudun. Dammit, Jace, he was MINE!* Jace made a quick motion, and something like a tiger made of solid light and dapples of shadow, Jace's prime fighting construct, tore itself out of the air and descended on the other *vaudun.*

Where are the rest of them? I thought, and heard another one of Gabe's short sharp cries. *Engaged over there,* I thought, turning on my heel, my tapline into the city's dark heart pulsing with Power. I kept the shields steady, juggling them as I bolted back for Gabe and Eddie. Jace could handle himself.

The Skinlin was growling as he fought with another Shaman, this one a wizened old nut-brown man with streaks and dapples of red paint on his face. Gabe, swearing and spitting, her face contorted into a mask of rage, was dueling a tall mercenary—he wasn't a Nuevo Rio, too pale, sandy blond hair, but he wore an assassin's rig and used a short thrusting sword. Plasbolts whined. One splashed against the edge of my torn shimmershield, and the resultant Power-flare nearly knocked me to my knees. I staggered, my forward momentum pushing me, just like riding a slicboard—and I threw myself on the two Nuevo Rios edging for Gabe's back.

One of them clipped me on the shoulder with a thrown knife before I cut him down, pain blooming along my nerves like spiked oil, the other engaged me— he was a huge hulking mass of weightlifting muscle and black-market augmentations; I smelled salt-sweat-sweet Chill on him before I made my cut and a bright jet of arterial blood splashed out of his neck. He was still trying to come for me when I took off his right hand with the plasgun still clasped in it. I finished by whirling and opening his belly with two cuts, my own battle-yell stinging my throat and dyeing the air red. *Chillfreaks, I hate Chillfreaks. I thought Nuevo Rios were more into hash anyway.*

Then it was over. I stood, panting, watching the blood gurgle, hearing the last choking gasps as the Chillfreak died, his eyes dimming, the spark exiting his chemical-abused body. *"Anubis et'her ka."* I breathed. *That was for Lewis, you sack of Chill shit.* The thought slid across my mind and was gone as soon as it came.

The plasbolts had stopped. Eddie's growling still sounded from behind me, and I heard Gabe taking in harsh tearing gulps of air. Clatter of steel. Running feet. A long, low howl of abused breath, snarling, a flare of familiar Power. Jace.

I stared blankly down at the body in front of me. The street was now deserted, but eyes glittered in the shadows. If we left the bodies, they would be stripped and harvested in minutes.

Chillfreaks, I thought, and shuddered. *I hate the motherfucking Chillfreaks.*

Three things I hated: the Mob, Chillfreaks, Santino. Each one of them had stolen something from me—Santino stole Doreen, the Mob had helped steal Doreen, and Chill and the Mob had stolen Lewis and fucked up too many bounties to count.

Japhrimel's hand closed around my wounded shoulder. I flinched—I hadn't even sensed him behind me. That was starting to weird me out. "You're hurt," he said quietly, and his hand bit down, a hot snarling mass of Power forcing its way into the wound. I gritted my teeth, feeling muscle knit itself together—I'd been so pumped on adrenaline I'd barely noticed the strike. "My apologies."

CHAPTER
29

I poured a full glass of brandy, handed it to the demon, and took a long pull off the bottle. It was good stuff, silken-smooth, igniting like a thunderball in my belly.

Jace slugged a hit of vodka. Eddie cursed as Gabe swabbed at his arm with peroxin. I waited a few moments, exhaled, took another pull from the bottle, my other hand white-knuckled on my sword. My bloody sleeve flopped.

"Careful with that, Danny," Jace said. "I need you sober."

"Fuck you," I said. "Why does the Corvin Family want me, Jace? What aren't you telling me?" *You swore you were free and clear of the Mob when you met me, and I believed you. Silly me.*

He shrugged. "Don't worry about the Corvins, sweetheart. I'll take them down if they so much as touch you."

"You still *work* for them, don't you, Jace? That's why you didn't want to talk about it. Once Mob, always Mob. You can't take them down."

Jace's face was bloodless under a mask of sweat, grime, and a spatter of blood high on his left cheek. "I bought myself free of the Corvins, Danny. They don't own me." He took another slug of vodka, smacked the shotglass down on the counter. The sharp sound crackled in tense air.

I took another hit off the bottle, turned to look at the demon. "Jaf?"

He shrugged, too. Goddamn shrugging men.

He's not a man, he's a demon. The thought struck me with almost physical force. I stopped, staring at him. When had I started thinking about him as if he was human? That didn't bode well. I tipped the bottle up to my lips again, but Japhrimel set his untouched glass down on the bar and took the bottle from me, his fingers hot against mine. "No, Dante," he said softly. "Please. I will not allow you to be harmed."

Well, that's comforting, I thought. And oddly enough, it was. "Okay," I answered, letting go of the bottle. The brandy settled into a warm glow behind my breastbone. "So the Corvins want me alive. What the fuck for? And—" A horrible thought struck me just as I finished turning to face Japhrimel.

He set the bottle down beside his glass, watching my face. "Dante?"

I stood stock-still, frozen, my entire body gone cold. Abra told me Jace is working for the Corvins . . . *The Corvins want me alive, and they're paying so much . . . someone else is leaning on them, someone big . . . Jace and the Corvins. He's one of them. Once Mob, always Mob.*

"Danny?" Gabe must have caught my sudden stillness, because she was staring at me, too, her dark eyes wide. "Danny?"

I swallowed. "I've got to go up to my room," I said, hearing the queer breathlessness in my voice. I sounded like a young girl viciously embarrassed at her first party. "Excuse me."

I was halfway to the door before Japhrimel fell into step beside me. He said nothing.

"Danny, what's wrong?" Gabe called. *"Danny!"*

I found the grand wide staircase and started to climb, the premonition beating under my skin. Premonition— and shock. It couldn't be. It couldn't be.

But he betrayed me once, didn't he? Left without a word—what do you want to bet he was called down here by the Corvins and that's why he left? Abra warned me . . . she knew. And now he's so willing to help . . . so very hospitable, stay in my house, it's safer there, he said he bought himself free of the Corvins but I know the Mob, you never get free. Even if he bought something from them, they can squeeze him until he hands over an ex-girlfriend, can't they?

My brain shied away from the cold, logical conclusion. I didn't want to believe it.

The demon stepped behind me, soundless, his musky aura closing me in, a shielding I ignored because I didn't have time or concentration to spare to shake it aside. He only touched me once, a subtle push on my blood-crusted shoulder when I almost got lost in the hallways. When we reached the blue room, I shoved the door open and bolted inside, trembling. Stopped.

The room, instead of blue, was now white. Heavy fragrance drenched the air.

Flowers. White flowers. Lotuses, roses, lilies, scattered over the room as if a snowstorm had dropped its blossoms. Gooseflesh raced up my arm, spilled down my back; my teeth chattered and my nipples drew up hard as pebbles. The flowers lay on every flat surface, even the floor, the smell was stifling, heady, and cloying. They piled on the bed, fluttered near the window, and I could see the bathroom was full of them, too.

Santino had sent blue flowers to Doreen. Great sprays and cascades of flowers in every shade of blue. I still couldn't look at irises or blue roses or cornflowers without shuddering.

"Dante?" Japhrimel definitely sounded alarmed now. He closed the door, then stepped aside, his long coat brushing his legs with a soft sound. "My shields are intact; only the house servants could have—"

"They were probably delivered and brought up by the staff." I sounded like I'd been punched in the stomach. "Look, I need to change. And pack my bag." I flattened my free hand against the door to brace myself. "Can you get me out of here without Jace's shields reacting?"

"Of course," he said, lifting one shoulder and dropping it. *All things should be so easy*, that shrug said. "What is this?" he asked. "Did your former lover perhaps—"

"Santino sent all his victims flowers," I said numbly.

The demon stilled, his eyes turning incandescent.

"He knows," I continued. "He knows I'm here, and looking for him. And I'm a Necromance. He's picked me as his next victim."

"Dante—"

"That means I won't have to worry about finding him," I said. "He'll find me." I laughed, but the sound was gaspy, panicky. The world roared underneath me, spinning carelessly away, almost like a slicboard but my feet slipping, slipping—

"Dante." He had me by the shoulders. "Stop. Breathe. Just breathe." His fingers bit in, and he shook me slightly. My teeth clicked together. I tasted apples, and the sour smell of my own fear.

A whooping breath tore between my lips. My left shoulder gave a livid crunching flare of pain, shocking me back into myself. I found myself shaking, my hands trembling, the demon's chin resting atop my head, his smell enfolding me. His arms closed around me, the feverish heat of Hell flooding my entire body. I was sneakingly grateful for it—I was cold, so cold my jaw clenched, my teeth chattered, and goosebumps rose everywhere. He had my sword—had I dropped it or had he just taken it from my numb fingers? That was three times he'd taken my blade. Was I really getting sloppy? When I was younger, I never would have dropped my blade.

"Breathe," he murmured into my hair. "Simply breathe. I am with you, Dante. Breathe."

I rested my forehead against the oddly soft material of his coat, filled my lungs with the musk smell of demon. Alien. It steadied me. The lunatic urge to sob retreated.

"Calm," the demon said. "Steady, Dante. Breathe."

"I'm okay," I managed. "We have to get out of here."

"Very well." But he didn't move, and neither did I.

"We have to find a place to stay," I said, "and I have to . . . I have to . . ."

"Leave it to me," he answered quietly.

"I've got to pack." I sounded steadier now. *"Anubis et'her ka. Se ta'uk'fhet sa te vapu kuraph."* The familiar invocation bolstered me.

He didn't move until I did. I rocked back on my heels and he let me go, his arms sliding free. His face was blank, set, his eyes burning holes. The mark on my shoulder throbbed insistently. He held my sword up, silently, and I took it from his hand. "Thanks." I was shaky, but myself again.

Japhrimel nodded, watching me. I wasn't sure what he was looking for, but he examined my face as if the Nine Canons were written there. Heat, a purely human heat, rose to my cheeks. "It is my honor," he said quietly. "I swear to you on the waters of Lethe, Dante Valentine, I will allow no harm to come to you."

"Santino—" I began.

A swift snarl crossed his face. I flinched.

"We will find a way to kill him, you and I. Pack your bag, Dante. If you are determined to leave this place, let us go quickly." He sounded utterly calm, the kind of calm that could draw a razor through flesh with only a slight smile.

"Sounds like a good idea," I managed. The flowers stirred. More thunder rumbled above the city, and a slight cool breeze stole in through the open window, ruffling petals, swirling the cloying stench of dying blooms against my face. I swayed in place. Japhrimel reached out, his golden fingers resting against my cheek for a moment. The touch made my entire body glow with heat. "Japhrimel—"

"Dante," he replied, his glowing eyes holding mine. "Hurry."

I did.

CHAPTER
30

The bodega was deep in the stinking well of Nuevo Rio, a small storefront marked with the universal symbols of Power: signs from the Nine Canons spray-painted on the front step, a display window showing small mummified crocodiles nestled among *grisgris* bags and bottles of different holy waters, lit novenas crowding on the step, each keyed to a shimmer of Power. The smell of incense from the fuming sticks placed near the door threatened to give me a headache, along with the breathless sense of storm approaching that hung over the city. I adjusted the strap over my shoulder, then rubbed at my dry, aching eyes. Japhrimel leaned on the counter, bargaining with the *babalawao* in fluent Portogueso. The woman had liquid dark eyes and a Shaman's thorn-spiked cruciform tattoo on her cheek; the cross shape and thorns told me she was an Eclectic Shaman—rare here in Rio for a native to be an Eclectic. She eyed me with a great deal of interest, stroking her staff at the same time. The staff thrummed with Power, as did her tiny bodega, and I counted myself lucky that I didn't have to fight her. She was tall, and moved with a

quick ferret grace that warned me she was very dangerous indeed.

I was faintly surprised to find Japhrimel knew Portogueso, but I suppose I shouldn't have been. Demons
like languages as much as they like technology, and have
fiddled with both for a long time.

He finally looked back over his shoulder at me. "Carmen says we're welcome to stay up over the shop," he
said. "Come. You need rest."

I shrugged. "How likely is it that we'll be tracked
here?"

He showed his teeth. "Not likely at all," he replied,
and I didn't press him for details. He probably wouldn't
give them anyway. "She is of the Hellesvront—our
agents," he continued, immediately proving me wrong.

"You have agents? Hell has human agents?"

"Of course. Human and others."

Then why didn't they track down Santino? I decided
not to ask. The bodega felt like Abra's store—dusty, old,
the same smell of chilis and beef. Yet the *babalawao*
wasn't like Abra—she was powerful, true, but human.
Only human. She swept her hair back over her shoulder
and regarded me coolly, her eyes moving over my di-
sheveled hair, dusty sweat-stained clothes, and white-
knuckled grip on my katana. She asked one question,
and Japhrimel shook his head. His inky hair lay still
against his skull. He didn't seem to sweat even in this
malicious wet heat.

Hell was hotter, anyway.

The woman led us to the back of her store, sweeping
aside a curtain woven into bright geometrics that writhed
with Power. A narrow staircase threaded up into darkness.

Japhrimel touched the woman's forehead. She nodded,

her brown skin moving under his hand, and grinned at me, her teeth flashing sharp and white. "*Gracias, filho*," he said quietly.

"*De nada*," she said, and returned to perch on her barstool behind the glassed-in counter. Glass jars of herbs twinkled behind her, and a rack of novena candles threw back the gleam.

I climbed the creaking stairs, the demon's soundless step behind me. We reached a low, indifferently lit hall, and a single door. I opened it, and found myself looking at a small, plain bedroom. An iron mission-style bed with white sheets and a dun comforter, a single chair by the empty fireplace, a full-length mirror next to a flimsy door leading to the Nuevo Rio version of a bathroom. I heaved a sigh. "I like this much better," I said shakily.

"No doubt." Japhrimel crowded past me into the room. It suddenly seemed far too small to contain him. The window looked out onto the street. I shut the door while he made one circuit of the walls, Power blending seamlessly to hide us. I dropped my bag on the bed, wishing I'd had room for more than one change of clothes. *It won't be the first hunt I've finished dirty,* I thought, and flipped open the messenger bag's top flap. I had to dig a bit to retrieve my datpilot. "What's that?"

"I need contacts," I said, waiting while the plug-in and the H-DOC established a linkup with the hand-held device. "Since we can't use Jace's, I'm going to have to look for anyone who has dual warrants in Saint City and in Nuevo Rio. That should give me a place to start. If nobody I know is in town we'll have to buy information, and that could get expensive."

"What information are we pursuing, then?" he asked, finishing his circuit of the room and making a brief gesture in front of the door. The whole building groaned a little, subliminally, and I felt a flutter in my stomach as the Power crested, ebbed. The room was now shielded—and if what I Saw was any indication, also invisible to prying eyes.

I took a deep breath. The medicinal effects of the brandy I'd taken down were beginning to wear off. My knees felt suspiciously weak. "I need to know two things: first of all, if Santino's running the Corvin Family from behind. And second—" I tapped into the datpilot, setting the parameters for the search, "I need to know what Jace has been doing these past three years."

CHAPTER
31

The next day was hot and breathless, thunder rumbling off and on, the light taking on a weird gray-green cast. I spent most of the day trying to sleep, sprawled on the small bed. Japhrimel dragged his chair up to the side of the bed and watched me, his green eyes veiled. I didn't speak much. I slept thinly, tossing and turning, waking with my katana still clenched in my hands and the same muggy heat lying over the city.

And Japhrimel's green eyes resting on me, oddly dark. Glazed.

My mind kept worrying like a dog with a single bone, over and over again.

Jace. The Corvin Family. Jace. Santino.

Jace.

The afternoon was wending toward evening when I finally sat up on the bed, tired of retreading the same mental ground. "Do you think he's betrayed me?" I asked, without even knowing I was going to open my mouth.

"I don't know," the demon answered, after a long, still pause. He rose to his feet like a dark wave. Demon-smell washed over me. He'd kept the window open, but the air was so close and still that the fragrance clung to the room. "You need food."

"I'll be fine. There's hunting to do." I stretched, my back cracking as I arched, then I swung my legs off the bed, came to my feet, and picked up my bag from the floor. A few moments divested it of everything I wouldn't need tonight—I piled extra clothes, the spare plasgun, and some other odds and ends on the bed. Japhrimel watched expressionlessly as I clumped over to the bathroom door, and was still watching when I came out. I buckled on my holster, checked the plasgun, and slid it in. Shrugged into my coat, immediately starting to sweat again. I finally gave my hair a short, vicious combing and braided it back.

"Do you think he's betrayed you?" he finally asked me when I checked the action on my main knives.

"It's looking pretty fucking possible," I said. "If what Abra told me is any indication, he ran with the Corvin Family even before he came to Saint City. You don't ever escape the Mob. And if Santino's running the Corvins from behind, they might be running Jace—or he was using me to pressure them for something. Or maybe just holding me until the Corvins reached a point in negotiations with Santino . . ." I trailed off. "It's very possible." I slipped my turquoise necklace on over my head, settled the pendant between my breasts. Japhrimel didn't reply. I finally settled my bag strap across my body. "What do you think?" I asked him.

His jaw set. "Do you truly wish to know?"

I nodded. "I do."

He shrugged, clasping his hands behind his back. "My opinion? He wants you far too badly to give you up to this Family," he said. "All the same, it would be fool-ish to trust him."

"If he wants me so much, why did he leave me?" I flared, then closed my eyes and took a deep breath.

"It seems we must discover this," he answered. "Do you care for him, then?"

"I used to," I said, opening my eyes and looking down at my free hand, clenched in a fist. "I'm not so sure now."

"Then do not decide yet," was his equable reply. But his face was full of something dark. I didn't want to know.

It was my turn to shrug. "You have agents in the city, you said."

He nodded. "They are already searching for informa-tion. Quietly, so as not to alert our quarry."

"That's good." My conscience pricked me. But that was ridiculous. He was a *demon*. He wasn't human. He wasn't even close to human. "Hey . . . you know, I . . ." Was I blushing? I was. Why?

I don't have time for this.

I approached him cautiously, laid my hand on his shoulder. His smell closed around me, vaguely comfort-ing. "Thank you," I said, tilting my head back to look up into his face. "Really. I really . . . well, thank you."

One corner of his mouth quirked up slightly. It was by far the most human expression I had ever seen on him. "No thanks necessary," he said quietly. "It is my honor."

"Do you really think I can kill Santino?" I asked.

His face changed. "We have no choice, either way. I will do all I can to protect you, Dante."

"Good enough." I dropped my hand. "Let's go find our first contact."

CHAPTER
32

The police net plug-in gave me a current map of the city and tag-locations of landmarks loaded from my datband to my datpilot; the DOC told me who was in town. It wasn't too hard to find a familiar face. Whatever city Captain Jack was infesting, he always hung out near the prostitutes.

We visited five bordellos before we hit paydirt. I scanned a two-story building and brushed against weak, familiar shielding. After running into Captain Jack on four bounties, one of which had almost cost me my life when he turned traitor and sold me to the criminal I was hunting, I could tell his shielding even through a building reeking of sex and desperation. It was an unpleasant skill. "Come with me," I told the demon, pushing through the crowd. "Look dangerous. Don't kill anyone unless I do, okay?"

"As you like." He shadowed me as I crossed the street. We ended up on the doorstep, two Nuevo Rio prostitutes eyeing us. They made no move to stop me as I strode past them. The heavies guarding the door—two rippling masses of black-market augmentation—examined me, looked at the demon, and stepped back.

It was kind of useful, having Japhrimel around.

Inside, the place was done in threadbare red velvet, waves of perfume and hash smoke, naked women pressed against lace, offering their breasts and other things. One bronzed Nuevo Rio man, reclining on an overdone mahogany and black satin couch with a guitar in his supple hands, plucked out a mellow tune—an accompaniment to the girls' blandishments. Two customers, neither of them Jack, stared at me with wide eyes. Seeing a fully clothed woman carrying a sword in a Nuevo Rio bordello must be a huge shock.

I scanned the room—no, the Captain was up on the second floor. It figured.

The madam came fluttering out in a pink synthsilk robe, a tall and heavily lipsticked woman, her thinning hair padded out with horsehair. She carried about fifty extra pounds, and I felt the skin on my nape prickle. The three whip scars on my back gave one remembrance of a twinge, then subsided as I took a deep breath.

At least being a Necromance had saved me from being a sex worker.

She fired a chattering stream of Portogueso at us, and Japhrimel answered her with a few curt words. She paled, and he held out two folded notes—Nuevo Rio paper. Currency for those without datbands.

She snatched the notes from his hand and leered at me. I turned my cheek so my emerald sparked at her, and she almost fell over backward in her haste to get away. If the Nuevo Rios were easier with Shamans and demons and *loa*, they were even more frightened of Necromances. They had old legends here of the spirits that walked in Death and the humans that could talk to them—while Shamans were mostly acceptable, a Necromance definitely was *not*.

I took the stairs two at a time, following the pattern of instinct, intuition, and Power. A long hall, some open doors with women standing in them, their usual catcalls dying on their lips as I came into sight; other doors were closed, the reek of sex and hash in the air thick enough to cut. I tapped in, shaping the Power deftly, and by the time I smacked the door open and came face-to-face with a half-naked and disgruntled Captain Jack I was all but humming with invisible force. Any more and I'd go nova. It alerted him to my presence, of course, but by then it was too late for him.

"Hesu *Christos*—" he began, and I was on him, driving him to the floor, my sword within easy reach. I had him in an armlock. Japhrimel hushed the naked, screaming girl on the bed by the simple expedient of clapping a hand over her mouth. He dragged her to the door and tossed her out, then tossed a few more Nuevo Rio notes after her. *How much money does he have?* I thought, and leaned into the armlock.

Captain Jack, weedy from hash overuse, his ribs standing out, still possessed a great deal of wiry strength. I was actively sweating by the time he finished cursing and heaving, his sweat-slick skin sliding under my fingers. He'd gotten old. His dreadlocked brown hair was streaked with gray, bits of glittering circuit-wire wrapped around dreads and twisted into runic shapes, dusty from the plank flooring. He called me something filthy. I got my knee in his back and applied a little pressure. He settled down a little.

"What the motherfucking hell do *you* want?" he

snarled. The demon, his face expressionless, leaned against the door, his arms folded across his chest.

"What I always want, Jack. To see your sweet face," I leaned over and purred in his ear. "Taking a vacation from Saint City, pirate? I'm on a legitimate hunt and you've got warrants. If you don't want your ass hauled in and cored in a Nuevo Rio prison, you might want to consider being a little more polite."

"Bitch," he hissed. His long thin nose pressed into the dusty planks; spittle formed on his thin lips. He'd pawned his golden earring, I saw it was missing. The tattoos on his shoulderblades—twin dragons, with no significance or Power—writhed on his skin. He was a bottom-feeder, with only enough psi to avoid being taken into wage slavery, not enough to qualify for a trade or even as a breeder. "Whafuck? Don't got nothing on you, I ain't seen you in years—"

"It's not me I'm asking about," I said quietly. "I want to know why Jace Monroe blew into town three years ago. Give, Jack, or I'll break your fucking arm and haul you in, I swear I will."

He believed me. "Christos," he moaned. "All I know's Jace was in the Corvins . . . bought himself out six months ago, foughta running street war with them. He's . . . big man now, lots of credit and a mean network. On the way to becoming a Family himself, he's filed . . . agh, lay *off*—for incorporation."

"*Sekhmet sa'es,*" I breathed. "And? Why did he come here? There must be rumors."

"Corvins made him a deal: Either he come in or they ice some bitch he was seeing. Lay *off*, willya? You're breakin my fuckin arm!"

"I'll break more than that if you keep whining. Who's he working for now?"

"You! Goddammit, woman, he's working for you! That's the word! Let up a little, come on, Valentine, *don't*!"

"Quit your bitching. Who's leaning on the Corvins to put my ass in a blender? Huh? Who?"

"Some big dude!" Jack moaned, his eyes rolling. "Don't know! Five million credit and a clean slate for bringing you in. Whole city's lookin' for you—"

"That makes you the lucky one, doesn't it." I eased up a little on the pressure. "You must have heard rumors, Jack. Who's pushing the Corvins?"

"Same as always, the big dick Corvin. Jace was their front man in Saint City, man. Goddammit, lay *off*!"

"Jace was their front man three years ago?" That was something I hadn't guessed.

"Hell, he's been working for them his whole life! Ran off about six years ago, worked mercenary, they let him go for a while and then sank their hooks in good when he started seein' some bitch up Saint City way. I ain't been back there for five goddamn years, Valentine, I don't know who he was screwin' up there! Lucas will know, go bother him!"

That was unexpected news. "Lucas Villalobos? He's in town? Where?"

"Man, do I look like a fuckin' vid directory?"

I shoved. He screamed, the sound of a rabbit caught in a trap.

"*Las Vigrasas!* He hangs out at Las Vigrasas on Puertain Viadrid, goddammit, motherfuck—"

I looked up at the demon. He nodded slightly, understanding. It sounded like Jack was telling the truth.

I gained my feet, scooping my sword up; watched Captain Jack struggle up to hands and knees, then haul himself into a sitting position, facing me. "Hesu Christos," he moaned. "Look at this mess. You used to be such a nice girl, Valentine."

"Yeah, I had to grow up. Sucks, doesn't it." My lip curled. "Thanks for your time and trouble, Captain."

"Fuck you," he spat, his watery brown eyes rabbiting over to the demon and halting, wide as credit discs. He crossed himself—forehead, chest, left shoulder, right shoulder—while I watched, fascinated. I'd never seen Captain get religious before. *"Nominae Patri, et Filii, et Spiritu Sancti—"*

Does he think Japhrimel's going to disappear in a puff of brimstone? I thought, feeling a sardonic smile tilt one corner of my mouth. "I never knew you were a Novo Christer, Jack. I thought fucking so many prostitutes would have made you irreligious."

He kept babbling his prayer. I sighed, backed up a few steps, eased for the door. It wasn't wise to turn your back on Captain Jack.

I made it to the door before he broke off long enough to glare at me. "I hate you, Valentine," he hissed. "One of these days—"

Japhrimel tensed. His eyes flared. I reached behind me for the doorknob. "Promises, promises," I said, twisting the knob and opening the door. "If you go running to Monroe, tell him he'd better pray his path doesn't cross mine."

"They'll catch you!" Jack screamed. "The whole city's lookin' for you!"

"Good luck to them," I said, and ducked out of the room. Japhrimel followed me.

"Shall I kill him?" he asked quietly as we made our way down the hall. The entire bordello was silent, waiting. "He threatened you."

"Leave him alone. He hates me for a good reason."

"What would that be?"

"I killed his wife," I said, checking the stairs. Looked safe enough. "Come on. Let's go find Lucas." My jaw set, and fortunately, Japhrimel didn't ask me anything else.

CHAPTER
33

Las Vigrasas was a bar. The street it crouched on lay under a drift of trash, furtive shadows sliding from place to place, danger soaking the air. I shivered, peering at the front of the bar from our safe place across the street. Japhrimel had suggested watching the place for a few minutes, and I'd concurred.

I scanned the place carefully. No real Power here, this was a blindhead bar. It was asking for trouble, walking in there. Some places weren't very hospitable to psis.

A lonely sign with a peeling *L s Vig asa* painted on it swung slightly in the freshening breeze. The air was so muggy, even the breeze didn't help much. Bullet holes and plasgun scorches festooned the buildings.

I took a deep breath. "What do you think?" I asked him.

I can't believe I'm asking a demon his opinion, I thought. *What the hell is wrong with me? Then again, he's my best backup, at least until I find this Egg thingie.*

"I think this is a dangerous place," he said softly. "I would ask you to be careful, but—"

"I'll be careful," I said. "Look, don't hesitate in there. You see someone go for me, take them down."

"Kill them?"

"If necessary." I paused. "I trust your judgment."

His eyes sparked briefly, turning bright laser-green, and then just as swiftly darkened. "You do?"

"I guess so," I answered. "You haven't let me down yet."

He didn't answer, but his eyes held mine for a long moment.

I finally eased out of the shadows and crossed the street, skirting mounds of rubble and trash. I didn't have to look—Japhrimel seemed melded to my shadow. Three steps led up to Las Vigrasas's swinging door; I heard rollicking shouts from behind it, a barrelhouse piano going. I pushed the door open, grimacing inwardly at the feel of greasy wood against my fingers. A roil of smell pushed out—alcohol, vomit, cigarette smoke, the stench of an untended lavatory, unwashed men.

Eau de Nuevo Rio bar, I thought. *I wish Gabe was here*.

That startled me. I wasn't used to hunting with anyone in tow, but it had been nice to have Gabe around. At least she was honest—or I hoped so. Then again, she had suggested staying with Jace, and contacted him.

It truly sucks to doubt your friends when you only have one or two of them, I realized.

I strode into the bar, Japhrimel behind me. Cigarette smoke hazed the air. The dark and sudden quiet that fell over the raucous drunken pit warned me. *Oh, what the hell*, I thought. *In for a penny, in for a motherfucking pound*. My emerald spat, sizzled, a green spark drifting down to the floor.

A long bar crouched on the left side of the room, tables and chairs scattered to my right. I stepped down, my boots making quiet sounds against the wood of the stairs and then a muffled deadened sound as I stepped onto the oiled sawdust.

Dark eyes watched me. Several Nuevo Rios, lean tanned men in clothes very much like mine, plasguns and old-time projectile guns openly displayed. There was a smattering of Anglos—I scanned the bar once, and found a familiar slouched set of shoulders. Lucas stood with his back to the door, leaning against the bar.

I knew better than to think he didn't know who had just come in from the cold.

I made it two steps across the sawdust before the bartender spat something in Portogueso, a long deadly-looking shotgun in his brown hands. He wore a stained apron and a sweat-darkened white shirt, oddly luminescent in the gloom.

Japhrimel said something in reply, and the air temperature dropped by at least ten degrees. Nobody moved, but there was a general sense of men leaning back. I waited, eyeing the bartender, my peripheral vision marking everyone in the room. Lucas wore a Trade Bargains microfiber shirt, like me; run-down jeans and worn engineer boots. But he also wore a bandolier, oiled supple leather against his shirt; his greasy hair lay lank against his shoulders.

The bartender spoke again, but his voice quivered slightly. I watched the shotgun.

Japhrimel said nothing, but the air pressure changed. I felt like a woman holding a plasgun over a barrel of reactive—my pulse ran tight and hot behind my wrists and throat, my nape tingling, my skin bathed with Power.

Five seconds ticked by. Then the bartender dropped his shotgun on the bar. The wood and metal clattered. I tensed, bile whipping my throat. *Do all these places have to smell so bad?* I thought, and then, *If I didn't have Japhrimel with me, someone would have tried to kill me by now.*

It was awful handy, having a demon around.

The bartender raised his hands, backing away from the shotgun. His pupils dilated, the color draining from his face. Pasty and trembling, he slumped against the fly-spotted mirror sporting shelves of dusty bottles. Glass chattered.

I pantomimed a yawn, patting my lips with the back of my hand. My rings flashed. I walked across the saw-dust, skirting a table where three men had a card game set out. I glanced down at the table—poker. Of course. A pile of metal bits lay in the middle of the table. One of the men caught my eyes and hurriedly looked down at his cards.

I made it to where Lucas leaned against the bar. A glass full of amber liquid sat at his elbow.

"Valentine," he said, not turning around. His voice was a whisper, the same whispered tone Necromances affected after a while. It made me shudder to hear. "Thought you'd come looking for me."

"I hate being predictable," I said carefully. "I want information."

"Of course you do. And I'm the only honest fucker you can find in this town that won't sell you." He shrugged, one shoulder lifting, dipping. "What you paying?"

"What you want?" I kept my katana between us.

"The usual, *chica*. You got it?" His shoulders tensed.

"Of course, Lucas. I wouldn't come here otherwise."

Letting you walk inside my mind isn't a price I want to pay, but I have no choice.

He turned around then, slowly, and I took a step back. Japhrimel's fingers closed around my shoulders, and I found myself with the demon plastered to my back, my sheathed katana raised to be a bar between me and Lucas Villalobos.

He was five inches taller than me, compact with muscle, his lank hair hanging over a pale, wasted face. His eyes glittered almost-yellow in the uncertain light.

The scar ran down his left cheek, a river of ruined skin. Was that where his tattoo had been burned away? I didn't know, he never told. I gulped. Lucas was a lot older than he looked; something in the hooded twinkle of his eyes and the almost-slack set of his mouth made that age visible. He wouldn't die, though. You could gut him, slit his throat, burn him alive, but he wouldn't die.

Death had turned His face from Lucas Villalobos. Nobody knew why, and it was worth your life to ask.

"You want to know about Jace Monroe," he whispered. His smell, dry as a stasis cabinet, brushed against my nose.

I preferred the stink of the bar. Power pushed at Lucas would simply be shunted aside; he didn't cast spells. No, he merely killed; hired himself out for protection work and assassinations. It was expensive to have the Deathless on your side—but worth it, I'd been told.

I never wanted to find out. Even going to him for information scared me. This was our third time meeting, and I sincerely hoped as I did every time that it was our last.

Nobody else in the bar spoke. Japhrimel was tense behind me, heat blurring through my clothes. The smoky smell of demon began to drown out every other scent in the bar—and for that, I was grateful. My mouth tasted like cotton—and bile.

"Tell me," I said simply.

He shrugged. "Not much to tell. He was born into the Corvins, I think. Far as I know, he's Deke Corvin's youngest son. Word is, he planned his escape for a long time, hoofed out to Saint City, and started doing mercenary work. Then something happened he didn't count on." Lucas shrugged, picked up his glass. Drained it, his Adam's apple working. "Idiot fell in love with a girl. Old man Sargon moved in for the kill, fouled up a job of hers, then let Jace know that if he didn't come back and fly right, he'd take out a contract on the girl. Jace caved, came home like a good little boy." Lucas's yellow eyes mocked me. "Stupid bitch didn't even bother coming out to Nuevo Rio to find out what had happened."

"I'm sure she had her reasons," I said, matching his quiet tone. Our words dropped into the profound silence of the bar like stones into a pond. "Who's running the Corvin Family from behind, Lucas?"

"Nobody I know of," he whispered, setting his empty glass down with finicky precision. "Sargon runs the Corvins, with an iron fist. Jace just bought himself free legally—and extralegally, the streets are still bleeding from his nightside war with the Corvins. He's incorporated under a Mob license of his own. Surprised?"

"Not really," I said. "Once Mob, always Mob. Who's looking for me, Lucas?"

"Whole damn city," Lucas returned. "You're worth hard cash, good credit, and a clean slate to several interested parties. Jace is combing the sinks for you and your pet demon there. Boy's got a real hard-on for you."

"I'm sure it will pass," I said. "Give me something real, Lucas."

"I don't have anything else," he said. "Someone wants you alive and unharmed. Every bounty hunter worth a credit is pouring into the city. You can't hide forever."

"I don't want to hide," I said. "I'm after Santino."

If I'd thought the place was quiet before, it went absolutely still now. Nobody was even breathing once I spoke that name.

Lucas went even paler. "Then you're on the track to suicide," he whispered. "Take my advice, Valentine. Run. Run as fast as you can, for as long as you can. Steal whatever bit of life you can. You're already dead."

"Not yet I'm not," I said. "You can tell whoever you like. I'm gunning for Santino, and I'm going to take him down."

Lucas made an odd wheezing sound. It took me a moment to realize he was laughing. Cold sweat broke out on my back.

Lucas finally wiped tears away from his hooded yellow eyes and regarded me. "You can't kill that fucker, Valentine. Not from what I've heard," he said. "Now get out of here. I don't want you near me."

"What about payment?" My fingers tightened on my katana.

"Don't want it. Get the fuck away from me before I decide to take you in myself."

"Good luck," I said dryly. "I don't want any debt to you, Lucas."

"I'll see you in Hell, Valentine. Get the fuck out of here, now." His eyes slid up, regarded the demon. "Go out and die well."

I didn't wait to be told twice. I backed up, cautiously,

Japhrimel moving with me, oddly intimate. Then he slid to the side, and I turned around. He walked behind me as I retraced my steps. I looked back over my shoulder once, when I reached the stairs, and saw Lucas pouring into his glass from a bottle of tequila. He filled it to the brim, then lifted the bottle to his lips and took two long gulps, not stopping for breath. He looked shaken.

Now I had officially seen everything.

CHAPTER
34

The stink of the street outside was almost fresh after the close, reeking air of the bar. I filled my lungs, walking quickly, Japhrimel matching me step for step. He didn't speak, and neither did I. We reached a slightly better-lit part of town. He touched my shoulder and pointed out a small restaurant; I didn't demur.

It was a little hole-in-the-wall cantina, and I ordered two shots of tequila to start off with. The waitress eyed me, nervously touching the *grisgris* bag around her neck. I didn't care anymore. Finally she took Japhrimel's money and hurried off.

I sank back into the cracked red vinyl booth, then leaned forward and rested my forehead on the table, trembling. Thunder muttered in the far distance.

"Dante." His voice was calm. I could feel his eyes on me.

"Give me a minute," I said, my words muffled.

He did.

I took in deep ragged breaths, trying to force my heart to stop pounding. Jace was a Corvin. He'd never told me—and I'd never guessed. Not even when Abra had told me Jace was Mob had I guessed he was a blood Corvin.

The second-to-last job I'd gone on before he left—that had been the Morrix fiasco. I'd barely escaped alive. I'd told Jace about it and he'd been worried, of course—any time your lover gets shot during a routine corporate-espionage, you can legitimately get worried—but he must have had a better poker face than even I'd guessed. He had lied to me about his origins, and I'd swallowed it like the fool I was.

And Lucas turning down payment was unheard-of. Whatever he knew about Santino, he wasn't going to tell—and he considered me already dead.

I was seriously beginning to wonder if he might be right. I was Santino's next victim.

And Jace might be working for the demon who haunted my nightmares.

The waitress brought the tequila. Japhrimel murmured to her, and I heard the rustle of more money exchanging hands. *I wish I'd learned Portogueso,* I thought, and slowly sat up. I took the first shot of tequila and tossed it back, hoping the alcohol would kill any germs on the dirty shotglass. Fire exploded in my stomach and I coughed slightly, my eyes watering.

Japhrimel sat bolt upright on the other side of the booth. I watched the front window of the restaurant for a little while—we'd taken a booth in the back, of course, so I could have my back to the wall. The water from the tequila-burn rolled down my cheeks; I scraped it off with the flat of one hand, keeping my katana under the table.

He examined me closely. I contemplated the second shot of tequila.

Finally, he reached over and took the shot glass in his

golden fingers. He lifted it to his lips and poured it down, then blinked.

"That," he pronounced, "is unutterably foul."

I coughed slightly, and giggled. The sound was high-pitched, tired, and more panicked than I liked. "I thought demons liked liquor," I said. The slick plastic tabletop glowed under the high-intensity fluorescents set in the plasteel lamps hanging from chains, made to look like old-fashioned lamps.

"That seems to be something other than liquor," he replied.

I took in a shaky breath. The banter helped. "Do you have any ideas?" I asked him. "Because I've got to tell you, I'm fresh out."

He nodded, the light running over his inky hair and even face. "There might be something . . ." He trailed off, closed his eyes briefly. Then he looked at me. "I've ordered food. You must take better care of yourself, Dante."

"Why?" Another jagged laugh escaped me. "I have it on good authority I'm not going to live long enough to have it matter. Everyone keeps telling me I'm going to die." *Including that little voice that happens to be my better sense,* I added silently. I held up a finger. "I'm Santino's next victim." Another finger. "The Corvins want me unharmed, presumably for delivery to an interested party." I held up a third finger. "Jace is a Corvin. A *blood* Corvin. What does this add up to? Me being fucked, that's what it adds up to. Santino's a *demon.* If *you* can't kill him, what chance do I have?"

Japhrimel looked down at the table. He said nothing.

"Lucifer's set me up to die, hasn't he?" I said it quietly. "There's no way I can kill Santino. I'm supposed to distract Santino while you get the Egg. And when I die, it's *too bad, so sad, but she was only a human after all.*" My fingers ached, gripping my katana's sheath. "Tell me if I'm wrong, Tierce Japhrimel."

He placed his hands flat on the table. "You're wrong," he said quietly. "The Prince believes you can kill him. You did survive him once, after all. And now you have me, not a human *sedayeen*, watching over you. I may not be able to kill him myself, but I can help you—and keep you alive and free long enough to kill him. And once we recover the Egg, I will be free." His eyes swung up, found mine. "*Free*, Dante. Do you know what that means? That means I can do as I please, no commands from the Prince, no shackle to my duty. *Free*."

His eyes blazed, his mouth turning down in a grimace. I watched, fascinated, almost forgetting my sword. It was the most emotion I'd ever seen from him.

I swallowed dryly. I'd never heard of a free demon before. Lucifer must be desperate to drag me out of my house and offer a demon like Japhrimel complete freedom. "What would you do if you were free?"

He closed his mouth, dropped his eyes again. There was a long pause before he shrugged. "I do not know. I have an idea, but . . . so much may change, between now and then. I have learned not to hope for much, Dante. It has been my only true lesson."

I took this in. I was beginning to feel more like myself now. "All right," I said. "You haven't led me wrong so far. So what's this idea of yours?"

"Eat first," he said. "Then I'll tell you."

I tapped my lacquered nails on the tabletop. "Okay." I checked the front window again, nervous for no discernible reason. "So what did you order?"

"*Arroz con pollo*. I am told it's quite good." He didn't move, hands flat on the tabletop, eyes down, shoulders straight as a ruler. His black coat and inky hair drank in the light, oddly glossy under the fluorescents. "Does it surprise you, that he would not tell you his Flight and clan?"

I shrugged. "I never would have dated him if I'd known," I admitted. "But still."

"Indeed." He waited for a few heartbeats. "He went back to his clan to protect you, it seems."

"He could have told me. Left a note. Something. Look, I don't want to talk about this. Can we pick another subject?"

He nodded, his left hand suddenly moving, tracing a glyph on the tabletop. I watched for a few moments, then looked at his face, studying the arc of his cheekbone, his lashes veiling his eyes, the curve of his lower lip. "I have a thought," he said.

"Lay it on me." I tapped my fingernails on the plastic. My rings were quiescent, dark.

"Sargon Corvin," Japhrimel paused, traced the glyph again. "In the name-language of demons, *sargon* means 'bleeder' or 'despoiler.'" He looked up again. This time his eyes were dark, and I felt my pulse start to hammer again. He looked thoughtful. "So does *Vardimal*."

It was near dawn as we headed back for Carmen's bodega. Japhrimel was right, the world started to look a little less grim once I had some food in me to balance out nerves—and the tequila.

Nuevo Rio was hushed, the night people streaming toward bed and the day people not yet awake. That meant that the crowds had thinned out, and there was less cover for an Anglo Necromance trailed by a demon. I was a little more sanguine now, though. After all, I had a demon on my side.

And I was beginning to think he was trustworthy.

We turned the corner onto a long, empty street with boarded-up windows, Japhrimel pacing next to me, his hands clasped behind his back. I carried my katana a little more easily than I had before, since it didn't seem likely that I'd need it in the next few minutes.

"So what's this grand idea of yours?" I asked, checking the sky. Pale pearly dawn was beginning to filter through the lowering clouds, and the breathlessness of an approaching storm had intensified, if that were possible. I longed for rain, for lightning, for anything to break this tension. I hate muggy weather.

"You may not like it," he said, his head down and his hands clasped behind his back.

"Does it give me a better chance of killing Santino?" I asked, checking the street again. My nape prickled. Nerves, probably. It had been a hell of a night.

"It does. Yet . . ." Japhrimel trailed off again. "You do not trust me, Dante."

I shrugged. "I don't trust anyone, not until proven." That sounded rude, and I sighed. "You're okay, you know. But my jury's still out until you tell me this idea."

"Very well," he said. But he didn't explain—instead, he glanced up at the sky too, then down at me.

"I'm waiting," I reminded him.

"I would wish to give you a gift," he said, slowly, as if he was choosing his words carefully. "A piece of my Power. It will make you stronger, faster . . . less easy to damage."

I thought it over, skirting a puddle of oily liquid. The

pavement here was cracked and dangerous, small sink-holes yawning everywhere. My neck prickled again. I was too nervous. Too strung-out. I needed sleep, or a fight . . . or something else entirely. "What's the catch?" I said finally.

"I am not sure you would wish to be tied to me so closely," he answered. "And the process is . . . difficult, for humans. Painful."

I absorbed this. "You would . . . what, make me into a demon?"

"Not a demon. My *hedaira*."

"I've never heard of that."

"It's not spoken of," he said. "It . . . ah, it requires a . . . ah, a physical bond . . ."

Was that *embarrassment* in his voice? Another first, the first time I'd heard a demon groping for words. "You mean like Tantrik; like sex magick?" I ventured, feeling my cheeks heat up. *I'm blushing. Anubis guard me, I'm blushing.*

"Very similar," he agreed, sounding relieved.

"Oh." I mulled this over, stepping over another puddle. Gooseflesh raised on my back, a chill breath on my sweating skin.

Why am I so nervous?

I opened my mouth to say something when Japhrimel froze between one step and the next. I halted, too, closed my eyes, and sent my senses out, winging through the predawn hush.

Nothing. Nothing but the demon next to me, and the persistent static of city Power—

—and a smell like cold midnight and ice.

My entire body went cold, my nipples drawing up hard as pebbles, my breath catching.

"Dante," Japhrimel said quietly. "Run."

"No way," I whispered. "If he's here—"

"Do not be foolish," he whispered fiercely, catching my arm and shoving me. "*Run!*" His hands flickered, came up full of silver guns.

My katana whispered free of its sheath, metal running with blue light and Power, runes twisting along its surface.

And then all hell broke loose.

I'd like to say I was of some use once the fighting broke out, but the only thing I remember was a huge stunning impact throwing me to the ground, my katana still clenched in my hand, and Japhrimel's roar of furious agony. *Plasgun bolt,* I thought, *I didn't expect a plasgun bolt from a demon.* And darkness swallowed me whole.

CHAPTER
35

*C*old.

After the heat of Nuevo Rio, the cold crept into my bones and twisted hard. I moaned, trying to lift my head. My left shoulder burned mercilessly, my right wrist clasped in something hard and chill. Stone under my fingertips.

It took a while before I could open my eyes. When I did, the darkness didn't change. Either I was blind, or locked in a place with no light.

Both were equally possible.

For a few vertiginous minutes after I woke up, I couldn't even remember my own name. Then it all came flooding back.

Plasgun. I'd been hit with a plasgun bolt, set on stun. That explained the temporary blindness—if I was blind—and the way my entire body felt as if it had been ripped apart and put back together wrong. A plasgun charge was the worst thing for psionics; it drained and screwed up Power meridians, as well as giving a hell of a headache.

I moved slightly, and the sound of metal dragging over stone reached my ears.

Chained. I was chained to the stone. A metal cuff clasped my wrist.

I took in a deep ragged breath, moaned again. Yanked on the chain. I was underground, I could tell I was underground, in the dark. My rings scraped stone as I pulled on the chain, metal clanking, another moan echoing against the walls.

Stop it, a cold, calm voice intruded on my panic. *Get hold of yourself. You're not dead yet, so look around. Use that famous wit of yours, Danny, and try to figure out why you haven't been killed yet.*

Santino. He'd been there. Had he snatched me? If so, I *had* to think, I had to.

I shut my eyes again. The squirming worm of panic under my breastbone started to grow. I had to pee, and the darkness was absolute, and the cold leaching into my bones made me shiver, like the cold of bringing a ghost back.

Anubis et'her ka. Se ta'uk'fhet sa te vapu kuraph. Anubis et'her ka. Anubis, Lord of the Dead, Faithful Companion, protect me, for I am Your child. Protect me, Anubis, weigh my heart upon the scales, watch over me, Lord, for I am Your child. Do not let evil distress me, but turn Your fierceness upon my enemies—

Light bloomed, a faint blue glow. I hitched in a shuddering breath. My eyes popped open.

My rings were dead and dark. The glow came from my katana, lying on the other side of the stone cube with my bag and my coat, thrown in a heap. My plasgun was gone; so was the katana's scabbard. *Oh, thank you*, I thought. *Thank you, Lord. Thank you.*

A faint heat bloomed inside my chest. My shoulder

ached fiercely, as if a hot poker was being drilled into the flesh. What had happened to Japhrimel?

And why leave me my sword? I was deadly with edged metal.

Then again, Santino had faced me down with a sword before and won; he'd taken the plasgun, which was the only thing faster than a demon. Santino might not fear me even if I had my other weapons.

Let's hope that's his first mistake.

I was trapped in a featureless stone cell with a drain in one corner. A faint sour smell came up from the drain. I wriggled across the floor, not trusting my legs yet.

The chain fetched me up short. I wriggled around, stretching, but the katana was still a good six inches away and I couldn't twist any other part of my body near enough due to the narrowness of the cell. I finally settled on my stomach, staring at the katana's hilt.

I was drained. I had not even an erg of Power left. Taking a plasgun bolt will do that, scramble and drain your Power meridians. I'd either have to wait for a recharge, or . . .

I stretched out my left hand. My shoulder burned. The faint blue glow helped immensely, even though I could see no way out of the cube. *Don't worry*, I told myself, *if there's a way in, there's a way out.*

I lay on my back, my left hand out and reaching, stilled myself. *Anubis,* I prayed, *You have shown me Your favor. Give me my weapon, please. Don't let me die chained like an animal. Please, my Lord, help me, for I have served You faithfully—*

I strained, every muscle singing in agony, my heart speeding up, my breathing rising. The blue glow stuttered.

I inhaled, waiting for the space inside me where the god lived to open.

—blue crystal pillars, a flash of light, the god's face, turning away from me. My emerald, flashing, a song of creaking agony.

My katana's hilt slammed into my palm. I gasped, shocked heart and lungs struggling to function—the body needed Power to survive; to drain myself so completely was dangerous, my heart and lungs could stop and tip me into Death's embrace.

When I regained consciousness, I had my katana in hand. The Power vibrating in the blade trickled into me. It helped.

In the glow from my blade, I examined the cuff around my wrist. It took a moment to snag the blade on the strap of my bag, and then once I had my bag I dug in to find my lockpicks. They were there—I said a silent prayer of thanksgiving while I worked on the ancient lock. It took a while, and one fit of whispered cursing at my numb fingers, but I finally tickled the lock open.

Wearing my coat helped with the chill. I settled my bag under the coat, against my hip, and held my katana.

There, I thought, *that's definitely better.*

I took a few moments to lean against the wall and breathe. The stone cube was windowless, doorless, with nothing but the drain in one corner. There was no Power in the walls that I could sense, but when I closed my eyes and felt around me I discovered two things—that I was still in Nuevo Rio, because the Power here tasted like ashes and tamales and blood, and that there was a dead spot on one wall, where the stone didn't resonate like stone should.

First things first. I relieved myself into the drain,

wishing I'd packed some toilet paper in the bag. *Really*, I scolded myself, *you should have known that you'd end up in a stone dungeon with no facilities. That's how these things always end up, isn't it? Who kidnapped me? If it's Santino, why am I not dead? And why in the name of the gods did he leave me my sword?*

Then I zipped myself up and walked over to the dead spot. The ceiling gave me only about an inch of clearance; if I'd been any taller I would have had to hunch.

I had enough Power now to reach out and tap into the city's well again, thankful I'd had a chance to acclimate. Being locked in this cell with backlash would not have been good.

With the tapline secure and my throbbing headache easing as the Power soaked back into me, I touched the dead spot on the wall. It appeared to be stone to my fingers.

I stared at the stone, and my left shoulder gave a crunching flare of pain. I transferred my katana to my left hand, blade-down so the glow from the steel would give me light, and reached up with my right, sliding my hand under my shirt. The ridged loops of scar pulsed under my fingers. Heat flooded me.

I saw, as if through a sheet of rippling glass, the city underneath me. Fire bloomed in several different places, and my right hand was up, clinging to something rough. Rain lashed down, unable to quench the fires, and there was an incredible noise. Then the world rushed up to meet me, boots thudding into pavement, and someone's soft throat gave under my iron fingers.

"If she is harmed," I heard Japhrimel growl, *"I will kill all in my path, I promise you this."*

I woke up lying curled on the stone floor, my katana's

hilt pressed to my forehead. I would have a nice goose-egg on my temple from hitting the floor. The tapline re-sounded as if plucked like a guitar string. "I gotta stop passing out," I moaned, tasting blood. I'd bitten the in-side of my cheek. "I'll never get out of here."

The tingle of Power told me I'd been down for about half an hour. *That doesn't tell me anything,* I thought, *who knows how long I've really been down here?* Hunger twisted my stomach.

I settled down cross-legged in front of the dead spot, staring at it. The lack of Power here told me *something* was here, and chances were it was an entrance.

I started to breathe, deep circular breaths. Opened the tapline as far as my aching head would allow, soaking up the Power of the city like a sponge. Three-quarters of the influx went into my rings; they started to sparkle against my fingers. The other quarter I used to start fashioning a glyph of the Nine Canons—*Gehraisz,* one of the Greater Glyphs of Opening.

If it didn't blast the door off its fucking hinges, at least it might blow away some of the shell of illusion over the door and give me something to work with. I waited, building the glyph carefully, the faint glow from my katana fading to a dim foxfire glow.

It took a long time for my rings to come back to life, meaning that my Power meridians were settling back into normal. Then all the available Power went into the glyph. It started to pulse, folding up in the air and glow-ing a fierce silvery-white. Looped and spun, three-dimensional, and I drew it back. Like an arrow, like a cobra coiling itself to strike.

I waited, humming the low note the glyph was keyed to, at the very bottom of my range. I juggled the glyph,

forcing an overflow line down into the floor of the cell.
If the glyph rebounded or the door was trapped, I didn't
want the backlash. Let the stone take it.

There was an endless moment of suspension, everything paused, the world stopped like a holovid still, and
then the glyph released, hurling itself toward the dead
spot in the wall.

A brilliant flash of light seared my eyes, and my left
shoulder sent a bolt of hot pain through me. When I finished shaking my head to clear it, I saw it had worked.

An ironbound door with a handle and a keyhole stood
in front of me. I let out a long satisfied breath.

"Okay," I whispered, hauling myself to my feet. My
left leg had gone to sleep, and I shifted back and forth,
gasping as the pins and needles bit my flesh. "Looks like
I'm back in the game."

CHAPTER
36

*W*hat felt like an hour but was probably only fifteen minutes later, I pushed the door cautiously open, my katana held ready. Stairs hacked out of stone rose up in front of me, and I sighed. *Of course not. It couldn't be easy, could it?* I climbed cautiously, my shaking legs protesting, my back on fire, my shoulders tense as bridge cables and my glutes singing a song of agony.

I reached the top of 174 stairs and found another door. This one was more resistant to my lockpicking skills, and I was beginning to gasp with panic, imagining being trapped underground, when it finally yielded. It creaked open, slowly, and revealed the very last thing I expected.

A large high-ceilinged room done in white. White marble floor, a large white bed with mosquito netting draped over it, a fireplace made of the same white marble. A white leather chair crouched in front of the empty fireplace, and a white rug lay on the floor at the bed's foot. I had to look twice before I recognized it as a polar bear's pelt. My gorge rose. I pushed it back down.

The tall French doors across the room were open, and the filmy white curtains fluttered on a sultry breeze. I heard the sound of falling rain, smelled oranges.

Out. Get out. Get out of here.

I made it halfway to the windows before he spoke.

"Impressive, Ms. Valentine. Lucifer's faith in you is well-placed, I expected another six hours before you came through that door. I hope your temper has calmed."

His voice was chill, high-pitched, and soaked with murderous Power. And then I smelled it—ice and blood, blind white maggots churning in a corpse, the smell that had soaked my nightmares for five long years.

I turned, my sword held ready. Blue fire ran along the blade, dripped on the floor. Gooseflesh roared over my body.

Get down, Doreen. Get down—

Game over.

He stood by the fireplace, one long hand on the back of the chair, the black teardrops over his eyes swallowing the pale marble light. He wore a white linen suit, cut loose and tropical on his thin demon's frame. His ears poked up through a frayed mat of dark hair, coming to sharp points. My hand shook, but the katana stayed steady. My spare knife slid out from its hidden sheath in my coat, reversed itself along my forearm.

"Santino," I whispered.

"The very same," he answered, bowing slightly. "And you, my beauty, are Danny Valentine. I knew I'd meet *you* again."

"I'm going to kill you," I whispered.

"Certainly you want to," he replied. "But I would like to talk to you first."

That was just strange enough to make me blink. *He's a demon, he's tricky, be careful.*

"Who are you?" I blurted. "Are you Sargon Corvin, or Santino Vardimal?"

He nodded. "Both. And more. Come with me, Dante. Let me show you what Lucifer doesn't want you to see."

"I don't trust you," I snapped. My rings sparked. *Why did he leave my sword and my gear in there with me, if he wanted to kill me?* It didn't make sense.

But I knew how he liked to play with his prey.

"I didn't think you would. However, I have not killed you. If I wanted to, I would have while you lay unconscious in the street and saved myself all this trouble. Surely you can afford to listen before you attempt my murder?" He shrugged, a demon's shrug.

I wish Japhrimel were here, I thought, and hastily shoved the thought away.

"You're being used, human," he said softly. "Come with me. I'll show you."

Without waiting for my answer, he turned his back on me and paced across the room.

Don't follow him, Danny. Take the window, however big the drop is from there you can take it, get out, get out, get AWAY—

I found myself following, advancing, keeping my sword ready. If he tried anything, I'd kill him or die trying. *Why did he leave me my blade?*

The house was massive, mostly floored in white marble, done hacienda style. It would have been beautiful if I hadn't been so terrified. He led me down stairs and through rooms furnished with pieces worth more than I made in a year—apparently Vardimal had done very well for himself.

Just like Jace.

He didn't seem to notice I was following him, but as we walked down a long hall with columns on one side and paintings I didn't look at on the other, he began to talk.

"Lucifer wants me destroyed because I outwitted him. He never could stand that. Yet he is himself the Prince of Lies. He may know that I've managed to do it, I've succeeded where so many others have failed."

"You're not making any sense," I said numbly.

He led me into another hall, this one sloping downward. "You're right. I should tell you from the beginning." A pair of doors in front of him; he twisted the knobs and flung them open. "A long time ago, when Lucifer had finished twisting the genes of humans to fit his plans, the sons of his kingdom looked upon the daughters of Men, and found them fair. They came to earth and lay with them, and in those days giants roamed the earth."

I'd heard this story before. Another hall spun under my feet. *Where are all his guards and everything?* I wondered. *And Lucas told me Jace is a Corvin's youngest son.*

"Are you telling me you've bred with human women?" I said, my boots whispering over the slick marble. I was beginning to feel sick and dizzy from the backlash of Power—and terror. I was following Santino through his own lair. Close enough to kill him. I was close enough to kill the thing that had killed Doreen.

Why hadn't I attacked him?

Something else is going on here, I thought. The premonition buzzed under my skin, the vision Japhrimel had interrupted. Would it have shown me this if he hadn't short-circuited it?

"Of course not. Yet you're far more intelligent than you're given credit for. Human women are some of the most pleasant ways to pass the time. Why do you think Lucifer took an interest in your species? But no, I have not fathered a child. Not in the way you think. "

He turned down another hall, this one lit by high-end fluorescents, most of them turned off so only a faint glow showed me the marble floor and tech-locked doors, each with a handprint lock. "Have you wondered why Lucifer granted me an immunity, Dante? Because I am a scientist first and a demon second. Long ago, I did the grunt work for Lucifer's remodeling of your species. Before demons could *play* with humans, humans had to be . . . well, helped along a little."

My gorge rose again. He talked about playing with humans as if it were slightly shameful, slightly loathsome, the way a Ludder would talk about going to a sexwitch House. Santino stopped in front of a blank, anonymous door, laid his hand on the printlock. Green light glowed, and the door shushed aside. "Come inside."

I followed him, the chill of climate control closing over my skin. It was a lab—fluorescent light flickered, computer screens glowed, and the temperature was about sixty-five degrees, shocking after the heat outside. Along one wall was something I'd seen before at the Hegemony psi clinics—a DNA map, twisting on a plasma screen, numbers and code running in the lower left corner. One whole wall was taken up with liquid-nitrogen–cooled racks of sample canisters behind glass, each neatly labeled. I had the sick feeling I would recognize the names on some of those labels. Each canister was a life, probably holding an internal organ, or a vial of blood—and a slice of human femur, with its rich big core of marrow. Just the thing for genetic research.

So many, I thought, the racks and rows of canisters

gleaming softly under the bright pitiless light. *So many deaths.*

Santino turned to face me again, and I lifted my sword. Blue light ran over the blade. He looked thoughtful, the black teardrops over his eyes holes of darkness. "I'm sterile, Dante," he said. "I couldn't breed with a human woman even if I wanted to. To breed, a demon has to be one of the Greater Flight of Hell—and he must also become one of the Fallen. I can't do that. So I escaped Hell and came here, in search of something very special."

My throat was dry. "You weren't taking trophies," I whispered. "You were taking *samples.*"

He beamed at me, razor teeth gleaming, his high-pointed ears wriggling slightly. "Correct!" he said, like a magisterial professor talking to a gifted but sometimes-terribly-slow student. "Samples. I felt sure that the key to the puzzle lay in psionics. Humanity exhibits some rather bizarre talents as a result of demon tinkering; if I could find a certain strain of genetic code I could reach my objective. I adopted several psionics and sponsored research in the Hegemony, but they move too *damnably* slow, even for humans. I decided to do the work myself, and for that I needed other samples. I was running out of time. I knew that the more time passed, the greater the chance Lucifer might decide to create another demon, and find the Egg missing." His fingers stroked the glass over the sample canisters, his claws making a slight *skree* against the smooth surface.

"What objective? And what *is* this Egg thing?" *Kill him*, my conscience screamed. *Revenge for Doreen, don't listen to him, KILL him!*

But if I was being used, I wanted to find out *why.*

Lucifer had told me none of this. *Japhrimel* had told me none of this. Which brought up the question of what they really wanted—what deeper game was being played here? I'd wondered why they had let him roam around earth for fifty years.

"Come." He led me through the lab, out another tech-locked door, and into a hallway that was more like a colonnade, an enclosed garden lying still and steamy under the Nuevo Rio rain, an assault after the climate control of the lab room. He turned to his left and I followed numbly, the door almost clipping my bootheels.

This garden was lit with a kind of orange glow—the light pollution from the city. He stopped at a techless door, this one white and etched with a strange design of an unearthly bird done in gold leaf. Santino turned to face me, and I shuffled back quickly, raising my blade. He laughed, a high-pitched giggle that echoed my nightmares and made my heart turn to dumb ice in my chest.

"We are an old and tired race, Dante, and our children are few and far between. Almost none are born without Lucifer's intervention, and he is *most* stingy in giving his help. To breed, a demon must go to the Prince as a supplicant." The black teardrops over his eyes somehow managed to convey the impression of a wide smile. "You want to kill me, Dante, because I took those precious human lives. But those lives were taken in service to a greater good—breaking the hold the Prince of Darkness has on your world and mine. I've finally done it, Dante. I've birthed a child that can challenge the Prince himself." He reached behind his back, twisted the doorknob, and backed into the room. "Come and see."

I followed him, cautiously. *Don't trust him, Dante! Kill him now! Kill him or run!*

It was a nursery. Slices of dim light fell through iron bars on the windows. Toys scattered across the hardwood floor, and plush rugs too. I saw a rocking horse, and a set of chairs around a table low enough for a little person. Wooden blocks lay scattered near a fireplace. And on the other side of the room, Santino stalked toward a low queen-sized bedstead wreathed in mosquito netting.

I followed, my boots occasionally kicking a small plush animal. *Dear gods,* I thought, *he has children here? What kind of kids are raised by a demon?*

"Lucifer rules because he is powerful," Santino whispered, his voice buzzing with secrecy. "But not only that—he rules because he is *Androgyne,* almost like a queen bee, capable of reproducing. It took me forty-five human years, but I finally found out how to birth another demon Androgyne. All it takes is the proper genetic material and engineering, Dante." He paused, maybe for effect. "Engineering by the scientist Lucifer used to create humanity in the first place—and material taken from a *sedayeen,* perhaps. A human psionic with the ability to heal, an almost-direct descendant of the *A'nankimel*— the demons that loved human women, and raised families with them eons ago. Until Lucifer, fearing the birth of an Androgyne on earth, destroyed them."

It made a twisted kind of sense. I approached the bed slowly, step by step. Needing to see.

"Demon genes don't lose their potency as human genes do," he whispered. "Witness the growth of human psychic powers, the fantastic blossoming of those powers during the Awakening—"

"Shut up." I sounded choked.

In the bed, under the smooth expensive sheet, was a pale-haired little girl about five years old sleeping the sleep of childhood innocence. Her long hair tangled over the pillow; I heard the faint whistle of her breathing. I tasted salt, and bitter ash. I knew that face—I had seen it before.

She lay on her back, one chubby arm upflung. Her forehead was odd, because there was a mark that glittered softly green on the smooth skin. My cheek started to burn. *An emerald. I wondered why Lucifer had one.* I could tell this emerald wasn't implanted—it was too smoothly and sheerly a part of her skin. Almost like a jeweled growth. It made me deeply, unsteadily sick to think that maybe my own emerald was an echo.

"There are two branches of human psionics that are almost directly descended from the *A'nankimel,* with the necessary recessive genes for my purposes. One branch is the *sedayeen,* who hold the mystery of Life. The other . . ." He paused again as I stared at the child on the bed.

The child that wore Doreen's young face.

"The other," Santino said, "is the Necromance."

"This is—" My voice was a dry husk. "This is why you—"

"This is why I took samples," he said softly, persuasively. "Who do you think rules both worlds, Dante? Who do you think is the king of all you survey? It's *him.* We are all his slaves. And I have the Egg, and the child that can topple him from his throne."

I swallowed, heard the dry click of my throat. "You killed her for *this*?" I rasped, and my eyes tore away from her sleeping face to Santino's grinning mask.

"Yes," he said. "I made a mistake, though. I shouldn't have killed her. I needed a human incubator, once I harvested the marrow and discovered she had all the requisite characteristics. It took all the cash and illegal gene-splicing that the Corvin Family could supply me with to bring this little one to pass. The human governments are too slow. But I did it. I found the shining path of genes that even Lucifer couldn't find with all his bloody tinkering. Now that I know *how*, I don't have to kill. All I need are female *sedayeen*—and Necromances—of certain Power, to blend with the codex in the Egg. I can make as many Androgynes as I want, capable of reproducing—"

"You killed her for *this*?" My voice rose. The child on the bed didn't stir. I heard her even breathing, slightly whistling through the nose. She slept like a human child, with deep complete trust.

"Think of it, Dante," he said. Softly, persuasively as Lucifer himself. "You can be the mother of a new race that will topple Lucifer from his throne. You'll be the new Madonna. Your every need—"

I backed up, kicking a small stuffed toy. "You killed her for *this*." I could say nothing else.

"What is one small human life compared to freedom, Dante?" He stepped forward. I raised my sword yet again. The blue glow from the blade intensified, and Santino flinched. It was only a small twitch, but I saw it.

A blessed blade will hurt him, at least, I thought. I heard Japhrimel's voice—*she believes.* Of course I believed—I *saw* the gods, I saw the Lord of Death up close. I had no choice but to believe. And that belief itself could be a weapon.

Maybe a blessed blade can even kill him, I thought.

"You didn't just kill Doreen. You slaughtered her while you laughed," I said. "You're no more a scientist than any other lunatic. You're just a different species of psycho, that's all." *There's a window behind me. Oh, gods. Oh dear gods.*

He waved his long elegant fingers, as if I were bothering him with trifles. Just like a fucking demon. "They were the mothers of the future, they died for a *reason*. Don't you understand? *Freedom*, Dante. For demon and human alike. No more Prince of Lies behind the scenes, everyone bowing and scraping to his whim—"

I was about to break for the window when the air pressure changed. Thunder boomed. The mark on my shoulder gave another screaming twinge.

Japhrimel. My heart leapt.

Santino's face twisted into a mask of rage. He lunged for me so quickly I barely saw him move. My sword jerked, blurring down as I threw myself sideways and back, toward the open window. His claws clanged off the blade. There was another shuddering impact, and I heard the unmistakable sound of Japhrimel's roar. The sound tore the air and left it bleeding. Santino snarled, whirling with balletic grace. He bolted for the bed and I scrambled forward, thinking of his claws and the little girl. I was too slow. Shock and the recent loss of Power and the swimming weakness dragged me down.

He scooped up an armful of bedding and the child's slight form, and his clawed hand came up. Metal flashed. The impact caught me high in the chest, the coughing roar of a projectile weapon splitting the air, my boots dragging along the floor in slow motion, my katana clanging on hardwood. I fell, my head cracking against something unforgiving—maybe one of the blocks.

How strange, I thought. *He shot me. Why did he shoot me? You'd think a demon would be more creative.*

I lay there, stunned, for what seemed like a long muffled eternity. Then I tried to roll onto my side. A bubble of something warm burst on my lips. I heard footsteps. Plasbolts. And Japhrimel's scream of agony. Pain bloomed in my chest, a hideous flower.

More footsteps. I tried to roll onto my side again. No dice. Just more pain. Bubbling on my lips—

—blood it's blood I'm dying, I'm dying—

"Oh, my God. Oh, God. He shot her, he *shot* her—" Jace's voice, high and breathless. "Goddammit, *do* something!"

A growled curse in a language I didn't know. But I knew the voice. A gigantic grinding shock against my chest.

"—leave me," Japhrimel snarled. "You will *not* leave me to wander the earth alone—*breathe*, damn you, breathe!"

Another shock, smashing through my bones. My left shoulder, torn from its socket, liquid fire in my veins. I gasped. Darkness tingled on the edges of my vision. I smelled flowers, and blood, and the musky smell of demon, drenching and absolute.

"You will not leave me," Japhrimel said. "You will *not*."

I tried to tell him to chase Santino, to kill him, to save the little girl—but before I could, Death chewed me with diamond teeth and swallowed me just as I hitched in breath to scream.

CHAPTER
37

A voice, reaching into the darkness.

I stood on the bridge, irresolute, my feet bare against cold stone. I felt the familiar chill creeping up my fingers, up my arms.

My emerald flashed as the souls fluttered past me, streaming over the bridge. The cocoon of light holding me safely on the bridge dimmed.

Why was I here? I wasn't pulling a soul back. Was I? I could not remember.

I looked at the other side of the bridge, the other side of the great Hall. The blue crystal walls rang softly, whispering a song I almost understood. I could feel it pressing in upon me, that great comprehension of Death's secret, the mother language from which all Necromance chants derived. The current of souls pushed at me, the emerald's light weakening, my cocoon of safety shrinking.

Yet that voice cajoled, pressed, demanded. I saw the god, His form shimmering between a slender Egyptian dog and some other form, a shape of darkness that seemed to run like ink on wet paper even as I looked at it.

My lips shaped the god's name, but the syllables

sounded alien. The crystal walls shuddered, and for a moment I saw stone, a great grim drafty stone hall, with a dour-faced King upon a throne at the far end. The throne was crusted with gems, glittering madly, and at the King's side sat a Queen with a face like springtime. I felt my mouth shaping alien words, desperation beating in my throat. I wanted so badly to understand the secret language, to feel the clasp of the god's arms around me as I laid my head on His chest and let the weight of living slip from me—

BOOM.

The sound startled me. It seemed to take forever for me to turn around. Before I could, the sound came again, as if a gong was being beaten, a brazen sound, pulling me back.

BOOM.

I struggled as if through syrup. I wanted to stay.

I wanted to stay dead.

BOOM.

One of the souls streaming past me halted, held up a pale hand. Formless as all souls were, a crystal drapery of unique energy, still it seemed I knew it, could put a face on it.

BOOM.

"Go back," it said. "Go back."

BOOM.

I opened my mouth to protest. Shimmering, the soul brushed my cheek.

BOOMBOOM.

"Go back," Doreen said. "Save my daughter. Go back."

BOOMBOOM. BOOMBOOM.

Then I understood it was not a gong or a brass bell. It was my heart, and I was called back to the world.

Dizziness. Cold seeping up my arms. Voices.

"Call her back!" Eddie, yelling, the bass in his voice rattling my bones.

My heartbeat thudded in my ears. To be forced back into a body was excruciating, even worse than being shot.

"Dante!" Japhrimel, howling.

"Danny! *Danny!*" Jace screaming at the same time. Cacophony. "Let me *go—*"

Scorching pressed against the side of my face. A hand.

Gabe's chant stopped, the last throbbing syllable shattering inside my head. I gasped a breath like knives. My chest hurt.

A great scalding wave of Power lashed me. I cried out, weakly, convulsing.

"Do not leave me," Japhrimel husked. "Do not leave me, Dante."

"Goddamn you, Eddie," Jace hissed, "let me *go* or I will *kill* you."

Light struck my eyes like a newborn's. I reacted the same way, screaming, raw from the lash of Japhrimel's Power and Gabe's Necromance. Japhrimel closed his arms around me and rested his chin on my head. I gasped, screamed again, muffled against his chest. The scream degenerated into sobbing. I cried because I had been wrong, and because I'd been right. I cried because the comfort of death was denied me. I cried because I had been dragged back into my weary body and shackled again.

And I cried in relief, clinging to Japhrimel the demon. He was solid and warm and *real*, and I did not want to let go.

CHAPTER
38

I was weak but lucid by the time we got back to Jace's mansion.

Eddie covered Jace with a plasgun most of the time. Gabe, paper-pale with exhaustion and bloody all over (most of it was mine), piloted the hover. I didn't ask where it had come from—if it was Jace's, it was all right, if it wasn't, I didn't want to know. All three of them—Gabe, Eddie, Jace—looked as if they had been through the grinder. Eddie's left arm hung limply by his side, Jace's face was covered in blood from a scalp wound and most of his shirt was torn off, stripes criss-crossing his torso. Gabe's clothes were tattered, filthy, smelling of smoke and blood and something suspiciously like offal.

Japhrimel carried me. His face was shuttered, closed, his eyes dark, a smear of my blood on one cheek. Santino had shot me in the chest. Otherwise, his dark coat was pristine. He occasionally stroked my cheek, sometimes glancing at Jace while he did so.

I didn't want to know. I had the uncomfortable feeling I'd find out soon enough.

I was too tired to think. My brain reeled drunkenly

from one thought to the next, no logic, nothing but shock.

The city lay under a pall of smoke. It looked as if a full-scale riot had gone down. I saw several craters, but the rain had intensified and was drowning the fires. The aroma of burning filled the air, even inside the hover. When we touched down at Jace's, it was a relief.

Inside, Gabe herded us all into a sitting room done in light blue and cream. Eddie shoved Jace down on a tasteful couch. *I hope he searched this room,* I thought, tiredly, *Jace could have a weapon stashed in here.*

I shivered. It would be a while before I took another Necromance job. If I went back to the borders of the land of Death too soon I would perhaps be unable to come back, training or no training.

"Okay," Gabe said, stalking across the room to a walnut highboy and tossing it open to reveal liquor bottles, "I need a motherfucking drink."

I cleared my throat. "Me, too," I said, the first words out of my mouth since leaving Santino's hideaway. "We need to move quickly," I said, as Japhrimel carried me to the couch facing Jace's. Instead of setting me down, he simply dropped gracefully down himself, still holding me. A little rearranging and I found myself in his lap, cuddled against him like a child.

A child. I shuddered at the thought. But it was comforting, his heat, and the smell of him.

Gabe groaned. "Give me a minute, Danny. I just found out one of my friends is a fucking traitor and yanked you out of Death's arms. At least let me have a bourbon in peace."

I cleared my throat. "Pour me one," I said, husky, my

voice almost refusing to obey me. "We've got big-time problems."

"I would never have guessed," Eddie growled. "You get into more fucking trouble, Valentine. That thing nearly burned down the entire goddamn city looking for you."

I barely had the courage to look up at Japhrimel's face. "You did that?" I asked.

He shrugged. "I had to find you," he said, simply.

I let it go. Instead, I started telling my story with the accompaniment of rain smacking the windows. Gabe knew me well enough not to interrupt, and Eddie watched Jace. Halfway through, Gabe handed me a glass of bourbon and settled down stiffly in a chair, her split lip and black eyes combining to turn her thoughtful expression into sadness. I downed the liquor, coughing as it burned the back of my throat, then continuing. By the time I got to the child sleeping in the bedroom, Japhrimel's eyes were incandescent. He had turned slowly to stone underneath me.

When I finished, Gabe drained the rest of her drink. Silence stretched through the room, broken by a low rattle of thunder.

Then she leapt to her feet and hurled her glass across the room, letting out a scream as sharp as a falcon's cry. The shattering glass didn't make me jump, but the scream came close.

She half-whirled, and pinned Jace with an accusing glare. "*Traitor!*" she hissed. "You *knew!*"

"I didn't know a goddamn thing—" he began. Eddie growled.

"Let him talk," I said, quietly, but with a note of

finality that cut across the Skinlin's rumbling. "And while he does that, Gabe, can you take a look at Eddie's arm?"

They all stared at me for a moment. Then Gabe moved stiffly to the hedgewitch and touched his shoulder. Some unspoken agreement seemed to pass between them, and Eddie's shoulders sagged just a little. More thunder crawled across the roof of the sky. I was so tired that for once it didn't hurt me to see Gabe press her lips to Eddie's forehead—but I did look away. I looked at Jace, who was paper-pale, the tic of rage flicking in his cheek.

"Talk fast," I told him. "Before I decide it was a bad idea to do that."

"I didn't know a goddamn thing," he said, harshly. Gabe started poking at Eddie's arm, and I felt the vibration of her Power start. She was doing a healing. I shuddered—every time she pulled on Power, it was like another astringent stripe against my abraded psyche. She had pulled me back from Death.

"Why didn't you tell me you were a blood Corvin?" I asked. *Are you part demon, Jace?* The question trembled on my lips. My skin crawled.

"I'm *not*," he said, sagging into the couch back. His hair was matted with blood and water. We were a sorry-looking group—except for Japhrimel, who was untouched except for the swipe of my blood on his cheek. "I was *adopted* by one of the Four Uncles—Sargon Corvin's adopted sons—because of my psi potential. That's what gets you into the Corvins—psi. I hated every goddamn minute of it, Danny. Once Deke Corvin died I made my escape and I ran as far as I could . . . and then I met you."

"You knew Sargon Corvin, the head of your fucking Mob Family, was Santino?" I asked, very clearly.

"No," he answered. "Gods, no. I swear on my staff, I had no idea. Nobody's seen Sargon for years except the older uncles—they give all the orders, supposedly from him. I thought the great Sargon was a motherfucking myth, Danny. Nobody was allowed into the Inner Complex—where we found you. That's where all the gene research went down, they were heavy into illegal augments and gene splices because it made money—that's what I knew. I didn't know. I thought Sargon was after you for revenge, since my street war with them killed all three of the surviving Uncles. They died hard, too. I've had my hands full while you were up in Saint City moping." He dropped his head back, leaning against the couch, and swallowed, his Adam's apple bobbing. "He would know that the only way to hurt me would be to kill you, Danny. That's why I left you, and why I insisted you stay here during this little hunt of yours."

"Why didn't you tell me you were a Corvin? You should have told me." I tried not to sound hurt and failed miserably. I was just too tired.

He laughed, dropping his chin to look at me. "Everyone knows how you feel about the Mob, baby. I never would have gotten past your front door."

"So you lied to me."

"I love you, Danny," he said, closing his eyes and tipping his head back onto the couch. Dark circles stood out all the way around his eyes. He was unshaven, gaunt. "I didn't have a *choice*. Not if I wanted to stay clean; if I'd told you who I was, you would have ditched me. I wanted to be clean for you. I was *out*, until you went on the Morrix job. They threatened to kill you. The only thing I could do was disappear and hope they would leave *you* alone." He sighed. "Sargon's been too busy to bother with you, I'd guess, while he perfected this fucking process of his and I slipped my chain and started giving him trouble. Until you came back and shoved yourself in his face again. I didn't *know*, Danny. If I had known, I would have killed him myself. Or tried to, at least. Why don't you ask your pet demon what he knows about all this?"

"Watch your mouth, *human*," Japhrimel said quietly, his tone completely cold. "Did the Prince know that Santino has gone so far as to create an Androgyne, he would have brought Hellesvront—Hell-on-Earth—to bear on this Corvin Family, and wiped them from existence. This affects him far more than it affects you."

Jace snorted and opened his mouth. "Shut up," I said. "Just shut up."

Japhrimel lifted his free hand and stroked my hair back from my face. "You should rest, Dante."

"What about the little girl?" I asked, craning my neck to look at his face. "Did you know Santino was trying to breed a new kind of demon?"

"Not a new kind of demon," Japhrimel said. "An extremely rare kind of demon. Lucifer is the Prime, the first Androgyne from whom all demons are descended— the younger Androgynes are either his vassals or his lovers. It is not a thing spoken of to humans."

I let out a long sigh. I was so damnably tired, my eyelids felt like lead. "So you knew. What does it mean, Japhrimel? I'm tired, and I died back there. I'm feeling kind of stupid, spell it out for me."

"The Egg is a sigil of the Prince's reign," Japhrimel said. "It holds the Prince's genetic codex and a portion of his Power—so much Power that he cannot leave Hell without it. Santino can access the genetic codex by virtue of his function as one of Lucifer's genetic scientists, but the Power locked inside the Egg is not his to use. If another Androgyne unlocks the Egg, the balance of power in Hell itself will shift. The Androgyne with the Egg will control Hell—and who will control the Androgyne?"

"Santino," I breathed. I believed it. I didn't need the canisters or the vision of the little girl with Doreen's face to convince me any more than I already was. Demons played with genetics the way they played with technology—some scientists said our own genes were proof of that. It was one of the greatest scientific mysteries, hotly disputed and contested by Magi and geneticists—could demons theoretically interbreed with humans? Only no demon had done so for thousands of years, if they ever had—if you could believe the old stories about demons marrying human women and giants roaming the earth.

I thought of the rows and rows of canisters and shuddered. Santino had figured out how to make another Lucifer, a Lucifer he could use for his own ends? A lovely little malleable, controllable genetic copy of Lucifer—using Doreen's genetic material in the process.

And now he wanted to use mine. Or maybe just my body as an "incubator." *You could be the new Madonna,* his voice whispered in my memory, soft and chillingly inhuman.

I shuddered. I had escaped being assigned as a breeder in Rigger Hall; I didn't want to be turned into one now for a crazed demon. And what about other *sedayeen* or Necromances, possibly kidnapped and forced to incubate more of the filthy little things?

I should have been angry. Japhrimel had omitted to tell me far more than Jace had, but I only felt a weary gratefulness that the demon was here—a gratefulness I didn't want to examine more closely. Silence stretched through the room. Eddie hissed a curse between his teeth, and Gabe murmured an apology, bandaging his arm.

"He's playing for control of Hell itself," the demon said quietly. "And if that happens, he will gain control of your world as well."

"He says it's for freedom," I answered. Exhaustion pulled at my arms and legs, wrapped my brain in cotton wool.

"Freedom for Vardimal, perhaps." Japhrimel shrugged. The movement made my head loll against his shoulder.

I closed my eyes. It was so hard to think with exhaustion weighing me down.

"So what now?" Gabe said.

"Now I get a couple hours of sleep, and I do what I should have done in the first place."

"And what is that?" Japhrimel didn't move, but his arms tightened slightly. If I hadn't been so tired, I might have thought about that.

Sleep was stalking me a little more gently than Death had. It was the expected reaction; most people fell into a deep sleep after being yanked back from death. It was the psyche's method of self-defense, trying to come to terms with brushing the Infinite. "I'm going to get up, and find my sword, and hunt the motherfucker down. Alone."

"Not alone," Gabe said. "We'll tie you up if we have to, Danny. Don't start that again."

I was about to tell her to back the fuck off when I passed out. The last thing I heard was Japhrimel's voice. "If I did not leave her at Death's door, I would not leave her now. I will take her to bed."

CHAPTER
39

I slept for twenty-eight hours.

Plenty of time for Santino to get away.

When I finally surfaced, it was to find myself tucked naked into a large dark-green bed. The climate control was on, so the room was cool, even though fierce early-morning sunlight stabbed through the windows. I blinked at the light, propping myself up on my elbows.

My entire body ached, the reverberation of the plasgun bolt and Power backlash. I'd pushed myself far beyond the limits of pain-free Power use. I would be lucky to escape a migraine in the next twenty-four hours.

My shoulder didn't ache, though. I touched the scarring of Japhrimel's mark and had to steel myself against a wave of painful nausea.

"I'm here," he said, and turned from the window. I hadn't seen him there, maybe dazzled by the sunlight. Maybe he hadn't wanted to be seen. "Rest, Dante."

"I can't rest," I said, tasting morning in my mouth. "Santino—"

"He's being tracked. You will not be helpful if you do not rest." He approached the bed silently, his black coat floating on the sunlight. "Events are moving, Dante. The

Prince, now that he knows what Santino was attempting, has placed the full resources of Hellesvront under my control. Every Hell-on-Earth agent is looking for Santino. He will not long escape our attention."

I sat up the rest of the way, gingerly, and rubbed at my eyes. "Unless he goes where there aren't any people," I said. "Human agents aren't any good if he stays out of sight like he's been doing for the past fifty years." And besides, he was *mine*. I'd started this hunt, I was going to finish it.

He shrugged. "Not all the agents are human. Vardimal is a scavenger, despite his contempt for humans. He needs people, hungers for them. Hellesvront will find him."

"What the hell are the demon police getting involved for? They can't *kill* him. I should know, I tried. Where are the others?" I asked, squinting up at him. I wanted to see his face, couldn't.

"The other Necromance and the earth-witch are sleeping. Your former lover is sealed in a spare room, but otherwise unharmed." Japhrimel's tone changed slightly. He sounded . . . disdainful. His eyes glowed with a light of their own. Backlit by the sun, he looked like a shadow with bright eyes. "I would speak with you of something else, Dante."

"If Vardimal's a scavenger, what does that make you?"

"I am of the Greater Flight, he is of the Lesser. I am not bound by his hungers." Japhrimel shrugged, but the movement wasn't as fluid as it usually was.

"Is that why you're the Devil's assassin?"

He bared his teeth in a facsimile of a pained grin. "I am the Prince's assassin because I am able to kill my brothers and sisters without qualm, Dante. And I am his assassin because he trusts me to do his bidding. I would speak to you of—"

I didn't want to know. "Is it true?" I asked him. "*Sedayeen* and Necromances—is it true?"

He was silent for a long time. Then, "It is true; *sedayeen* and Necromances do carry recessive genes closely related to demons. I would speak to you about—"

Gods. I'm human, I thought. *I'm not a demon. I know I'm human.* "Later," I said, and slid my feet out of the bed. The blessed warmth of the covers was matched only by the blessed coolness of the climate control. "Get the others. We've got work to do."

"You should eat something," he said, stepping back slightly. Retreating into the sunlight. "Please."

"I'll make you a deal." I gained my feet in a rush, too happy to be vertical to care if I was naked. Besides, he was a demon, he'd probably seen plenty of naked women before. "You get the others here by the time I get out of the shower, and I'll eat breakfast while we plan." I headed for the bathroom, heard his sharp intake of breath. "What?"

I stopped, looking over my shoulder. My knees were shaky, but I felt surprisingly good despite having been shot and dragged back from death.

"Your . . . scars." Japhrimel's voice was flat again.

"They don't hurt anymore," I lied. "It was a long time ago. Look, Japh—"

"Who? Who did that to you?" Now there was a tinge of something else in his voice. Was it anger?

It was my turn to shrug. "It was a long time ago, Japhrimel. The . . . the person who did that is dead. Get the others. I'll have breakfast while we plan." I forced myself to take another step toward the bathroom. Another. *That's what you get for walking around naked in front of a demon,* I thought, and managed to make it to the bathroom, flicked on the light, and shut the door behind me before I looked down at the other mass of claw scars on my belly. My ribs stood out, each one defined, my hipbones sticking out sharply. I'd lost weight.

I blew out a long whistling sigh between my teeth. My legs trembled. I looked up, meeting my own eyes in the mirror. I'd faced Santino again, and survived.

Miracles did happen.

"Maybe this job won't kill me," I whispered, and tore my eyes away from my gaunt face to go take a shower.

Gabe looked a lot better, especially with her long dark hair clean and pulled back. Eddie still favored one arm, but Gabe's healing charm had apparently sped his recovery—as well as hers. Her black eyes were now a yellow-green raccoon mask, and her split lip looked less angry.

Jace was unshaven and moving a little stiffly, but his eyes were clear. He lowered himself cautiously into the chair Japhrimel placed for him. Gabe didn't even spare him a look. Eddie, shaggy and direct as ever, stared at him for a full twenty seconds, lip lifting in a silent snarl.

I sat cross-legged on the bed. It felt good to be dressed in clean clothes, and felt even better to be clean myself, my hair damp from the shower and smelling like sandalwood. Japhrimel, expressionless, produced my katana. The sheath was lost, so I balanced naked metal across my knees. "Okay," I said, once we'd all settled in. "Breakfast is due up in a quarter-hour. Japhrimel's checked the staff here and says they're trustworthy. I'm going to start tracking Santino as soon as—"

"Wait a minute." Gabe held up her hand. "How in Hades are you going to find him without alerting him? He's got a day's head start, and he's a demon—Magi magick might find him, but if he's on his guard it might just put him in a snit. And we can't afford to have you come down with another case of backlash. There's a limit to the amount of abuse you can take, Danny—*despite* what you seem to think."

I held up my hand. "Gabe," I said with excessive patience, "we may not be able to track *him*, even with Dake's little toy. But he's got the kid. And the kid's at least half Doreen; I shared my mind and my bed with her. I can find the kid, we're bound by Doreen's blood. Where she is, Santino will be."

Gabe shrugged. She glanced at Jace, seemed about to say something, and stopped.

"What about this kid?" Eddie asked suddenly. "What the demons gonna do with her?"

I looked up at Japhrimel, who shrugged. His eyes darkened, more strange runic patterns slipping through their depths—but he looked down at the floor, as if avoiding my gaze. "The Prince will perhaps take her as a lover," he said, "or as a vassal. Androgynes are precious, and she is far too young to challenge his rule."

"Like hell," I said. "I'll take care of the kid. I owe it to Doreen. Lucifer didn't contract me to bring the kid back, he contracted me to kill Santino and return this Egg thing. He doesn't even need to know about the kid. You haven't told him, have you, Japhrimel?"

Please tell me I've guessed right and he hasn't told Lucifer about the kid.

Silence crawled through the room.

"You would ask me to lie to the Prince," Japhrimel

said, finally. He stood at the side of the bed, his head down, his eyes hidden, hands clasped behind his back. His coat rustled slightly; I wondered again why he wore it.

"You can't trust a demon, Danny," Jace piped up. I ignored him, watching Japhrimel. His reaction told me he'd kept his mouth shut. If he hadn't told Lucifer about the little girl, he had to have guessed I would ask him not to.

He finally tilted his head back up, his green eyes meeting mine for a long moment. It wasn't hard to hold his gaze anymore. "I have not . . . told Lucifer of the child, only that Vardimal was attempting to create an Androgyne. I did not think it wise, as Lucifer would perhaps seek a different means of effecting Santino's capture. That would endanger you, Dante." He paused, his eyes holding mine. *Here it comes,* I thought, amazed I'd been able to predict him for once. "However, to *lie* to the Prince after Santino is dead . . . I will do as you ask," he said, "but in return, I will ask a price."

I shrugged. "I expected as much." My throat went dry. "What price?"

"I will tell you when the time comes," he said. "It is nothing you cannot pay."

"Danny—" Jace sat bolt upright.

"Shut up, Jace," I said, my eyes fixed on the demon. "All right, Japhrimel. It's a deal. Gods grant I don't regret it."

"I would speak with you privately, Mistress," he said, formally, nodding slightly. That managed to hurt my feelings—so we were back to *Mistress*, were we?

You will not leave me to wander the earth alone. Had

he really said that, or had it been some kind of near-death hallucination?

I shook the thought away, hair sliding over my shoulders. "Soon enough. Gabe, I need you and Eddie at full strength. Do what you have to do to get there. We're hitting the trail soon as possible. Before twelve hours I need a work-up of every bit of munitions we can beg borrow or steal. *Everything*. Plasguns, assault rifles, projectile guns, explosives, everything. Eddie, I need as many *golem'ai* as you can make before we leave—and firestarters, too. You're the best Skinlin I know, and the mud-things will even the odds for us. Jace—" He flinched as I said his name, his shoulders hunching protectively. "Get yourself up to full strength and outfit us. We need transport, supplies, and passports into Mob Circle."

"Mob Circle?" Eddie actually sputtered. "Are you *crazy*?"

"We can't travel everywhere in the world just on a hunt," I said. "If Santino goes into any Freetowns, Mob Circle passports will give us some kind of protection and a place to sleep. Can you do that, Jace?"

He was paler than I'd ever seen him. "You'd trust me?" he asked, his blue eyes stuttering up to mine then sliding away, as if he couldn't stand to look at my face. "You'd trust me to do that?"

"I'm not going to *forgive* you," I told him. "I'm just going to overlook the fact that you took up a year and a half of my life with a complete lie. You do this for me, and we're even, your debt's paid. After this job, I never want to see your face again. If I see you after this is over, I'll fucking kill you—but if you help me take Santino down, I'll let you go your own way. Alive. All accounts balanced."

"Danny—" he began.

"You lied to me," I hissed. "Every time you touched me, it was a lie. And you didn't come clean when I came here, either—you *kept* lying to me. What, were you thinking I'd never find out?"

"You never would have—" he began.

"Well, we'll never know now, will we? I never had the chance." I shook my head, looking away to where the sheaf of sunlight fell into the green room, pure light glowing on every surface. It was nothing like the clear light of Death, but it was close enough that my heart twisted. The room was beautiful, clean, and made my entire body hurt. I wanted to be home, with Santino dead and the Devil's lies and little games out of my life. "Either you do this for me, or I'll kill you, Jace. It's that simple."

I don't know if it was my level tone or the way my face felt frozen, or maybe it was just the way my fingers touched the katana's hilt, but Jace believed me. He stared at the floor, his jaw working.

"Fine," he finally said. "If that's the way you want it, that's the way we'll play it."

"Good." I looked up at Japhrimel, who was wearing a faintly startled expression. "Japhrimel?"

He shrugged again, one of those faint, evocative movements. Nothing to add or subtract, and he wouldn't talk to me in front of them. Fine.

"Okay," I said. "That about covers it. Let's get moving."

Jace hitched himself up to his feet with a single measuring glance at Eddie. The Skinlin sat absolutely still, his eyes slitted, his hair tangling over his forehead. "I'll start working on passports and supplies," Jace said. "The staff will bring you breakfast, and whatever else you need."

I nodded.

He strode from the room without giving me a second glance.

Gabe whistled, shaking her head. "Are you crazy?" she said. "What if he's still working for Santino?"

"He's not. If he was, we'd all be dead." I sighed.

"You're letting him off easy," Eddie snarled.

I knew it. Ten years ago I might have gone after Jace just on principle. But I was just too tired. And the vision of all those canisters behind that glass shield, Santino's claws skritching against the glass, wouldn't go away. So much death, who was I to add to it? I was a Necromance. It was my job to bring people back. I was so tired of killing.

"Danny?" Eddie snapped his fingers to get my attention. "You're lettin' him off easy. You should fuck him up at the least, break a few bones. He—"

"Relax, Eddie," Gabe broke in, reaching out with her bare toes to rub his knee. "She knows what she's doing. The munitions aren't for a frontal assault on Santino, are they, sweets?"

"Of course not," I said. "They're for erasing whatever's left of the Corvins from the face of the earth. And Jace is going to do it himself. If he fails, we don't get any blowback, because Jace will be dead and his Family just another failed attempt at cutting out turf. If he succeeds, Santino doesn't have a Mob Family to do his dirty work, I'm free of the Corvin Family for good—and Jace will owe me a big-ass favor, since he'll be free too. *Really* free, not just street-war free."

"The *golem'ai* and the firestarters?" Eddie asked, comprehension dawning over his hairy face.

I suppressed a shudder. The *golem'ai*—semisentient mud creatures a Skinlin could create from organic matter and pure magick—made my skin crawl. "Those," I said, "are for Santino."

CHAPTER
40

*W*e had a nice, if hurried, breakfast; the thick Nuevo Rio coffee-with-chicory did a good deal to dispel the cobwebs and ease my pounding head. Japhrimel was oddly silent, watching me eat, occasionally walking to the window and gazing out, his hands clasped behind his back. I didn't want to know. His silence seemed to infect all of us. Maybe there was just nothing left to say. The maids who came to clear away breakfast were both pale, their hands trembling, stealing little glances at me out of the corners of their eyes.

I couldn't even work up enough steam to care. You'd think they'd be used to psions, working for a Shaman.

I finally sent Gabe and Eddie to do their work and yawned, looking down at my katana. Oddly enough, the blade didn't seem to be reacting to Japhrimel's presence—it should have been spitting glowing blue as it had every other time he'd touched it.

Then again, after dealing with Santino and almost dying there was precious little Power left in the steel. I'd have to recharge before I could make my blade burn again. It was a kind of torture—the longer we waited, the more prepared we were to kick Santino's ass, but the more time he had to dig himself into a bolthole it would cost us blood to crack.

The door shut behind Eddie, and Japhrimel turned on his heel, sunlight falling into the bottomless dark of his coat.

"Okay." I slid my feet off the bed and stood up, the katana whirling in an ellipse that ended up with the blade safely tucked behind my arm, the hilt loosely clasped in my hand and pointed downward. "You've been acting weird, even for a demon. What's up?"

He shook his head, light moving over the planes of his face. I took a closer look.

I'd thought he was plain, his face saturnine and almost ugly. I'd never noticed the exact arch of his eyebrows, his thin mouth half-quirked into a smile, or the high impossible arcs of his cheekbones. It was nothing to compare to Lucifer's beauty, of course . . . but he was actually kind of easy on the eyes. "Spit it out," I persisted. "You said you had something to discuss with me?" My bare feet curled against the hardwood floor, and I shivered. I was so used to the blanket of Nuevo Rio heat by now that the climate control was a little chilly.

Japhrimel took one step toward me. Then another. His eyes burned, seeming to make the sunlight on his face slightly green.

He approached slowly, his hands clasped behind his back, and finally ended up looming over me, less than a foot away. The musk smell of demon drenched me, his aura sliding over mine. I tilted my head back to look up into his face. "Well?"

He shook his head again. Then he unclasped his hands. His left hand came up, cupped my right shoulder, heat scorching through the material of my shirt. His eyes caught mine.

My heart gave a huge thudding leap. "Japhrimel?" I asked.

He slid his left hand down my right arm, and his fingers curled over mine. He took the katana's hilt from my hand, the sword chimed against the floor. I would have lunged for it, but his eyes held mine in a cage of emerald light. "Dante," he answered.

His voice was no longer the robotic, uninflected flatline it had been before. Instead, he sounded . . . husky, as if he had something caught in his throat. I blinked.

"Are you—" I began to ask him if he was all right, but his eyes flared and the words died in my throat. He didn't sound okay.

Then, the crowning absurdity—he slowly, so slowly, dropped down to his knees, his hand still holding mine. He wrapped his other arm around me and buried his face in my belly.

Nothing in my life had ever prepared me for this.

I stood rigid, uncertain. Then I lifted my free hand, and smoothed the rough inky silk of his hair. "Japhrimel." I said, again. "What—"

"I failed," he said, his breath blurring hot through my shirt to touch my skin. I barely understood him, his voice was so muffled; he pressed against me like a cat or a child. "I *failed* you."

"What are you *talking* about?" My own voice refused to work properly. Instead, I sounded like I had something lodged in my windpipe, strangling my words, making me breathless.

He looked up, his arm still pressing me forward. "I knew you were not dead," he said, his eyes blazing so brightly I almost expected to smell scorching in the air. "For I was not returned to Hell. Yet I did not know what Vardimal would do to you—keep you alive to torture you, or wait until I reached you before he killed you. I *did not know*, Dante. I failed to protect you, and you were taken."

"It's all right," I whispered. "Look, you couldn't know they'd paste me with a plasgun bolt. Even you can't out-run one of those. It's not your fault, Japhrimel."

"I found myself faced with a vision of an existence without you, Dante. It was . . . unpleasant." His lips peeled back from his teeth in a pained snarl that tried to be a smile.

You will not leave me to wander the earth alone. His voice traced a rough line through my memory.

I smoothed his hair. The inky darkness was silky, slightly coarse, slipping through my fingers. "Hey," I said. "Don't worry about it. It's all right now."

I sounded awkward even to myself. *He's a demon, Danny. What is he doing?*

"You will hate me, Dante. It cannot be avoided."

A jagged laugh snapped out of me. "I don't hate you," I admitted. *Great, Danny. He's too old for you. He's not even human.*

But he came for me, I protested.

Only because he's got a stake in this. He's playing with you, Danny. He's playing. Nobody could ever—

I don't care, I thought. *He doesn't look like he's play-ing. I don't care.* "But you're a—"

"You must know," he said. "I am no longer demon."

What? I stared at him, my fingers stopping, curling into his hair. "What the *hell* are you talking about?"

"I am no longer demon," he repeated, slowly, looking

up at me. He was queerly pale under the even golden tone of his skin. "I am Fallen. I am *A'nankimel.* I have set you as a seal upon my heart; I will not return to Hell." His arm tensed, and so did his fingers holding my right hand.

My mouth went dry. "Um," was my utterly profound response.

He waited, patient and expectant, staring up at my face.

I regained the power of speech in a spluttering rush. "You mean . . . what do you . . . I mean, I . . . um, why do you . . . ah. *What?*"

"I am yours," he said, slowly, as if spelling it out for an idiot.

"Why?" I could have kicked myself. *How do I get in these situations? I'm chasing one demon and I have another kneeling at my feet and oh my dear gods, what am I going to do?*

"Because you are the only being in eternity who has treated me as an equal," he said, his arm tightening a little more. My knees buckled slightly. "You have *trusted* me; you have even defended me to your precious friends. I have watched you, Dante, in daylight and in shadow, and I have found you fair."

"Um," I said again. "Japhrimel—"

"My price for silence to Lucifer is this: Do not send me from your side," he whispered, still watching my face. "When you have killed Santino, allow me to remain with you."

"Um," My brain seemed to be working through syrup. "Ah, well, you know, I can't have a demon hanging around."

"Why not?" he asked, logically enough. "You court

Death, Dante. You have found nothing to live for; you walk alone. I have seen your loneliness, and it gives me pain. Besides, it seems you are foolhardy enough to need me."

It occurred to me that I should protest about this, but it was hard to find an objection in the soup my brain had become. Common sense warned me to be cautious—after all, he was a demon, and demons *lied*. That was the first rule in Magi and Ceremonial training—beings that weren't human had nonhuman ideas about the strict truth of any situation. What was in it for him?

And yet . . . He had stood behind me when I faced Lucas Villalobos. He'd tried to follow me into Death. And he'd burned down damn near a third of Nuevo Rio looking for me.

But Lucifer has him by the balls, too, I thought.

"What about your freedom?" I finally asked him.

"When we win my freedom, it is mine to do with as I will," he said. "I will stay with you, Dante. As long as you allow it, and perhaps after."

I chewed on my bottom lip, thinking about it. I had no way of knowing if he was telling the truth. "Why now? Why tell me this *now*?"

"I told you there was a way," he said. "I wish to give you a part of my Power, Dante, and I must do it quickly, before I become more *A'nankimel* than I already am. It will bind me to your side and your world will become my domain. There is only a short time for me to bond with you before I fall into darkness and a mortal death." His arm loosened a little, but I couldn't have gotten away if I tried, because he rose to his feet, my right hand still trapped in his left. I had to tip my head back to look at him. My heart pounded and my palms slipped with sweat, and I had the lunatic idea that maybe I would start screaming, once I got my breath back. Something about his eyes was making it difficult to breathe.

"Oh," I said, and wished I hadn't, because he smiled. It was a gentle smile, and my entire body seemed to recognize it.

His free hand came up, cupped the side of my face. "Courage, *hedaira*," he said, softly, his breath touching my cheek. Then he leaned down, and his mouth met mine.

It's said by the Magi that demons invented the arts of love, and I was tempted to believe it. The kiss tore through me, lightning filling my veins, the smell of him invading me, making me drunk. Blood-warm, his darkness folded around me, and I shuddered, my hands coming up and clasping behind his neck. My entire body arched toward his, he tipped me over onto the bed. I didn't care.

He bit his lip, and the smoke and spice of demon blood filled my mouth. I gasped for air, swallowing, choking on the scorching-hot fluid, his Power wrapped around us both. I was too far gone to think, nothing but a welter of sensation, my throat burning, eyes closed, his hands tearing at my clothes, finding bare skin and burning me all the way down to the bone. I cried out twice, shaking and shuddering, wet with sweat, my heart exploding inside my chest. And when he drove his body into mine I nearly lost consciousness, screaming, thrashing away from pleasure so intense it was like the chill-sweet darkness of Death. It was like dying, being held in his arms while the Power tore through me, remade me, and finally drove me down deep into twilight. Again.

CHAPTER
41

*T*he soupy half-conscious daze lasted for a long time. I would surface for long enough to remember where I was—completely naked, in a demon's arms, lying in one of Jace Monroe's beds—and then my mind would shiver back into a kind of halfsleep. My entire body burned, changing. He held me when my bones crackled, shifting into new shapes; things moved under my skin, internal organs changing and moving, my heart pulsing lethargically. He murmured into my hair, his voice taking away the pain and bathing me in narcotic drowsiness.

It ended with a final flush of Power that coated my skin, sealing me away. I came back to myself with a rush.

Japhrimel lay next to me, my hair tangled over his face, my head pillowed on his shoulder. His fingers, no longer scorching-hot but merely warm, trailed up my back and I shuddered. "It's done," he whispered. For the first time, he sounded tired. Exhausted.

"It hurt," I said, childishly. That was the first shock— my voice wasn't my own anymore. Instead, it was deeper, full of a casual power that gave me gooseflesh.

Or would have given me gooseflesh, if my skin hadn't been so—

I looked at my hand. Instead of my usual paleness—a Necromance almost never went out in daylight unless forced to it—I found my hand covered with golden, poreless skin. My nails were still crimson and lacquered with molecule drip, I still wore my glittering rings, but that just made my hand look even more graceful and wicked. "Anubis," I breathed. "What did you—"

"I have shared my Power with you," he said. "There was pain, but it's over now. You share a demon's gifts, Dante, though you are not demon yourself. You will never be a demon."

A kind of dark screaming panic welled up from behind my breastbone. But I was too tired—or not precisely tired. I was numb. Too much had happened, one shock after another. I was too emotionally drained to react to anything right now—and that was dangerous. *Numb* meant *not thinking straight*, and thinking straight was the only thing that was going to keep me alive. "You did *what*?"

"You are still everything you were," he pointed out. "Now you are simply more. And Vardimal will not be able to kill you so easily."

"*Sekhmet sa'es—*" I pushed myself up, trying to untangle my body from his. A few moments of confusion ended up with me sitting, the sheet clutched to my chest, staring at him. Bare, hairless, golden chest, his collarbones standing out, and behind him, glaucous darkness lay on the bed. *So that's why he never takes it off*, I thought, and had to put my head down on my knees. *They're wings. Oh, my gods, they are wings*—I hyperventilated for what seemed like ages, Japhrimel's hand on my back, spread against my ribs. The heat from his touch comforted me, kept the gray fuzz of shock from blurring over my vision.

Finally the panic retreated. But it was a long time before I looked up and found that the room was going dark. "How long has it been?" I asked.

"Ten hours or so," he replied. "It takes a short while for the changes to—"

"I wish you hadn't done that," I said. "I wish you'd warned me."

"You would not have allowed it if I had," he pointed out. "And now you are safer, Dante."

"How safe?" I couldn't believe I was having this conversation with a naked demon. Then another more terrible thought struck me. "Am I still a Necromance?"

"Of course," he said. "Or at least, I presume so."

"You *presume* so?" Okay, so maybe I wasn't numb, just stunned. I stared at him, my breath coming fast and short. My heart pounded.

No, not numb. Stunned, and numb, and terrified.

"I presume so," he said. Dark circles ringed his green eyes. "I have never done this before."

"Oh, great," I mumbled, and looked down at the side of the bed. My clothes lay in a shredded heap. "Japhrimel—"

"You could thank me," he said, his eyebrows drawing together. "If you were a Magi—"

"I'm *not* a Magi," I interrupted. "I'm a Necromance. And I'm *human*."

"Not anymore," he said shortly, and levered himself up from the bed. "I told you, I will not allow you to be harmed. I swore on the waters of Lethe."

"Shut *up*." I bolted up from the bed, yanking the sheet

with me. It tore right down the middle. I stood there, looking at the long scrap of green cotton clenched in my hand. "Gods," I breathed, and then looked wildly around.

I found myself across the room, with no real idea of how I'd gotten there. As a matter of fact, I collided with the wall, and plaster puffed out in a cloud. *Faster than human*, one part of me thought with chilling calm. *I'm faster than human now. That will come in handy when I go after Santino.*

I untangled myself from the wall, shivering. Stared at my hands. My golden, perfect hands.

"Why?" I whispered. "Gods above, *why*?"

"I swore to protect you," he answered. "And I will not let you leave me behind, Dante. No one, demon or human, has treated me with any kindness—except you. And even your kindness has thorns. Still—"

I clapped my hands over my ears and bolted for the bathroom. Japhrimel watched this, expressionless.

The vision that confronted me in the bathroom mirror made my stomach revolve. *Or do I even have a stomach now?* I thought. I looked . . . different. My tattoo was still there, quiescent against my cheek, the emerald glittering slightly. But otherwise . . . my face wasn't my own. Golden skin stretched over a face I didn't recognize—but there were my dark eyes, now liquid and beautiful. I looked like a holovid model, sculpted cheekbones, a sinful mouth, winged eyebrows. I touched my face with one wondering fingertip, saw the beautiful woman in the mirror touch her exquisite cheekbone, trace her pretty lips.

I looked like a demon. There was only a ghost of the person I used to be left in my face. Japhrimel's mark remained on my left shoulder, but it was a decoration instead of a scar, etched into my newly perfect golden skin. And my hair, Japhrimel's inky black—but long, falling over my shoulders in choreographed strands.

My flat stomach, lightly ridged with muscle, showed no more marks from Santino's claws. I twisted around, pulling my hair up, and strained my neck to examine my back in the mirror. No ridged thick whip scars. I couldn't see my ass in the mirror, but I felt along the lower curve of my left buttock and found no scarring there either.

Gone. They were gone. All except Japhrimel's mark on my shoulder. I dropped my hair over my back, shuddering.

The disorientation made me grab at the counter. I tried not to do it too hard, but my nails drove into the tiles. My hair fell over my face, tangling, tempting. I still clutched the piece of green cotton sheet in my other fist.

"Anubis," I breathed out, and closed my eyes, shutting out the vision. I sank down to my knees, sick and shaking, banged my head softly against the cabinet under the countertop. My breath shivered out of me. "*Anubis et'her ka . . .*" The prayer shivered away from my lips, a more terrible fear rising out of my panic-darkened mind. What if the god no longer answered me? What if the emerald on my face went dark, what if the god no longer accepted my offerings?

I choked on a dark, silty howl that filled my throat. I felt the inked lines of my tattoo shift slightly, and tried to breathe. If I could breathe, if I could just *breathe*, I could find a quiet space inside myself and see if the god allowed me back.

Japhrimel gently freed my fingers from the tile. "Hush," he said, and knelt down. He took me in his arms. "Hush, Dante. Breathe. You must breathe. Shhh, hush, it is not so bad, you *must* breathe." He stroked my hair and kept whispering, soothingly, until my shallow gasps evened out and I could open my eyes. I clung to him, the material of his coat soft against my fingers.

Now that I knew what it was, it made me slightly sick to think about touching it. But he pressed his lips to my forehead, and the warmth of that touch slid through me, exploding like liquor behind my ribs. "You must be careful," he said. "You will damage yourself if you try hard enough. That will be unpleasant for both of us."

"I hate you," I whispered.

"That is only natural," he whispered back. "I am yours now, Dante. I am *A'nankimel*. I have Fallen."

"I hate you," I repeated. "Change me back. I don't want this. Change me *back*."

"I cannot." He stroked my hair. "You have a demon to hunt, Dante."

I couldn't help myself. I started to giggle. Then chuckle, then roar with panicked laughter.

You have a demon to hunt, Dante.

I was still laughing like an idiot when Gabe kicked the door to the bedroom in, Eddie right behind her.

CHAPTER
42

I crouched in the bathroom, a towel haphazardly wrapped around me. My throat burned from laughing until I screamed, and screaming until my voice broke.

Outside, raised voices. Japhrimel had driven them back into the room and stood guard, not allowing any of them to come near the bathroom.

Gabe: *I don't care what you think, that's Danny in there. You can't—*

Eddie: *Used to be Danny. That goddamn thing did something to her!*

Gabe: *What the fuck did you do? Answer me, or I'll—*

Japhrimel: *Injuring me, if it is possible at all, will harm her. You don't want that. I can calm her, if you leave. Leave now.*

Eddie: *Shoot the fucker, Gabe, shoot him!*

Japhrimel: *Shooting me might possibly harm her. And if she is harmed I will kill you both. This was the price I demanded of her, and she has paid. It is a private matter.*

Eddie: *Shoot the fucker, Gabe! Shoot him!*

Gabe: *Shut up* both *of you. Or I'll shoot you both. What the hell happened to Danny? What did you do to her? You'd better start talking.*

Long tense silence. Whine of an active, unholstered plasgun. Then another sound, footsteps. Drawing closer. Feet in boots, a familiar tread.

Japhrimel: *Don't, human. She is dangerous.*

Jace: *Fuck you.*

The door slid open, a slice of light spearing the darkness. I put my head on my knees, curling even more tightly into myself.

He didn't turn the light on. I smelled him, rank with dying cells. *Human*, a smell I had never noticed before. Would I smell it everywhere, this effluvia of decay? How did Japhrimel stand it? How could *I* stand it?

He didn't walk into the bathroom. Instead, he stood in the door for a moment, looking. Then he slowly bent his knees, knelt down, and crawled into the bathroom on all fours.

The darkness wasn't helping. Neither was the electric light that poured through the door. Nothing was helping. Nothing would ever help again.

He stopped just inside the door. I huddled against the antique iron bathtub, making a small breathless mewling sound. The sound wouldn't stop, no matter how hard I drove my sharp new teeth into my perfect new lips. My datband was blinking. It had to be reset—I didn't scan as human now. I scanned like a genesplice, like an aberration . . . like something *other*. He told me I wasn't a demon, I was *hedaira*—but what the fuck did that *mean*?

Jace eased himself to the side, sitting with his back against the wall. He sat for a few moments, and then, slowly, he reached up into his linen jacket and pulled out—of all things—a pack of cigarettes.

He never used to smoke, I wonder if he got those from

Gabe, I thought, and my breath hitched. The small wounded sound I was making quit, too.

"Mind if I smoke?" he said, quietly.

My breath sobbed in.

He lit up. The brief flare of the lighter seared my eyes. I huddled back even further, the soft helpless sound rising to my lips again. But he didn't do anything, just inhaled some synth hash smoke and blew it out. "It's a nasty fucking habit," he said, his tone pitched low and intimate. "But you've always got to have a pack, in case some petty thug you're trying to ease needs one. You know?"

I said nothing. Squeezed my eyes shut. Patterns of Power shifted in the darkness under my eyelids, patterns I had never seen before. Part of a demon's Power. Shaking at the edge of my control, straining to leap free.

He tapped the ash onto the tiled floor next to him. The tiles were dark-green, with lighter green ones scattered every fourth or fifth tile. It was pretty, and kind of soothing.

He took another drag. "I must have seen thousands of these in my time," he said. "Smoked a few, too. Have to take detox every six months, but it's worth it to see someone relax when you offer them a stick. You know they used to call these fags? Used to make them out of tobacco 'stead of synth hash. *Nicotiana.* Eddie still grows some of that shit."

My breathing eased out a little. His tone was so normal, so familiar. I opened my eyes, resting my cheek on my naked knees. Watching him.

He finished the smoke and ground it out on the floor. I heard low shuffling sounds out in the bedroom. Gabe's hiss, the slow static of Japhrimel's attention. Japhrimel was trembling, too, a fine thin tremor racing through his bones. I could feel it in my own body, the demon's need of me.

Like an addiction.

"I remember one time I was talking to this guy," Jace continued, lacing his fingers over his knee and leaning back into the wall, "and I had to find out what he knew. He was uncooperative . . . they'd already put him through the wringer by the time I got there. I took a look at the situation, and settled down in a chair. Then I offered him a cigarette. I had the information in five minutes. Useful things."

More silence. Jace tilted his head against the wall. I caught the gleam of his blue eyes.

"You remember that little slicboard shop we always used to get our boards tuned at? You still ride a Valkyrie?" He waited.

I was surprised to hear my own voice. "After jobs, sometimes." I sounded flat and bored. My breath hitched; my beautiful new voice was ruined and husky— but still lovely. It still made the broken glass on the floor shiver slightly; I felt Japhrimel listening intently.

"You always loved Valkyries," he said. "I think what you liked best about riding a board was the flying. The adrenaline. Made you feel alive, right?"

A tear trickled down my cheek, touched my knee.

So demon-things can cry, I thought. It was the first sane thought, and I grabbed it like a shipwreck survivor.

"I miss Saint City," he said. "That noodle shop on Pole Street with the fishtank on the far wall. And that hash den we used to drink at—the one with the great music."

My throat was raw. "It closed down," I whispered. "Two hookers ODed in a week. On T-laced Chill."

"Shit," he said easily. "Damn shame. They played RetroPhunk all the time. And Therm Condor."

"Ann Siobhan," I supplied finally, my voice shaking.

"The Drew Street Tech Boys," he said after a considering pause. "Audiovrax."

I seemed to be slogging through mud to think. "Blake's Infernals."

"Krewe's Control and the Hover Squad," he said.

"I hated them," I whispered.

"Did you?" Now he sounded surprised. "You never told me."

"You loved them." My voice caught on a hoarse sob.

"You bought me all eight discs," he said, scratching at his cheek. "Damn."

"I incinerated them," I admitted. "After you left."

"Oh." He paused. "I'm sorry, baby."

It sounded like he meant it.

"Why didn't you tell me?" I whispered, my voice raw.

"I was trying to protect you, Danny. If you'd known, you'd have come riding into Nuevo Rio with your sword out, to 'save' me. That goddamn honor complex of yours would have gotten you killed. Just like you're trying to get yourself killed avenging Doreen."

"I have to," I said. "I *have* to." I choked on the words. Rigger Hall had taught me how to be hard—but to be hard was no use without your honor. Honor was everything. And honor demanded I avenge Doreen, even if it killed me.

Even if it turns me into a genesplice aberration? I wondered, and my breath jagged out, a low moaning sob.

"I know," he answered, softly, intimately. "You can't

be anything else, Danny. I always liked that about you. Right out to your fingernails, you just can't be anything other than what you are."

"Look at what he did to me," I whispered.

"So what?" Jace said. "You're still *you*. Still my pretty Danny Valentine. And while you sit in here moaning about it, your prey is either getting away or digging into a hidey-hole." He shrugged, his shirt moving against the tiled wall and making a little whispering sound. "We need you to finish this hunt, Danny. Gabe needs her own revenge on the Saint City Slasher. Eddie needs Gabe happy. I need Sargon Corvin dead so I can start living again and maybe prove to you I ain't so bad. You're letting us down, Danny. Come on."

I shuddered. It should have been a transparent ploy, but it needled me. I *was* letting Gabe down—she'd dropped everything to come with me. And Eddie loved her. It must eat at him to see her unhappy.

A deep racking cough shook me. I wiped at my face with bladed hands—my hands weren't even my own anymore. But they would do what I asked them to do. I finally raised my head to find Jace watching me. He didn't look nervous, but the set of his shoulders told me he was tense.

"I need some clothes," I said huskily.

"You got it," Jace said. "Anything you need, baby."

CHAPTER
43

$\mathcal{G}$abe examined my face. "Hades," she breathed, then handed me my sword.

I took it, cautiously. But no blue fire bloomed on the blade, and it didn't hurt me.

I glanced at Japhrimel, who stood expressionless by the window. Darkness pressed against the glass, the sound of rain tapering off. I wondered if the city was still burning. "Blessed weapons won't react to you," he said quietly. "Ease your mind, Dante. Your blade is still your own."

I looked at the curved length of steel, closed my eyes, and thought of Santino. Opened my eyes.

Blue ran weakly along the slight curve of the blade. *Anubis*, I prayed, *I beg of You, answer me.* I let out a shaky breath. Felt my tattoo shift on my cheek, the emerald sparking. Relief burst inside me. It still worked. And if my blade was still blessed, I was still one of the god's own chosen.

"Well," Gabe said. She wore her long black police-issue coat, a plasgun holstered under her left arm. I couldn't see her sword. She put her fists on her hips. "Damn. Better than an augment, I guess."

It was her attempt at humor, and it failed miserably. I was still grateful for it, though. "And so cheap," I said, my own failed attempt at levity.

Silence stretched inside the wrecked bedroom, a thin humming silence. The bed was reduced to matchsticks and springs and strips of material, the chairs splintered. The curtains were torn, and there were a few impact-marks on the walls. I took this all in.

"Sorry about the room, Jace," I finally said, not meeting his eyes. My voice was indeed ruined, husky but still perfect. I sounded like a vidsex queen.

"It's okay." He leaned against the door to the hall. His staff leaned next to him, the bones moving uneasily in the charged air, clacking against each other. "I wanted to redo it anyway."

Eddie, his arms folded, hulked behind Gabe, stealing furtive looks at me and then at Japhrimel, who looked just as he always had—except for the dark rings around his glittering eyes. He looked tired and somehow more human than I'd ever seen him. I felt his unwavering attention, his back to the window but his entire body focused on me.

"Where are we at?" I asked, and didn't dare look Gabe in the eyes. I didn't think I could stand to meet her worried dark gaze.

She cleared her throat. "I've managed to get a nice stockpile of munitions. Eddie can have three *golem'ai* ready for Manifest in two days. And he's put together eighteen firestarters. Forty-eight hours, and we're as ready as we can be." She looked at Jace.

"I've got Mob Circle passports for all of us," he said quietly. "And my second is already handing out the weapons. We've declared war on the Corvins, they just

don't know it yet. Funny thing is, there aren't any of the
Inner Circle left in the city. They've vanished, probably
gone with Sarg—um, Santino. I've given the orders to
take out their holdings. As for us, we've got supplies,
and world-class transport. I'm ready to go whenever you
are."

"You're staying here," I said. "You've got to coordinate—"

"I'm going with you," Jace disagreed mildly. "If you
don't like it, tough. I've got my own score to settle with
Sargon Corvin. Or whoever the hell he is."

I looked at him, my fingers tightening on the hilt.
Gabe stepped back. Eddie slid his arms around her, and
they stood, watching me.

A kind of black fury welled up behind my breastbone.
I swallowed, looking down at my sword. Blue light glittered along the ringing blade. "Get me a map," I said, finally. "Let's see if I can track Doreen's blood. If I can't,
we still have Dake's tracker. We can hope Santino hasn't
set up countermeasures."

I felt rather than heard Gabe's sigh of relief. Jace nodded, took his staff, and left the room. Gabe followed,
pulling Eddie by the hand. The Skinlin sidled past me.
Gabe paused at the door.

"Danny?" she said.

"Hm?" I steeled myself, looking at the glitter of blue
fire along the steel. Power. The changes had settled into
me, and I felt the same humming force that lay over
Japhrimel flooding me. So much Power—I didn't even
need the city's well of energy now. My brain shuddered
away from the implications. *I could tear this whole damn
house apart.*

"You're still my friend," she said, firmly. "No matter what you are, you're still my friend."

Startled, I half-turned to look at the door, but she was gone, dragging Eddie after her.

That left me alone with Japhrimel.

He studied me across the burning air. Finally he moved slightly, clasping his hands behind his back. "I am not sorry," he said.

"Of course not," I said. "You're a demon."

"*A'nankimel.* Not demon. Fallen." His eyes did what his hands didn't, touched my face, roamed over me. "I will not give you up, Dante."

"I don't belong to you," I flared.

"No," he agreed. "You do not."

I swallowed dryly. "Why? Why did you do this?"

"If you were merely human, Vardimal might kill you." Japhrimel cocked his head to the side. "Now you are neither human nor demon. *Neither man nor demon may kill him*, that was the immunity given to him by the Prince in return for his services."

That brought up another question. "What's Lucifer going to think of this?"

For a long moment, Japhrimel examined me. Then one corner of his mouth quirked slightly up. The slight smile made my heart pound. "Ask me if I care."

"Do you care?" My breath caught on the last word.

"No."

Well, that about summed everything up. Except one thing.

I stepped around a pile of splinters that had once been a chair. Approached him cautiously, my boots grinding against the plaster dust and small bits of wreckage on the floor. I held my katana to the side and stopped less than a foot from him, close enough to feel the heat radiating from him. His eyes held mine, but he didn't move.

"Did you mean any of it?" I asked him. "What you said?"

He nodded. "Of course, Dante. Every word."

His eyes glittered feverishly, and a faint, almost-human flush crept up his cheeks.

I believed him. Gods help me, but I believed him.

"You're going to have to tell me what all this means and what exactly I am now," I said finally. "After I kill Santino." *There's a whole lot about my life that I'm going to sort out once that motherfucker's dead.* The thought was welcome—it sounded like me. At least I sounded like myself inside my own head.

"When he is dead, I will explain everything," Japhrimel agreed. "My apologies, Dante. But I am not sorry."

I licked my dry lips. "Neither am I," I said harshly. He deserved the truth. "I . . . I just . . . it's a shock, that's all." It took more courage than I thought it would, but I reached up and rested my fingertips on his cheek. "I never thought I'd even *consider* dating a demon." I was still searching for levity and failing miserably.

His shoulders sagged. He closed his eyes, leaning into my touch. We stood there for a few moments before I took my hand away, and his green gaze met mine. His eyes seemed strangely dark now.

"Now come on," I said. "We've got a demon to kill, and the Egg to get back, and Doreen's little girl to save. We'll do some planning."

CHAPTER
44

*T*hey ate dinner in the ornate dining room while I examined the map and checked my gear. I'd lost my scabbard, but Jace had an antique katana hanging on his study wall, so I took its scabbard. It was better than nothing.

We weren't anywhere near ready yet, but I felt a whole lot better about the deal.

I settled cross-legged in front of the fireplace, the chill of climate control playing over my face, staring at the map. It unrolled in front of me, Hegemony territories in blue, Freetowns in red, Putchkin in purple, and the wastelands where nobody lived in white. There was precious little white—mostly around the poles and one spot in Hegemony territory, the Vegas Waste where the first and only nuclear bomb of the Seventy Day War had dropped.

Why do all these rooms have fireplaces? I thought. *It's Nuevo Rio, it never gets cold here.*

Gabe and Eddie held a fierce whispered conference, silverware clinking against plates. Jace said nothing, staring at his plate as if it held the secrets of the universe. Japhrimel stood by the French doors leading out into the

courtyard-garden, slim and dark and utterly impenetrable.

I held my hand over the map, trying to feel anything.
Nothing. Nothing at all.

I sighed. Then I drew one of my main knives out of
my coat.

Silence fell.

I set the blade against my hand.

"Dante?" Japhrimel's tone was cool, but the snarl
below his voice warned me.

"Calm down," I said. "Easy. Blood's what I'm tracking, let me work."

He said nothing else, but I felt the weight of his eyes
on me.

I drew the blade against my palm, willing the blood to
come out. The new golden skin was a lot tougher than
human skin; I almost had to force my flesh open. A thin
line of smoky-black blood welled up.

My breath hissed out between my teeth. The slash
began to close almost immediately.

I closed my eyes and my hand, slippery hot blood
burning in my palm. Held my hand over the map.

"Doreen," I whispered. *Doreen.*

I had found her while on the Brewster job, the one that
had made my reputation as a hunter, not just a Necromance. I'd taken the contract and tracked down Michael
Brewster, psychopath and serial killer; brought him back
from the Freetowns to the Hegemony justice system, getting shot at, knifed, almost gang-raped by a Circle of
Magi, and nearly burned alive in the process. It had been
Doreen's distraction at the warehouse that had bought
me enough time to escape the Magi and go to ground,
and I'd hunted Brewster down with increasing panic

after that. The day after he was processed into lockdown, I flew back on the red-eye hover transport and sprung her from that whorehouse in Old Singapore, using most of the bounty credit to pay off her tag fee and threatening the pimp into letting her go.

She'd been in bad shape. I guess that when the rogue Circle couldn't have me, they went for her. One psion almost as good as another, and a *sedayeen* couldn't even fight back like I would have. Might have, if I hadn't been spell-tied and chained.

Who was I kidding? I knew I wouldn't have been able to escape that without her help. Leaving her there was a shoddy fucking way to repay her for that, but I'd had no *choice*.

It had taken a long time for either of us to get any real sleep after I brought her to Saint City—she would scream in the dark for months, nightmares torturing her until I woke her up. My bare skin on hers, her mouth meeting mine, our hair tangled together in the safety of my bed.

You saved my life, she would often say, *I owe you, Danny.*

And I'd always reply, *You saved mine too, Reena.* I wouldn't have survived that job without her. Or the years that followed, while I learned how to work the mercenary field and started tracking down criminals. The house I bought with the bounties became *our* house: she had always wanted a garden and after Rigger Hall I had wanted a space all my own. As a Necromance I needed space and quiet, the house was the only piece of Doreen I had left.

And Doreen had given me the greatest gift of all: she had taught me how to *live* again.

Her pale hair, cut short and sleek; her dark-blue eyes. She'd worked in a Free Clinic in the Tank District and also patched up mercenaries and psis when they played too rough. Quiet and serene, her mouth always tilted into a smile, her eyes always merry. The Saint City psionic population closed around her like a protective wall. Psionic healers—*sedayeen*—were pacifists to a fault, they couldn't stand to hurt anyone. The pain they inflicted would rebound on them. They were helpless. So we all watched out for her—but it had done no good.

The flowers, blue flowers. I knew now that they were Santino's gift to the "mothers of the future," but back then, all I had known was the threat to Doreen's life.

And Gabe had been the only cop who believed me about the danger Doreen was in.

I had moved Doreen from safehouse to safehouse, but the flowers always found her. Gabe and I had taken turns standing guard, frantically trying to dig up the murderer who seemed intent on stalking her. Once we blew his human cover—once we knew it was Modeus Santino we were looking for and his company was seized—he went underground, and we had a week of breathing room before the flowers showed up again and the last desperate endgame started. Always one bare step ahead, moving her around, hiding first in one part of the city, then another—

—and Santino had probably known all the time, I realized. Had probably simply played cat-and-mouse with us, allowing us to spirit her away, drawing out the final coup, finally moving in for the kill—his "samples"—in that warehouse. Gabe had been called away on another case, Eddie had gone for supplies, and it was only me and Doreen, hiding in a shattered hulk of a pre-Hegemony building.

Slippery blood in my palm. I felt the Power take shape.

My cheek ignited, the emerald singing a faint thin crystal note. I *reached* into that place I had not touched since her death, the place inside me where her gentle presence had gone.

—Slight sound, scraping, a high thin giggle in the dark. Doreen whirled, her pale hair ruffling out. I leapt to my feet, sword ringing free of the sheath, spitting blue fire. I shoved her and she fell, scraping both palms and crying out thinly. Rumbling sound—the freight hovers, rushing past the warehouse; here in the shattered part of town they ran a lot closer to the ground.

Explosions. No—projectile fire. And the whine of plasbolts. I tracked the sounds—one gunman, firing at us both. No—Doreen was trying to get up, but he was firing at me, he wanted her alive. I pushed her toward the exit.

"*Get down, Doreen. Get down!*"

Crash of thunder. Moving, desperately, scrabbling . . . fingers scraping against the concrete, rolling to my feet, dodging the whine of bullets and plasbolts. Skidding to a stop just as he rose out of the dark, the razor and his claws glittering in one hand, his little black bag in the other.

"*Game over,*" *he giggled, and the awful tearing in my side turned to a burning numbness as he slashed; I threw myself backward, not fast enough, not fast enough.*

"*Danny!*" *Doreen's despairing scream.*

"*Get out!*" *I screamed, but she was coming back, hands glowing blue-white, still trying to heal.*

Trying to reach me, to heal me, the link between us resonating with my pain and her burning hands—

Made it to my feet, screaming at her to get the fuck out, Santino's claws whooshing again as he tore into me, one claw sticking on a rib, my sword ringing as I slashed at him, too slow, I was too slow.

Falling again. Something rising in me—a cold agonizing chill. Doreen's hands clamped against my arm. Warm exploding wetness. So much blood. So much.

Her Power roared through me, and I felt the spark of life in her dim. She held on, grimly, as Santino made little snuffling, chortling sounds of glee. The whine of a lasecutter as he took part of her femur, the slight pumping sound of the bloodvac. Blood dripped in my eyes, splattered against my cheek. Sirens—Doreen's death would register on her datband, and aid hovers would be dispatched. Too late though. Too late for both of us.

I passed out, hearing the wet smacking sounds as Santino took what he wanted, giggling that high-pitched strange chortle of his. His face burned itself into my memory—black teardrops over the eyes, pointed ears, the sharp ivory fangs. Not human, I thought, *he can't be human, Doreen, Doreen, get away, run, run—*

Her soul, carried like a candle down a long dark hall, guttering. Guttering. Spark shrinking into infinity. I was a Necromance, but I couldn't stop her rushing into Death's arms . . .

I came back to myself with a jolt. Tears slicked my cheeks. Japhrimel knelt on the other side of the map, his fingers clamped around my wrist. My finger rested on the map, far south of Nuevo Rio, in the middle of a field of white and the paler non-Hegemony blue of ocean.

An island in the middle of a cold sea. Almost in

Antarctica. The last place anyone would look for a demon.

"That's where he is," I said, husky, my voice making the map flutter against the floor, held down by my finger. "Right there."

Japhrimel nodded. "Then that is where we will go," he said. "Dante?"

"I'm fine," I said, wiping at my cheeks with my free hand. "Let go."

He did, one finger at a time. I looked over at the table.

Gabe's fork paused in midair. She watched me, her pretty face pale, her emerald flashing as the tat shifted against her cheek. Eddie stood, his chair flat on the floor as if he'd tipped it over. Jace had pushed his plate away and was staring at me, blue eyes wide, fever spots of color high in each pale cheek.

"Finish your dinner," I said. I sounded like Japhrimel, the same flat voice, loaded with a full-scale plasgun charge of Power. "Then get some rest. We've got work to do soon."

CHAPTER
45

$\mathcal{T}$he house slept.

Gabe and Eddie were asleep, and Jace had finally stumbled off to bed, rubbing his eyes. They would need their rest.

I didn't want to sleep. Instead, I walked slowly through the empty halls of Jace's mansion, my footsteps echoing. I didn't know where I was headed until the front door loomed up ahead of me, and I put my hand flat against it. The Power contained in Jace's walls resonated, slightly uneasy, and I calmed it as I would a rattling slicboard.

"Where would you go?" Japhrimel asked in my ear, appearing out of the darkness with only a sigh.

I shrugged. "I'm not going anywhere, I just need some air."

"And?" His voice was calm, almost excessively calm.

I didn't answer. Twisted the doorknob, let myself out into the night.

Outside, the plaza in front of Jace's house stretched away, expanses of white marble. The edges dropped down, sheer rock, until the suburbs of Nuevo Rio splashed against the cliff. He'd chosen this place for security, I guessed, and metaphorical height.

Japhrimel closed the door behind me. I paced out onto the flat white expanse, glancing up at the sky. Clouds scudded in front of a quarter-moon, I had no trouble seeing. Demon sight was far better than human eyes. I could see every tiny crack in the marble, every pebble and dust mote, if I looked for it.

Japhrimel, silent, halted at the bottom of the steps leading to Jace's front door.

"So what am I?" I asked finally. The stink of human Nuevo Rio, the sharp tang of Power, vied with the night wind and the persistent smoky fragrance of demon. "What *exactly* am I?"

"Hedaira," he replied, his voice weaving into the night. "I am Fallen, Dante. And I have shared my Power with you."

"That tells me a lot," I said, my hand tightening on my swordhilt.

"Why don't you ask what you truly wish to ask me, Dante?" He still sounded tired. And forlorn.

"Can I kill you?" I asked, in a rush of breath.

"Perhaps."

"What happens to you if Santino kills me?"

"He will not." Stone rang softly underfoot as Japhrimel's voice stroked it. His voice was almost physical now, caressing my skin as nothing else ever had. It reminded me of the barbed-wire pleasure, so intense it was agony, of his body on mine.

I turned back, saw him with his hands clasped behind his back. His eyes gleamed faintly green. The darkness of his winged coat blended with the darkness of night, a blot on the white stone. "That's not an answer, Tierce Japhrimel."

Saying his name made the air shiver between us. He tensed.

My thumb slid over the katana's guard. His dark eyes flicked down, then back up, a glitter showing on their surface from the moon. The pale crescent slid behind clouds again, and he went back to being a shadow. If I concentrated, I could see his face, decipher his expression. "You do not want to question me," he said. "You want to fight."

"It's what I'm good at," I said, wishing he hadn't guessed.

"Why must it always be a contest, with you?" I could see he was smiling, and that managed to infuriate me.

"Why don't you carry a sword?" I avoided the question.

"I have no need of one." He shrugged. "Would you like me to prove it?"

"If you can beat me, Santino will—"

"Santino preys on *humans*," he said. "He is a scavenger. I was the Prince of Hell's Right Hand, Dante."

"What did you prey on?" I tried to sound rude, only managed to sound breathless.

"Other demons. I have killed more of the Greater Flight of Hell than you can imagine." His lips peeled back from his teeth, one of those murderous slow grins.

I tried to feel afraid. Every other time he'd grinned like that my skin had gone cold with terror. Not now. Now my breath caught, remembering his mouth on mine. Remembering his hands on my naked skin.

I almost drew my katana, five inches or so of bright steel peeking out. No blue glow.

He still smiled, watching me.

"Did you plan this? Or did Lucifer?" I swallowed, wishing for my normal human terror with a vengeance that surprised me. I never thought my own fearlessness would be so scary; I'd lived with comfortable fear for so long.

"Lucifer did not plan this, Dante; he will be exceedingly displeased. No demon *plans* to Fall. To become *A'nankimel* is to give up much of the power and glory of Hell." He shrugged again, his hands still clasped behind his back.

"You can't go back?" I asked. "What about . . . what about being free?"

He shook his head. "There are other kinds of freedom. My fate is bound to yours, Dante. I am bound to finish the Prince's will in this matter, and then . . . we shall see, you and I, what compromise we can reach."

I closed my eyes.

You're so sharp and prickly, aren't you? So tough. Someday you're going to find someone you can't bamboozle, Danny, Doreen's voice echoed through my memory. *Someone's going to find out what a soft touch you are, and what are you going to do then?*

I'm not soft, I had replied, and changed the subject. And Doreen had giggled, her fingertips sliding over my hip, a soft forgiving touch.

I'd met Jace at the party we threw to christen the house, and he started coming around after Doreen died, doing repairs, showing up once or twice while I was on a job to watch my back, and going out on a limb for me during the Freemen-Tarks bounty, the one that had given me the worst case of nerves from a bounty ever. I still had nightmares about being trapped in the rain, Tarks beating me with a crowbar until Jace appeared out of nowhere and took him down. Even when Jace had started to actively court me I'd kept him at arm's length. Everything had to be a fight between us, and he seemed to enjoy the battles as much as I did, exchanging sharp word for sharp word, finally a sparring partner I didn't have to hold back and be careful of.

I opened my eyes, looked down at my blade, peeking out between hilt and scabbard. Slid the blade home. It clicked back into the sheath, useless. What was I going to do, try to kill him because he'd made me stronger? If Santino couldn't kill me now, if I was quicker and tougher because of what Japhrimel had done . . .

I didn't realize I was walking toward him until he moved down off the bottom step, opening his arms, enclosing me in the warmth of a demon's embrace. I sighed, my shoulders dropping, the weight of uncertainty slipping away. In his arms, I could breathe. As if he carried around the only sphere of usable air on the planet.

He kissed my forehead, gently. Fire sparked through my veins, recognizing the touch. "If you wish to fight me, Dante, fight me." His lips moved against my new skin. "If it will ease you, I will play that game. Or we can devise new ones."

I hadn't thought it possible that a demon could seduce me. But seduction was what demons did. Cajoling, enticing, fascinating, tempting—they made it into sport, and had a long time to practice.

He kissed my cheek, the corner of my mouth; I tipped my head back, a small pleading sound escaping me, and his mouth met mine. This kiss wasn't like the first—it was gentler. Softer. A sharp, greedy demon I could fight.

Japhrimel, gentle, sharing his mouth with me as if he was human, and mine—I had no defense against that.

Japhrimel led me through Jace's house, his warm fingers in mine. I cried without a sound, tears sliding down my cheeks as he closed the door of yet another bedroom behind us. He wiped away the tears, tenderly, and I forgot to weep as he told me silently everything I had always wanted to hear.

CHAPTER
46

*I*t's a ten-hour hover flight," Jace said. "You said we needed something that could go over water."

I eyed the freight hover, tucking a stray strand of hair behind my ear. It looked like a garbage scow, dirty and blunt-nosed. Her name—*Baby*—was permasprayed on her hull in pink. "Any particular reason why you chose this piece of trash?"

"Watch." Jace lifted his wrist and tapped his datband. He was grinning, an expression he usually reserved for when he'd won a card game

The hover—almost as big as a freight transport—vanished. My jaw dropped. I saw the marble plaza, the smoke drifting up from Nuevo Rio in the background, hover traffic beginning to slide through the city once more—but no garbage scow.

I lifted my own datband and scanned. Then I dug in my bag and extracted my datpilot, scanned again. I thinned my shields and tried to find any electromagnetic disturbance.

Nothing. If I hadn't watched it vanish, I would never have guessed.

"Gods above and below," I said. "How did you—"

"Hegemony military tech and a little extra," he replied, his golden hair shimmering in the reflected light from the vast marble courtyard. "I've got a great Tech guy, and your demon's been pretty useful. Invisible to radar, deepscan, magscan, and psi. It's faster than it looks, too. And it's combat-equipped, fore-and-aft plas-cannons—"

"Yeah, but does it have that new-hover smell?" Eddie snorted. He handed me a small plas package full of six gray crystalline nubbins, each as big as my thumb. "Firestarters. Be careful, okay?" But his eyes didn't quite meet mine. I didn't blame him. I had trouble looking in the mirror, and I was living inside this new body.

Gabe shrugged, her coat settling against her shoulders. "I've got the map," she said. "Let's get this show on the road, huh?"

"One second." Jace pressed his datband again, and the hover reappeared. "She only looks ugly, guys. She's got a heart of gold." He produced his chromium hip flask.

An ash-smelling wind touched my hair. Nuevo Rio had stopped burning, but it would be racked with gunfire again as soon as Jace's lieutenants moved out into the city. Hours of frantic planning had narrowed down to this: if his network succeeded, Jace would take over all the Corvin Family's assets in Nuevo Rio and probably elsewhere in the Hegemony. It was the accepted method for a Family to start out, in murder and fire after all the legal paperwork of incorporation was done. And we hoped it would distract Santino—he was arrogant enough to think that if we were attacking the Corvin Family, we weren't going after him, right?

Wrong, I thought.

Jace unscrewed the flask, took a swig. Rolled it

around in his mouth. Tossed it back. "We who are about to die, salute you," he said. Handed the flask to Gabe, who glanced at me.

"A sort of ritual," I said. "Every time we started a job, we would take a slug and give a quote. Good luck."

She shrugged, took a hit, and coughed, her cheeks flushing pink. "Let the gods sort them out," she said, and grimaced. "Hades love me, that's foul."

Eddie took the flask, took a long swallow. "*Fortis fortunam iudavat,*" he growled. Coughed slightly, blinking watering eyes. "God*dam*mit, Jace, what *is* that?"

"Jungle juice," Jace replied. He was smiling, and his eyes glittered madly. Fey.

Eddie handed me the flask. If it was a gesture, it was a good one. I tipped it into my mouth, a long swallow, felt it burn fiercely all the way down. I coughed, my eyes watering. "*Go tell the Spartans, passers-by; That here, obedient to their orders, we lie.*" It was just as awful as every other time I'd tasted it. I gave the flask back to Jace, who watched me for a moment. Had he been watching the flask meet my mouth, the way my throat moved as I swallowed? Maybe.

Then he passed it over my shoulder to Japhrimel, who stood dark and silent as ever. "Take a swig and give a quote," Jace said. "You're one of us."

I don't know what it cost Jace to say that, but I was grateful. I bit my lip, sinking my teeth in, but nobody looked at me.

"I suppose he is," Gabe chimed in. "He saved Danny's life."

"And got her involved in this in the first place," Eddie snorted. She elbowed him, her emerald glittering in the late-morning sunlight. The afternoon storm was just beginning to gather on the horizon, a dark smudge. I could smell approaching rain and nervous peppery adrenaline from them all. Except Japhrimel.

Japhrimel took the flask, lifted it to his mouth. A single swallow. His eyes dimmed slightly. *"A'tai, hetairae A'nankimel'iin. Diriin."* He handed the flask back to Jace. "My thanks."

"Don't mention it." Jace tipped the flask, poured a smoking dollop out onto the marble, and then capped it deftly. "Well, if we're going to make a suicide run, let's get on with it."

"Let's hope it's not suicide," Gabe said dryly. "I've got property taxes. I can't afford to die."

CHAPTER
47

I watched out the window as the dark nighttime ocean slid away underneath us. Japhrimel leaned against the hull on the other side of my window, looking out as well. The hold was fitted with utilitarian seats, the entire back section filled with crated supplies. I hoped we didn't need everything we had brought—we could hunt Santino for months on what we'd packed. If I had to spend months doing this I *would* probably go crazy.

Gabe, strapped into the captain's chair, piloted us with a deft touch. Eddie paced down the length of the hover's interior, silently snarling, whirled on his heel, paced back, stared out the front bubble, then whirled back and repeated the whole process. He was readying the *golem'ai* to be released. They were a Skinlin's worst weapon, the mud-things. I felt a small shiver trace up my spine.

Jace leaned back in his chair, his eyes shut. It was his usual prejob ritual, to sit quiet and still, maybe going over the plan in his head, maybe praying, maybe silently chanting to a *loa*. The thorn-twisted tattoo on his cheek shifted slightly.

And me? I sat and stared at my hands, clasped loosely

around my katana's hilt. Golden skin under my rings. Light sparkled under the amber and moonstone and silver and obsidian. They rang and shifted with Power constantly now, demon-fed.

I had far too much now, too much to control. Power jittered in the air around me, working its way into my brain, teasing and tapping and begging to be used. I slid my katana free, just an inch or so, and watched a faint blue glow play over the metal. The song of my runespelled blade, familiar, resonated under the whine of hovercells.

I looked up at Japhrimel, who studied the waves, his profile sharp and somehow pure in the blue light. I blinked.

His eyes were no longer bright laser-green. Instead, they were dark, dimming. I gasped, shoved my katana back into its sheath. "Japhrimel?"

He glanced at me, then smiled. It was a shared, private smile that made my breath catch. *I was lying in bed with him this morning,* I thought, and a hot flush slid up my cheeks. "Your eyes," I said, weakly.

Japhrimel shrugged. It was an elegant movement. Would I share his grace? The crackling aura of Power that followed him around? *There are worse things,* I thought, and then flinched. *No. I'm human. Human.*

No, I'm not. I realized for the umpteenth time, my fist clenched on my katana's hilt.

"Dark now," he said. "Probably. I am glad of it."

"Why?"

His smile widened slightly. "It means I am no longer subject to Hell," he said shortly. "Only to you."

"So you're technically free? You could walk away from this?" I persisted.

"Of course not. It simply means that once the Egg is returned to Lucifer, I stay with you."

"I'm not so sure I'm comfortable with that," I answered, and went back to staring out the window. "What is he likely to have on that island, Japhrimel?"

"Several rings of defenses, human guards, other things." Japhrimel still leaned against the hull. "It is impossible to guess. Best just to wait and see."

"Like a standard hit on a military installation," Gabe supplied from the front. "Can't tell until we get there, going to have to just go loose and fast. Not enough time for proper intel."

We'd gone over this before, but the conversation was comforting. Better than the silence, anyway. But something was bothering me, some question I couldn't quite frame.

"Well, if we're invisible, we can recon a little before we send their asses to hell," Eddie growled. Then he glanced at Japhrimel. "No offense."

Japhrimel blinked. "None taken."

I watched the sea heaving below. I'd never liked the sea. Anything that big and unpredictable gave me the willies. Ditto with thunderstorms, some of the Major Works . . . and demons.

The question clicked into my conscious mind as I sat staring out the window. *Just how exactly did Santino escape Hell?* He was scary, much scarier than any human monster I'd faced. But still . . . I'd *seen* Hell now, and it didn't seem likely that Santino had possessed the kind of Power necessary to wrench himself out of the Prince's grasp, especially with something so valuable as the Egg. Of course, the Egg wasn't often used . . . so it was probably guarded.

Guarded by a demon Lucifer thought he could trust.

My eyes traveled up Japhrimel's coat, fastened on his profile. I did *not* want to be thinking this, especially since I'd spent the morning rolling around in bed with him. He hadn't let me down yet; I could ask him the hard questions later.

If there *was* a later.

We had about four hours before we reached the island, and then we had to find whatever installation Santino had there, and then we had to crack it and kill him—and rescue the little girl.

Doreen's daughter. Or Doreen cloned. Lucifer cloned with a bit of Doreen. One-quarter? One-half? How much? Did it matter? Of course not. I owed Doreen. If nothing else, she had given me my body back, made it possible for the terrified girl inside me to finally go to sleep and the adult begin to come out.

Oh, come on, Danny! I thought, lifting my katana, resting my forehead against the sheath. I was glad we were running dark, so I couldn't see my reflection in the windowplas. *What are you going to do with a demon child? Play mommy? Send her off to school and hope she doesn't burn the whole goddamn place down?*

Doesn't matter, I answered. *You can't hand a little kid—Doreen's kid—over to Lucifer. You just can't. What will* he *do to her? You owe Doreen. She saved your life at the expense of her own.*

I sighed. Here I was, sitting in a retrofitted garbage scow, dragging my best friend—and who qualified as my best friend now if Gabe didn't?—and her boyfriend into this. And Jace. And Japhrimel, but *he* could probably take care of himself.

Could he? Why the hell was I worrying about *him*?

I lowered my katana, drummed my fingernails on the hilt. "Japhrimel?"

"Dante."

"Are you . . . are you vulnerable, now?" I sounded a lot less certain than I wanted to.

"Not to humans," he said, shortly. "To some demons, perhaps. Not many."

"Is Santino one of them?"

He shrugged. "I am not worried about him."

"That's not an answer."

"You have grown more perceptive."

"And you're giving me the run-around. Which means he could hurt you."

"The Power contained in the Egg might conceivably damage me. However, I am not the one he wishes to capture." Japhrimel was a statue of darkness now, only his skin faintly luminescent.

"He *shot* me. I doubt 'capture' is on his laundry list where I'm concerned."

"If he wanted to kill you, he would have eviscerated you, Dante. He could have. Instead, he only shot you, knowing we were close enough that your condition would delay us. He obviously means to recollect you at his leisure. Which means he has a plan."

That didn't help me feel any better. I opened my mouth, but Jace beat me to it. "It doesn't matter," he said. "As soon as my Family moves on the Corvins, all Santino's neat little plans go out the window. He won't have any resources left to fuck around."

"I doubt your move on him is unanticipated," Japhrimel said quietly. The hover rattled. I tensed in my chair, and Eddie growled.

"Still doesn't fucking matter," Eddie growled. "We're

taking him down." He swung around to pin us all with a ferocious glare. "I ain't come all this way and been beat up and stuffed in two hovers to let him get off with just a spanking. 'Sides, we got *the* Gabriele Spocarelli. An' Jace Monroe. And Danny Valentine version two, kickass demon Necromance with her own pet demon boy. And you've got Eustace Edward Thorston III, Skinlin sorcerer and pretty pissed-off dirtwitch berserker." He showed his teeth, lips peeling back. "He hurt my Gabby," he continued softly. "And I'm gonna make him *pay*."

I blinked. It was the longest speech I'd ever heard from him.

Gabe didn't twist around in her seat, but I could tell from the set of her shoulders that she was smiling. Japhrimel had turned, and was regarding Eddie with a faintly surprised look. Jace grinned, his eyes closed, his head lolling against his seatback.

I cleared my throat. "Thanks, Eddie. I feel better," I said dryly.

And the funny thing was, I did.

CHAPTER
48

*H*oly motherfucking shit," Gabe whistled out tune-lessly. "Would you look at that."

"What about the radiation scans?" I asked.

"Flatline. They can't see us," Jace said, leaning over Gabe's shoulder, buckling his rig. "Ogoun . . ." he breathed. "Damn."

"Impressive," Gabe giggled. It was a carefree, girlish sound, but it set my teeth on edge. "Looks like a bad holovid villain's hideaway."

Below us, the icy sea broke foaming against sheer cliffs. The island was a hunk of rock rising from ice-floes, and the castle crouched atop it, spires of stone rearing up from darkness, decked with tiny yellow and blue points of light. It looked like something out of a Gothic fairytale, spire upon spire, screaming gargoyle shapes torn out of the stone.

"Get me a laseprint of that," I said, and Jace's fingers danced over a keyboard. The computers hummed. A laseprinter droned into life. "Are you *sure* we're invisible?"

Eddie tore the paper free. "Looks like antiaircraft batteries here, here, here, and here," he said, smacking the printout down on a small foldout table. "If they knew we were here, they'd blast us out of the sky."

I passed my palm over the smooth paper. We'd done our final equipment checks. All that remained was to actually drop out the side hatch and start causing trouble. "Jace, get me a couple of different views. Gabe, keep us going slow. Magscan shielding is no good unless we drift a bit."

"I know, Mom," Gabe sneered. "Let me fucking drive, okay?"

"They are unaware," Japhrimel said. "Dante, this place is heavily guarded."

"Good," I said. "The more confusion, the better."

Jace laid another two printouts down. "More?" he asked, and my eyes met his. It was a moment of complete accord, the kind we used to have while we were working together.

"Can you penetrate the shielding?" I asked.

"That is no trouble," the demon answered, his eyes never leaving me. "Santino has no demon shielding; if he did, Lucifer could track him. He is naked here, depending on secrecy."

"Good." I spread my hands over the printouts. "Japhrimel, make sure I don't bleed through," I said.

He nodded. "Of course."

I *focused*, looking for the link I'd followed before. It was weak—the child wasn't Doreen, and she wasn't human. But then again, neither was I. Not anymore.

I followed the thread-thin cable stretched tautly over the roiling sea below. Reaching. *Reaching.*

Contact.

—who are you—

The voice was neither male nor female, but it was

familiar, as familiar to me as my own. A wave of heat sparking up my arms, into my bones, my heart pounding, mouth full of copper.

Disengage, ripping free, link open, too open, salt against raw wound, Doreen, the memory of Doreen tilting her head back, her hands full of blue-white fire, her blood everywhere—

—who are you—

The *contact* stretched. My mental "fingers" froze, unable to let go, as whoever it was—*the kid? But no kid can be this strong*—examined me like a fly caught in a glass.

I stumbled back. Japhrimel caught my shoulders, steadied me, absorbed the backlash of Power. He rested his chin on top of my head. "Dante?"

"Fine." I said. My fingertip glued itself to a space on the printout. *Whatever that is, it's not a kid. It looks like a kid, but it's not a kid. But it's Doreen's, and I promised.* "She's here. We'll hit here hardest and extract her."

"Sounds good," Gabe said. "I'll put ol' Betsy here on autopilot."

I looked up at Eddie. The shaggy blond Skinlin hitched his leather coat higher on his shoulders, then checked his guns for the umpteenth time. "Maybe you should stay here, Gabe," I suggested.

"Fuck that," she returned equably, her fingers tapping an AI pilot deck. Coordinates entered, she slid out of the captain's chair and picked up her rig, buckling herself into it. Projectile guns, plasguns, knives, and triggers for various spells settled into their accustomed places. Even in a rig she looked impossibly elegant. "I'm not about to stay in here while you go have all the fun."

"You can pilot this thing; we need a getaway driver."

"Quit fussing, Mom." Gabe rolled her eyes, shoved a

pin through her braided hair. "Why don't *you* stay up here and cover us?"

"That's Jace's job," I returned. Then I looked down at the printouts. My finger rested over one of the yellow points of light, low down on the south side of the castle, in one of the most difficult-to-access parts. "Japhrimel, can you . . . umm, fly?"

"I can get you into that window, Dante," he replied. "I can't carry more than one, though."

"Don't worry about us," Gabe piped up. "We brought slicboards."

"I don't suppose I can talk you out of this." I rolled my head back; Japhrimel's lips met my temple. Jace glanced down at the printouts. I tore my finger away from the table with some difficulty, shook my hand out. My heartbeat took on the usual prejob pace—too quick to be resting, too slow to be pounding, adrenaline flooding my bloodstream.

"Wait a minute," Jace said. "I'm not staying here. You need backup."

"I've got Japhrimel," I said, without thinking about it.

There, it was out. Jace's mouth twisted down at the corners. Japhrimel's arms tightened slightly. The mark on my left shoulder flushed with velvet heat.

"We're too small a group to leave someone topside," Eddie said. "We need everyone we've got down there making trouble."

I hunched my shoulders. "You're all fucking crazy." I put my hand out, palm-down, over the table. "All right. We all go in together."

Gabe placed her hand over mine. "All together, and the gods help us."

Eddie covered our hands with his hairy paw. "Fuck 'em all," he growled.

Jace, then. "I won't be left behind," he said. "Not on something like this."

Japhrimel paused, and then slid to the side. He laid his hand over ours. "May your gods and mine protect us," he added judiciously.

"I didn't know demons had gods." Gabe grinned. It was her combat grin, light and fierce.

We broke as if at a prearranged signal, and I looked up at Japhrimel. "Be careful, okay?" I rubbed my katana's hilt with my thumb.

His face was as grim and murderous as I'd ever seen it. The eerie green glow from the instruments bathed him in a radioactive aura. "Do not worry over me, Dante. I have fought many battles in my time."

I looked down at the printouts, my mouth dry. The place was massive, and I had no clue where Santino would be hiding.

Jace opened the side hatch as the hover drifted. "Datbands?" he yelled over the sudden roar of wind, water, and pressurized airseals. The commlinks in everyone's ears crackled into life. I shook my head—I hated commlinks, but I couldn't spare the concentration keeping a telepathic five-way link open would cost me.

I held mine up, Gabe and Eddie copying me. We were all three keyed into the hover's intranet, which meant we could track each other with our datbands. Gabe extracted a long NeoSho slicboard from a crate in the pile of supplies. I checked my plasgun for the fiftieth time. Eddie took the NeoSho and Jace pulled out his Chervoyg. The hum of powering-up antigrav filled the air.

Gabe grinned. "See ya in the funny papers," she

yelled, and ran for the door. Eddie followed, coasting his slicboard out into the jetstream and leaping, the green-yellow glow of Skinlin sorcery limning him. *He's triggered the* golem'ai *to start the distraction*, I thought, and shivered. The mudlike creatures gave me the willies. "Japhrimel," I yelled over the noise, "just cause as much damage as you can once we've grabbed the kid. Level the whole place, if you can."

He nodded curtly, his coat beginning to stream and flap, separating in front. I swallowed hard. Jace dropped out the hatch, two plasguns already in his hands, his sword tucked through his belt. I took a deep breath. "Catch me?" I yelled, and Japhrimel nodded.

I didn't wait for more, simply ran for the hatch and launched myself into the night. Before I could lose my nerve.

CHAPTER
49

*W*e certainly made an entrance.

We were too-small targets for the antiaircraft battery, and by the time I found myself yanked up in Japhrimel's hands, the first *golem'ai* had Manifested. It was seven feet tall, built out of what looked like sentient humanoid mud, with glowing yellow spotlight eyes. It landed on the battlements with a thud, and screams drifted up over the sound of the waves and the punishing icy wind.

Cold. It was brutally cold. The wind sliced through me. Jace bobbed and wove underneath us, skating his slicboard fast through a collage of plasgun bolts—*where are those coming from,* I thought, and tossed a firestarter into the wind. A breath of Power made it arrow off toward the outcropping where human guards crouched, raking us with plasgun fire. The resultant explosion briefly turned the night a lurid orange, and I saw Gabe and Eddie had already reached the south side. Gabe wove among plasbolts with incredible grace, as if she was tagging slow hovers back in Saint City; I heard her voice raised sharply as Japhrimel glided, angling to keep us out of the way of the plasbolt crossfire. One gun emplacement exploded; I caught a whiff of Gabe's Power. She'd used a firestarter.

Picture this, then: the whole battle happening in seconds. Jace's share of the firestarters crackled, he was sowing them in a criss-cross pattern, taking out a whole tower. Stone crumbled, I heard his whoop of bloodthirsty joy. Then he went streaking over the battlements, sword in one hand, plasgun in the other, almost losing his slic as a plascannon bolt clipped the edge of his shielding.

We were on the north side, Japhrimel and I, about to make the sharp banking turn that would bring us back around and drop us into position to run for the spot in the castle where I'd felt Doreen's kid. There was a bank of guns here, too, beginning to move on their gimbals to focus down on the other three. "Drop me!" I yelled, flicking a firestarter, and wonder of wonders, Japhrimel obeyed.

I hit hard, rolling, and he was right behind me. I took the first two almost before I knew what was happening, my body moving with instinctive speed and precision. I leapt, catching the iron bar that the gunner was standing on, found his ankle, and yanked. He tumbled off into the wind, a human cry escaping him, lost in all the ruckus.

"Heavy fire," Eddie gasped.

"I'm on it," I snapped, shimmying up, hearing the clatter of gunfire while Japhrimel dealt with the other human guard. My conscience would prick me later—but they signed up with Santino, they took their chances. I swung the plascannon and yanked back on the trigger-bolt, praying—

Prayers answered. The bolts raked the other end of the wall, exploding cannon after cannon and crackling. I scrambled down, whirling as Japhrimel shouted something shapeless I understood anyway, and flicked another firestarter at the cannon as he grabbed me and flung us both out into empty air. "Now, isn't that better?"

Japhrimel coasted around, ducking under a stray bit of debris. "Let's get this over with," he yelled. I glanced down—we were losing altitude fast.

"Direct me, Danny," Gabe's voice crackled over the commlink.

I was happy I could. "Two windows up, straight in front of you, that's where the kid is. Pull up and watch your left, there's a bunch of plasgun coming your way."

"Got it," Eddie snarled, and flame bloomed again. A concussive *boom!* raked the night, stone and glass shattering. I heard thin human cries; another klaxon started to blare. More lights started to blaze in the massive pile of rock. *Holy fuck,* I thought, *we're doing a full-scale frontal assault on a demon's hideaway and getting away with it.*

Then things started to get interesting.

I didn't want to see how Japhrimel was flying—or gliding, actually, since we seemed to be falling pretty rapidly. He aimed for the kid's window and I spent a few moments with my eyes closed, *feeling* for her, letting him take care of it. The flare of her presence was close, so close—

"Dante?" Japhrimel's voice in the commlink.

"We're in," Gabe said. "What the—"

"Danny!" Eddie yelled. *"He's here! He's here!"*

"Burn the entire fucking place down, Japhrimel!" I screamed, and the entire world went soundless white as Japhrimel pulled on all the Power he could reach. A thin white-skinned shape blew out on the backwash of the explosion; my entire body screamed. It might have been Santino, my prey, falling through cold empty air.

If it's him, that won't kill him, I thought. *Not even a drop like that will kill him, he's a demon even if he's a weak one he's too strong, too slow, we're moving too slow—*

Jace nipped neatly inside the hole torn in the south side of the castle. Japhrimel let go of me and I tumbled through empty frozen air, faster-than-human reflexes saving me as I slammed into the stone wall. The *boom!* of another explosion rattled the wall; I jackknifed into the hole, my fingernails plowing stone and cold air plucking at my hair, landed on a wooden floor littered with shards of glass, broken stone, and wooden splinters.

The room was a nursery, again, stone floors holding pastel hangings in a faint attempt to make it less grim. Toys scattered, burning, across the floor. A huge ornate mahogany bedstead crouched in one corner, and I saw a stray gleam of light from the emerald in the child's forehead as it gave one amazing flash of light. My own emerald rang, answering it.

"Oh, no—"

Eddie screamed. The smell—ice and cold blood, maggots and wet rat fur—triggered my gorge. If I'd had anything in my stomach I would have spewed. I didn't know demons *could* throw up. *Santino.* It was his smell, he'd been here, I *knew* he'd been here. So it had been him falling from the room.

Gabe lay, broken and bloody, against the far wall. Of course—she'd been the first in, and Santino had been here, probably expecting us as soon as the commotion started. How badly was she hurt? I didn't have time to think about it; Eddie would take care of her.

Eddie gained his feet, shaking his shaggy head. It looked like he'd fetched up hard against the other side of the steel door to this room; his hair was singed and he was dirty from stone dust. He ran for Gabe. *Don't let her be hurt,* I prayed. *don't let her be hurt—*

Jace grabbed my arm and hauled me up as Japhrimel landed inside the room, coat folding around him as he rolled. He gained his feet and whirled, seeing me, then nodded. He strode toward Gabe and I shook free of Jace, bolting for the bed.

The little girl sat straight up, her dark eyes huge. The only uncertain light came from burning reflected in through the massive hole in the wall, glass from the lamp in the ceiling crunching under my boots. I reached the bed, stared down at the girl.

This is no child, I thought. *What am I doing?*

"Go," Japhrimel said. "Go, take her back to the ship. She'll live."

"He ripped her stomach out!" Eddie screamed, but Japhrimel caught his shoulders, his eyes sparking for a moment with the old green flame.

"I have mended her, she will *live*, dirtwitch. As you value her life, *go!*" Then Japhrimel pushed him away.

"What about Santino?" Jace yelled.

I held out my hands.

The girl looked at me. The cacophony—klaxons screaming, human cries, antiaircraft fire—they were filling the sky with bolts, trying to hit something—faded away.

She has Doreen's eyes, I thought, and the child nodded.

It wasn't just that she was beautiful, because she was. She looked as if Lucifer and Doreen had been melded into one small, perfect entity, the emerald in her forehead singing softly. It wasn't that she put up her hands and smiled at me. It wasn't even that she smelled familiar—some combination of fresh-baked bread and a unique smell that something in my subconscious recognized.

It was the shadow of knowledge in her dark eyes, and the absolute lack of fear. I knew she had somehow been waiting for me. Had somehow *known* I was coming, and accepted it. The knowledge chilled me right down to my new bones.

She's not human, I thought. *What if it's best to leave her with Santino?*

I scooped her up and turned, ran for the others, her hot, chubby arms wrapped around my neck.

Eddie had just finished triggering the third *golem'ai.* Screams. The heavy, ironbound door leading into the rest of the castle resounded with shouts and thuds. They were breaking in. Santino's human army was on its way.

Where did Santino go? How long will it take him to get back up here?

I didn't have time to worry about it.

I shoved the girl into Jace's arms. He took her before he realized what I was doing, and I pushed him out of the hole in the wall, his slicboard whining and taking the kinetic energy I supplied. *Too much Power, sorry about that, Jace—* "Get her to the ship, Jace! *Move!*" Japhrimel hauled Gabe up, Power thundering in the confined space and dyeing the air with diamond-dark, twisting flames. Gabe flopped in his arms, but Japhrimel had said she would live.

Eddie took Gabe's limp weight. Her slicboard lay twisted and useless against the far wall. "He went that way—" Eddie screamed, pointing at the hole in the wall, his face a mask of rage.

I grabbed him by the collar and shook him. "Get Gabe out of here! *Move it!*"

I didn't have to tell him twice. He bolted for the hole in the wall, Gabe in his arms, blood dripping from her long dark braid. *I hope she's still alive, if she dies goddammit Santino I'll kill you twice—*

"Danny, get out of there," Jace yelled, the commlink crackling in my ear. "Hurry up!"

Japhrimel started toward the hole in the wall.

Oh no, I thought. *I am not leaving. I have business to finish here.*

I turned toward the door, my katana sliding free. I dropped the borrowed scabbard, tore the commlink out of my ear, and fitted the plasgun into my left hand. Took a deep breath. Japhrimel twisted away from the hole in the wall, his boots skidding. Had he really thought I would leave without doing what I came to do?

As long as Santino was alive, I would never be able to rest again.

Japhrimel's lips shaped my name as I took in a deep breath, my blade blazing with pitiless blue light that threw sharp reflections through the ruined room. I pointed the plasgun at the door, where a circle of white-hot glow told me they were using lasecutters to break in.

"*Santino!*" I roared with all my newfound Power, and squeezed the plasgun's trigger just as the demon Vardimal broke through the wall behind the bed, mahogany splinters flying like shrapnel, stone turning to dust and icicle shards. The shockwave caught me and threw me against the stone wall, and I almost lost my sword when

I hit with a sickening thump that shivered yet more stone from the roof and wall.

Japhrimel let out a sound so huge it was almost soundless and hurled himself at Santino.

Who threw up one clawed hand that held something glittering, made a complicated twisting motion, and tossed the glitter straight at Japhrimel.

The Egg! The thought seemed to move through syrup.

I gained my feet in a shuffle, hearing groans from the ruins of the door. The plasgun bolt had smacked into the cutter's field and caused a chain reaction, plasbolt reacting with the lase energy and freeing a whole hell of a lot of violent energy. It's a basic law of dealing with plasguns: *never shoot at reactive or lase fields.* Nobody caught in *that* would want to fight anymore—not if they were human. If I'd been human the concussion might have killed me.

I launched myself at Santino as the small glittering thing, no bigger than my fist, smacked Japhrimel in the chest—and blew him through the wall and out into the night with a sound that made a gush of blood drip down from my ears and nose. I shook my head, dazed for only a split second. The drilling pain flashed through me and was gone, the warmth of the blood freezing against my skin in milliseconds. My breath puffed out, turned to a tissue-thin cloud of ice crystals, fell straight down.

Japhrimel! I skidded to a stop, facing Santino, whose claws cut the cold air. Our feet crunched in glass and tinkling stone shards as he moved, circling.

He didn't look happy to see me. "*Fool!*" he hissed. "The *fool.*"

My katana circled. The rest of the world faded away. Here he was, right in front of me.

My revenge.

"Santino," I hissed. The entire world seemed to hold its breath, the shape of my vengeance lying under the fabric of reality, rising to meet me. "Or Vardimal. Or whoever the hell you are."

"You can't kill me," he sneered. "Neither man nor demon can kill me. Lucifer assured me of that."

I showed my own teeth, boots shuffling lightly, quickly. "I am going to eat your fucking heart," I informed him. *I'm not a man or a demon, Santino. Your immunity doesn't apply.*

"You could have been a *queen*," he snarled at me, the black teardrops over his eyes swallowing the light. "You could have helped me kill Lucifer and take the rule of Hell! But no, you stupid, silly *human*—"

"Not human," I said. "Not anymore."

He bared his teeth again. "Who do you think helped me *escape* from Hell?" he screamed, my blade flashing up as we circled. "He's *Lucifer's* assassin! His Right Hand! He's *used* you—"

That answered the question that had been teasing the back of my mind since this whole thing started—of how exactly Santino had escaped Hell. I should have been enraged at Japhrimel for hiding that from me, I should have been wondering what else he'd hidden. What other secrets he might have kept. But with my revenge in front of me and Japhrimel's blood filling my veins, I could have cared less.

"I don't fucking care," I hissed, and my own voice tore more stone from the ceiling and sent it pattering down in a drift of dust. "I've come to kill you, you scavenger son of a bitch, for what you did to Doreen. And every other woman you murdered."

And then there was no more time for talk, because he moved in with that spooky invisible speed of demons.

I parried his claws, my katana ringing and blazing with blue fire. He screamed, a horrible drilling sound of awful agony, the plasgun tore out of my hands but I hooked my fingers and swiped at him, hot black demon blood spraying and freezing in the too-cold air. Something had happened when he'd thrown that thing at Japhrimel. It was too cold even for Antarctica.

He leapt on me, his compact weight knocking me off my feet. We tumbled, and his claws tore at me, a horribly familiar gush of pain. I screamed, forgetting I was no longer human, and did the only thing I could.

I jackknifed my body, using his momentum as well as my own, and flung us both out into the night as I buried my katana in his chest, shoving with every ounce of preternatural strength Japhrimel had given me. The blade rammed through a shell of magick, through muscle and the carbolic acid of demon blood, and the agony of the blade's shattering tore all the way through me.

One of the shards pierced his heart. I flailed at him with my claws, his throat giving in one heated gush that coated my face and hands and instantly froze, almost sealing my nostrils. If I hadn't been screaming, I might have suffocated.

I was still hacking at him with my claws when we hit the water, his slack lifeless body exploding out in noxious burning fragments. The shock of that hit drove all breath and consciousness from me, and I fell unresisting into the embrace of the ocean, waves crackling and freezing closed over my head.

CHAPTER
50

I floated. Face-down.

Stinging. Cold so intense it burned. Lassitude creeping up my arms and legs.

No. A familiar voice. Familiar fingers on my cheek, tipping my head up. *No, don't, Danny. You have to live. You promised.*

I didn't promise! I wailed silently. *Let me go! Let me go, let me die—*

You have work to do. Doreen's voice, gentle, inexorable. *Please, Danny. Please.*

Floated. Sinking. Even a share of a fallen demon's Power couldn't keep me alive for long in this. Something had happened—Santino had done something, that small glittering thing had hit Japhrimel—

Santino. I'd killed him. I'd watched his body dissolve under my fingernails, I'd torn through his throat. He was, indisputably, dead and scattered on the freezing ocean. No little bit of him would be left.

I killed him, I pleaded. *I did it. I got revenge for you. Isn't that enough?*

No, she replied, solemn. *Live, Danny. I want you to live.*

It hurts too much, I keened to her.

Blue crystal glow, the bridge under my feet. For one dizzying moment I was between two worlds—the Hall of Death, its blue directionless light pouring through me, Anubis standing tall and grim on the other side of the bridge; and the real world, where I floated face-down under a sheet of broken ice. For one infinite moment I was locked under the pitiless, infinitely forgiving gaze of the Lord of Death, weighing, evaluating, His black eyes fixed on mine. *It hurts too much,* I told him. *Please don't make me go back.*

He shook His sleek black head, once, twice. I struggled—*no! Let me stay! Let me stay!*

Then He spoke.

The Word boomed through me. It was not His name, or any Word of Power. It wasn't the secret name I held for Him, my key to the door of Death.

No.

It was my name—only more. It was my Word, spoken by the god, the sound that expressed me, the sound that could not be spoken aloud. My soul leapt inside me, responding to His touch. The god took the weight from me, briefly, let me feel the freedom, the incredible *freedom*, rising out of my body, leaving the world behind, the clear blue light becoming golden, the clear rational light of What Comes Next.

Then it dwindled to a single point in the darkness, and I rammed back into my body, fingers clamped in my hair, yanking. I was torn from the water's embrace, glazed with ice, choking, coughing, the landing lights of the garbage scow named *Baby* exploding through the darkness. Jace, his lips blue, tangling the plasnet around us both and we were yanked up together, his arms and legs wrapped around me. We broke through the airseals and into the warm interior of the hover, and the hatch slammed closed as the peculiar weightless pressure of a hover quickly ascending pressed down on me.

I coughed and choked, spluttering.

"*Breathe*, you stubborn little bitch—" Jace shivered and cursed, raging at me. Water washed the decking, rapidly melting ice shrinking under the assault of climate control.

"Is she alive?" Eddie said from the front. After the deafening noise, the quiet of the hover's interior and someone speaking normally was a muffled shock.

"She's alive," Jace said, and flung his arms around me again. Water dripped. My fingers and toes tingled and prickled. "Gods *damn* you, Danny, don't you *ever* do that to me again." He kissed my forehead, examined my fingers and my dark rings, wrapped me in a spaceblanket that started to glow, heat stealing back into me. My teeth chattered. My right hand was twisted into a fist, and I couldn't unloose it.

"G-G-Gabe—"

"She'll live. Your demon friend patched her intestines back together up there in that room, damndest thing I ever saw. She's lost a lot of blood, but she's stable and the medunit's monitoring her." Jace kissed my cheek, pushed sodden strands of dark hair back from my face. "Don't *ever* do that to me again, Danny. I thought he'd killed you."

"The k-k-k-k—" I began.

"The kid's fine. Curled up in a seat with a spaceblanket. She's asleep." Jace coughed. "Look, Danny—"

"Japhrimel?" I whispered.

Jace shook his head. "There was a hover—another

hover. It might have scooped him up, I don't know. We looked for him, Danny. We really did. The entire god-damn island's broken down and iced over, I don't think anything survived that. If we hadn't been airborne we'd have been toast. What *happened*?"

"I killed him," I whispered. "I killed Santino. He threw s-s-something at J-J-aph . . ."

"We couldn't find him," Jace said. "I'm sorry, Danny."

I clapped my fists over my ears, huddled under the spaceblanket, and started to cry. I'd earned it, after all.

CHAPTER
51

*T*welve hours later we floated over an oddly quiet Nuevo Rio. Dry and finally warm again, I sat in the seat next to Doreen's daughter (I couldn't think of what else to call her), watching out the window as morning lay over the city. Jace had moved up front next to Eddie, and the comms up there were crackling with messages. Gabe lay across a table, strapped down and deep in a sedative-induced slumber, the medunit purring as it monitored her and dripped synthetic plasma and antibiotics through a hypo into her veins. She'd wake up with a headache and a sore gut and spend a week or so recuperating, but she'd live.

The Corvin Family was gone. Just . . . gone. They hadn't even put up a real fight. Jace was now the owner of a hell of a lot of Family assets.

When I looked back at Doreen's daughter, I saw she was awake. In the light, her eyes were wide and clear, and dark blue. Like Doreen's.

Exactly like Doreen's.

She watched me gravely, a small child with frighteningly adult eyes, far too much Power and knowledge swimming in their depths. For a few moments, we sat like that, one tired, sobbed-out half-demon Necromance and one small demon Androgyne child.

I can't handle this, I thought. Then, *I have no choice.*

I finally managed to clear my throat. "Hi," I said quietly. "I'm Danny."

She watched me for a few more seconds before she responded. "I know," she said, in a clear light voice. "He told me you would come."

My mouth was dry and smooth as glass. This wasn't normal for a kid.

Like I knew what was normal for a kid. I never spent any time with children if I could help it. "Who told you?" I managed. "Santi—ah, um, your daddy?"

She nodded, her pale hair falling forward over her face. "*He* said he was my daddy," she confided, "but I don't think he was. My real daddy talks to me inside my head at night. He has green eyes and a green stone like me and he told me you would come for me. He said he would send you."

She seemed to expect some sort of reply. It was obvious who her "real daddy" was. Either Lucifer had some way of communicating with her, or she was precognitive, or . . . My brain stopped sorting through alternatives. It didn't matter. Lucifer already knew about the kid, I'd bet. I'd also bet that Lucifer had known about Santino's "samples." Or if not known, guessed. The Prince of Hell was no fool.

Why then had Japhrimel promised not to tell him?

"I promised your mommy I'd take care of you," I said rustily. *Oh, gods, Danny, you've done it now.*

The little girl nodded solemnly. "You're not like them." She pointed at the front of the hover, where Jace and Eddie conferred in low worried tones. "You're not like my real daddy either."

"I hope not." I shifted uncomfortably in the seat, the spaceblanket crackling as I moved. "What's your name?"

"I'm Eve," she said, matter-of-factly. I flinched. *Of course*, I thought, and watched as her dimples came out. She smiled at me. "Can I have some ice cream?"

"I don't think we have any, kiddo." *Japhrimel had to live on blood, or sex, or fire,* I thought. *What does this girl eat? Oh, you are not ready for this, Danny. Not ready at all.*

The hover circled slightly, and began to drift downward toward Jace's mansion.

"Um, Danny?" Jace called. "You may want to come take a look at this."

I hauled myself up, and the little girl pushed her blanket off and shimmied down from her seat. She held her small perfect hand up. "Can I come, too?" She wore a short white babydoll nightie, and her chubby feet were bare. I fought the urge to pick her up off the hover's cold metal deck.

"Okay," I said, and took her hand. It was warm in mine—a demon's touch.

Like Japhrimel's. Was he dead? Or had Santino's men taken him? What could they do to him? Was he injured?

I made my way up to the front, holding the girl's hand. "What's up?" I peered out the front window.

"Take a look." Jace glanced up at me. "How's the kid doing?"

"She seems okay," I replied.

Below us, the familiar blocky outlines of Jace's mansion

grew larger as the hover slowly dropped. On the wide marble expanse of courtyard in front, two sleek limo-hovers crouched, and four police cruisers.

"Fuck me," I breathed, forgetting the child's small hand in mine. "What the hell?"

"I was hoping you could tell me," Jace said. "I'm incorporated and operating under codes, so I'm fairly sure they're not here to roust *me.*"

"*Sekhmet sa'es.*" I was too tired to come up with a good plan. "No chance they're here for you, Eddie."

"'Course not, unless they'd like to arrest Gabe for fucking almost dying," he said, with no apparent growl in his voice. He must be exhausted. "What do we do, Danny?"

I wish they would stop nominating me as the idea man, I thought. "Nothing else to do," I said. "Drift on down and land, but keep the motor running until we're sure we won't need it. Jace, can I have a commlink?"

"Of course," he said. "What do you want me to do, Danny?"

"Stay here with the kid," I answered, glancing down at Eve. The little girl looked up at me, as if I were the only person in the hover. "If they take me, get the kid somewhere safe and wait for me to show up."

Jace swung out of his chair, not even bothering to argue with me. I felt a weary relief. Was it normal to feel this way? So tired, but unable to sleep.

No sleep. Not until I finished this game. And it *was* a game, I'd been pushed from square to square all along.

I took the child back into the hold and settled her back into the chair, tucking the blanket around her again. When I finished, Jace was standing by a crate of supplies, a strange expression on his face. His hair curled into a halo, drenched in ice water and then dried in climate control. I probably didn't look very good either.

"What?"

"Nothing," he said. "Let me find a commlink."

Eddie piloted the hover down. We landed with a thump. "Sorry," he called back. I slipped the commlink in my ear, settled my wrinkled coat on my shoulders, made sure my knives were easy in their sheaths. My right hand ached deeply, all the way down to the bone. If I were still human, I might be maimed.

I knelt down in front of Eve, who watched me with Doreen's eyes. "I've got to go talk to whoever this is," I told her. "You stay with Jace until I get back, okay?"

She nodded. "It will be all right, Danny. My daddy says so," she said, her clear piping voice oddly adult.

"Great," I answered grimly, and stood up. The ground swayed underfoot, or maybe it was just me. "Jace, I want you to promise. Promise you'll take care of her if I—"

He shrugged. "You know I will, Danny. Go on, get this over with." His blue eyes skittered over to the girl, back up to me.

I nodded, then Eddie popped the side hatch. I hopped down to the marble, almost losing my balance. The heat hammered at me, Nuevo Rio back to its old, bad, sunny self. *I wish I was home,* I thought suddenly, and that surprised me, too. I hadn't felt like Saint City was home for a good two or three years.

One of the limo-hovers opened its side hatch. A set of steps folded down.

I swallowed. I had a fair idea of what could be waiting in there.

I strode across the burning white marble and toward the sleek black hovers, trying to keep my shoulders straight and wishing I wasn't dirty, bloody, air-dried, and so close to crying my throat ached keeping it all in.

CHAPTER
52

The inside of the limo-hover was done in all different shades of red. Crimson, cardinal, burgundy, magenta, carmine, lobster—I blinked, stepping onto plush carpet at the top of the stairs. The air swirled with the smell of *demon*, smoky musk, and I took a deep breath. It was as if I hadn't been breathing until now. Whatever demons used for air, this hover was full of it.

That's why she smells familiar, I realized with no real surprise. *She smells like him. Like Lucifer.*

The Prince of Hell lounged elegantly on a huge circular red-velvet couch, his booted feet crushing the velvet. I gave the surroundings a tired glance—wet bar, tinted windows, doors probably leading to a bathroom and a private bedroom. There was a sunken tub in one corner, bubbling and frothing with a clear viscous fluid that didn't look even remotely like water.

Lucifer's golden hair burned among the redness. He was dressed, of course, all in black silk, loose elegant pants and a long-sleeved, Chinese-collared shirt. The walls were done to look like expensive red damask wallpaper, and heavy velvet drapes muffled every sound.

I swallowed. "The decor sucks," I said, too tired for

any bowing and scraping. I cradled my right hand in my left—it was really starting to throb as adrenaline wore off.

"Good afternoon to you, too," Lucifer replied, his voice stroking and tapping at my ears. A thrill like old tired fire ran through me—I was too exhausted to really respond to him. If I'd had any more energy I would have been worried about it. "Have you brought me the Egg?"

"Nope," I said. "But Santino's dead. And you didn't really want me to bring you the Egg anyway, that was Japhrimel's job. Looks like he did it, because you're out of Hell and feeling frisky."

Lucifer held up one elegant golden hand. I could look at his face now, without my eyes blinking and watering. His smell folded over me, teased at my hair, permeated my clothes. My bones rang with his nearness, a vibrating electricity that made me want to go to my knees. I fought the urge.

A fine golden chain wrapped around his beautifully manicured fingers. "The once-demon Japhrimel brought me this," he said, twirling a diamond-glittering oval on the chain. The hum of Power filled the air. I couldn't look directly at the glittering thing, it hurt even my eyes.

My throat was desert-dry. "So that's what that was." Santino had thrown the Egg at Japhrimel, to fend him off.

"Indeed. Vardimal managed to unlock a fraction of the Egg's power and threw it at Tierce Japhrimel. The only thing that could possibly hurt my Eldest—because it is *mine*, and therefore dangerous to my line. Any demon would be grievously injured by it. Except, of course, myself. I am the Prince." Lucifer sounded amused. He cocked his golden head. "Where is the child, Dante Valentine?"

I shrugged. "That's what you were after all the time, wasn't it? Doreen's kid. The Androgyne. You let Santino alone until he did what you couldn't, and now you have everything."

"The *sedayeen* was never more than a template, Dante. The Egg contains my genetic codex, and pure Power. It is a mark of my reign and a useful tool."

"You knew the whole time. You *knew*. You just couldn't afford to have anyone else know Santino had done what you couldn't, so you had to find a human to do the dirty work. And all that tripe about the Egg being broken—" I shook my head, a lump in my throat. My voice sounded husky and harsh next to his smooth persuasive tones.

"Think if Vardimal *had* managed to raise the child undisturbed, Dante. Imagine him ruling Hell, and our Hellesvront agents on Earth, through that child. That is what 'breaking the Egg' means. Breaking the chain of command, breaking the rule of Iblis Lucifer."

I had one of those sudden flashes of instinct that made my back chill with gooseflesh. *He's not nervous,* I thought, *but he is tense. Where's Japhrimel? What game is he playing now?*

I glanced back toward the side hatch. It had silently closed. I was alone in a hoverlimo with the Devil. And wonder of wonders, it looked for all the world like the Devil was scared of little ol' me. "That hover at Santino's lair—that was you, or your agents. They brought you Japhrimel, and the Egg. And Santino's dead. Case closed, contract terminated, bargain fulfilled." I didn't want to say it, but I had to anyway.

Lucifer tipped his perfect head back, his green eyes crawling over me. "Aren't you going to ask about Japhrimel?"

The thought that had been tormenting me all the way back from the island slammed into the forefront of my mind again. *Who do you think helped me escape from Hell? He's Lucifer's assassin, his Right Hand! You've been used!* "I doubt you'd tell me the truth if I asked," I said. "Why waste my breath?"

"He is *A'nankimel*, Fallen. I can no longer use him, and he has tied himself to you. Besides, I promised him his freedom." Lucifer seemed to sink even further into the cushions. "I never thought to see the day my assassin was brought low by a human woman."

I got the distinct idea that Lucifer was not pleased with this turn of events.

Now we come to it, I thought clinically, wishing I had my sword. "So? He's free. Fine."

Lucifer blinked.

I suppressed a tired urge to giggle.

"Let me be perfectly clear, Dante: you do not want to play with me."

I shrugged. "I'm not playing, Lucifer. I don't care anymore. I just want to go and get some sleep." I spread my hands—my new, golden-skinned hands, sparks from my rings popping in the charged air. It felt like a thunderstorm was gathering.

For all I knew, one was.

He sat up, his boots touching the floor. I tensed. But he only leaned forward, hands on his knees. "Very well then. Here is your choice. Give me the child, and I will give you Japhrimel."

That did it.

I tipped my head back and laughed. It started out as a giggle, blew through a chuckle, and ended up full-fledged howling mirth. I laughed until tears squirted out of my eyes and my stomach hurt. When the laughter finally faded in a series of hitching gasps I wiped my eyes and regarded the Prince of Hell.

"Go fuck yourself," I said pleasantly, "if it will reach. If you think I'm going to hand an innocent kid— *Doreen's* kid—over to you for gods-alone-know-what you want to do to her, you've got another think coming. You made the bargain with Japhrimel that he had his freedom when he finished this job, and he finished it. You can't keep him, you sorry son of a bitch, and I'd like to see you try. He'll eat you for breakfast." I took a deep breath, my rings sparking, Power cloaking me in close swirls. "Let me give you a piece of advice, *Iblis Lucifer.* Don't ever try to double-cross a Necromance. As scary as you are, *Prince*, Death's bigger *and* badder."

I finished my speech with my hands on my hips and my chin held high, my right hand flaring with pain as I balled it into a tight fist. Lucifer didn't move. His eyes glittered, that was all. No wonder he was afraid—if Santino could challenge him with Eve, Lucifer probably thought I could too, if he pissed me off enough.

"How do you think you will feed her, Dante? Or teach her to live in the human world? Hell is separate from earth for a *reason.* You cannot raise an Androgyne." He said it softly, silk brushing my ears, whispering in my veins, tapping behind my heartbeat.

"I promised," I said. "I promised to take care of her. I don't want Hell or any fancy-schmancy deals. You should have told me everything at the beginning, Lucifer. She wasn't part of the deal. Let Japhrimel go."

I waited. The air turned prickling-hot. I didn't move, meeting his eyes, finding out that I only had to be too tired to care before I won a staring match with the Devil.

He finally spoke again. "Japhrimel is no longer a demon," he said quietly. "Any bargain I made with him does not apply. I will keep him in Hell, enchained, tortured for as long as his life lasts. And I will be certain to let him know that you could have saved him from his fate, and did not."

"You really are a piece of work," I said, my left hand creeping toward my knifehilt. Left-handed? I couldn't kill the Devil left-handed. "I am *not* handing a kid over to you, you freak. And if you go ahead and torture Japhrimel—which I don't recommend—you'll just be a fucking grifter. How will that look—the Prince of Hell has to welsh on a deal? You're already known for being a liar, now you're a cheat, too—"

I didn't even see him move. One moment I was standing there, hands on hips, talking smack to the Prince of Hell. The next instant, he had me by the throat, his grip crushing-strong, holding me against the side of the hover as casually as he might hold a kitten by the scruff. "I am being merciful," he said softly, pleasantly, "because you have been useful. You are under the *illusion*—" His hand tightened, here, and I kicked fruitlessly, "that you have a *choice*. Do not interfere with the child, and I will let you and Japhrimel live out your miserable lives unmolested."

What happened to being my friend? I struggled, black spots dancing over my vision. His fingers were like iron bars even for my newfound demon strength. Something crackled in my throat; he eased up a little. I managed a little bit of air. "Fuck . . . you . . ." I croaked, and his eyes blazed. He didn't look so pretty when he was angry.

My left shoulder began to burn. Faintly at first, but steadily. The black spots danced over my vision. I kicked, weakly, once, twice.

"Ah." Staring over my shoulder, out the window, he dropped me like a pile of trash and I coughed, rolling onto my side and rubbing my throat. Blessed air roared into my lungs. It took me two tries to get to my feet. The side hatch of the hoverlimo was open, white sunlight from the Nuevo Rio day pouring up and making a square on the ceiling.

I half-fell out of the hover and down the stairs, sharp edges biting into my hip, smacking my head on one. The skin split and blood dripped down my face. I landed in a heap on hot slick stone and scrabbled to my feet.

The child—Eve—stood by the garbage scow, the fierce sunlight making her hair seem even paler, glittering. Her eyes blazed, incandescent blue.

And Lucifer stood in front of her.

"No—" I choked, scrambling over the marble. "*No!*"

The Prince of Hell knelt slowly, sinking down, a black blot on the carnivorous white of the day. I saw Jace, braced in the side door of the hover, shaking his head as if dazed. Lucifer held up the Egg, and settled the thin gold chain around Eve's neck.

She smiled up at him.

My abused body couldn't go anymore. My feet tangled, and I fell. Lucifer rose like a dark wave, and the child put her arms around his neck and hugged him, resting her head on his shoulder.

Just like a little girl with her daddy. My gorge rose. But demons weren't human—and human rules didn't apply to them. For all I knew, all of Lucifer's bed-buddies were his children. He was the Androgyne. The first.

Then Lucifer turned on his heel, took three steps, and lifted one golden hand. His hair ran with sunlight, a furnace of gold, glittering unbearably. I heard the whine of hover displacement, didn't care. I saw Iblis Lucifer rip a hole in the fabric of reality and step through as if going from one room to another. Flame licked the corners of the hole he made, and the last thing I saw was Eve smiling over his shoulder, her blue eyes fixed on me, calm and tranquil and utterly inhuman. Power rippled, rent the air, nausea spiking under my breastbone.

Something thudded on the marble. Jace's boots rang—but the thump was from behind me. He reached me, dropping to his knees with a heavy sound, grabbing my shoulders. We watched together as the limo-hovers lifted into the sky, quickly, then dived over the well of Nuevo Rio. The police cruisers made one circuit of the mansion and then slid down into the city, going back to patrol probably.

Game over. Lucifer wins.

Jace cursed, shook me. "Danny! *Danny!*"

"What the *fuck?*" My tongue felt too thick for my mouth.

Jace's arms crushed me. "Fuck, Danny. What happened? The kid heard his voice on the commlink and just walked out; she said her daddy was here to get her."

I groaned. "I hate this line of work," I husked dryly, then looked back over my shoulder, to where the limo-hovers had rested.

Another black blot on the pavement, this one with short ink-black hair.

"They tossed him out," Jace said into my hair. "Danny—"

"Help me up. Help me *up.*"

He dragged me up to my feet, steadying me as I swayed.

"What the *fuck* is going on out there?" Eddie yelled from the hatch.

"Go back," I told Jace. "I'll be fine."

"You're not fine," he shot back at me. "Look at you. Your hand—your *throat*—"

"Go make sure Gabe's okay," I said, and shoved him away. "Go on."

Maybe I shouldn't have done that. He took a step back, his face going cold and hard as the marble under us. I think I watched Jace Monroe age five years in that one moment, his shoulders slumping, his blue eyes gone pale as frost.

"Danny," he said. "You're not seriously . . ."

The heat poured down on us like oil from Nuevo Rio's blue sky. "Go on, Jace. Go."

I turned away. Limped toward the crumpled dark shape lying against the whiteness. Too still. He was too still.

"Danny," I heard Jace say behind me, shut the sound out. I didn't care.

It took me a long time to limp across the marble. I finally reached him and went down on my knees. He lay twisted against the smooth slick stone, legs shattered, his face unrecognizable. Nothing could possibly be that broken and live.

I flattened my left hand against his shredded chest. His wings lay bent and broken, tattered, draped across him. He had stopped bleeding. Smoke threaded up from his wings, his blood burning, burning.

"No," I whispered. "No."

His eyes were mere slits, glazed over. "Japhrimel?" I whispered. The mark on my shoulder had stopped its flaming pain. Now it was cold, all the way down to my bones. Numb cold, the cold of shock.

No spark of life. I touched his throat, pried up one ruined eyelid and peered at his eye. No pulse. No reaction in the pupil. Just the steady drift of smoke rising from him.

My head dropped. I sighed. The sound seemed to go on forever. My throat pulsed with pain.

I *reached*, with all the Power I had left. I tried to find the spark of life in him. I rested my left palm on his body and closed my eyes, searching, but nothing was there. This was only a shell.

Japhrimel was gone.

Free. He was finally free. Lucifer had killed him—or let him die.

I didn't realize the tears splashing his battered face were mine. I bent over him for a long moment, frantically searching for any sign of life, and then settled back on my heels, cold in the middle of the furnacelike sunshine. The flames began in earnest, eating his demon body, self-combusting with a smell like burning cinnamon.

Then I tipped back my head and howled to the uncaring blue sky.

EPILOGUE

*G*abe was fine. Shaky, battered, weak from blood loss, and possessed of an interesting new set of scars where Santino had ripped her belly open, but fine. She lived, and after a couple of days she called me to say Eddie had stopped rampaging through the mansion threatening to break windows. I stayed in a hotel down in Nuevo Rio, a cockroach-infested place where I had to listen to screaming and the pops of projectile guns outside my window every night. Gabe also told me Jace was going to give them the *Baby*, and they planned to fly the garbage scow back to Saint City. Eddie had wanted a hover anyway.

I said nothing, just listened to her on the phone and then slowly closed the sound of her voice away, setting the receiver down in its cradle. Good for them.

I flew first class in a passenger transport. My right hand was an awkward claw, but I got around with my left just fine. It would take me a long time to bless another sword if my hand ever straightened out.

I carried the urn with me. It was black lacquer, beautiful, and heavy. Pure fine cinnamon-scented ash, scraped together from white marble and carefully placed in the urn's embrace. Every speck of ash I had been able

376 Lilith Saintcrow

to find had gone into the urn, left by Lucifer as a parting gift maybe. Just to rub everything in.

Jace did not see me off at the dock. I didn't expect him to. I'd left his mansion like a thief in the middle of the night, carrying Japhrimel's ashes with me. Jace hadn't tried to find me or talk to me.

Good.

It was while I was sitting in the hover, resting my head against the side of the seat, that everything became clear. Of course Japhrimel had helped Vardimal escape Hell. It made sense, especially since Lucifer probably *let* him do it, figuring that Vardimal wouldn't find anything of value among humans, even humans carrying the strain of the Fallen—psions. What Lucifer didn't know, and Japhrimel probably didn't know either, was that Vardimal had taken the Egg. And when Lucifer found that out, suddenly Vardimal wasn't so little a threat. If Lucifer hadn't known about the kid then, he'd probably guessed when he found the Egg gone and took notice of the human world again; finding out that Vardimal, true to form, had been taking samples from human psychics and had then disappeared. And at some point, Lucifer had made contact with Eve—way before I did, but probably by following the same link of blood I'd followed. Only his link with the child would be stronger, since it was his genetic material, and I only had the fading echo of my love for Doreen and our shared human link.

And if Lucifer had been unable to leave Hell without the Egg, all of a sudden it became necessary to attack Vardimal from a direction the scavenger demon wouldn't see coming. No demon would think that the Prince would hire a human.

Lucifer had been playing to retain his control of Hell;

Eve was another playing piece with potential value as a *created* Androgyne. It would be child's play for Lucifer to reverse-engineer and find Vardimal's "shining path of genes," securing his own grasp on the reproduction of other demons. And it probably piqued the hell out of Lucifer that Vardimal had managed to do something the Prince couldn't.

Vardimal had been playing for control of Hell itself. Japhrimel had been playing for his freedom, and just when it seemed possible that he might live out the game, Lucifer had killed him for letting Vardimal escape—never mind that Lucifer allowed and probably facilitated it.

It was all very logical, once I got a chance to think about it. Simple enough.

Me? Just a human tool. I'd been playing for my life. And here I was alive, and the demon who lied to me was dead. I'd killed Santino at last, but Lucifer had Doreen's kid. If that made us even, it also made me the loser.

Maybe Lucifer hadn't expected Japhrimel to turn me into whatever I was now. And that was a problem—just what the hell was I? Japhrimel had expected to be alive enough to explain it to me when everything was said and done. Maybe he miscalculated just how deeply Lucifer would detest the idea of anyone winning anything from him—even his assassin, whom he'd thrown away anyway.

The transport finally docked, and I waited until everyone else had a chance to get off before I made my way out into the hoverport, breathing in the Saint City stink again, feeling the cold glow of my home's Power rasping against my flesh. It took me bare seconds to adapt, because I wasn't . . . human.

I caught a cab home, the urn cuddled against my belly, and found myself in my own front yard again, under a blessedly cloudy Saint City sky. A faint light rain was misting down, decking out my garden with small silvery beads of water. I'd need to weed soon, and tear up half the valerian. Dry out the roots to use for sleeping-tea.

If I could ever sleep again, that was.

I unlocked my door and stamped my feet on the mat. My familiar, soothing house folded around me.

I carried the urn into the stale, quiet dimness of my house. The hall had that peculiar odor of a place where nobody has breathed for a while, a house closed up on itself for too long.

Halfway up the stairs, the niche with the little statue of Anubis was just the same as it had always been. Dusty, but just the same. My house was still here, still standing. It was only my life that had been burned to the ground.

I settled the urn between two slim vases of dead flowers—I had forgotten to throw them out before I left—and lit two tall black candles in crystal holders. Then I trudged up the rest of the stairs, one by one. I draped my coat over the banister, unbuttoned my shirt, freed my hair from its filthy braid. Somehow washing off all the crud hadn't seemed worth it.

My personal computer deck stood in the upstairs study, next to the file cabinet where Santino's file had rested. I flicked it on and spent a few moments tapping.

When I finally signed on to my bank statements, I sat and stared at the screen for a long time.

I was no longer Danny Valentine, struggling mercenary and Necromance.

I was rich. Not just rich—*phenomenally* rich. The breath slammed out of me while I sat there, staring at the flickering screen. I would never have to worry about money again—not for a long, long time, anyway.

And just how long would I live, cursing myself, knowing I'd been outplayed by the Devil in a game I hadn't even known I was going to be sucked into? All things being equal, I was lucky to still be breathing.

I looked at the numbers, my pulse beating frail and hard in my throat and wrists. At least Lucifer hadn't welshed on that part of his promise.

I logged out and switched the deck off, then sat looking at my hands in the gathering twilight. The blessed quiet of my house enfolded me.

My hands lay obediently in my lap, golden-skinned and graceful. The right was still twisted into a kind of claw, but if I tried I could move the fingers a little more each day. My wrists were slender marvels of bone architecture. If I scrubbed the dirt off my face I could look in a mirror and see a demon's beauty under a long fall of dark hair, the emerald glowing from my cheek.

Would I still be able to enter Death? I was pretty sure . . . but I didn't have the stinking courage to find out for sure. Not yet.

Empty. I was an empty doll.

You will not leave me to wander the earth alone. Had he meant it?

Had the only thing Japhrimel not planned for been *me*? Or had I been part of his game?

Somehow, I didn't think I'd been something he'd planned. Call me stupid, but . . . I didn't think so.

The breath left me in another walloping rush. I blinked. A tear dropped from my eyelid, splashed onto my right hand.

I might have sat there for hours if my front door hadn't resounded with a series of thumps.

My heart leapt into my mouth. I tasted bile.

I made it down the stairs slowly, like an old woman. Twisted the doorknob without bothering to scan the other side of the door. My shields—and Japhrimel's—still remained, humming and perfect over the house. Nothing short of a thermonuclear psychic attack could damage my solitude now.

I didn't want to wonder why Japhrimel's shields were still perfect if he was dead. Maybe demon magick worked differently.

I jerked the door open and found myself confronted with a pair of blue eyes and slicked-down golden hair, dark with the creeping rain. He stood on my doorstep, leaning on his staff, and regarded me.

I said nothing. Silence stretched between us.

Jace shoved past me and into my front hall. I shut the door and turned around. Now he faced me in my house, through the stale dimness.

We stared at each other for a long time.

Finally he licked his lips. "Hate me all you want," he said. "Go ahead. I don't blame you. Yell at me, scream at me, try to kill me, whatever. But I'm not leaving."

I folded my arms. Stared at him.

He stared back at me.

I finally cleared my throat. "I'm not human anymore, Jace," I said. Husky. My voice was ruined from scream-ing—and from the Devil's hand crushing my larynx. I was lucky he hadn't killed me.

Or had he deliberately left me alive? To wander the earth. Alone.

"I don't care what you are," he said. "I'm not leaving."

"What if I leave?" I asked him. "I could go anywhere in the world."

"For fuck's sake, Danny." He pounded his staff twice on my floor, sharp guncracks of frustration. "Get off it, will you? I'm staying. That's it. Yell at me all you like, I'm not leaving you alone. The demon's dead, you need someone to watch your back."

"I don't love you," I informed him. "I won't ever love you."

"If I cared about *that* I'd still be in Rio with a new Mob Family and a sweet little fat-bottomed *babalawao*," he shot back. "This is my choice, Danny. Not yours."

I shrugged, and brushed past him. Climbed the stairs, slowly, one at a time.

I hadn't made my bed before I left, so I just dropped myself into the tangle of sheets and covers and closed my eyes. Hot tears slid out from between my eyelids, soaked into the pillow.

I heard his footsteps, measured and slow. He set his staff by the bed, leaning it against the wall the way he used to. Then he lowered himself down next to me, fully clothed.

"I'll sleep on the couch, if you want," he said finally, lying on his back, staring up at the ceiling.

"Do whatever you want," I husked. "I don't care."

"Just for tonight, then." He closed his eyes. "I'll be a gentleman. Buy another bed and clear out that spare bedroom tomorrow . . ." His voice trailed off.

"I don't care," I repeated. Silence descended on my house again, broken only by the soft sound of rain pattering on my roof. The sharp tearing in my chest eased a little, then a little more. Tears trickled down to my temples, soaked into my hair.

He must have been exhausted, because it took a very little time before his even breathing brushed the air, his face serene with human unconsciousness and age. Sleep, Death's younger sister.

Or oldest child . . .

I lay next to Jace, stiff as a board, and cried myself into a demon's fitful sleep.

Don't miss *Dead Man Rising*,
the sequel to *Working for the Devil*
by Lilith Saintcrow
Here's an exciting preview . . .

The cavernous maw of the warehouse was like the throat
of some huge beast, and even though it was large and
airy claustrophobia still tore at my throat. I swallowed,
tasted copper and the wet-ratfur reek of panic. *How do
I talk myself into these things? "Come on, do a bounty,
it's easy as one-two-three, we've done a hundred of them."
Sure.*

Darkness pressed close as the lights flickered. *Damn
corporate greed not putting proper lighting in their
goddamn warehouses. The least they could have done is
had the fluorescents replaced.*

Then again, corporations don't plan for hunters taking
down bounties in their warehouses, and my vision was
a lot better than it used to be. I eased forward, soft and
silent, broken-in boots touching the cracked and uneven
floor. My rings glinted, swirling with steady muted light.
The Glockstryke R4 was in my left hand, my crippled
right hand curled around to brace the left; it had taken
me weeks to shoot left-handed with anything like my
former accuracy. And why, you might ask, was I using

a projectile gun when I had two perfectly good 40-watt plasguns holstered in my rig?

Because Manuel Bulgarov had taken refuge in a warehouse full of plastic barrels of reactive paint for spreading on the undersides of hovers, that's why.

Reactive paint is mostly nonvolatile—except for when a plas field interacts with it. One plasgun blast and we'd be caught in a reaction fire, and though I was a lot tougher than I used to be I didn't think I could outrun a molecular-bond-weakening burst fueled by hundreds, if not thousands, of gallons of reactive. A burst like that travels at about half the speed of light until it reaches its containment edge. Even if I could outrun or survive it, Jace certainly couldn't, and he was covering me from the other side of the T-shaped intersection of corridors faced with blue barrel after blue barrel of reactive.

Just like a goddamn bounty to hide in a warehouse full of reactive to make my day.

Jace's fair blond face was marred with blood that almost hid the thorny accreditation tat and the spreading bruise up his left cheek, he was bleeding from his shoulder too. Ending up in a bar brawl that alerted our quarry was *not* the way I'd wanted to do this bounty.

His blue eyes were sharp and steady, but his breathing was a little too fast and I could smell the exhaustion on him. I felt familiar worry rise under my breastbone, shoved it down. My left shoulder prickled with numb chill, a demon's mark gone dead against my flesh, and my breathing came sharp and deep, ribs flaring with each soundless gasp, a few stray strands of hair falling in my face. *Thank God I don't sweat much anymore.* I could feel the inked lines of my own accreditation tat twisting and tingling under the skin of my left cheek, the emerald set at the top of the twisted caduceus was probably flashing. *Tone it down, don't want to give the bastard a twinkle and let him squeeze off a shot or two.*

Bulgarov didn't have a plasgun—or at least, I was reasonably certain he hadn't had one when he'd gone out the back door of the PleiRound nightclub and onto an airbike with us right behind him, only slightly slowed down by the explosion of the brawl. After all, the PleiRound was a watering hole for illicits, and once we'd moved and shown we were bounty hunters all hell had broken loose. If he'd had a plasgun, he probably wouldn't have bothered to run. No, he would have turned the bar into a firezone.

Probably.

I'd almost had Bulgarov, but he was quick. Too quick to be strictly normal, though he wasn't a psion. I made a mental note to tell my scheduler Trina to tack fifteen percent onto the fee, nobody had mentioned the bastard was genespliced and augmented to within an inch of violating the Erdwile-Stokes Act of '28. That would have been nice information to have. Necessary information, even.

My shoulder still hurt from clipping the side of a hover as we chased him through nighttime traffic on Copley Avenue. He'd been keeping low to avoid the patrols, though how you could be inconspicuous with two bounty hunters chasing you on airbikes, I couldn't guess.

It was illegal to flee, especially once a bounty hunter had identified herself as a Hegemony federal officer. But Bulgarov hadn't gotten away with rape, murder, extortion, and trafficking illegal weapons by being a law-abiding jackass who cared about two more counts of felony evading. No, he was an entirely different kind of jackass. And staying low meant that it bought him a little more time without the Hegemony patrols getting involved in the tangle, making it him against just two bounty hunters instead of against full-scale containment teams. It was a nice move, and sound logic—if the two bounty hunters weren't an almost-demon and the Shaman who had taught her a good deal about hunting bounties.

My eyes met Jace's again. He nodded, shortly, reading my face. Like it or not, I was the one who could take more damage. And I usually took point anyway, years of working bounties alone made it a tough habit to break.

He was still good to work with. It was just like old times. Only everything had changed.

I eased around the corner, hugging the wall. Extended my awareness a little, just a very little, feeling the pulse thunder in my wrists and forehead; the warehouse was magshielded and had basic corporate security on it, but Bulgarov had just walked right in like he owned the place. Not a good sign. He might have bought a short-term quickshield meant to keep him from detection by psions or security nets, just what I'd expect from him. Tricky bastard.

Concentrate, Danny. Don't get cocky because he's not a psion. He's dangerous and augmented.

My right hand cramped again, pointlessly; it was getting stronger the more I used it. Three days without sleep, tracking Bulgarov through the worst sinks in North New York Jersey, taxed even my endurance. Jace could fall asleep almost instantly, wedged in a hover or transport seat while I crunched data or piloted. It had been a fast run, no time to catch our breath.

Two other bounty hunters—both normals, but with combat augments—had gone down trying to bring this guy in. The next logical choice had been to bring a psion in, and I was fresh from hunting a Magi gone bad in Freetown Tijuana. From one job to the next, with no time to think, perfect. I didn't *want* to think about anything but getting the next bounty collared.

I would be lying if I said the idea of the two extra murder charges *and* two of felony evading tacked onto Bulgarov's long list of indictments didn't bring a smile to my face. A hard, delighted grin, as a matter of fact, since it meant Bulgarov would face capital punishment instead of just filling a prison cell. I edged forward, reaching the end of the aisle; glanced up. Nothing in the rafters, but it was good to check. This was one tricky sonofabitch. If he'd been a psion it would have made things a little easier, I could have tracked the smears of adrenaline and Power he'd leave on the air when he got tired enough. As it was, the messy sewer-smelling drift of his psychic footprint faded and flared maddeningly. If I dropped below the conscious level of thought and tried to scan him, I'd be vulnerable to a detonation circuit in a quickshield, and it wasn't like this guy *not* to have a det circuit built in if he spent the credit for a shield. I could live without the screaming migraine feedback of cracking a shield meant to keep a normal from a psion's notice, thank you very much.

So it was old-fashioned instinct doing the work on this one. *Is he heading for an exit or sitting tight? My guess is sitting tight in a nice little cubbyhole, waiting for us to come into sight, pretty as you please. Like shooting fish in a barrel.* Sekhmet sa'es, *he better not have a plasgun. He didn't, I'm almost sure he didn't.*

Almost sure wasn't good enough. *Almost sure*, in my experience, is the shortest road to *oh fuck.*

Jace's aura touched mine, the spiked honey-pepper scent of a Shaman rising around me along with the cloying reek of dying human cells. I wished I could turn my nose off or tone it down a little. Smelling everyone's death on them was not a pleasant thing, even if I of all people know Death is nothing to truly fear. And whenever I thought about it, the mark on my shoulder seemed to get a little colder.

Don't fucking think about that, Danny. Nice and cautious, move it along here.

A popping *zwing!* made me duck reflexively, calculating angles even as I berated myself for flinching. *Goddammit, if you heard the shot it didn't get you, move move move, he's blown cover, you know where he is now!* I took off, not bothering to look behind me—Jace's aura was clear, steady, strong. He hadn't been hit.

More popping, clattering sounds. Reactive paint sprayed as I moved, blurringly fast, faster than a normal human could. My gun holstered itself as I leapt, claws extending sweetly, naturally, my right hand giving a flare of pain I ignored as I dug into the side of a plastic barrel, hurling myself *up*, get *up*, and from there I leapt, feet smacking the smooth round tops of the barrels. My rings spat golden sparks, all need for silence gone. The racks holding the barrels swayed slightly as I landed and pushed off again, little glowing spits and spats of thick reactive paint spraying behind me as lead chewed the air. *He's got a fucking semiautomatic assault rifle up there, sounds like a Transom from the chatter, goddamn cheap Putchkin piece of shit, if he had a good gun he'd have hit me by now,* then I was almost under the floating panel of a hover platform. Its underside glowed with reactive paint, and I could see the metal cage on top where the operator would guide the AI deck through manipulating the dangling tentacles of crabhooks to pick up five racks at a time and transport them to the staging-area. A low indistinct male shape crouched on the edge of the platform, orange bursts showing from the muzzle of the semi-automatic rifle with the distinct Transom shape. He wasn't aiming at me now, he was aiming *behind* me at Jace, and the thought spurred me as I gathered myself and leapt, fingers sinking into the edge of the platform's corrugated metal and arms *straining*, the deadweight of my body becoming momentum as I pulled myself up as easily as if I was muscling up out of a swimtank. Almost overbalanced, in fact, still not used to the reflex speed of this new body, proprioception still a little off, moving through space faster than I thought I was. *Don't hit Jace, you motherfucker, or I'm going to have to bring you in dead and accept half my fee. Don't you dare hit him, you piece of shit.*

Gun barrel swinging, deadly little whistles as bullets clove the air, a smashing impact against my belly and another against my ribcage; then I was on him, smacking the barrel up. Hot metal sizzled, a jolt of pain searing up my arm from the contact, then fading as my body coped with the damage. He was combat-augmented, reactions quicker than the normal human's, but I'd been genetically altered by a demon, and no amount of augmentation could match that.

At least, none that I'd come across yet.

I tore the Transom away and grabbed his wrist in my cramping right hand, setting my feet and yanking sharply down. An animal howl and a crunch told me I'd dislocated his shoulder. Fierce enjoyment spilled through me, the emerald on my cheek giving one sharp flash, the *kia* bursting from my lips as I struck, *hard*, ringed fist ramming into the solar plexus, pulling the strike at the last moment so as not to rupture fragile human flesh, my rings turning my fist into a battering ram, psychic and physical power wedded to a strike that could kill as well as daze. The *oof!* sound he made might have been funny if I hadn't felt hot blood dripping down my ribs, the slight twitching as a bullet was expelled by preternatural flesh lower on my belly. *Ouch*. It stung, briefly, then smoothed itself out, black blood rising and sealing the seamless golden flesh. Another shirt ruined. I was racking up dead laundry by the ton now.